HAWK
CHANNEL
CHASE

HAWK CHANNEL CHASE

TOM CORCORAN

K&
YP

THE KETCH & YAWL PRESS
MARATHON, FLORIDA

ISBN-13: 978-0-9788949-7-9
ISBN-10: 0-9788949-7-9

The Ketch & Yawl Press, LLC
2315 Overseas Highway
Marathon FL 33050
or
PO Box 5828
Lakeland FL 33807

Visit our Web site at www.ketchandyawl.com
Visit the author's Web site at www.tomcorcoran.net

Printed in the United States of America.

First Edition

For my son, Sebastian H. Corcoran

-with appreciation for assistance, support and time:

Richard Badolato, Les and Dona Bernier, Pat Boyer,
John and Laurel Boisonault, Benjamin "Dink" Bruce,
Bill Bramblett, Eric Christensen, Marty Corcoran,
Nathan Eden, Carolyn Ferguson, Dinah George,
Jim Harrison, Nancy Harris, Lorian Hemingway,
Sandie Herron, Matt Lockwood, Chris Robinson,
Carolyn and Jim Inglis, Jerry and Elsie Metcalf,
Doyle Smith, Marshall Smith, David Standish,
June Vail, Franette Vaughn, Katie Wagner,
and Charles Wood.

HAWK
CHANNEL
CHASE

1

THE MAN AT MY screen door looked like a former pro halfback. He was about forty, had iron-hard eyes, a deep tan, dark hair, a square jaw and huge arms. On an island where bright tropical-print shirts are as common as sunglasses, his stood out as garish. There wasn't a drop of sweat on his face, and I suspected that his haircut had cost more than his shoes.

I had begun the day drinking coffee, listening to a Townes Van Zandt album and cleaning dust from the high sides of my ceiling fan blades. A pure South Florida kill-time task that promised to be the most thrill-packed half-hour of my week. The man didn't look like a vinyl siding salesman or religion peddler. I decided to give him a minute of ear time.

He launched his spiel without revealing his identity or confirming mine.

"Mr. Rutledge, straight to the point. I'm here to offer you one-point-one for your house. You'll have six weeks to vacate."

He wanted to make me a homeless millionaire.

Dumb-ass me, I said, "Let me think about it."

His eyes filled with pity. "You heard the part about the money?"

I nodded and understood that puzzlement, not pity, had formed his expression. He had expected a fatter reaction to his big bucks offer. I was too stunned to give up a reaction, much less a celebration.

"Do you want to step inside?" I said.

"I'm fine out here."

"How am I so blessed that my place is a target?"

He shrugged a whatever. "You're the lucky dog for location."

"Like every other house in Key West?"

He turned and feigned a judgment scan of the lane. "That about gets it. It's your palm-trees and flora, your fishing shorts and rum-drink lifestyle. It's the Caribbean and you can drive to it." He smirked and jammed his right knuckles into his flat left hand. "That's a great slogan. I just made it up."

"Some people on this island see all that as negative."

He slid his eyes back to mine. "How would that be?"

"We feel like victims of geography."

He exhaled a half-laugh through his teeth. "Every one of you came here for geography. You and your neighbors were tourists to start with, right? And, take my word, that post-sale trip to the bank is a great high. If you could let me know inside of seventy-two hours, my mobile number's at the upper right..." He pulled a card from his shirt pocket, poked it through a slit in the door's screening. "We need to fix this slim little hole before the skeeters find it and carry you off."

"Great advice," I said, but he'd started to walk. Except for the card he hadn't offered his name, but where would etiquette fit in? It was all about the money.

I watched him scope his surroundings, alert for business prospects or immediate threats. I amended my first impression. He probably wasn't an ex-football player. With his quirky yard-bird mannerisms, he moved more like a former prison handball champion. He turned right on Fleming. A moment later I heard two vehicle doors slam. I watched a dark green Yukon accelerate toward White Street. Tinted windows, of course, so I couldn't see the rest of the team.

It didn't matter what they looked like. He and his colleagues were errand boys for someone with cash flow as strong as the Gulf Stream. The business card for Worthwhile Investments, LLC, showed a string of capital-letter designations after Bob Catherman's name. They told of seminars and continuing education with no guarantee that anyone but Bob might benefit. They offered no promise that the man might be less mercenary in future visits. I knew that he would be around again—like the dust on my slowly turning fan blades.

I HAD RETURNED TO Key West the previous night after three days on Bimini. I needed to write a job summary and invoice for my photography—product shots of a hot sauce sold out of Pineland, Florida. The gig could've been done on Pine Island, so I assumed the whole exercise was an excuse for the company owner—a retired light-tackle guide—to write off a Bahamas trip. I didn't complain. Who could bitch about fresh fish at every meal, including breakfast, boating the Yellow Bank, or a couple evenings spent bouncing between Big John's, the End of the World Saloon, and the Big Game Club? All while collecting a pay check.

I knew I'd return to Key West at a late hour, so I left messages for Bobbi Lewis, my confidant and lover, on her cell voice mail and at her home on Big Coppitt. She had called back before I was home to bemoan overwork, to beg off meeting my arrival, to promise quality time, soon. It was my turn again. I tried her direct line at the sheriff's office.

She picked up. "I've had less than eight hours' sleep in three days, so tonight might not be…"

"Sleep here, detective," I said.

"We'd want a week's worth of something else, darling. I catch myself making small mistakes. I have to rest before they get big and I hurt someone."

"I will sit here awaiting your call," I said.

"Thank you, Alex. Try to keep your hand out of your shorts. Or does that sound greedy on my part?"

I spent the afternoon running lightweight errands, catching a sundown beer at Schooner Wharf, running into some friends from St. Augustine and joining them for a light supper at Blue Heaven. I let a backlog of Bahamas fatigue guide me to my pillow well before midnight.

THE NEXT MORNING AROUND nine the handball halfback knocked again on my door. A glance through the screening told me it wasn't a pressurized follow-up on his offer to buy my cottage. Bob Catherman had aged ten years, had lost his tropical flair and much of his bulk. This was a lost soul, new to the territory, and he was about to share baggage. He didn't speak, barely made eye contact, but entered when I opened the screen door.

"Coffee's gone," I said. "I can make a new pot."

He sat on a cushioned chair, focused downward as if inspecting the porch floor for splinters. "That might help," he said. "Maybe the caffeine will work backward and put me to sleep."

I opened the small window between the side porch and kitchen and went to brew a pot of Bustelo. "If you want to talk," I said, "I can hear you in here."

"It'll wait," he said. "I've been talking to walls for eighteen hours. Right now I need eyes and ears."

I kept quiet while I poured water and scooped dry grounds. A strong flash of "Why me?" blitzed my thoughts.

"You wouldn't have a cold one?" he said. "Like an appetizer for the coffee?"

I had two bottles left from a six-pack bought before Bimini. I popped them and returned to the porch. In contrast to Catherman's dismal appearance, the morning sun, muted by screen mesh, lighted the bougainvillea and reminded me why I hadn't jumped at the man's cash offer of a day earlier. But I wasn't sure why I had opened the second beer, or felt compelled to drink with this forlorn man only two hours after sun-up.

Some kind of gut reaction.

I carried his to the porch. He grasped the bottle as if its contents might save his life, but he didn't tilt it back. He rested it on his knee and watched a damp ring form on the press line of his khakis. Then he shifted his gaze downward, used his free hand to rub his eyes and appeared to be organizing his thoughts, perhaps choosing his words. On closer look I decided that his shoes probably cost more than his haircut. I listened to a neighbor's air conditioning compressor kick on. Music from fifteen yards away told me that a rude guest over at the Eden House had downloaded a chorus of "Kokomo" for a max-volume ringtone. Breaking rules of the hotel and mankind. Aruba, Jamaica, my ass. A perfect reason to proscribe the death penalty for selected misdemeanors.

Two minutes passed before Catherman lifted his head and tried to say something. A moment of silent eye contact ended with, "You're a photographer."

I was hoping for something more informative. I couldn't think of a response that wasn't redundant. Respectful of the man's distress, I waited him out.

He said, "You've built quite a reputation for yourself."

Another one requiring no answer, though it could have been a negative shot rather than positive. To move things along I said, "How so?"

Catherman still hadn't tilted back his beer. He leaned to one side and pulled from his trouser pocket a wrinkled bank envelope stuffed with currency. "I want you to take pictures of my daughter. She's photogenic. You won't have trouble making her look wonderful. This is a token retainer. You can bill me your regular day rate beyond this, and I'll cover your expenses without question."

Like the brush of a frond, a stroke of apprehension painted

5

goose bumps on my arms. I assumed the bills were hundreds; his "token" retainer looked fat enough to be three or four grand. He wasn't shopping for a photo shoot. I knew my answer ahead of time but I couldn't ignore the man's pain, the agony of a stranger.

Thankful that I had opened it, I took a slug from my bottle and said, "How long has she been missing?"

A minute of silence informed me that my guess was dead on.

"She's only nineteen," he said. "Her name is Sally."

Keep it rolling, I thought. "Is she here in the Keys? Does she go to school?"

He nodded. "Full load at the community college. She works the checkout counter at Colding's Grocery on Summerland, right where Monte's Restaurant used to be. She's been here since the start of summer. She lived all these years with my ex in Sarasota, but down here she's started to bloom, to use her talent. *Solares Hill* just printed an article she wrote about snorkeling."

"Could she have met someone who..."

"No way." He looked away from me, stared beyond a column of ferns inside the porch to a place more distant than Dredgers Lane. "Every customer in the place, that grocery, every co-worker the past four months, has appreciated her smile, her openness. Even the idiot boss man treats her like a human while he bullies his other employees. But there's no way, no chance in hell she would run off, even go out to dinner without calling me first. It's not something I drilled into her mind or ordered her to do. It's the way she is. God knows she didn't get it from her asshole mother."

The coffee maker quit gurgling and barking. A Conch Train went south on Frances, its driver droning memorized patter about architecture.

"She didn't come home from work yesterday?"

"Right. She made it to class—an eleven-o'clock that ended at ten after noon—but she never made it to work at two. She works two-to-eight or nine, depending on the day of the week. They said they called her cell a few times, then the home number. I found their message at home last night."

"She have her own car?"

"The only orange Mazda Miata in the Keys. You can see it a mile away. But nobody's seen it."

"How does my being a photographer bring you to me?"

"That's not the reputation I'm chasing."

I stared at him for a moment then put the money envelope on the porch table and went to the kitchen. "You still up for a cup?"

"Black's good," he said. "Could I have another cold one to go with it?"

"All out. You can finish mine, if you want. One sip missing."

He looked at the open bottle for a moment then extended his arm. I placed the beer in his grasp.

AFTER ANOTHER COUPLE OF minutes, a ceremony of alternating slugs of coffee and sips of beer, he got down to it. "I heard you helped find a nut case who was killing ex-Navy dudes. I also heard you helped bust a sheriff who had snuffed his mistress. You've got a rep of knowing how things work in the Keys and how to make things happen."

"Those last two things," I said, "I'm no different than anyone else who's been here a few years. I've adapted to my environment. You hear stuff, you see things happen, you understand more of it but never all of it. But law enforcement—or private investigation— they're not my dream vocations. They're down below my last choice. I got into a couple... umm..."

"Situations?"

"Right," I said, "and the only safe exit was to pinpoint the guilty. I don't have special skills to flash in the marketplace."

"You think it was luck?"

"Mr. Catherman, I've run good luck past my lifetime allotment, if there is such a thing. What I've done—it's no more than picking up a kid who's fallen off his bike. Or helping someone in the library who's dropped a stack of books. There's been no plan of attack—ever—no expertise or bravado, no grace under fire."

"You're running yourself down."

"What, you've got a dossier on me?"

"No, I was filling the air with words. But dealing with killers, you sure as hell were being more than charitable."

"I was finding the shortest road to survival," I said. "When those episodes were behind me, all I wanted was to go back to taking pictures."

His expression went to a touch of anger then faded to mild disbelief. It was his turn to wait me out, so I took a break to gather the facts. For some reason I sensed that Catherman could drag me into a situation more complicated than he'd outlined. His cash wad was fatter than required for finding a runaway nineteen-year-old. His mercurial body language—from his aggressive salesman persona to his meek hurt daddy to the mixing of coffee and alcohol—threw me warning signals as well. I had to wonder how much drama or paranoia lay behind his obvious desperation and dread. Or how much peril.

Then he chugged the whole beer.

"Surely you've talked with the police, the deputies," I said.

He nodded. "Last night twice and again this morning. They reacted like I'd dropped in to complain about a crack in the sidewalk, most notably Detective Lewis. She acted like it was her tenth missing person of the week and she was damn tired of people losing each other."

I let that one ride without comment. I knew that most agencies didn't consider a person "missing" until twenty-four hours had passed.

"This was the last cold one?" said Catherman.

I nodded.

"A first-class bitch," he said. "She asked if I had questioned her friends about enemies and possible foul play. I told her I thought that was her job. She said her job was to talk to fathers just discovering that their daughters had hormones too."

I offered a tempering, "Cops have their weird days."

"Right," he said. "I have mine. But this county's like a lot of others. They've got weird cops who mostly have bad days. I carried a snapshot of Sally to give them and this Lewis didn't even ask me for it."

I stared at him and said nothing. I knew that Bobbi was capable of the hardness Catherman described, but always for a reason. Perhaps she had scoped his offbeat mannerisms, decided to keep his anxiety level in perspective.

"Right," he said. "I need to concentrate on the real problem."

"Can I ask a question without having you pissed off at me, too?"

He lifted a shoulder. "Go for it."

"Does Sally have a girlfriend or two she might confide in? Close friends who know things a parent might never know—no matter how perfect their child?"

His jaw clenched, his eyes went beady for an instant. Then he nodded. "She carpooled to school with a girl from Summerland Key until the girl dropped her morning class on Tuesdays and Thursdays. Her name's Mikey Bokamp."

"What's her opinion on Sally's disappearance?"

"I haven't... Why don't you ask her yourself? That can be your first step in putting together a portfolio. Here..." He tilted sideways, pulled out his wallet, extracted and handed me a small head-and-shoulders color photo.

He'd been right about photogenic. Shoulder-length pale brown hair with streaks of yellow. Skin the tone of clean white sand and blue, low-mileage eyes. Sally radiated innocence, wholesomeness. She looked like an optimist, a natural cheerleader, a walking-around good mood.

"With your expertise I guess you could shoot circles around that picture," he said. "What are your specialties, portraits or sunsets or what?"

He was trying to butter me up, so I didn't respond. I thought of that sequence of letters on his business card, his professional designations, whatever they were. His line of work—if he really held a bona fide real estate license—practically demanded that he train in negotiation, psychological puppetry, whatever their sugarcoated term might be. They turn into manipulators with all that "win-win" hokum. I've often believed that "win-win" could best be defined as two smiles and one screw.

WE LISTENED TO A neurotic woodpecker tap an aluminum rain gutter across the lane. A waft of kitchen-prep odors—what I would peg as capers, mushrooms and olive oil in a white wine reduction sauce—came through my screening. The restaurant down on Grinnell finally had opened for lunch, a promise of good eats. A reminder that I might need to buy a bathroom scale.

"You shoot for, like, national magazines, or what?" he said.

I placed the photograph on the table next to the money envelope. "I've done that, yes. Three or four advertising agencies outside the state."

"So you don't just work locally..."

"I was in the Bahamas this past week. I have Costa Rica scheduled for early November and four days in Sanibel right after that. How long have you been in real estate?"

"Not very damn long," he said.

"How do you get all those letters after your name on the business card?"

"Cram courses in Miami and the Internet. For some you go to one or two seminars and some you sign up once a year. Why do you ask?"

Instead of saying "Just nosy," I shrugged.

"I ran the press room for a commercial printer in Clearwater until three years ago. The sales people were always drunk so the business went south. They downsized and kicked me to the sidewalk. The shift work caused my divorce, but I was still trying to get back with my ex. Having no work at all flat did in my chance of that. So I came down here, and one thing led to another. Turned out to be best anyway."

"Sometimes change is good," I said. "Were you trying to buy every house in town?"

"Certain houses, certain sizes. My client wants privacy, places that are off the beaten track."

"Even if it's only seventy-five yards off the beaten track?"

"That's a long way in a small town. Are you and I making progress here?"

It was my turn to think clear thoughts and select proper words. I juggled the missing young woman's odds on the spectrum between voluntary departure and outright abduction. These were the Keys—anything could happen and usually did. If she had vanished by her own decision, she probably was in fine shape. If someone had grabbed her, had she been targeted because of her fundamental innocence? I dropped that line of thought. Who can define "target" in the mind of a sicko? Plus, that same sweetness could prevent her father or friends from imagining that she might, someday, engage in sex or make awful choices in her romantic pursuits.

I couldn't muster a post-crime image of the young woman in the photo hurt or flung dead on the roadside or dumped in the ocean. I trusted, for the moment, that she was alive, having a better time than her father thought possible.

It made it easier for me to turn him down.

"Mr. Catherman, I'm not licensed to be an investigator and I can't pretend to be a cop. In the eyes of the police, that makes me a pest. If they choose to see it another way, I would be a fraud and a felon. And right from scratch, looking for Sally, whom I've never met—and I don't know how she thinks or what she does with her days—how could I do any better than you?"

"How about experience and success?" he said. "How about guts and local knowledge?"

"My entire track record consists of getting out of jams. I don't know the first damned thing about finding and working my way into—to borrow your term—situations. I never had to locate anything. It always found me."

"You're saying my money's no good."

"I'm saying..."

"Why have you been wasting my time?"

"Just to give you free beer and a hot drink. Your time, my porch. Ears and eyes better than walls. You were a wreck I wanted to salvage."

"Why did you ask me all those questions? To pull my chain?"

"Maybe to help you focus on more than your shoelaces."

"As we say in my field, time is of the essence. Have you got Mason jars buried out back?"

"Come again?"

"First you blow off my purchase offer. Now you're giving up an envelope full of cash. You're too good for the job, too rich to help a guy in real need? You must have money buried in the yard."

I shook my head. "You can't put a dollar value on your worry. I can't put a price on my reasons."

"You put me through all this yammering and pissing and moaning just to say no?"

"I wanted to show you a workable pattern of thinking. But, yes, the legwork is up to you. I can't invent a new occupation just because... "

Catherman jerked to his feet and bloomed into the bulky jock he'd been two days earlier. "You can kiss my ass, fucknut. You have pissed off the wrong guy."

12

"If you didn't want to be pissed, you shouldn't have knocked on my door."

He almost pushed the screen door off its hinges, almost fell down the short stairway. Five steps into the yard he said, "You just fucked any chance of selling this dump for a million-plus."

"In that case you owe me five bucks for the beers."

He shook his head with exaggerated disgust and headed toward Fleming, again checking the lane for concealed, undefined dangers. I stared at his back, sensed an odd chill, and wondered what experience in his past gave him his insight to "weird cops who have mostly bad days."

I told myself to think thoughts that wouldn't jinx the status quo. Told myself to believe in the absolute power of pretty-picture cheerleaders, the warm promise of walking good moods.

2

In Bimini I had feasted on conch salad and snapper seviche, and a massive craving flew home with me. I could score seafood from Sam Wheeler, my close friend who ran light-tackle trips in the lower Keys. Or buy fresh at the fish market on Eaton, but I needed green peppers, onions, lemons and a bird pepper, plus a bag of key limes to replenish my Old Sour bottle. I also wanted to fix my beer shortage. I braved the midday heat to pedal the Cannondale to Fausto's.

I was riding back up Fleming, balancing groceries and a six of Amstel Light, when Marnie Dunwoody flagged me down in front of the library.

"Question," said Marnie. "If you don't want to answer, say so." She wore her standard work casual—khaki slacks and a polo top, sunglasses dangling from a braided lanyard. Her expression looked more harried than relaxed. "I mean, you're his best friend, and I'm about to put you on the spot. Tell me to shut my trap, and I won't be offended."

"I can't refuse until you ask."

In thirty seconds we had created a traffic jam. Cyclists in the bike lane, utility vehicles wide as tennis courts barging up the narrow street. I pulled my bike to the sidewalk, and we moved to the library's palm garden, one bench removed from a wino reading the

15

Money section from *USA Today*.

Marnie had occupied a pedestal since the week I met her in the early 1990s. Her athletic grace and natural height weren't factors— they simply added to her elevated stature. Nor was my admiration founded on the fact that she shared a home with Sam. If she had been a cop instead of a reporter, her investigative skills could have taken her to the top of that profession too. She wrote well, never bent or extended the truth with the hope of selling extra news- papers. I had never seen her back down from a scornful attorney, a slimy commissioner, a sleazy businessman, a bitchy tourist. Her finest success was her refusal to formulate articles ahead of time then plan her questions and facts to match a prejudice or a lazy way out.

Marnie perched so close to the bench edge that I feared a slight shift might drop her ass to the stone walkway. She held back tears and began with the tap of a sledge: "I think Sam's seeing someone else."

All I could do was shake my head. The simplest question in his defense was how could he find time? Somehow I found the wisdom not to voice that thought. "Not on the sly, Marnie," I said. "Not without telling you first."

"Why not the sly? If he met someone, wanted to test the water, he'd have to give up his housemate. He'd have to squander a long- term love. Why not run a test drive, say, the first few weeks, see if his newfound squeeze made the grade?"

"Because he's beyond honest. How long have we suffered the pain of his truth? He also knows you'd customize his dick with a rusty garden tool. Where would he meet another woman, anyway? It's not like he hangs in bars."

"He charters to both sexes, Alex. His clients tend to be success- ful, wealthy and sociable. Female fisherman, on average, tend to be lookers."

I still disagreed but kept my mouth shut.

"He didn't come home last night," she said. "He pulled the same thing ten days ago and twice before, three weeks and a month ago. Each time he claimed that he slept on his boat, but his skin gave him away. Lots of windburn and no mosquito bites."

"It's hard to get windburn in a bimbo's bed."

She looked at the wino then back at me. "If you're out in a boat, it's easy to get laid and not get caught. It's rough on the knees and elbows, but it can be done."

For a moment my thoughts wandered.

"Several times, Alex, if that's where your dirty little mind..."

"He called yesterday afternoon," I said. "He bitched about an awful morning charter and another odd one for today."

"What did he say about yesterday?"

"Word for word?"

"Or verbatim, your choice. I can take it."

"The angler was late to the boat, rude to the dockmaster. He announced to Sam on the way out of the harbor that he wanted to chop a tarpon into steaks to freeze and ship to his brother in Dubuque. He lied about his fishing skills, which became evident on their arrival in the Snipe Keys. After the jerk flubbed three casts, Sam restarted his motor and beelined back to the Bight. He refused the man's check and pointed him out to all the guides at the dock to make sure that no one else would take the schmuck back to the backcountry. He called the guy a flaming, full-tilt, unrelenting asshole."

"Is that more than he usually says about his clients?" she said.

"Sure, but most are repeats—no surprises."

"So, thinking back," said Marnie, "what does all that sound like?"

I didn't have to ponder long. "An overtold lie."

"And you don't know who she is?"

"He talked about this other guy for today and tomorrow. Can't we assume it's some circumstance other than a woman?"

"Like he's sneaking off to church, Alex? You think he's volunteering at a Big Pine soup kitchen?"

"Like we give him the benefit of the doubt. Because he's Sam."

She shook her head. "That's the reason for no benefit. Sam's a man with zero speed bumps. Now he's hit three and we're supposed to ignore them? If we were counting strikes instead of bumps, he'd be out."

"He's a man of integrity. So far, they're your bumps, not his."

"Your words were 'overtold lie,' Alex."

"Then trust my judgment. You can't condemn the man for having fewer mosquito bites than you see fit for punishment."

"Damn. I put you on the spot and you dodged it," she said. "Clever man."

The wino threw down his Money section, stood and stomped on it. "If I was a CEO and had a parachute, I wouldn't take all that money from my shareholders, no sir, no ma'am. And I'd damn well be one right now if my Chrysler hadn't been stolen before that job interview in '84. That ripped-off car led me to poverty and a life of shame, and I swear I regret it."

The man stormed out of the garden like a saint on a mission.

"Is that the way I'm acting?" said Marnie. "Like I'm the hub of the universe? I've had a double dose today. I'm brainwashed and bottled up."

"Work issues?"

"Some crap went down before sundown last night, but there's a lid on it. The sheriff's people in the Lower Keys scrambled—even the crime scene techs who don't get bothered unless it's a sure mess. Suddenly it's a non-event. We know their techs got U-turned on US 1 because the *Miami Herald* stringer was right behind their van. They told us to pull back, then screwed their mouths shut tight."

"False alarm or what?" I said.

"They're trying too hard to make it look like that. I don't buy it."

"Maybe FDLE claimed jurisdiction," I said. "Maybe a drug sting went bad."

"Or a politician's kid, or a cop's wife, or a mayor's mistress, a rich man and his dog. Maybe a jackpot, a Saudi spy. Or any of two dozen other system loopholes."

"A rich man and his what?"

"Please forget I said that," she said.

"Did you check the airport? See if a private helicopter or a small plane went down? The FAA could have put the clamps on it."

"That's good, Alex. I'll check but they've always been open before. When that Cessna hit the tether..."

A year earlier, a private plane not only entered Fat Albert's restricted airspace, but struck the cable that secured the surveillance balloon to its base on Cudjoe Key. A chance in ten million—and three people died.

"Or some Cubans came ashore," I said. "All it takes is one tourist to see ten or twelve scruffy people on the beach to start a panic."

"Cubans happen all the time, Alex, unless Fidel himself caught a ride to Miami. Whatever, it pisses me off. It's a keep-a-secret virus that's trickled down from the feds to the staties to the locals. Mark my words. In three years you'll need to give your thumb print and an eyeball scan to pay your goddamned water bill."

"If there's still any water." I waited for a loud motorscooter to pass. "Do you have any idea which key they were scrambling to?"

"I got the impression it was Sugarloaf, but no one was saying. You need to get your groceries home." We stood and she quick-hugged me good-bye. "Now that I feel better for having learned nothing, I need to chase a story at the court house."

I FOUND CARMEN SOSA on my porch recliner, her palm pressed to her forehead.

"Is this meditation?" I said.

She didn't respond. I stopped and stared, waited for her to speak.

Except for a two-year hiatus, Carmen had been my neighbor on Dredgers Lane since I bought my house. Her parents, Cecilia and Hector Ayusa, bought their home across from mine about twenty-five years before I arrived. That's where Carmen grew up. After high school she married, moved to a two-bedroom on Staples and gave birth to a daughter, Maria Rolley. The marriage went south, she divorced the loser, and landed a job with the Postal Service. Hector learned about the cottage at the end of the lane before the owners listed it. He staked a claim for Carmen and helped with the down payment. Throughout Maria's childhood, she and her grandparents have loved the proximity.

A few years ago Carmen and I tried to be lovers. We went through the motions of an affair for a month or two, then called the game on account of friendship. Our friendship has endured.

She finally lowered her hand. I saw tears.

"I feel guilty," she said. "I think I'm happy but I can't be sure."

"You're on the glad-sad spectrum. It's the in-thing today, so don't feel lonely."

"Don't give me shit right now, Alex."

"You got offered a ridiculous amount for your house?"

She raised her eyebrows, inhaled deeply, bugged her eyes and exhaled. "So did my parents. And you must have gotten an offer, or you wouldn't have guessed so quickly. Is someone trying to buy the whole lane?"

"It'd make sense, for the right multi-millionaire."

"I think I'm going to throw up."

For a moment, I did too. I've always known that I counted on Carmen, but at that moment I understood my need, my attachment. Having her move away would turn me into a shaky boat with a slipping anchor.

I sat on a canvas chair and replayed my joy in watching her

daughter grow up, being "Uncle Alex." Hector and Cecilia for years had been my link to island history with their stories, their love of the island and human nature, their humor and the old Conch nicknames. Hector's best friend Ed Sawyer, long deceased, was always Gabby Frijoles. I couldn't count the times Cecilia had proudly shown me the 1948 edition of the cookbook published by the Key West Woman's Club. Each recipe was reproduced in its creator's handwriting. Her entries were adjacent to submissions by island legends such as Floy Thompson, Betty Moreno Bruce, Lorine Thompson, Thelma Strabel, and Helen (Mrs. Oliver) Griswold. One faced a woodcut by Martha Watson Sauer, the WPA artist who remained in the Keys until she died in 2005 at age ninety-three. Sharing those memories and details had made me feel more a part of the island, the community I had chosen as home.

Plus, I knew exactly what Carmen had been through, dumping a loser husband, raising her daughter alone, sticking close to her parents, surviving financially. And now the changing island, the economic wedge...

"There is one other thing," said Carmen. "Remember Carol Anne?"

"Your high school co-conspirator in craziness," I said, "now in central Florida."

"Right, she divorced Bobby Dudak and moved with her son Jason to Ocala the day before Hurricane Georges. As of last night and for no more than five days, Jason and his pal Russell are sleeping on my living room floor. Remind me never again. "

"Down here early for Fantasy Fest?"

"They say they're not here to party. They're here to reclaim their lost youth. Russell's dad, Ovie Hernandez, sold his house on Von Phister when the kid was three, and took him to Ocala, too. The boys want to find jobs, stick around, get in touch with what they missed growing up away from the Keys."

"The Honda with the yawning chrome tailpipe I saw yesterday?"

21

Carmen nodded. "They live out of their backpacks and subsist on junk food and diet soda. They've got a lead on an apartment which can't come too soon because I'm totally uncomfortable with young Russell. I don't like the way he looks at my daughter. Maria's twelve going on sixteen. She doesn't need close-up college-age boys in her life."

"Jobs doing what?" I said.

"I think they'd settle for anything. I can't imagine they're presenting a positive image to prospective employers. The way Jason wears his shorts, he looks like he's got a load in his diaper. Russell has a line on washing dishes in some restaurant. He said the whole kitchen crew was about to be arrested by Immigration."

"Pretty good inside info for a kid new to the island," I said.

"They've got their ears to the ground—or the Duval concrete."

"Being under twenty-five helps with the language," I said. "You want me to chat them up, be a male presence, be the bad guy if I have to?"

"Let's wait another day or two," she said, standing to leave. "Maybe if you see them tomorrow."

"I'll introduce myself, ask for a progress report. Speaking of employment, why aren't you at work today?"

She shook her head. "They boogered up the schedule again."

I PUT AWAY THE groceries and took a time-out in the bamboo rocker, secure in knowing that my ceiling fan was sending me healthy air. On top of the cleansing effect Bimini had had on my brain, the beer I'd drunk during Catherman's visit demanded that I grab a nap. Then again, the disturbing news delivered by Marnie and Carmen ensured that I wouldn't fall asleep. My perfectly good morning had turned into a tabloid day.

Bob Catherman carried the backing to offer me tall cash for my home. But my reluctance to locate his daughter didn't mean I was bluffing, pushing him for more money. Every word I had spoken in defense of my photo work was true. I had no desire to be a soldier of fortune, a gumshoe, a night sneak, a fixer. I didn't want to get rich by solving the myriad problems of the wealthy. I wanted to earn enough to keep my checking account fluid, maybe park a little for the future. I had learned over the years that solvency was a prime requirement in maintaining a Keys lifestyle. Not that it wasn't a tougher challenge as years passed, as Key West became known to the world's upper crust, as taxes rose to fund changes to meet the needs of a more demanding population. I took what some might call naive pride in maintaining that solvency without selling out.

I called Detective Bobbi Lewis's work number.

She caught the second ring. "Call you back, Alex? Say an hour? It's a bitch of a morning."

Go lightly, I thought. "What's the matter? Robberies, car wrecks or politics?"

She hesitated a beat too long. "A mountain of the usual. Lemme go right now." She clicked off.

Shitfire, I thought. I love you too. I hung up and slapped the wall.

The phone rang, and I was tempted to run for the door.

So I did. After a morning of crazy bullshit, I deserved a break, a late lunch at Louie's Backyard. Let the message service earn its keep. Give the old Triumph 650 Bonneville some air, eat a fancy-damn salad on the Afterdeck and listen to the ocean under my barstool.

I TOOK WHITE STREET, running in light traffic until I tried to turn right on Von Phister. Two wobbly tourists in the bike lane and a Dodge pickup on my ass prompted me to venture 100 yards farther. A beautiful day in paradise, and what was my hurry? I caught a green at Flagler, turned, then spotted Sam Wheeler's funky Ford

Bronco parked near the corner of Whalton. The area was residential, and Sam was supposed to be fishing. Unless the old Bronco had broken down and he had abandoned it, the only sense I could discern was that his client lived nearby. I couldn't think of anyone who lived along that stretch. But I knew there was a plausible explanation—if Sam cared to volunteer it.

IN AN EXPANDED OLD Conch house, Louie's Backyard dominates the beachfront where Waddell meets Vernon. The Afterdeck, wedged between an elegant dining patio and the waters of Hawk Channel, has been a refuge for twenty years. It's a mix of fashion and funk, rich tourists and all brands of locals—pillars of the town and dregs of the harbor. I've been there hundreds of times and never seen the water the same color, the wind from the same direction. I probably have viewed more lovely sunsets from that deck than most people see in a lifetime. My stability has wandered each time Louie's closed for an annual break or hurricane repairs. I worry that I am one of those terminally drawn to the combo of alcohol and salt water, a drooler camouflaged by nautical lingo and a fisherman's ball cap. I have no desire to become one of the loopy ones.

The peace I needed went down the tubes. I found Sheriff Fred "Chicken Neck" Liska with one of his ops officers, Dick Wonsetler, drinking lunch at the tide line. Like his boss, Dick was a veteran of the Key West police force. I didn't know much of his history, but he always looked fatigued, always wore the sneer of a man who disliked his job, maybe his whole life.

Liska was the cop who had drawn me into photographing crime scenes. It had started when he was a city detective, three or four small jobs that expanded into actual sleuthing. He plugged me into several more gigs after being elected Monroe County's sheriff and still called once in a while, despite my constant refusal of forensic work. We never talked about the times I had saved his ass. I knew that rubbing it in would only incite him to call more often. Local rules dictated that it was better to store blue chips than to spend them in public. I had never interacted with Wonsetler.

The men were seated at the far end of the bar, their backs to the water's glare. Liska held a mixed drink in a tall glass. Wonsetler was waving an empty Corona bottle at the server, ordering a fresh one. The Afterdeck was all but empty, with three other men at the bar, a young woman working behind it and, in the heat of the day, no one at the tables. Odd, I thought, that Liska was with only one of his two operations officers. That fact suggested that it wasn't a strategy meeting, a business lunch. It was a hump day escape.

I walked over to shake hands. Up close, Liska looked hangdog and war weary in one of his old disco shirts, the period attire he'd forsaken when he'd quit his city job to run for sheriff. "Did I miss a BeeGees concert? ABBA on the beach?"

He put a disgusted look on his face, swiped at his shirt with the backs of his fingers. "Some days you don't give a shit."

"Remember you once told me about a certain person having bad luck with a love affair?"

"I don't know what you're talking about."

I knew he was fibbing, probably for a good reason. I assumed it was because of the man to his right.

I let it drop. "No big deal. I was trying to remember a name."

"Thanks for the background," said Liska. "I still don't know who the fuck you got in mind."

"You're sporting a cheerful outlook today," I said.

"Do my job for a month, Rutledge. Then tell me outlook."

I backed away. "I'm going to feel sorry for you, Sheriff, but I'm going to do it over here." I found a tall chair at the far end of the bar, asked for a menu and, on impulse, ordered a mojito. I had a beer for breakfast. Why not rum before sundown? Just this once.

Ten minutes later the ops officer went into the restaurant. I assumed he'd gone to the men's room. I stood, walked over to

Liska but said nothing.

"Look, Rutledge, I don't play social games. You know as well as I do, the only important gossip in town comes from dental hygienists and legal secretaries."

"I'm not looking for trash talk, sheriff. I need a dose of counseling."

Liska considered my phrasing. "First, just for today, call me Fred. Second, you didn't hear this from me. I sympathize with your plight, you might say. The lady's got issues. She can be her own worst enemy."

"You told me she had a fling a few years ago and got double-whammied."

"Right," he said. "The guy bought the farm in a plane crash and that was when Deputy Lewis—before she made detective—found out he was married."

"You also said that she'd had couple of boyfriends after that. They didn't work out."

"I know where you're going, Rutledge. You're perceptive and you're right. Two of them were fellow deputies."

"And of those two..."

"Both left the sheriff's office before I took over. And, yes, one of them has been in the Keys for the past three weeks. He works for another agency and he and Lewis have been in touch. That's all I know and all I want to know."

"That might explain a few things," I said.

"They're all flaky, from time to time," said Liska. "That one I was seeing, five, six years ago? She told me once... her name was Carla. I don't think you met her. She said denial made her the happy woman she faced each day in the mirror. She worshiped her own bliss. She couldn't find enough bad history to deny."

"And you became excess?" I said.

"I declared myself such. Here comes Wonsetler. Go the fuck away."

Mission accomplished, with a typical Liska send-off. Now I knew why Bobbi Lewis had been running hot and cold. The insight offered me no relief, no clues toward salvaging our romance.

I returned to my mojito. Two boardsailors, college-age kids, male and female, swooped toward the beach and changed direction in the shallows. Silence engulfed the Afterdeck. The young woman wore a huge sports bra and a skin-toned thong that was lost in the shadow of her ass crack. It was a matter of perspective and perception. I guessed that every man present would bet his own home that she'd been naked from her belly button down.

A man two stools away from me broke the spell. He leaned toward Liska and said with a slur, "Hey, I overheard. You really the county sheriff?"

Liska shrugged and stared at the man for a moment.

"What was all that horseshit yesterday, sheriff? I couldn't go home."

"Am I supposed to ask you what shit?" said Chicken Neck. "You got questions, call the office."

"Bay Point. They wouldn't let me go to my house. They finally let me go to my house and nobody could tell me why they wouldn't let me go to my house. That, by any doofus explanation, is horseshit, wouldn't you say?"

I could see Liska sizing this up as far too public. "I'll have to check and let you know. Write down your phone number for me."

"They evacuated the neighborhood, sheriff. You didn't know?"

Liska stared at him.

"Come on, sheriff, pile it a bit higher. We can stick a fork in it."

Stone-faced, pissed, Liska said nothing. Everyone within earshot expected the bartender to stifle the heckler. That wasn't happening. Miranda was about one-third the guy's size.

"My neighbor didn't answer his door, sheriff. He saw them making our other neighbors leave their houses. They all had to get into their cars and drive away. So he pretended he wasn't home. He saw all those county cars surrounding that vacant house on stilts. He

27

couldn't see what had their attention, but he saw more unmarked cars than he'd ever seen in one place. Car after car after car. Some of them didn't even have license plates, sheriff."

"Sounds like a movie script to me," said Wonsetler.

"My take, too," said Liska. "UFO flick or a sea monster epic. Subtitles, flaming eyeballs."

"Well they stayed so long that someone brought in pizza. They spread it out on the hood of an unmarked cruiser, pizza, two-liter jugs of Pepsi, what have you. A damn picnic."

"That wouldn't have been our people," said Wonsetler.

"You're flaming out your stupid, frigging..."

Everyone but the drunk saw it coming. He was grabbed by the restaurant owner's son and hustled toward the deck's exit. It was probably the quickest the man had walked backward in years.

Liska nudged Wonsetler, tilted his head toward the exit. The men pushed back their bar chairs, stood, and reached for their wallets. Liska waved a fifty, indicated that he'd cover the tab. He must have felt me staring at him. It took him a while to look my way. He growled, "Don't fucking ask."

Liska and Wonsetler walked toward the next-level dining patio so they could exit through the lobby entrance, probably to avoid the man who had been eighty-sixed. At the top of the short stairway a man in a business suit approached Liska.

"You left a message?" he said.

Liska nodded and made a "shh" sign—his finger to his lip. The three men departed through the inside dining room.

I borrowed the bar's phone, called Marnie, and got her voice mail. I let her know that the non-event on Sugarloaf was the real thing, an official non-event.

I hung up and stared at the dregs of my drink.

Someone tapped my shoulder. Twice, lightly.

3

"If I bought two Bacardi 8 mojitos, which is more than I need, would you drink my second one?" A sugar voice, shoulder-length honey blonde hair, five-eight, in a pale gray woman's executive suit—jacket, slacks, white silk blouse. On closer look, small earrings, a small platinum Rolex on her thin left wrist, a single silver bracelet on the lightly tanned right arm. Difficult to miss: the elegant diamond wedding ring. She placed a large paisley-patterned tote on the bar and eased into a teak curved-back bar stool.

"I'll drink both if you say the word," I said. "What are we celebrating?"

She caught the bartender's attention with two raised fingers and pointed at my empty glass. "We like the fact that I finally tracked down Alex Rutledge, the well-known magazine and advertising photographer. We like the weather and we love this restaurant and we have nothing to do until whatever time is suppertime."

"I worry about the possibility that you're an attorney or a judge."

"Neither." She leaned forward and began to remove her jacket. Always the gentleman, I stuck out my arm to assist. I hadn't seen her unbutton the blouse, but when she lifted her elbows two garments came off. I was left holding laundry and she was wearing an expensive-looking and immodest bathing suit top. I caught the momentary crescent of aureole as the suit top's hem hung on a nipple.

She stuck out her hand. "Lisa Cormier. Atlanta and points south."

I left that one alone.

Our server, the lovely, mischievous Miranda, stood ready to confirm the drink order. In her eyes-front frozen expression I detected a trace of astonishment at the disrobing and a good-natured reproach for my having glimpsed private skin.

Lisa Cormier looked down at her breast, said, "Shocking," and adjusted her garment. She looked back to Miranda. "You must love working here."

"Most of the time. Did you say two mojitos?"

"I did." Lisa turned to me, said, "Bacardi 8, right?" then peered southward to the pastel blue-green water. "God, I love this place. I live most of the year on the cloudy side of a baby foothill that's damp and cold except when it's incredibly hot and dusty. That's when I ache for the beach. I ache from my neck to my knees."

Somewhere in the distance, over toward Simonton, a siren wailed then quit.

"You just arrived in town?" I said.

"Two weeks ago. And please don't think I've been stalking you. I asked the woman inside at the podium if you ever came in here. She pointed you out."

"The fact that I liked Bacardi 8, that was just a good guess?"

"Key West is a small town," she said. "We have mutual friends, and I happen to prefer that flavor, too."

I was ten yards from the ocean with a sunny wide-angle view of twelve-mile horizon. But I felt more claustrophobic than I might in a dark, cold cellar. As if the next things on the menu were batting eyelashes and a pistol in my ribs.

Miranda placed our drinks on square cardboard coasters. She gave me a grin far too wide, then moved away to chat up a tourist.

Lisa raised her glass to propose a toast. I hefted mine, drank it in one slam and said, "Gotta go. Thanks for the kind words."

"Maybe I've muddied the waters," said Lisa Cormier. "I was coming around to a job offer. My husband needs advertising photography. Will you stay for another minute, let me make a call here?"

I looked at Miranda, wished I had taken a few minutes for food then realized I hadn't paid for my first mojito. While I settled my tab, Lisa made her call. All I caught was, "Hi, Honey," and muffled conversation.

Then she handed me the phone.

"Mr. Rutledge, I'm Copeland Cormier. Can you meet me in the lobby of the La Concha Hotel in, say, twenty-five minutes?"

"Is this about location work, product shots or stock from my files?" I said.

"It's location, local, a minimum of three days."

I glanced at Lisa Cormier. She stared at the rows of liquor bottles behind the bar, slowly sipped her mojito through its straw.

"Are you with a magazine, Mr. Cormier?" I said.

"Can I explain everything when we're face-to-face? I assure you, Mr. Rutledge, I have no intention of wasting your time."

I handed the phone back to Lisa and said, "Okay."

She conveyed my assent to her husband, spoke another fifteen seconds then flipped the thing shut. "It'll be fun to work with you," she said, pushing her hair behind the ear closest to me. "I've learned that most locals know who you are, but very few know you well."

WITH NO COINS IN my pocket for high-rent meters, I parked my Triumph near the library on Fleming, walked past the Key West Island Book Store and entered the La Concha through its Duval Street entrance. My soles squeaked as I weaved through a forest of potted date palms. I found refuge in the elevated sitting room adjacent to the lobby. Under twelve vertically rotating fan paddles on a long horizontal post, I studied a massive mahogany bookcase—now a Hemingway shrine. An Underwood manual typewriter, a bust, a modest book collection. Even the room's leather sofas and chairs, the tables' steamer-trunk motif, and the tufted ottoman had a rustic author-in-Kenya feel. I thought I heard the distant trumpeting of an elephant. Then I heard it again. It was a cruise ship's whistle summoning the flock for departure.

The La Concha had seen more downs than ups since its mid-1920s debut. Several times in the late seventies I visited a friend who spun records from WKWF's third-floor studios—the only part of the hotel open at that time except for a rooftop lunchroom and saloon. On those evenings when I smuggled clandestine beers and a stack of my own record albums through the threadbare lobby to the studio, the seedy, half-asleep desk clerk advised me to use the unswept stairs rather than the balky elevator.

The elegance these days amazed me—marble flooring, tasteful art, the sturdy furniture, unbleached cotton, black leather, over-sized pillows in mock-carpetbag fabric—and all those palm trees. There was no piped-in music. I heard only the motor whine of the huge ceiling fan, muffled voices from the registration desk, and distant murmurs from the restaurant nearer the sidewalk.

COPELAND CORMIER ENTERED THROUGH the driveway portico. There was an obvious age spread, but he matched his wife in style.

He was distance-runner slender, maybe six-one, one-eighty max. He wore the ultimate in light-tackle fashion. Sage green Beach Crocs, a ventilated long-sleeve flyweight shirt, matching sage pants with knee-level side pockets and a couple days' worth of chin stubble and cheek sunburn. Stylish sunglasses hung from his neck on a woven leather cord. He carried a khaki long-brim Columbia nylon hat (which dangled a "hat saver" leash) and a faded Crips-blue Bass Pro bandanna. I assumed that he would ask me to shoot action photos on a guide skiff. That was more appealing than my fear as I had left Louie's—that the Cormiers wanted kink shots of themselves in a four-bills-a-night hotel suite.

He spotted me, took the short stairs to the sitting room in two steps and stuck out his arm. We shook hands without exchanging names. He looked around for a bellman. "Can I order you a coffee or a drink?"

"I'm fine for now," I said, wishing for coffee or water. "Let's talk business."

"You're a good friend of Sam Wheeler, the fishing guide."

A light bulb went on—along with alarm bells. Was Marnie right? Was Lisa Cormier the new attraction for Sam?

"Is that a question?" I said.

"Oh, no, Mr. Rutledge. An absolute statement of fact."

He paused so that I could respond. I waited for him to continue.

"I've known Sam for almost twenty years," he said. "Ours was a captain-client deal that turned into friendship and trust. Sam has told me about your friendship and a bit of your history. He mentioned, in particular, a little misadventure you two shared in Miami several years ago..."

Again a stranger knew too much. I was ten seconds away from bolting.

"Is that so?" I said.

"Indeed. Your saving the life of a city detective impressed me. I laughed for days thinking about Sam sending the FDLE's satellite tracking device northward on a tractor-trailer."

The "fisherman" was angling outside of my comfort zone. "This isn't about a photo gig," I said. "What other tidbits have you stockpiled?"

"Sam also said that you'd suspect me of being—let's say 'unfriendly.' He gave me a key fact that would confirm the confidential nature of our conversation—so you and I can continue our talk."

"That would be *your* talk."

"Correct," he said. "So here's the deal maker. When Sam wants to leave an object at your home that he wants only you to find, a piece of equipment he might loan you, there's a hiding place. He would place it on a hook between your house and your outdoor shower's east wall. Behind the soap dish, hidden by overgrown crotons."

I ran that one through my memory for a good minute. I couldn't recall ever telling anyone about the pistol stash—even Carmen. Sam would never have had a reason to tell anyone, even Marnie. I squashed the thought that Marnie, had he ever told her, might spill our secret.

"He would hang it by its trigger guard," said Cormier.

"Got it," I said.

He nodded. "Does that mean you trust me?"

"Why isn't Sam here to introduce us? Is he in danger?"

"For the past day or two he's had good reason to take precautions. Why don't you hear me out, then decide for yourself?"

"I'll listen to what you have to say."

"Good." He handed me a business card and gave me a moment to study it.

Dr. R. Copeland Cormier
Director of Surgery
Buckhead-Vargo Memorial Hospital
Atlanta, Georgia, USA

"Let's go for a walk," he said.

"Let's stay right here."

"This is a lot more public than you think."

I glanced around, saw no one within earshot or who appeared to care about two men shooting the breeze in Hemingway's sitting room. While I was certain that the hotel had video surveillance, I couldn't imagine hidden microphones.

But I was there for Sam. I'd let Cormier call the first shots.

"Go out to Duval," I said. "Go left, cross the street, and walk into St. Paul's. Up front and left of the central sanctuary there's an alcove with four pews and a communion rail. I'll be there in four minutes."

"Make it three, please," said Cormier. "I'm a practical man, short on prayers." He descended to the main lobby, put on his sunglasses and strode toward the Duval doors.

I gave him a minute so I could bid goodbye to Ernest's ghost and approach the registration desk at the rear of the lobby. A smiling hotel management major with a brushed brass name tag asked if she could help me.

"I need to leave a short note for one of your guests, Eliza. I would appreciate the loan of a ballpoint pen and the outright gift of a piece of paper."

"Certainly, sir." The pen was at hand; it took her an embarrassing ten seconds to locate a blank sheet of hotel letterhead. "Would you rather use a house phone to leave voice mail?"

"I would rather leave the note. Can you make sure Dr. Cormier receives it?"

"Of course..." She turned to her computer monitor while I wrote: "Mary had a little lamb but Eliza had cute cheeks." I folded the note, began to write Cormicr's name on the outside.

"How is he spelling his name?" said Eliza.

I told her my best guess.

"No one in the hotel has that... Not even close, starting with C." She poked a few more keys. "Nothing in the Ks, either. Cormier?" She tried two or three alternate spellings then looked up and shook her head. Her face showed more frustration than I felt. I supposed from the start that he wasn't a guest.

"Maybe he hasn't checked in yet." I wadded the note and stuck it in my pocket. "I'll call back in a couple hours and leave that voice mail. Thanks for your help."

———

A MAN ON A TRICYCLE towed a two-wheeled cart full of beach gear down Duval. A cooler, an umbrella, a chair, a portable stereo and a tarp. A leashed Dalmatian walked ahead, no doubt anxious to play in the ocean.

Someone and his dog had figured out the climate and locale.

I swear I know the formula. I just can't make it happen.

The chapel, with a half dozen stained-glass windows swiveled open, smelled cleaner than the sidewalk and street. Its peace welcomed me until a straight-pipe Harley at the Eaton Street stoplight tarnished its sanctity. I took a moment to cut off my ringtone and drop five bucks into the donation box. Cormier, the only other person in the sanctuary, sat in the center pew of the military alcove. With his hat removed his hair looked darker than his facial stubble. I entered the pew and sat five feet away from him.

"Sam's involved in important, risky work," he said. "His contributions have been quite valuable."

My soup kitchen remark to Marnie Dunwoody was about to bite me in the ass.

"You make it sound like charity," I said.

Cormier nodded once. "The beneficiaries are innocent Cuban nationals."

"Steering refugees to safe landing spots?"

"It's not that simple," said Cormier, "and not that local. He makes nighttime trips to Cojimar. He delivers legitimate pharmaceuticals to doctors on the island."

"Legit... from a medical standpoint?"

"Right," said Cormier. "But his trips are not legal. This country's arbitrary laws regarding business with Cuba could be held over our heads."

"So... the danger comes from the expansive hand of law enforcement?"

"A small part of it," he said. "We consider jail and lawyers to be costs of doing business. We worry more about the transport cow-boys who shuttle humans and contraband in either direction for a price. We donate legitimate drugs. They think our missions cut into their profit potential, and they resent our presence."

"Why don't you pay the bad boys to run your supplies?" I said. "Make them part of the team?"

"They could skim or steal loads, let the drugs roast in the sun, or jack up their transport prices and threaten to expose us if we com-plain. Once we let them in the door, there'd be no getting rid of them."

I pondered his tale while a stereo inching south on Duval broad-cast a battle of fifty kettledrums versus thirty mooing cows.

After waiting out the thumps Cormier said, "I know you came here to hear my pitch, but can I ask you a couple of things?"

"You can ask."

"Has anyone come to you in, say, the past several days asking about Sam?"

I shook my head. "Nope."

"How about asking for personal info about yourself—or offering some kind of too-good-to-be-true deal?"

I flashed an image of Catherman on his first visit. But I shook my head.

"How about bogus-sounding phone surveys or someone who knows both you and Sam asking about him, what's he up to lately, that sort of question?"

I flashed an image of Marnie, distraught over Sam's unexplained absences.

"Nope."

"Your, girlfriend, or however you refer to Detective Lewis. Has she asked about Sam?"

"She hasn't even asked about me," I said. "Who's the 'we' you mentioned, as in 'We consider that a cost of doing business.'"

"I assume you know the concept of 'need-to-know' in classified data."

"When I was in the Navy it meant, 'Please don't load me down with secrets I can't use.'"

"Right. So I'm going to tell you enough to satisfy your curiosity. Sam assured me that you would respect our level of caution. Are we on the right track?"

"I'm all ears," I said.

"I co-founded... or brought together a group of successful people who want to make a difference. There are five of us, three doctors and two tactical types. We call ourselves Doctors with Deep Wallets."

"Same concept as Doctors Without Borders?" I said.

He shook his head. "We admire Medecins Sans Frontieres. We pay attention to their effective methods, but we have no connection and narrower goals."

"You probably don't have their money or support."

"No," he said. "And they have the world's media on their side, at least in the free world. We—most assuredly—don't share the same methods. We prefer total anonymity. We wallow in our secret self-satisfaction, with the occasional glass of fine wine."

"Where does Sam fit into your organizational chart?" I said. "Is he a tactical type or the hired help?"

"Let's call him core member number six, except..." Cormier looked upward to a stained glass window.

"I assume we just hit a 'need-to-know' snag," I said.

"For now, yes—we have issues that I can't discuss with you. I can assure you that Sam's fine. He probably needs you to explain to Marnie that he won't be home for a few days. A message from you would offer a degree of confidence. Right now, out of respect for her occupation, she can't be told about his trips to Cuba's north coast."

"Why do I need to know any of this?"

"Three reasons," said Cormier. "First, so you could deal with

Marnie. Also, Sam felt that someone local—that means you—should understand the dynamics of our operation, the nature of his involvement. He also feared that you would answer to your own curiosity and start trying to figure out his actions. He didn't want you to turn over stones that, for the moment, are best left alone."

"All this build-up, this stealth meeting, is this your way of asking me to do nothing except bullshit Marnie?"

"The church was your idea," said Cormier, "though I caught the irony. Helping Sam Wheeler calm Marnie doesn't sound like a stretch among friends. Revealing details of our enterprise was not my idea, believe me."

"Why all the sudden commotion?" I said. "Why is Sam laying low?"

"We have a system to monitor the safety of our group members. It's fairly simple, and one man hasn't called in for two days."

"Go back to your twenty questions," I said. "Mutual friends, deals too good to be true."

Cormier spoke with forced calm. "I'd like to hear about anything you felt was out of the ordinary."

"Talking about two deals," I said, "from one man. I don't know if this falls into your category, but..."

Cormier's eyes flashed. "Offers or deals?"

"I didn't agree to a thing. My guess is that each is kaput."

"Please," he said.

I explained Bob Catherman's home purchase offer and my refusal to bite. That got no reaction from Cormier. I described that morning's follow-up, Catherman's changed appearance and his fake big-dollar offer to hire my photo skills. Cormier interrupted to apologize for using a job ploy to draw me to the La Concha. Then he apologized for interrupting, asked me to continue, but I'd said it all.

"Did you see the vehicle Mr. Catherman was driving?"

39

"Yesterday, a dark-colored Yukon or Suburban," I said. "This morning I didn't notice."

"With tinted windows? Tint darker than legal?"

It dawned on me. A dark, tinted Yukon or Suburban was a typical federal ride. The vehicles could have been Secret Service vans or DEA surveillance, Homeland Security or Border Patrol. "Am I taking you into the shit?"

"That was our doing," he said. "You're letting me know its depth."

We sat in silence for a minute. It might have been a good time to say a prayer for Sam, but he wasn't into prayers and my mind was sifting facts, failing to find a pattern.

I said, "Are you really a fisherman?"

"People believe what they want when they see certain things. I travel a lot and this outfit provides fine camouflage in many countries. I would rather be thought an angler than an invading businessman or a Peace Corps hippie or a Red Cross junior executive."

"Do you ever consider the number of Americans who could use your aid?"

Cormier gazed at the ceiling, considered his answer. "We doctors never knew each other until we volunteered for Baghdad a while ago, the same month, same year. We all chose to help our soldiers in a war zone. We got housed in a poorly ventilated mobile home in the Green Zone. When they found work for us, it was fucking intense. When we sat around—with vodka from Kazakhstan rather than fine wine—we figured there must be a better way to donate, to lay our asses on the line. We'd all done inner-city work and, for many different reasons, found it unfulfilling. So, yes, we considered fellow countrymen. We all felt that the more anyone gives to Americans, the more Americans expect freebies to continue indefinitely."

We all have opinions, I thought. I had no comeback for him.

"I think we've covered everything," said Cormier, "except for a

40

couple of warnings. You should consider your home and cell phones insecure, open lines to anyone with the technology to intercept. And bear in mind, even if you don't talk, they will know who you've dialed."

"But I can't control who calls me," I said. "What else?"

"Would you mind meeting my wife for another drink around 7:00, give or take a few minutes? Some place other than Louie's—your choice."

I wasn't happy with the prospect of joining them in their mess. And I almost said, "Another offer too good to be true." But keeping Sam's ass out of a grave, a prison, or the deep blue sea was the only reason for my sitting in the church, plotting against the government or the human smugglers or a combination of the two. "Let's make it Prime 951," I said, "the steak house on Caroline."

"One of our favorites," said Cormier. "She'll have her bells on."

And her shirt, too, I hoped.

"If she's there when you walk in," he added, "don't sit next to her. Don't act like you know her. Let her make the move to you."

Another good time to clamp shut my mouth.

I GAVE CORMIER A one-minute head start. On my way out of the church I saw a slight movement in an archway about four feet above me. I stepped aside then stepped back. Ah, sweet paranoia. A nesting dove, worried that I was there. You can't ask for more protection than a church.

Fat good it would do.

4

I PARKED THE TRIUMPH in its custom-built, weather-tight shed—now worth about sixty grand on the Catherman scale—and walked down Dredgers Lane to check on Carmen. Her two-year-old Passat wagon sat in its usual spot, half on the lane's pavement, half in her grass-and-gravel lawn. The boys had wedged their battered Honda between two croton bushes. An empty bike rack rode its rear end. A bumper sticker screamed END WAR NOW! I couldn't argue with the sentiment, but I wondered who, exactly, might pull up behind the car, read the message and possess the power to act upon it.

Carmen walked out the kitchen door as I approached to knock. "The boys are out job-hunting. Maria and I are going to Mickey D's for chicken wraps."

"Everything smooth?" I said.

Her face clouded. "Hector and Cecilia want to sell. They've got no social life here. All their friends who are still alive have moved to the new island, that circle around Ocala with the forty-mile radius."

"They'll get a good chunk of change for that house," I said. "They'll never worry again about money."

"My mother—in a rare moment of clear thinking—came up with this. We sell this cottage and Maria and I move into their house. I can buy them a nice place in central Florida and I'll inherit the big house—with less capital gain if I ever sell."

"Do I have to beg you to stay?" I said.

"I have no choice, Alex, although my love life could use a change of venue. I'd need transfer approval from the Postal Service and two of my fellow-workers have already applied for Ocala. I'd be so low on the list, I might have to wait for two or three years."

"Your longevity's worth sticking with the post office?"

"The way I hear it, every decent job in Ocala's already gone. Most have been taken by people who've already left the Keys. Anyway, there's a house for sale near Carol Anne, like a block away. If it checks out okay, we can buy it and they'll be close to her. That's a huge relief."

Not for my selfish self, I thought.

"Thanks for letting me weep on your shoulder at noon." Carmen turned to her daughter. "I wasn't really crying, honey. Figure of speech."

Maria rolled her eyes. "Mom, you never cry. Your eyes perspire. Can we go now?"

I WAS TWO STEPS into my house when the phone rang. Bobbi Lewis, contrite. "Sorry I was short at lunchtime," she said. "I spent the morning with Chicken Neck and two big-shot out-of-town cops. They treated me like a servant, and Liska put up with it."

"That doesn't sound like our sheriff. He sees 'suits' as leaches programmed to steal cases—or the limelight. He hates to cooperate."

"Well he was kissing ass with this pair, but they were in Hawaiian shirts instead of spiffed up like bankers. It's only taken about thirty years for non-locals to learn the value of blending in."

"What was the occasion?" I said.

"If I knew, I couldn't tell you."

Translation: she knew but wasn't going to blab.

"When did Liska phase himself back into disco style?"

"Never happen, Alex. This morning he looked like a model from a Brooks Brothers catalog. Button-down blue oxford cloth, Italian loafers, pressed khakis. His dance fever days are behind him."

That didn't square with his attire at Louie's. He must have gone home to change before meeting Wonsetler for their liquid lunch. Maybe he felt dirty in his office clothes, soiled by the silence imposed upon his whole department.

"Can I make up for my rudeness?" said Lewis. "You want to do something tonight?"

"What, walk downtown and chase the music?" It would have to be after my scheduled rendezvous with Lisa Cormier.

"I meant earlier, like dinner on me," she said. "I was thinking of splurging, going to Michaels."

What would it be, the showdown, the breakup? The sweet, romantic meal when she offers the age-old words, *"It's nothing you did or didn't do, Alex. It's all my fault, this need for a change."*

"How about a glass of wine at my house first?" I said.

"The restaurant has wine," she said. "See you at six-thirty?"

"I did a late lunch, Bobbi. How about eight-thirty?"

"Okay, seven-thirty." She hung up.

The caller I.D. window told me I'd had another call. I hit the speed button for message retrieval and punched my code.

Catherman: "Rutledge, I'm sorry I barked. I was way out of line. I'm asking you to reconsider. You probably tossed my business card, and I don't blame you. Here's where to reach me." He reeled off seven digits then added, "That or call Cecil Colding. He owns the grocery where Sally works. He's going to bat for us."

Bat?

Us?

I still had his card in my wallet. I sent the message to oblivion and tapped out Sam and Marnie's home number.

"I have to admit," said Marnie, "I drove over the Bight bridge.

45

No skiff, no car. Is it raining at your house?"

"Beautiful sunny day."

"It's pouring here," she said.

"I hope you mean actual wetness and not poetic metaphor."

"I don't have frigging time for pain poems, Alex. No haikus of the broken-hearted."

"Why don't we talk over a couple beers," I said, "share a few laughs with Vicki?"

"Well, I'm not..."

"Great. See you there." I hung up and pulled the plug from the wall.

I might have the makings of a successful spy. An eavesdropper on my phone line would have to know Vicki to understand where we were headed. I pocketed Catherman's card before I started walking down Grinnell.

SOME VETERANS CAME OUT of Vietnam damaged; all of them came out changed. Sam Wheeler had never discussed his experiences beyond the one-liners; battlefield words of wisdom, quick praise or disdain for books and movies about the war. I knew no details on the action he had seen, the peace of mind it had cost him to bring home a Silver Star. He once said, "If you fight crazy people with crazy logic, you force the other guy to share your fear. The more he has, the better your shot." Several years ago he volunteered to counsel Desert Storm and Iraq vets. It took him too far into his memories. He quit before it tilted his mental balance.

Sam and I had taken turns over the years owing each other for lunches, pep talks, physical labor, and arrest avoidance. He had saved my life twice, debts he wouldn't let me discuss. We'd reached a point of trust where odd requests went unquestioned, occasional peril was taken for granted. While certain aspects of our mutual respect came off as foolhardy to outsiders, to Bobbi and especially to Marnie, they felt natural to me—as opposed to macho—and as simple as foxhole dependability. We had become each other's back-facing eyes. It sounded like Sam was up to his ass in this operation. If he needed a hand, I'd be there with an arm.

THE SCHOONER WHARF CROWD was packed in for music and sunset. Sheltered from a brisk southeast wind, the leeward calm in the bar was thick with smoke and chatter. I signaled Vicki for a beer. She handed over an Amstel Light with a shrug; there were no seats in sight. I took my beer to the boardwalk where gas and oil fumes from the dinghy corral still had a fighting chance, as did grilled fish from somewhere upwind. Tarpon splashed under the decking and dock lines creaked as sailboats' high rigging swayed.

Also swaying—but counter to the wind and the world about him—my old friend Dubbie Tanner. He had made an art form out of false homelessness, living for years out of the trunk of a Chevy four-door, sleeping under bridges, hustling shots and beers from tourists who thought him quaint, a true island character. I happened to know that he earned a solid income from an old venture. He now owned a slum-on-stilts on Rockland Key where he showered and did laundry. His drinks-for-the-needy act remained active.

"Spare change, mate?" he said.

"What's new, Dubbie? What are the street secrets known only to you?"

"If you feel rich enough for the full list, here goes. Little Feat are recording at Shrimpboat Sound. They rented a house on Margaret and hired a healthy-food chef. Someone in the city planner's office might have taken a bribe. It might have been precisely fifty-two hundred, but you never heard that. A body—maybe two—was found on the beach at Bay Point yesterday morning. And my brewski is empty—from now until midnight."

"I heard none of it," I said. "Can I ask your source on Bay Point?"

He up-ended his beer. "Not while I'm drinking."

Marnie appeared. I gave Dubbie a twenty to go away.

"Have you talked to Sam?" she said.

"No, but I know that he's fine and there's been no one else."

"Sounds like hearsay. Were you trying to talk in code, or what?"

"Your presence is proof that I succeeded."

"My obvious next question," she said. "Why code?"

"Here's where you have to trust us both," I said. "And please don't decide that you need a drink to make the jump."

"What am I supposed to do, Alex? Chug a fucking Dr. Pepper and cheer for my missing lover?"

"All I can say is that he's in a slight jam and, as I suggested this morning, he's being true to his character."

"A slight jam as in life or death, or merely serious?"

"In the big picture we might call it turbulence," I said. "But you might want to treat your home phone like a party line."

Her face went to instant disgust. "Is the damned Pentagon interested in my hair appointments? My pizza orders? Is there an extra topping profile that will turn me into a 'person of interest?'"

I couldn't answer without saying too much. After a half-minute of silence I said, "Anything more on your no-content news story?"

Marnie mulled my words, stared up at the mast lights of the tall schooner *Hindu*. "The paper got an email, a Citizens Voice blast. It questioned a police blockade on Bay Point yesterday, so we know it wasn't Sugarloaf."

"It wasn't just a blockade," I said. "I heard some maniac bitching at Liska this afternoon on the Afterdeck at Louie's. They evacuated homes along one stretch. He saw it going down and pretended not to be home. The deputies had helpers in unmarked vehicles. I'm guessing they maybe found a body."

"I demand the maniac's name," she said.

"Don't know it."

"How did Liska react?"

"He didn't say squat. His mood could've darkened a coal mine."

"You know more than you're letting on," she said.

"What makes you say that?"

"When I saw you at the library, you had something on your mind. I could tell by the lines in your face."

"Always the reporter," I said, "sussing out her sources."

"Anything you need to unload?"

"I didn't think so until I got back to my house and talked to Carmen," I said. "A slick fellow in his mid-forties came by Monday, tried to feel me out on selling my cottage. I sent him away. He showed again this morning—looking like forty miles of bad road—and tried to hire me as a private eye. He said I had a reputation for crime solutions. He knew about Little Torch, even knew about Avery Hatch, back in the Stone Age. His nineteen-year-old daughter works at a grocery on Summerland but she's been missing for two days."

"At Murray's?"

"No, Colding's, the one farther up, where Monte's Restaurant used to be. I told him I made my living taking pictures, so he tried to pay me a tall stack of cash to take her picture."

"All you had to do was find her first?"

"I sent him away again. But that's not the punch line. He's also made offers to buy Carmen's cottage and her parents' house. Do you know what time it is?"

"Two minutes to seven. I want his number and the daughter's name."

I gave her the info and said, "Go slowly with this guy. This mess has him shook. He was a pompous dick, but his sanity was barely along for the ride."

FIVE MINUTES AFTER COUNSELING Marnie not to drink, I grabbed another beer and a roadie cup before hiking over to meet Lisa Cormier. If I ran through the humid October evening, hustled three hundred yards to the restaurant, I'd be a one-man sweatshop and five minutes late. If I walked and sipped warming Amstel and watched the evening sun fade from the tops of palm trees and utility poles, I might be ten minutes late. Damn, I like easy decisions.

It would be my last for a few days.

I CHUGGED MY BEER and ditched the cup in a trash bin before entering Prime 951. I didn't want to look low-rent on my arrival to secretly meet a glamorous society dame from Atlanta. I found six empty bar stools within four steps of the door. A sign of good planning—for the chronically thirsty and weary of leg. I sensed Mrs. Cormier about fifteen feet away—the only person at the bar—but didn't look at her. I pointed to a stool to inform the woman at the podium that I didn't need a dinner table, then dutifully kept my eyes on the bartender as he delivered a drink napkin and a wine list. For some reason, at that moment, I wondered if everything Copeland Cormier had told me in church was bullshit. I tempered the thought with the fact that Sam Wheeler had vouched for him. I then sharpened the notion—Sam's assurance had arrived by an indirect path.

I would have to be extra-cautious until I could talk to Sam. Starting with staying alert and not sitting with my back to the door.

"What choices do I have in the Merlot column?" I said.

The bartender waggled his finger at a list of by-the-glass pours. "Lady behind me wants to know if you're Alex Rutledge, famous photographer."

"That's my name. I'm not so sure about the rest."

"Run with it, guy. She's got your drink, and you're welcome to join her."

"Can you pick a red for me?"

"How about a head start," said the bartender, "like a favorite."

"There's a permanent soft spot in my heart for Gallo Hearty Burgundy. What does she do, sit there every night and wait for her dream date to show up?"

Too late I saw the warning in the man's eyes.

I felt her close behind me: "Call it what you want, handsome. My name is Lisa. Can I join you?"

"Where were you sitting?"

She sashayed and I followed to the far side of the bar, finally noticing the music that had played since I entered. Frank Sinatra singing a duet with Carly Simon. I chose the farthest barstool, next to the server station, too late realizing that we now faced an enormous television. I swiveled to face Lisa Cormier.

"More comfortable facing the door?" she said.

"Like the boss in a gangster film."

"It's also positive feng shui. What do you see when you look around the restaurant?"

Was I supposed to spot surveillance or a sniper? "Can I have a category?"

"I mean, with your photographer's eye."

I turned my head to scan the room. "Thick steaks and atmosphere battling for dominance, each side armed with large knives."

"More details, please."

"Ten-pound butcher blocks masquerading as supper plates, bourbon-soaked mahogany paneling and barrel-aged candles in sconces. An abundance of wide, dark wood window blinds. Exposed yet attractive air conditioning ducts. This may be more than you want to know, but the Kelvin temperature of the room's indirect lighting is flattering to skin tones."

She looked around, slowly nodding. "More yellows than blues, I get it. What do you see when you look at me?"

If I wanted to be a wiseass, I could describe the TV show reflected on her face by the marble bar top. I took a sip from the huge wine glass that had appeared before me. Without looking at her I said, "I see a woman comfortable with her loveliness, in no danger of having to wrestle the chub demons."

"What's lovely about me, in order of importance?"

Eyes front. "Your smile, eyes, face, hair, figure... and your confidence."

"You fired that back pretty quickly," she said. "One of your tried-and-true lines?"

"Did we come here for this discussion?"

She smiled. "The floor is wide open."

Now I looked at her face, noticed imperfections I hadn't seen at Louie's Back Yard—her eyes a touch too close together, an off-kilter dimple low on her right cheek—that made her more attractive. "You're acting a shade nervous, Lisa, like a lonely housewife here to pick me up. Is that part of the act, for observers we can't identify—who may not even be here?"

The smile froze, faded to anger. "Fuck part of the act and fuck observers," she said. "My husband dreamed up an altruistic nightmare. You think I don't worry my ass off? Every day I worry my heart out."

"Copeland said five people are involved. Are they all in the Keys?"

"He also forgets, there are six involved. I am not the frigging wallpaper."

"If you're looking to recruit a seventh," I said, "I doubt that my skills match the job requirements. Or that my commitment even comes close."

"Is that wine okay, or would you rather have 'Ocho' on the rocks—Bacardi 8—like mine?"

"Very good wine. If anything, I'm a bit hungry... oh, shit." I looked at my wrist. No watch, as usual. I pulled my cell phone out of the fisherman's knife pocket on my hip. It told me I'd missed a call before 7:00, probably while I was talking with Marnie at Schooner Wharf. I had turned off the ringtone going into St. Paul's chapel. I had forgotten to reset it.

I pressed a button, read the clock. "I have to be somewhere in eight minutes. It's a ten-minute walk."

Lisa Cormier looked at me like I was dumb as toast. "Half the time I use my cell, it's to warn somebody I'm going to be late."

"Your husband suggested I use it sparingly."

"Yes," she said. "If it wasn't for his paranoia, he'd be fearless."

I borrowed the bar's phone and white pages directory. Michaels' listing, with its clip-art palm tree, was easy to find in dim light. A woman answered.

"This is Alex Rutledge calling about a 7:30 reservation..."

"Sir, Ms. Lewis called about twenty minutes ago. She changed your reservation to seven o'clock tomorrow evening. She said, in case you didn't get her message before you arrived, she apologizes. It couldn't be helped."

"Thank you. See you tomorrow." I hung up the phone as the bartender placed two appetizer plates in front of us. They must have been ordered before I arrived. Lisa was baiting her trap with every conceivable treat. Next up, she'd hand me a motel room key, two condoms, and her panties.

"Why am I here?"

Lisa studied the rum in her glass, took a deep breath. "We haven't been able to reach Sam since you and my husband spoke in the chapel. We want you—and we believe Sam would want you—to pursue this search for the man's daughter. It may carry some relevance to our situation."

"I'd become one more person to worry about. Or don't I count?"

"We're not asking you to volunteer your skills, Alex. You take the man's money and give him a time limit. Three days ought to cover it, from our side of things. You do whatever you do, and we debrief once a day. By the third day, from our questions, you'll have an idea what this is all about. It's something we're prepared to trust you with."

"Are you throwing me to the wolves?" I said.

"Not the hungry ones. Treat it like you face each day. Be alert to danger. Keep an open mind, especially in daylight."

She made it sound so easy. Bob Catherman's cash. My tush hung on the line. Doctors with Deep Wallets reaping benefits I wasn't allowed to know about.

On the other hand, I could always screech to a halt, hand back the money. I might even get the chance to verify the mess with Sam Wheeler, perhaps feel good about helping to extract him from his undefined jam. Benefit of the doubt pushed me toward the hunt, toward finding the girl. Without direct word from Sam, I didn't like a bit of it.

"Please pay the bill and leave first," I said.

"You're with us?"

"I'll give Catherman his three days unless..."

"Unless Sam tells you to stop."

"Just for this moment, Lisa, get the fuck out of my brain."

"If it wasn't a mystery, it wouldn't be life. That's what my daddy used to say. Can you meet me tomorrow, like this, at 5:30 in Virgilio's?"

"Sure," I said. "But I mean it. Go away right now."

She began to speak but stopped. For an instant I saw true hardness in her face. It may be the Atlanta high road now, I thought, but only one generation removed from Appalachian tough times. She put four twenties under her drink napkin, sniffed a couple of times but still said nothing. She strode—as opposed to sashayed—to the exit, disappeared into the darkness of Caroline Street.

I DUG CATHERMAN'S BUSINESS card out of my wallet and asked again to borrow the bar phone. I dialed his number and identified myself.

"Mr. Rutledge," he said. "Where do we start?"

"With that bank envelope," I said. "Then, for a day or two, maybe longer, the 'we' part of it goes away."

"I'm supposed to sit and wait for the phone to ring? No fucking way."

"Do whatever you please, Mr. Catherman, but I won't play tag-team. I go solo or I stay home."

No response.

"It's your call," I said.

"Can you disabuse me of the thought that you've come aboard only for the money? I fear that you'll go through the motions with no concern for results."

"You came to me in the first place," I said. "Where was your fear of my intentions this morning?"

"I've had all day to think about everything in my world."

"I've built a photo career by giving my clients their money's worth. This time the difference is my lack of experience. But you have your opinions on that."

For some reason I suspected that his protracted silence was just for effect.

"I live on Cudjoe," he finally said. "It'll take me thirty-five, forty minutes to drive into town."

"That won't work for me," I said. "Have any deputies called you back on your missing person report?"

"Nope, not a word. Like I said before, they didn't really take a report."

"Did you go to the substation on Cudjoe as well as the sheriff's office on Stock Island?"

"Only the main office. That's where I spoke with that unpleasant woman."

"Can you meet me at 9:30 tomorrow inside the post office on Summerland?"

"I'll have money with me," he said.

"Bring me three grand. I'll give you three days, then it ends. Also, bring me more pictures. I'd like to see a variety. And a copy of her car registration... Her class schedule, too, if you can find it."

"How about four days for five grand?" he said.

"No."

I WALKED BACK TO the bar. Lisa Cormier's drink glass was gone. The bartender held a wine bottle just above my glass.

I shook my head. "My turn to drink rum, rocks."

"Gotcha."

"One other small detail," I said. "I know you didn't send those untouched appetizers back to the kitchen. My supper plans are down the tubes. There's plenty for both of us, right?"

5

A VOICE ORDERED ME to clean out the boat. I was awakened by the stench of fish left in the sun for days in an Igloo cooler. My pillow felt crusty and stank of booze drool. The odor was my breath; the pain behind my forehead the result of poor judgment—or a crappy job of counting my drinks. The upside was that I wasn't waking in someone's hedge, wasn't a guest of the city. I recall feeling odd relief when Bobbi Lewis had postponed our Last—my presumption—Dinner, and half-wishing that Lisa Cormier had slipped me a motel key instead of relaying her husband's request that I deal with Catherman. I wasn't sure I had the balance to stand and brush my teeth. I had no choice but to get out of bed. My bladder was calling the shots.

Twenty minutes later the coffee had done its trick. My hair was contained, the clothing was no longer yesterday's. Small matter that my eyes needed flushing, my face could have used a sand-blasting.

I thought seriously about returning to dreamland.

"Rutledge? Are you home?"

The voice of Beth Watkins—a Key West detective with maybe a year on the job—stood at the screen door. I'd be happier to see her smile than she'd be to view the wreckage of Rutledge. I began to ask why I hadn't heard her Ducati motorcycle in the lane but shut up when I saw her glum expression. Lieutenant Julio Alonzo, in his stretched-out city uniform, lurked on the stoop. Julio had pegged his gaze on an indeterminate spot about six feet off the ground and halfway to the lane pavement.

She had that look on her face. Someone close to me was hurt or worse.

I opened the door, stood aside to let them enter. "Who died?"

"What makes you think anyone's dead?" said Watkins.

"The gloom in your eye. The phrasing of your question confirms it."

"One of your neighbors."

That category included Carmen, her daughter and her parents. I wasn't about to trivialize by guessing, popping out names.

Watkins stared at me. Her skin was pasty, her hair more brown than yellow, as if she hadn't been outdoors in weeks. She wore a white polo shirt embroidered with a city logo, pressed dark blue slacks and a fanny pack-type pouch on the front of her belt. Alonzo now stared at the back of her neck, his eyes the tone of the ocean's surface on a chill, cloudy day.

"Well?" I said.

"You knew someone was dead?"

"What's with the tone, Watkins? Are you here to inform me of a passing or to question me as a crime suspect?"

Watkins kept her eyes locked on mine. "Tell me about your friendship with Jerry Hammond."

"That's not a name I know," I said. "Would you like some coffee?"

Alonzo moved sideways, a macho shuffle that let him block the doorway. What was I going to do, escape the prison of my own home?

Beth Watkins stared and said nothing.

"No one named Hammond has lived on Dredgers Lane as long as I've been here."

"Mr. Hammond lived on Eaton Street."

"Another world, detective."

"It's the next street." She pointed. "You hear that truck?"

I hadn't noticed the truck's rumbling exhaust until she mentioned it. Had I conditioned myself to ignore vehicles droning fifty yards away? "This lane hasn't changed in years," I said, "which is one reason I stay. Houses on Eaton get sold and remodeled and sold and bought again. It's a flipper's bazaar with vultures and temporaries and part-timers who hang just long enough to cut their dream deals. I have no reason to socialize with anyone over there."

"Over there is your back fence."

"My side fence. I never met my side fence neighbor. Only his dog."

"That's a bit strange, this close, you never met," she said.

"His taste in music sucked. I was forced to share too many loud evenings with Barry Manilow. I took that as a sampling of the man's personality."

"You never introduced yourself? No fence talk about bush trimming, maybe borrowing a rake?"

"Never laid eyes on him."

"Everyone in this town knew Jerry Hammond," said Lieutenant Alonzo, his Conch accent a reminder of past years. His put-down phrasing alerted me, told me to ignore him, to keep my attention on Watkins.

"Is this Hammond a victim or a bad guy?"

She let down her guard. "Maybe both, you never know. Could be, the bad got him killed."

"When?" I said.

"Nobody had seen him for two days," said Watkins. "A friend of his called and we sent in an officer. The place was unlocked."

"Last night or this morning?"

"A few hours ago," she said. "It was daybreak by the time we got the prelim scene crew assembled."

I imagined a traffic snarl on Eaton with detectives' cars and forensic vans. But I couldn't miss it: a fast-moving Harley suggested that the street was clear.

"Why does everyone know this man?" I said.

"He worked the post office for twelve years," said Alonzo. "He retired last summer. Then he volunteered at that Bahama Village music school."

"He worked with Carmen for twelve years?" I said. "She never mentioned him. He was her neighbor, too."

Watkins angled her head to check the lane toward Carmen's house. "We've heard that he and Ms. Sosa didn't share mutual respect. No one ever got a reprimand, but there was a history of minimal cooperation."

"Ah, strife. That can happen in the workplace," I said.

Watkins nodded. "We need to hope it didn't carry over to his dining room."

"Don't even think she could do it," I said. "Carmen's so anti-violence, she once tried to hire me to kick my own ass when I'd pissed her off."

"She may be able to give us some ideas."

"She's a good judge of character."

"You never even saw him, say, through the hedge?"

I shook my head. "I heard him or some frequent guest of his sing along with Barry, but I can't recall hearing anyone talk over there, ever. It's crazy, I admit it. Hammond was a total stranger who lived thirty yards from where I sleep and eat."

Beth nodded. "He's been in that house since the late nineties."

"I knew the woman who bought it in the early nineties," I said. "She bought it on a shoestring and paid it down with alimony. Spent five years fixing it to resell, and when she found a buyer I never saw her again."

"This island, it changes downhill," said Alonzo.

Watkins and I watched him try to scowl. His fleshy face refused to play. His expression remained the same.

"I was a barefoot kid," he said, "picking spanish limes, mangoes out of my yard, everybody know everybody. Sure as hell we know nicknames, their whole family, all the kids, their jobs. Key West is going away like a bar of soap, rubbed down to dime-size."

"I remember when you were a beat cop, Julio," I said, "harassing hippies on Duval. I didn't know anyone on Eaton back then, either. A lot changed, I'll give you that. But plenty is still the same."

"Cayo Hueso got trampled by Woodstock refugees," said the lieutenant. "You got another opinion, I'm sure."

"I take a bigger view of it," I said. "The Navy ran the island when hippies were still beatniks. Tourists came after the longhairs grew up and blended in. If you take a longer look, the spongers, cigar rollers, railroad and hurricanes, it's been constant change for two centuries."

Alonzo said, "The hippies may think they blended, but they ruined it."

He hadn't soaked up a word I'd said.

Puzzled by Alonzo's vehemence, Watkins tried to calm him. "You heard his complaint about part-timers, Julio," she said. "He wants our island to stay the same."

Alonzo's sullen eyes became slits as he glanced back through the screening. Now that Watkins had touched the topic, truck and moped sounds from Eaton Street became more persistent.

"I'm worried about our crime scene," said Watkins. "We need to make sure it's not being contaminated."

I took that to mean invaded by jurisdiction poachers from county or state law enforcement. It worked as an excuse to get rid of Alonzo.

The lieutenant shoved open the door but stopped and turned. "Lady, he's not talking about *our* island. I was born here and you weren't. He's talking about *my* island."

He stepped out, let the door slam and marched off. Ten paces away he raised his voice. "You bring the car, detective. I'll walk around the block like we used to do."

Beth Watkins observed a few ticks of silence then said, "From what I know, he's got a legit complaint."

"It's after-the-fact whining," I said. "The old-time Conchs have taken the money, house by house, for twenty-five years and left town with fat wallets. I've wondered all that time why more of them didn't stand up for their turf, reject the profits and defend the lifestyles they bemoan in hindsight. He can bitch all he wants, but it's like trying to hold back the wind with a sail."

"You've been saving that speech for a while."

"Maybe he's the only one left who bemoans the changes," I said. "Anyway, thanks."

"For chilling him out? It didn't work too well."

"For not asking me to take crime scene photos."

She hesitated, tried to decide on her wording. "Your proximity to the deceased disqualified you."

"In what way, Beth?" I said. "A 'person of interest' or a just a neighbor?"

She gave me an odd look. "Who dragged you away from advertising photos in the first place?"

"I still do magazine work and brochures. It's how I make my living."

"You know what I meant," she said.

"Sheriff Liska, years ago. Before he quit your desk at the city to run for office. I must have needed cash that month. Neither of us knew it was habit-forming."

"They wouldn't have called you back if you weren't good at it."

"What do you know about Bay Point?"

"That article in the paper this morning? Zip. I went to a party up there two months ago. It was dark. A year ago I observed while the county processed a crime scene... What am I saying? You were there."

"I'm talking yesterday," I said.

"What's to know? If it was county crap, I'm out of the loop. When was the last time you saw Mr. Hammond's dog?"

I shrugged and shook my head.

"Surely there's an answer to that one," said Watkins.

"Can I think about it and call you in a while?"

"When was the last time you heard Manilow?"

"Saturday night, around nine p.m."

"Four days ago."

"Three and a half days ago," I said. "Almost to the hour."

Beth nodded. "There was another reason I didn't ask you to take pictures. Are you still seeing Bobbi, your deputy?"

I almost shrugged but went the gentleman route and nodded.

"I know she pisses you off every time she calls you with a police photo gig. You deserve better treatment from a woman you're dating."

"How does that..."

"I didn't want to join her club."

"Whose do you want to join?"

She started toward the street. "Call me if you think of anything helpful."

I HAD LESS THAN an hour to get to Summerland, but I wanted to make sure that Carmen—if she was at home—knew about Hammond. I also wanted to meet her houseguests and check on their job- and home-hunting progress. Plus, their goal of reacquainting themselves with Key West had sparked my curiosity. I envied their search for the island life they had missed because of their parents' decisions. After years of watching the trickling exodus, I had lost hope of seeing many—or any—departed Conchs return to Key West.

63

———

I HIKED THE LANE and found the young men loading duffels, five or six Hefty Bags and several grocery sacks into their Honda. The shorter of the two hoisted a satchel while he pressed a phone to his ear.

The taller boy gave me a suspicious look then relaxed. "You must be Alex, the neighbor." He stuck out his hand. "I'm Jason Dudak."

"You guys packing to leave already? Giving up on the old island?"

"No way," said Jason. "That geek there is Russell—with his mama on the line. We're having a glory moment because in the last hour and..." he checked his watch, "in the last eighty minutes we both got jobs—plus a place to live."

"Fast work," I said.

"The jobs—we hustled a couple days. The apartment, some guy that works at Greenacres—the yard maintenance people who hired Russell—he said, 'You dudes need to score a crib, I got bunks.' His roommate split for the Ukraine owing him, like, sixty-five dollars."

"You didn't go with Greenacres?" I said.

"RPP Construction. Pounding nails, which will work some sweat out of me and keep me outdoors, both of which are good."

I knew the men who had started RPP years ago. It had changed hands several times, along the way earning a negative reputation. I once heard someone speculate that its initials stood for Rape, Pillage and Plunder.

"You going to live off the island?" I said.

The other boy approached, snapping shut his phone, reaching to shake hands. "I'm Russell Hernandez. Did you know me when I was little? Everyone I've met the past two days knew me when I was three years old."

"I missed you that time around," I said.

"Our new home is on Elizabeth Street," said Jason. "Four or five of us—we're not sure—in two rooms upstairs from the woman who

64

owns the house."

I had to laugh. "Sounds like the standard arrangement when I first hit town. I would've put up with anything, I was so happy to be here. I didn't know why I was so content, but I sure as hell felt it."

Russell clenched his fist in the air. "The first thing that got me was a whiff of Knights Key, like this combination of fish damp and salt and seaweed. It gave me a preview of Key West smells."

"Okay, but before that," said Jason, "we drove up that bridge at Tea Table Channel south of Islamorada. The road goes up and down like a dirt bike race track with green areas like city parks, bike paths snaking on either side. But seventy feet to our right and left, past that greenery, it was salt water, nothing but ocean as far west as I could see. It was the ocean with Naples one way and Havana the other."

"I'm for smells," said Russell Hernandez. "I wake up every morning, the air tells me that we made the right decision to come down here, to catch up with our lives. As far as looking around town, I haven't had time."

"Is Carmen around?" I said.

Jason opened the car door, got ready to hop in. "The princess went to school and Carmen went to work."

"Are you all moved out? Is this it?"

Russell said, "We travel light." He pointed to the Hefty Bags. "Our matching luggage. That's how we roll."

"Glad you wrapped up your deal so quickly."

"We're not done yet," said Jason. "We can't exactly relax at the beach. We'll be working in the weather and sun, so we need clothes. These Reef sandals won't cut it."

"Life stays complicated, doesn't it?" I said.

"Damn, you said it, amigo. Complicated."

6

I APPROACHED MY MEETING with Catherman with sporadic nausea. I blamed it on dread and distaste, denying the wave action of my hangover. Bob wanted one thing, a search for his daughter. Copeland Cormier—with Sam out of sight and Lisa running point—claimed to need information, nothing more. I wasn't privy to his goals. I couldn't imagine how a missing young woman might relate to his Cuban drug transfers.

Secrecy, implied risk, and my ass on the line. Not much of a job description. I would dive in with shit for knowledge, but that was okay. Doctors with Deep Wallets, no matter their agenda, wouldn't influence my queries. I wouldn't have to slant my questions. I could stay focused and still cover the favor asked by the Cormiers on behalf of Sam. If I tried to connect Sam to a nineteen-year-old new to the Keys, I could drive myself nuts. It helped to believe that he hadn't gone to the dark side. He wasn't thumbing his nose at state and federal laws for purposes other than altruism.

Then came the money. Now that I had taken the job, I had to take the man's cash. If I volunteered to work for free, I could ruin my credibility. If Sally turned out to be dead—from suicide, a double-suicide, or murder, I would feel lame for having charged a cent. But that was how Catherman wanted to play it. Plus, why be stupid about involving myself? Given Sam's need to hide and

Cormier's check-ins and other clandestine actions, cash in hand made sense before I started. If only for bail money and emergency room visits.

Before leaving the house I looked up Bokamp in the phone book. Two Lower Keys listings, neither for Mikey or the initial M, neither offering an address. If I could locate Sally Catherman's carpool friend, she might have ideas to help my search. I wrote the numbers on a scrap of paper, stuck it in my wallet. I also grabbed my Canon camera. Small as a deck of cards, it fits in a front pocket of my shorts—as well as the palm of my hand.

MARNIE'S BROTHER, BUTLER DUNWOODY, gave me a 1970 Triumph several years ago after someone torched my Kawasaki while I was doing Butler a favor. It's a classic T120R, hence the locked, custom-built mini-condo that keeps it mine and protects it from rain and salt air. It's my sunny-day ride for distances beyond bicycle range, and I often invent trips off the island to free my mind of cobwebs.

I chose it this time for low profile. Motorcycles are common in the Keys. It was less conspicuous, less memorable than my car.

I rode the Palm Avenue bridge, checked the Garrison Bight dock where flats guides keep their skiffs. Sam's slip was empty though he would have *Fancy Fool,* on a morning like this, in the Snipes or Marquesas. Also missing was *Flats Broke,* the Maverick skippered by Sam's friend Captain Turk. Again, normal for this time of day, this time of year. Not that I was forgetting my locale. In Key West what is normal, ever?

I drove across Stock Island with a group of lane-changers who competed for asphalt as they'd been taught for years by on-car cameras and racing analysts. The frantic pack slowed at Rockland Channel Bridge then funneled onto "Lower Shark," as Big Coppitt residents refer to their island—in parodic reference to the Shark

Key enclave one island eastward. Except for the new telephone switching boxes on raised platforms, I saw little evidence of Hurricane Wilma's flooding of several years back. I recalled the aftermath, the green trees and shrubs damaged and killed by salt wind and water. Offshore mangrove islands turned reddish-brown. Of course I couldn't see the waterlogged file cabinets and photo albums, the ruined dreams, displaced families. Like many storms, Wilma had put the worst hurt on those least capable of dealing with it. I'd been lucky at my place. Dredgers Lane had come within two blocks of turning into oceanfront property. In the weeks following the flood, when I wasn't helping friends discard furniture and appliances, I built shelves for the waterproof containers that now held all my film files and office records.

AT 9:32 AM I PEELED off my helmet in the Summerland post office parking lot. Catherman climbed out of a dark gray Porsche Cayenne SUV and began to walk toward me.

Be alert to danger, I thought, even in daylight.

I averted my eyes, fiddled with the motorcycle. I said, "See you inside."

He had the smarts to keep quiet and keep walking.

In a long room lined with post office boxes, he handed me the fat envelope. The place smelled of damp paper and shampoo, though I welcomed the cool air. No one else was in that wing. No one outside could see us. Catherman looked less disheveled than the previous morning. He wore a clean polo shirt, pressed Levi's, clean athletic shoes, a fresh shave. Studying his eyes, I saw more aging. But weak and tired, he was still a large customer.

Inside the envelope I found another envelope—presumably full of hundreds—plus photocopies of Sally's car registration, the picture page of her passport, her drivers license renewal notice, and three copies of the head shot—the innocent eyes that had grabbed me two mornings ago on my porch. He hadn't found a school schedule, but I could ask her friends about that.

I squeezed the sealed envelope between my thumb and index finger. "Unless this is fifties, it feels a little thick for three grand."

"It's five grand," he said. "That doesn't mean a fourth day is anything but your option. We're good for three—unless you feel compelled…"

"I won't, but…" I split the cash into two wads, then folded and stuck them in separate Velcro-closure front pockets in my shorts. I placed the envelope with the Sally-relevant material in my helmet padding. While I did this, no one entered or left the building. We were good so far unless a well-hidden security camera had documented our rendezvous.

"How you making out?" I said.

"For shit, since you asked. A third of the time I pretend she went to visit her double-wide mother. The rest of the time I sit awake, making lists, thinking of things I could do. Then I think of reasons none of them will work."

"Did you try again to report the stolen Miata?"

He nodded. "I spoke with an officer at the Cudjoe substation who sounded willing to help."

"Do me a favor, then," I said. "Call your insurance agency and tell them it's gone. Tell them you've heard talk in the Keys about a sports car theft ring working out of Homestead. Ask them to pressure the sheriff's office to catch the thieves."

"Okay."

"Then call the deputy and tell him that you're worried about getting dropped by your insurance company. Stress that you'd appreciate his checking for basic evidence. Especially fingerprints so the thief can be identified and busted."

"He needs me to tell him how to do his job?" Catherman's voice echoed in the empty room. I heard workplace joking and other chatter in the mail sorting area. No one was paying attention to us.

"Tell him to the point of slipping him, say, fifty bucks if you have to."

"And set myself up for a bribery bust."

"I don't think it's illegal to pay a cop to do his job," I said. "Or compensate him for the extra time it might take. It's not like you're trying to buy your way out of a citation. If they try to track a car thief and plug the right info into their system, they might stumble onto a kidnapper."

I knew it was wrong the instant I said it. Catherman caved as if he'd been kneed in the nuts.

"Sorry," I said.

"That's all right, Rutledge." He tapped his forehead. "The concept has been up in here for two days. Just hearing someone else say it out loud..."

"I like to work backward from the full-bad chance. That way we don't skip details. Clues that could take us to less-bad. Or give us a shot at neutral."

Catherman appeared to accept my strategy. "Do you always wear a crash helmet?"

"Always, and always long sleeves."

"Protect yourself if the bike goes down."

"I don't think much about accidents," I said. "The hours I spend on the cycle, I worry about sunburn. Which days does Sally go to school?"

"Every day but Tuesday—yesterday. But different times every day."

"Please leave before I do. But one last thing. Any boyfriends—here or in Sarasota?"

"No way," said Catherman. "Her school work kept her too busy. Back in Sarasota, I wouldn't know. She never mentioned or called anyone."

"Does she ever go up the Keys, say shopping in Key Largo or Miami?"

71

He shook his head, began to walk away. "I would have told you all these things yesterday morning. She went from home to school to work and back home."

"No social life at all?"

"What do you mean? She wasn't a hermit. I didn't keep her in a cage. She and her girlfriends went to the beach a couple times. I tried to take her out to dinner once a week. The Square Grouper, Boondocks, that place at the end of Drost Road."

"Thanks," I said. "That gives me a better picture."

"One last thing," he said as he went for the exit. "Don't contact her mother. Let me take care of that side of things." He pushed on the exit door and dropped his sunglasses. One lens popped out when they hit the tile floor.

"Fuck," he said.

"Not me, I hope," said a woman trying to enter the post office. She hurried past him before he could muster an apology.

OUTSIDE, THREADING MY CHIN strap, I saw them. The dark blue Dodge Charger on the far shoulder tipped me off. It sat an inch higher than the showroom version of that sedan and ran 18-inch wheels, telltales of a cop-duty handling package. A stubby antenna poked up from the center-rear of its roof. The driver had dropped his window six inches or so.

Any observer could see the open map and assume some daffy tourist had gotten his ass lost on the only road in the Keys. The other, thinking himself clever, had backed his maroon Impala between two forward-facing pickups in front of the hardware next door. He was staged for a quick exit. Both cars had "probable cause" window tint—dark enough to justify a traffic stop—for a civilian. It had taken thirty years for non-local police to under-stand the stealth value of tropical duds south of Miami. They still weren't compelled—or budgeted—to drive blend-in vehicles.

They'd have been less obvious in old Jeeps or Broncos. Even pink Bentleys or chrome-plated Hummers.

A promo sign in front of the hardware said: ""Small enough to know you, bigger than we look." The irony allowed me a two-second smile.

Catherman was behind another car waiting to pull out of the lot. It crossed my mind that I had forgotten to ask him to stay away from the grocery. I wanted him to go south and the Charger to follow. The six-cylinder Impala would be easier to evade and, unless they had an additional car to tail me, I would be free to roam in fewer than ten minutes.

Or maybe not, on the only road in the Keys. From where I stood, with twenty-four miles paved westward and ninety to Florida City, US 1 was a fool's freedom, no matter his vehicle. I couldn't outrun anyone.

The Porsche Cayenne's left turn signal eased my concern. Catherman pulled into the center lane and blended quickly into southbound traffic. I feigned inattention while the driver of the Charger dropped his map and raised his window. With a Honda van between me and the Impala, I snapped a picture of the Charger. He gave Catherman a five-vehicle head start then joined the flow.

I shifted into first, rolled slowly to a vending box and pretended to peruse newspaper headlines. Sure as hell, my movement inspired Impala. He inched far enough forward to give himself a 180-degree view. He also gave me a clear view of his small-radius "poverty" hubcaps on black wheels. Why don't they just paint badges on the side of their cars?

From that point onward I was solid on several things. Catherman and I each had a shadow, so someone knew of our meeting in advance. That meant his phone was tapped and my license tag number was now in the mix. It also gave probability to my home and cell lines being monitored before day's end.

The obvious fact: Cormier understood the playing field.

Another zinger: I had mentioned the bank envelope during the phone call. The listeners didn't know how much the envelope held. But I could bet they would love to confiscate it, make me go to a judge to explain and justify my ownership.

In no hurry to lead the Impala to Colding's Grocery, I kept staring at the *USA Today* and *Miami Herald* boxes. I needed to stop thinking like a criminal and tally facts from the beginning. A girl was missing. A senior agency had told the sheriff to bug off from a crime scene. A large number of agents had been mobilized. All lips were sealed. The public had no knowledge that a problem existed.

What would bring law enforcement heavies to town?

Work it through. Keep mimicking my study of front pages. I needed to think like a headline scribe. Refugees from Haiti or Cuba delivered by smugglers who charged by the head. Refugees killed and dumped to elude the Marine Patrol or Customs. Or killed because the payoff man didn't show at the drop point. Rival human-cargo gangs wanting to prove points, gain dominance. None of them, I thought, were big enough. It could be only one thing.

Nothing brought out horsepower, relentless investigation and door-pounding like the murder of a federal agent. If publicity had accompanied the scramble, the whole nation might know that an officer was dead or imperiled.

A fresh stream of two-beat scenarios rushed my thinking. Agents were targeted but the wrong two people were killed. The death of a crooked cop demanded a quick solution with zero publicity. A blown undercover operation or a dead federal informant—both of which required massive disconnect to escape the blame game. Sally murdered because her father was smuggling humans, drugs or cash. Or—after all, this was Florida—a non-event that had been politically chain-yanked into a mudbath.

On top of all that, Copeland Cormier felt that his pharmaceutical transport scheme had been put on the ropes by some aspect of the ongoing circus.

Still it was hard to connect the big scenarios with young Sally Catherman, a student new to the Keys. Unless she was dating someone on the smuggling team. Or a murdered cop. Or had dumped a jealous man with a gun and a badge.

If these fellows were as thorough as I now believed, they would have another team member watching Colding's. No matter where I went—they would know.

I had been grossly underpaid.

The only thing left to outrun was my imagination. I probably couldn't do that, either. I checked oncoming, twisted the throttle, and fell in behind a northbound pickup truck.

7

As I NEARED COLDING'S, a quarter-mile north of the post office, the truck in front of me turned on East Shore. With open road ahead, I decided to drag the Impala a few miles farther to see if I could shake him—or force him to commit to being on my butt. It would tell me how badly he wanted to monitor me, and I like going fast. Traffic had thinned, typical for the tourist off-season.

Going up the Niles Channel Bridge slope, not knowing what patrols might lurk beyond the crest, I kept it under sixty-five. Except for a flock of dive-bombing gulls above the bridge, my spook and I owned the highway. Once I hit the summit and could see most of Ramrod Key, I cracked it open, ran it up to eighty-five. It took him longer to reach speed but he hung with me—not bad for an Impala. It confirmed his gig. He ran fast knowing he could badge his ass out of a ticket.

Halfway across Ramrod I braked hard and went left into the Boondocks lot. To inform me that he was a true prick while I was a minor-leaguer, he didn't slow, missed me by two feet, then continued up the road. I expected to see him duck into the Chevron or the Looe Key Tiki Bar so he could loop back to monitor me, but he kept on rolling toward Middle Torch. The decline of my importance offended me. Maybe I had been passed to another babysitter. No matter what, I wanted to make a call.

Common sense told me that the coin phone outside Colding's Grocery was already a police party line. On the other hand, they couldn't tap every damn box in the county. I didn't see a booth at Boondocks Grille so I rode the quarter-mile to the Chevron. A deputy in a county green-and-white came toward me, southbound, cruising easy. Timing is everything. I had been lucky on my speed run. Also, the cop hadn't needed to whip back northward to chase a speeder. The Impala had slowed or pulled over.

I CALLED HIS HOME first. It was more wishful thinking than a hunch. I thought Liska would be able to speak more freely without subordinates lingering within earshot. No matter the conversation, I could read his mood, especially compared to his liquid lunch on Monday at Louie's. I expected his answering service.

To my relief he picked up. He grunted, sounded asleep.

"Do I still have to call you Fred?"

"Shit," he said. "Why did I answer this bastard?"

"Your steadfast devotion to duty?"

"Right now, Rutledge, my only allegiance is to the reclining chair. And I'm not running a hotline, advice to the lovelorn."

"Are you still running the Monroe County Sheriff's Office?"

I sensed a beat of hesitation before he said, "The eighty percent I usually run. A wise man plans for pockets of anarchy, even on slow days."

"I guess that's how a smart fellow plans his romances, too."

"Don't start," said Liska.

"Is Sally Catherman with you?"

"Oh, Rutledge, you fucking fool. Just the fact that you know her name..."

"Her daddy asked me to help..."

"Stop," he said. "Even I'm not privy and, believe me, I'm happy to keep my distance. It's only by chance that I learned their names

78

and I'm not that damn glad that I did. Did you sic the news monster on me?"

"The paper got a 'Citizens Voice' e-mail. Some Bay Point resident whining about roadblocks and evacuations. That got me Marnie, and I told her about that dork who mouthed-off at the bar."

Liska bought time, cleared his throat. Patience, I thought. The temperature in the phone booth must have been over 100. I hoped he was considering his moral commitment to his job. Or getting up steam to tell me how much he resented an outside agency treading his turf. Except for a close friend of mine—an ex-Key West cop—I had never met a federal interloper who had run for office, walked a beat or justified his actions to a skeptical city commission.

"How did she get my cell number?"

"I've never had your cell number," I said. "Maybe one of your employees. Your office isn't leak-proof. You've known that from the beginning."

"I can't tell you strongly enough, Rutledge, back off. This could poison your future, fuck up your credit, you name it."

"Just so they don't scar my face. I have to accept that my phone is wide open, my civil rights are being violated."

"What civil rights, fucknut?" said Liska. "Try a red flag on your passport. That's a lifetime sentence to high hassle."

That one got my attention. I had seen the ugly treatment given in airports to people with flags on their names.

"I'm curious," he said. "How come you're so hot-shit anxious to work for the girl's father when you tell me, every time I need your help, to take a walk?"

"It's a complicated deal," I said.

"Here's one that's not." He hung up on me.

CROSSING BACK TO SUMMERLAND I fought a southeast crosswind at the bridge crest. On another day it might have made a fun ride more sporting. The mid-morning sun's heat and minding the speed limit and not having my mind on sport made it a task. I spent more time checking my mirror than the road ahead while I tried to script my questions for the people at Colding's Grocery. If Sally Catherman's fellow employees saw her as a pain in the ass or boss's favorite, they might see her absence as positive. If they feared that her disappearance was connected to her working with the public, they might be afraid to talk with me. My first step would be to chat up the owner, to find out how he intended to "go to bat for us."

AT THE NORTHEAST CORNER of Summerland Key's busiest intersection, Colding's couldn't be more public. I checked the Mobil station and the office building lot across the street. No suspicious sedans—but that didn't assure me that I wasn't being watched. A gravel road lined with stacked lobster traps ran eastward from the grocery's parking area. The only vehicles in that direction belonged to commercial fishermen who tended to reinvest in their boats rather than their pickups. I couldn't picture an undercover agent borrowing a funky, stained, rusty, dented and lopsided truck. A Lexus SUV in front of the store's entrance boasted a LIMITED EDITION badge.

For the moment, apparently, I had no watchdog. It was just as well. Liska had put me in a mood to confront someone, and agents lose much of their humor when they take the gig. They aren't promoted for their charm, and have no patience with those who fail to see the serious nature of their mission. If I fumbled a one-on-one, resorted to chuckles and lies, I'd be illegally searched and taken to a cramped, ugly room to explain myself—and the cash still in my pocket.

I took my time setting the kickstand, hooking the helmet to a handlebar lock so it—and its hidden envelope—couldn't leave without me. One last look—no other cars.

"It's Rutledge, right?"

I recognized the voice of Frank Polan. He walked out of the grocery wearing unattractive, expensive-looking shades, an unattractive, expensive-looking polo-style shirt, and fishing shorts. I had encountered Mr. Polan twice in recent years during "situations."

"How you doin'?" he said. "Long time no."

"Frenzied. You?"

"Actually, a bit depressed. I just came out of this relationship, younger. She had the legs, the tits her ex-husband paid for, the cute face."

"Sounds wonderful, Frank," I said.

"But she had the kid and I ask you. I'm not getting any younger. What sense will it make, twelve years from now, to be teaching her kid to drive when the state is trying to pull my license for old age?"

"Good point."

"I wasn't all that turned on by the tits," he said. "Glad I didn't pay for them."

"So why be depressed?"

Polan admired his Lexus then shook his head. "I guess I'm happy, now that you mention it. Very happy."

If this is joy, I thought, please don't show me your flip side. "You know the owner of this place?"

"No," he said. "This is where Monty's used to be, where I ate lunch a few times a week. The county wouldn't let him expand or some shit—I can't remember. He must have pissed off a commissioner. They leveled Monty's and built this place two years ago."

"Good to see you, Frank."

"Come on by sometime. Call me. I'll take you out on one of my boats. You can bring some of those models you're always meeting. I'd rather see no boobs than store-bought boobs, you follow?" He winked. "Plus those models, I'm sure you know. They hate the tan lines."

"One of them might like you," I said.

"Too much to ask."

I REMOVED MY SHADES. It still took a half-minute for my eyes to adjust to the grocery. The place smelled of coffee, peach pies, laundry soap, and sausage spices. A store I would love to enter some other day, to inhale, inhabit and sample. One bored young woman sat on a stool at a front register. Her name tag said Alyssa. She wore a gray DKNY T-shirt, perused a National Enquirer and ignored me. A girl in a pink top and beige Bermuda shorts was stocking shelves. A slightly older woman at the deli counter along the rear wall was mass-assembling sandwiches. Her tag read: Honey Weiss. I asked her if Cecil was in the building. With a sneer disguised as a grin, Honey pointed at a closet-width unmarked door. "Go on in," she said. "He ignores knocks."

The reader at the register whispered, "But not knockers."

Cecil Colding half-stood when I entered, looked as if he was expecting me. He was an ad agency's ideal grocer. Male-pattern baldness, round head, trimmed moustache and a white Polyester blend short-sleeve shirt. The only missing piece was the pen protector. His office smelled musty though two-thirds of it was filled with cartons of store stock.

I introduced myself and explained my visit. Cecil pushed himself to the full vertical, walked halfway around his desk, crossed his arms and leaned against a steel file cabinet. He didn't offer me the chair next to my left leg.

"We were hoping you could provide some insight," I said.

He swiveled his head to one side, lifted his chin, perhaps trying to stretch a neck muscle kink. "I told the father I would do what I could. Mostly, I wanted to quiet him down. His stress level was fouling my sales atmosphere."

"How many customers did he drive away?" I said.

"Zip, nada. Thank God I cut it short. The chickadees were another story. They were starting to look frantic and I just can't have it."

Cecil's nasal voice carried no accent but he'd mastered a demeaning tone. I imagined he could say, "Nice day," and made it sound like someone's fault.

"You really aren't too worried about Sally's absence," I said.

He turned his head again as if trying to release a muscle spasm. "She wants her papa to think she's this pure little thing. Or at least give him room to believe it. Maybe you've seen the web statistics on virginity after, say, tenth grade. These days, after high school, the only thing pure with these girls is the line of crap they give their parents and boyfriends."

"Do you have any idea where Sally's basic impurities may have taken her?"

"Not a fucking one, but don't get me wrong. I wish you the best of luck. If you find her today or tomorrow, tell her she's suspended from the schedule, two days for every shift she missed so far. Tomorrow afternoon I got three interviews for replacement help."

"I'll make sure she understands that. If, say, she's anxious to return. And if she hasn't fallen victim to, say, foul play."

"What's foul play, dirty underpants?" Cecil laughed at his bad joke then at me for keeping a straight face.

"You mind if I ask your employees a few questions?"

"Do it quick," he said. "I'm not trying to roadblock you here. Go take two or three minutes, total, but no protracted interviews. Can't have them sloughing off, right? I don't pay the fuzzy-brains to speculate on tropical comings and goings."

"Any particular one be a better choice than the others?"

He shook his head, sneaked in a neck swivel. I finally realized it was a nervous tic. I could tell he was hedging.

"I challenge you, try to find a lick of sense out there on the floor. On second thought, Rutledge, you want to chat up my help, make appointments for when they're off the clock. Don't pester them while they're working. I got no say in their private lives. But I'm not running a singles bar."

Cecil Colding wanted me out of the hen house.

I exited, closed the door, and softly said, "Holy shit."

"Maybe unholy," said Honey Weiss. "Welcome to Colding's."

"You're making sandwiches for the evening rush?"

"No, for a boatload of night fishermen," she said. "Are you a rep? What are you trying to sell Cecil?"

"I'm a friend of Sally's dad. We're worried about her."

Honey nodded, tried to smile but looked grim instead. She looked over my shoulder. The shelf-stocker had walked up behind me. This one was Mikey. I had found her without trying. Her gray knit T-shirt said BIG PINK SOUTH BEACH. She looked about the same age as Alyssa but kept a reserved, quiet expression. She looked at Honey Weiss, as if for guidance or to urge her to say something.

I dug into my wallet but found only one business card. All it had was my name, the PO Box and my email address. Honey handed me a ballpoint pen. I almost wrote my phone number. A picture flashed in my head of a government snoop wearing earphones in a dark room listening to one of these young women, putting her name on a watch list. I wrote Carmen's number.

"Cecil asked me to hurry out of here," I said, "and I don't want to cause you problems. If you can help at all, leave me a message at this number, please. I'll meet you anywhere, you name it."

"Cool," said Mikey. "Rob's Island Grill. Or Square Grouper."

"Why there?" said Alyssa. "We can do a big lunch at Mangrove Mama's."

Alyssa wore a braided string necklace with a seashell dangling from it. Her ponytail was clumped into a bun, held by a green rubber band. She looked stuck in that realm between cute and beautiful, but she wasn't too young to upgrade, to be trading cheap meals for better meals.

Then, again, I had said "anywhere."

"I'll just have the salad." Alyssa waved her hands as she spoke then reached to touch my arm. "Tomorrow's my day off."

Honey appeared to enjoy it all. I watched her catch Mikey's eye and give her a subtle nod, perhaps permission to speak. I waited for Mikey to chime in.

It didn't happen. Cecil's door handle made a slight click. Alyssa and Mikey walked away. Honey went back to wrapping sandwiches in foil. By the time the boss poked his head out of the office, I was a customer. Under the watchful, perhaps suspicious eye of Cecil, I carried a small box of granola bars to the register. Up close I noticed Alyssa's metallic tongue decor. I paid with a five from my wallet—not from the wad of bills in my front pocket—then hit the exit.

THE GROCERY'S EMPTY PARKING lot did nothing to drop my pucker level. A scan of my surroundings turned up zilch. I felt more discomfort in not seeing anyone than I had with the Charger and Impala right in my face. I hadn't thought of my chat with Frank Polan as a comfort moment, but it beat standing there, pulling on my helmet, acting the bull's-eye.

The three women appeared both fearful of Colding and anxious to talk. Their worry about Sally appeared genuine. I needed to exercise what I had learned at sea in the Navy, and keep thinking a few more steps ahead of myself.

8

SPANISH MAIN DRIVE ON Cudjoe Key runs straight south from the Overseas Highway. A natural radar trap, the stretch offers a clear view in the rear view. If I were being followed, I would know. For one mile I saw only a squadron of senior tricycle riders from Venture Out, the upscale trailer park. At road's end I went right, hoping to catch Frank Polan at his coral-colored two-story home on Calico Jack Circle.

Bobbi Lewis had revealed to me a year ago that Polan had become wealthy through financial ventures kept clean by the constant vigilance of his attorneys. She knew because the deputies had done a background check on him after a shooting on his property. Polan, it turned out, was an innocent bystander.

I found him using a pole brush to chisel bird shit off the stairs to his elevated deck. He wore another pair of unattractive sunglasses, a tank top, a Speedo suit, a plastic mesh pith helmet and submersible sneakers. His shoulders and arms shined with sun oil. He didn't appear surprised to see me.

"It's okay to walk on the pea rock," he said. "I'm not as fussy as I used to be."

"That's good news, Frank. It'll reduce your stress."

"But what the hell," he said. "Try to stay on the stepping stones. You want a smoothie? I bought this very expensive blender, and I use organic fruits. It keeps down my sugar and makes me younger. Or I got beer somewhere, maybe in that fridge in the downstairs guest room. You can go look. I never have to buy beers. Visitors leave them behind."

"Thanks, but no. Your place looks great," I said. "You can't afford a yard man?"

"Oh, sure, I got the service, it comes once a week. But I keep my hand in. I replaced my treated wood with that new composite. I mean, I had it done. One less upkeep hassle. No more stain, no more sealer I gotta buy... You're right, it drops my stress level. But how do you stop this shit rain? Wouldn't our lives be better with no birds? We should teach every last one of them to fly to Iraq. They could birdshit the terror boys into submission."

Because I had come to ask a favor, I changed the subject. "You used to wear those big rubber Birkenstocks."

"They got too heavy and they boiled the tops of my feet. These Surfwalkers are like foot condoms, if they made rubbers with mesh which I'm glad they don't because of my opinion on rug rats. But I'm glad I bought these. I mean, what the hell." He waved his arm at his yard and boat ramp. "I can afford what I want."

"That's why I'm here," I said.

He took off his pith helmet. His hair was so closely cropped that his skull had a deep tan. "Come into the carport, out of the sun. I don't make loans for under fifteen percent. You should know that going in."

"I want to give you some money to hold for me. About four grand."

"You don't trust yourself not to piss it away?"

"Nothing like that," I said. "It's somebody else I don't trust. I figure, if I need someone to sit on my cash, why not a millionaire?"

Polan got an odd look on his face.

"Of course," I added, "that may be the exact person not to trust."

"You've got a point, there." Polan finally cracked a grin. "Maybe

I can put it to work for you."

"Or just hold on to it."

"Okay, I'll do that. It's the least I can do, and I always want to offer the least I can do. I'm that kind of guy. Come see my new backcountry boat, the Everglades. It draws maybe sixteen inches—a bit more with all your topless models aboard."

I almost made the mistake of following him to the dock. The view of Cudjoe Bay was a postcard dream, and Polan's array of boats, kayaks, jet skis and sailboards was equal to a five-star resort's. I stopped short, begged off, and explained to Frank that I had an appointment in Key West in an hour.

I kept some pocket money and gave Polan forty Ben Franklins. While he was double-checking my cash count the cell phone buzzed my hip. The little window flashed Bobbi Lewis's personal number.

"Frank," I said, "can I borrow your phone?"

"It's up in the kitchen, the first sliding glass door. Go around to your right, but..."

"Take off my shoes before I walk inside?"

"If you don't mind."

"Stress you haven't addressed yet, Frank?"

"Not really. I just washed the floor. I'm a very clean man."

BOBBI GRABBED MY CALL on the first ring. "Liaison."

"You want to liaison with me?"

"Alex? Why are you calling from a Lower Keys exchange?"

"I came to Cudjoe," I said. "I had to talk to a man about a possible job."

"Here in the Keys, Alex, so close to home? Won't that cramp your international lifestyle?"

"Aside from the November Bravo Rule, my style requires only frequent bank deposits."

"The November Bravo twins," said Bobbi. "No babies, no brides."

"Actually triplets," I said. "I've quit photographing bodies, too."

"No Bobbis?"

"You heard what I said."

"What else are you doing up there?"

What the hell did that mean? "Nothing. Talking out details."

"Are we still on for six-thirty?"

"How about eight?" I said.

"See you at seven." She clicked off.

"WHAT'S WITH THIS MONEY?" said Polan. "I won't ask how you earned it, but the story's on the paper. You got a safe buried under your bedroom floor?"

"What are you talking about?"

"Look at the dates. You're holding old money. These bills are from '96 and '99 and nothing newer. Which might be smart on your part. A friend of mine, getting divorced, his wife tried to put the screws. She told the tax office about his secret money stash. They went to look, made him open his safe. It was old money. He told them he saved it before he got married. They couldn't prove that he was hiding income. He got to keep it."

"But law enforcement might see it another way?" I said.

"Bingo," he said. "But I'm okay with it."

I assured Polan that his home was a masterpiece of clean.

"Okay," he said. "I won't spend your money on a power washer."

I RODE TOWARD KEY West feeling as if I had done nothing to earn a penny of Catherman's money. Beyond blowing the speed limit and badgering a slimy store owner, I had turned up diddley. Worse, I couldn't think of anything else to do except chase down Sally's classmates, maybe an instructor or two. Someone who might have clues to her habits or good friends. Or her bad habits and enemies. Maybe real private eyes have a secret checklist or standard routine that gets them results. Maybe I was still running at Bahamas pace, on a Bimini clock. A neighbor had been found dead and I hadn't taken a moment to think about it. My love life was floundering and I couldn't drum up an opinion. I wasn't in denial as much as disgust. One thing I knew for sure. At some point in the near future I would dump that spooky grin off Cecil Colding's face.

Astronomical note: during early autumn the afternoon sun is directly in your eyes when you ride toward Key West between mile markers 23 and 21. You can't see ahead at all and you don't have time to look behind. Crossing the bridge onto Upper Sugarloaf, I decided my best approach would be to stop for a think session. Stop the Triumph and stop worrying about being followed. There's a chance that I dreamed up this strategy because I was about to turn into Mangrove Mama's.

The restaurant bar was behind the dining patio. I pulled around back and found the missing car.

CATHERMAN HAD SAID, "THE only orange Mazda Miata in the Keys. You can see it a mile away." But no one could see it stashed in this parking area—two-thirds surrounded by trees and shrubs, three-quarters hidden from the highway. Blinded by the rollback-style tow truck's flashing halogen roof rack, I failed at first to notice the small car from twenty yards away.

The Storms Tow Jobs driver defined a modern-day biker. He was a bulked-out, ex-weightlifting, beer-drinking pirate with a POW-MIA logo bandanna head-wrap, full-arm tattoos, and a short leather vest over a black Sturgis T-shirt. A stout chain linked his trucker's wallet to a frayed belt loop.

I parked the Triumph, walked over to watch. "What's up?"

"If it's yours, you're too late, dude. It's ours for the time being." He tilted his head toward the restaurant. "These people called. It's been sitting here for three days."

"A friend of mine reported it stolen."

He shook his head, turned back to tightening straps. The name carved into the back of his two-inch belt read HARLAND. "I can spot stolen a hundred yards away. This thing, it's closed up and locked. No cut top, no broken window, no jimmied ignition. Your friend maybe took drunk, got fucked up, forgot where he lost it. Or she, whatever. It happens. Bad for them, good for me."

"Where you going to haul it?"

"Our locked lot on No Name Key," said Harland. "Tell your friend not to try to liberate it. Our guard dogs are plain ugly. We time their feedings by a random computer-generated schedule. It keeps them healthy and hungry. And... even if your friend's car is stolen, we still get our fees."

I was tempted to ride to Catherman's home, to tell him the news. But hurrying wouldn't change things. He couldn't get the vehicle processed and released any sooner than Harland wanted it to happen. And keeping it in secure storage might preserve evidence, if there was any to be found. With the car so carefully hidden and locked, a reasonable person might assume that Sally had put it there. Plus, I had overlooked one detail. Even though Bob Catherman had handed me five grand less than two hours earlier, I didn't know where he lived. I walked to my Triumph and peeled back the damp foam liner in my helmet. Its backing material had protected the envelope of pictures and photocopies. Catherman's address on Scabbard Road was printed on the envelope. It didn't prompt me to head his way.

I had imagined that finding the car would offer us a breakthrough. Instead it had handed me more things to ponder.

———

I HUNG THE HELMET on the bike and walked through the patio and into the bar. I didn't know the woman setting up for the late-afternoon rush.

I ordered an Amstel and said, "Do you know if Anne's working tonight?"

"She works at Square Grouper now. You must've been gone for a while."

"I live in town. I'm down there most of the time. But I've got to say, that's the first time I've ever seen a car towed out of here."

"That Miata, I wondered," she said. "Last couple months I've seen a cute little girl driving it on the highway. Our schedules must have caused that we passed all the time. I didn't know where she was going and she sure-as-shit didn't notice me, but it's hard to miss a car like that. Anyway, a man parked it here and got out, I don't know, Monday or Tuesday, right as I got here for work. I thought maybe he was leaving it for her, or she was driving his car and they were meeting here. That can happen. Last I saw, he was walking around to the front. Maybe he didn't go in the front entrance—maybe he got a ride out of here."

"Do you remember what he looked like?" I asked.

"Like a hundred other guys, I suppose. Not too tall or short, no clothing that stood out so I would have noticed. I guess I'm saying I can't bring a picture of the dude into my brain right now. Anyway, there was that car the next day, yesterday. So what does that make it, Monday he parked it? So the next day I think maybe it was stolen. This Key West cop comes like he does in most days for his after-work beer, to get stewed before he goes home to his bitch of a girlfriend. I tell him about that little car, how long it's been sitting there and it might be stolen. He tells me not to bother calling the county. They'd just tell me to call a wrecker. So, finally we did, we called the wrecker four hours ago. Took him long enough to get here, and it's not like its a hundred miles. Good thing it wasn't a real wreck."

Good thing I didn't ask a third question, not that I didn't appreciate her info. I slugged down my beer before the conversation could grow into a burdensome exchange of hunches and clichés.

I PULLED OUT OF Mangrove Mama's and twisted it on. The limit was forty-five and I was doing ten over in six seconds. A new medium-blue Mustang came toward me, doing about the same speed. It honked as it passed. It wasn't a car I knew—it looked to be a rental—but people like my Triumph. I watched it fade in my mirror. I didn't see it cut a U-turn. Before I reached the Crane Boulevard traffic signal, a mile west, the Mustang was on my butt and passing me. It slowed for the light. Sam Wheeler beckoned me to turn right and follow. A quarter-mile farther he went left onto Bad George Road and drove to the dead end.

With "dead" the operative description. The mudhole-pocked turnaround was the last repository of shit no one wanted. Chunks of docks, washing machines, used tires, a scattering of gravel from another era.

Looking more weather-beaten than usual, Sam climbed out of the low-slung GT while I unstrapped my helmet. He stared down the empty street for a half-minute to watch for company. He pressed a key ring button that popped his deck lid, then pulled three Beck's Lights from a cooler that was bungee-corded upright inside the trunk. Using yachtsman's smarts and the skin between his left thumb and forefinger as a fulcrum, Sam hooked one bottle cap under the sharp base of each of the others to lever them off. He returned the unopened one to the cooler.

We raised a quick, silent toast to the blue sky and our predicament.

"Catch me up," I said.

"You go first."

It took me four minutes to tell all. I described the real estate offer, the agent's return the next day and his attempt to hire me. I mentioned Marnie's concern, Lisa Cormier's come-on and Copeland's recruitment, their request that I look for the girl. Then the cash delivery, the spy boys watching the post office, and Cecil's attitude—which I described as more slimy than suspicious. I told him about the drunk at Louie's who blasted Liska about the Bay Point roadblock.

"It's still blocked where the road splits," he said. "They're letting in residents only."

Sam went for two more beers, came back and handed me mine. The man I had known for two decades to be rock solid and energized looked depleted. He sat and studied the bottle in his hand. "I've been trying to cut back."

"You been on the pussy trail?" I said.

"Trail, yes, but not that one. I should have guessed that she would worry in that regard. But that isn't it."

I looked him in the eye. "What is it? Is there any of the old Sam left in the shell?"

He risked a quick grin, really a smirk. "I saw this obese woman on Simonton Street last weekend with a T-shirt that said, 'It's Not Nice to Stare.' Half an hour later, out by the Bight, I saw a knockout. She was maybe forty-five, great legs, nice figure, beautiful hair. She was wearing a T-shirt that said, 'It's Not Nice to Stare.' So that begs the question. What do we nice guys do? Gouge out our eyes?"

"That's a passable version of the old Sam." I tried not to stare at the three or four days of stubble on his chin.

"This is my fish camp look," he said. "The girl you're looking for. Is her name Sally?"

I didn't move a muscle.

"Oh, fuck," he said.

"Do I give the man back his money?"

Perspiration streamed down his face. "No, keep looking for her.

Just act as if you don't know a thing. If her old man gets outraged and goes to the media, my dear Marnie included, we'll have a worse cluster on our hands."

"Do I want to know?"

He looked away, fixed his gaze focused down the road. "Can I wait to tell you? Now is not a good time."

A small brown dog ambled up the road, saw us, stopped and started to bark. Sam kneeled down, held out his hand, whistled softly. The dog, quieted, hurried over to sniff us out, then retreated to other territory.

"I spoke with Liska ninety minutes ago," I said. "I brought up Sally by name and he got upset."

Sam turned his head, closed one eye against the sun, waited for more.

"Liska said it was only by chance that he learned the names."

"He used the word, 'names,' plural?"

I nodded.

"Double fuck." He stood and looked around. "That's especially not good."

"Where's *Fancy Fool*?" I said.

"Hung on a davit in seawall suburbia, where it will stay. Totally out of sight."

"I saw the Bronco parked on Flagler."

"Right," he said. "The result of an evasive action."

"You found a GPS transmitter?"

Sam nodded.

I said, "They may have put something on the Triumph."

Sam grinned. "A GPS tracker device? They'd need a search warrant. Which is not to say they won't try. If you happen to find one in the next day or two, don't mess with it. They wire it to your battery and if their signal goes out, they know you're trying to evade. That could bring down a full-court press."

"You act like you're on the lam," I said. "You sound like you're in

96

the eighth inning of a doom game."

"Everybody's normal life is a doom game, Alex. I just hope I'm in the fourth or fifth inning. Certainly no farther than the seventh-inning stretch."

"I didn't mean life span," I said. "I meant this week."

"Shit, we may only be in the top half of the first inning."

"Where to from here? Are you through making deliveries to Cuba?"

"The first few times we knew that I was clear to go down and back. The last time I went, this past weekend, I had the same assurance. But I had to make use of my... call it local knowledge. I had to evade an ugly boat with multiple motors."

"So until someone straightens out the mix-up..."

"Right," he said. "The whole deal's on hold. Or washed up. Which is too bad because I know we were helping out."

"So I keep pretending to be a private eye?"

"Do everything you should be doing," he said. "Just don't do too good a job. If you learn something that, say, takes you to another level, that's when you back off and shut up and play stupid as a weed."

"Meanwhile, where will you be?" I said. "Full tilt or heavy whoa?"

"I'll be around. If I have to leave the county, I'll go up into Florida and find a down-and-out motel that will let me register without a credit card."

"Go stay with Annie Minnette."

"If things go as they I suspect they might—at least at first—she could be disbarred for harboring me."

"Have you got any money?"

Sam scratched his head, looked puzzled, then held out his hand. I dug out the ten Bens.

"Take it one day at a time," he said. "Whatever you'd give the father for his money, which I'll match. Double-dip your ass off."

"Not a cent," I said.

"Cash only," he said. "This is not a beer job. One thing, though.

See who she was with. Get a name. But cut the father out of your moves."

"I already did. Can I have one more clue?"

"Stay alert for the name Cliff Brock."

"Is that mister or sergeant or..."

"Mister—civilian," said Sam. "Though some are more equal than others."

"Is that the other name that Liska knew?"

"We hope not," said Sam.

I had never seen such a forlorn expression on his face.

"Is there anything you can do in person for Marnie?" I said. I'm not too good with it falling on me."

"I'll figure something tonight or tomorrow. Where's that pistol I loaned you a couple of years ago?"

"Back with you," I said.

"You got that concealed permit, right?"

"Last year."

"Next chance I get, I'll loan it to you. Make it a habit to carry."

"Let's not use that hook behind the shower," I said. "Copeland Cormier knows about it."

"Why should he be a worry?" said Sam.

"This is all new to me, captain. I trust only you, sunrise, sundown and the brakes on the Triumph."

"That may be one too many," he said. "That garage Carmen rents you for your Shelby, what kind of lock has it got?"

"Bingo," I said, and told him the combination. "There's an old Granday canned turtle crate in there. It's full of wax and WD-40 and towels."

"I'll wrap it in the towels."

"Maybe you should tell me one or two things that might constitute red flags. Reasons to carry a weapon."

He looked away, said nothing.

"Have I ever pushed you for anything?"

"Okay," he said. "Be alert to cops you've never met being far too friendly. Don't tell Copeland or his wife that you spoke with me. You're a wise man, Alex. If it gets hinky, you'll know when to back off."

"And for two beers you'd send me into a cave full of razor blades?"

He knew I was making light of the dilemma, but his tone went grim. "If anything weird goes down, get in touch with Captain Turk at the Bight. He's on our side. But don't talk to him before any odd shit comes down. Turk can get a little frantic."

"Does truly weird mean you'll be dead?"

A cell phone rang, not mine. It was in the fish-knife pocket of Sam's shorts.

"Just as you never saw me, you did not hear that," he said.

"In exchange for one favor," I replied.

"Name it."

"If I die, please keep an eye on my obituary. I hate the phrase 'sorely missed' and I don't know what it means, anyway."

Sam smiled. "It's a way of saying you pulled out too fast."

I let myself grin. "Thanks for the beer."

Explaining that he needed to be "up the road, right about now," Sam put our empties back in the Igloo, wedged himself into the Mustang, and dragged a dust cloud down Bad George.

I SAT ON THE TRIUMPH and viewed my surroundings. Two abandoned utility poles capped with insulators, aluminum scrap. A gutted Volvo. The upturned base of an office chair. A stripped, rusted-out motorscooter. Even the grass and shrubs looked depleted. I didn't hear birds, but a quarter-mile away the dog barked at a new target. A few miles to the south, one mile higher, a military jet hot out of Boca Chica sped toward the Gulf of Mexico.

I was back to playing solo.

99

9

THIS TIME I KNEW why Carmen Sosa was on my porch recliner, palm to her forehead. I locked the Triumph in its Shed Deluxe, tossed my helmet in the front room then joined her in the warm shade. An open bottle on the porcelain-top table dripped condensation. The wine glass in Carmen's other hand tilted almost to the point of spilling. She hadn't changed out of her postal service uniform.

"Your phone rang five minutes ago," she said. "You might have a message."

"It can wait," I said. "You're first in line. I'd rather plop down right here and share your..."

"Pinot Grigio. It's cold."

"You bet. I'll get a..."

"Your glass is right here behind the bottle."

"...and sit here and talk to you."

"About..."

"The death of a co-worker," I said.

"Not to mention neighbor."

"Whom I never knew and you never mentioned before." I placed my helmet on my threadbare director's chair.

She looked away. "He was the neighbor I denied. I wanted to think ignoring him would make him go away."

I almost said, "I guess it worked," but my self-censor clicked in.

I went inside to urinate. I had demolished a strict rule about drinking while driving. Sam's beers plus the one I slammed at Mangrove Mama's had been three too many for riding the motorcycle, but they hadn't inspired me to act crazily or head-butt a phone pole. They had combined to dissuade me from stopping at the college to inquire about the late Sally Catherman. From Upper Sugarloaf to Stock Island a tall thunderhead had chased me. I'd also had the Florida Highway Patrol on my tail from the Saddlebunch Keys to Key Haven. Instead of making me wish I had drunk fewer beers, he boosted my thirst for several more. I could've given him a run for his money like I did with the Impala on Ramrod. Why should I act intelligently when all those around me are making shit choices?

Now, at home, it occurred to me that the trooper had been put on my ass by a government agency with initials for a name.

I PISSED FOR TWO minutes. During that time I reminded myself that I had to meet Copeland Cormier at Virgilio's at 5:30. Meet with the man who had urged me to collect Catherman's money for a useless task, a job for which I had no skills. Sam hadn't appeared surprised by Cormier's request nor had he argued for a different approach. Both men had shown lack of respect for the father of a girl presumed to be dead.

Someone could think they knew Catherman and already had lost respect.

Hell, I thought. If the trooper had been sent by someone, what about Catherman? Had he come to Dredgers Lane as part of Cormier's scheme? If so, Carmen's plans to sell her home and move her parents to Ocala could be skunked from the get-go. I begged myself to return to reality. Sam wouldn't put up with that style of game playing.

I returned to the porch, poured some wine, my arms still twitching from road vibrations. I sat facing the door, wishing I could stop for the day and stare at my shrubs. Think about overdue yard work or wonder if I needed to clean more fan blades. The sympathetic buzz from the motorcycle engine stayed with me, helped me into the zone. But I popped out of my reverie when I wondered when Sam would hide his pistol in my garage.

Carmen sipped from her glass, shook her head. "If Hammond had ever touched Maria, I would *not* have killed him. I'd have chained him to a cop car and chopped off his balls, kicked them down the street and let his future keepers clean up the mess."

"Please don't repeat that in front of another soul. Why would he touch Maria?"

"Oh, I'm not sure he would. But there's always been talk of his taste in young ones—not cradle robbing, not under the line but almost. Hell, he spread most of the gossip himself. He made sure his pals knew that the 'sweet chickadees' were legal. He made no secret that he liked to taste them. That tidbit trickled through the office about once a year."

"You think some father..."

"That would be my first guess. That's what I told the detectives."

"Julio Alonzo said that Hammond volunteered at the Bahama Village music school."

"I'm sure the investigators will run that one down," she said. "The problem is, every little flute player in town will have to answer to some stranger about whether an old man fiddled with her panties."

"Unless they find his killer first," I said. "One that's unrelated to his..."

"Go ahead, I said it first," said Carmen. "His tastes."

Time again to stay silent. I reached over and poured for Carmen until she motioned for me to quit.

"Marnie came by and interviewed me about twenty minutes

ago," she said. "Everything I told her made me sound like I was a hit man or I'd bought one. She had fewer questions than I thought she might."

"She was being considerate," I said. "She's the type."

"Unlike the cops. I made her promise not to use my name in print."

"If you see her again, please tell her that Sam's in great shape and in control."

"That sounds iffy. Between you and me, she seemed a bit off her game."

"And it's a story that will wait until tomorrow," I said. "Speaking of which, I caught a good one from the boys this morning."

"I was going to celebrate. They found jobs and an apartment. All their crap is out of my house. I have to admit, they were fastidious about keeping their dirty laundry in their car and doing their own dishes. Shit, now I wish they were back, just for the sake of security, having two men around the house. With just me and Maria... Okay, change the subject. Have you heard from Bobbi?"

"Intermittently."

"You've got that look. Is she fast becoming the future ex-Mrs. Rutledge?"

"Dinner tonight on her plastic," I said.

"Think you'll get laid?"

"Too much to ask." The words came out before I realized that I was echoing Frank Polan.

"I can tell, you want this to work," said Carmen.

"That's been true from day one. Now I want it to be more like day one."

"Dreamer."

"You always call me a dreamer," said Carmen's daughter, Maria Rolley, through the screen door. "Are you the only one who's not one?"

"Where did you come from?" demanded Carmen.

104

"The day I was born or the last five minutes?"

Carmen looked at me. "The boys were here three days, and she turned into a wiseass."

"Will you drive me to Elizabeth Street?" said Maria. "Jason promised to loan me his Simpsons Tenth Season DVD when he gets it unpacked. It was buried in his trunk."

"It can't happen today, honey. But I don't want you to go alone, you hear? In about ten minutes I have to take your grandmother to Publix for rice pudding and Cajun crab boil mix." Carmen turned to me. "Cajun. All these years I thought my mother was Cuban. Thanks for the glass of wine. I'll put your bottle back in the fridge."

Covering herself from the judgment of the child.

"Tomorrow, after school?" said Maria.

"Maybe I'll take you over there tomorrow," I said.

"Cool." Without changing her expression, she walked away.

Carmen got up to follow her. "Alex, don't forget that phone message."

"Don't let this murder affect your decision to stay," I said, "or to move your parents away. We need to talk and think this through. You may be able to keep both houses and buy them a place in Ocala. Whatever rent you might get for your cottage would pay down an upstate mortgage overnight."

She tried to smile in response. It came off as a grimace.

BOBBI ON THE VOICE mail service: "Alex, I got tied up and I'll be a little late. Let's meet at the restaurant at seven-fifteen. Make it seven-thirty, and could you change the reservation?"

Tied up? The photographer's mind wanders...

Ah, yes, photography. I needed to turn on my printer and download the digital picture of the Dodge Charger. A little something to hand to Lisa Cormier. It wasn't any more than a side-on car shot. But it spoke of attempted work—of progress I hadn't made. I checked the time. Enough to print a five-by-seven and take the nap I should have grabbed after finishing my morning coffee. I inserted the flash chip and a sheet of matte photo paper, pressed three buttons and let the machine earn its keep. I called Michaels to bump up our dinner reservation. Then I set the alarm in my cell phone, gave myself a twenty-minute snooze.

It felt like the bell woke me five minutes later. I spent two minutes of quality time in the shower. I decided to walk to my meeting. If it didn't kill me, it might wake me up.

VIRGILIO'S IS AN OBLONG backyard bar behind La Trattoria, a restaurant on Duval. Half of the place is open-air, nicknamed the Rain Forest. The section under the roof is, much of the week, a night jazz club. Rather than barging through the restaurant, I entered by way of Appelrouth Lane. Lisa Cormier was not on the crowded patio. But her husband was inside, the sole customer at the bar. I wasn't sure whether to approach him, but he waved me over, grabbed and squeezed my upper arm like a proud uncle.

"Hey pal, what's up?" he said. "You just happened to drop in for a toddy?"

Cormier's breath smelled as if he'd been drinking cleaning fluid. He had gone to a tourist's outfit—in plaid Bermuda shorts, dark loafers without socks, and a tan guayabera shirt.

The bartender and server had that look on their faces. Cormier had done or said something strange enough to embarrass the witnesses.

Copeland slurred his words. "When I was a kid in college, I was in the Vegas airport on a layover between Los Angeles and Denver. I didn't have time to go into town, just to switch planes. And they had slot machines all over the terminal, and I didn't believe in gambling and I was probably too young to gamble. But I thought what the hell. I gave myself permission to risk jail time and one

106

twenty-five-cent piece. I had this feeling—what's the word, poetic... no, prophetic—that it would either make me a pocketful of money or give me an insightful message about my future. Are you with me so far?"

I nodded knowing that a disinterested shrug could backfire.

"It was the soul of that moment, and how do you explain such a thing? So I dropped the quarter and I yanked the lever, can you picture that? And you know what came up, Rutledge? A cherry, a cherry and a lemon, and in my youth I didn't get it. I didn't get it for years, for twenty years, however many. I didn't understand that message until about three months ago." He quit talking long enough to sip his drink. "You want a drink, Alex? Tell this fine man what you want."

"Right now I want to hear your story," I lied.

"My first wife, bless her soul, died in a car wreck near Memphis while the first George Bush was president, the father, the ex-CIA boss. My second wife, bless her soul, died on an operating table, not mine, thank God. Let's not call on vulgar slang, but those two women, when I met them, you get the idea. My third wife, I believe, is the lemon. I'll spare you the details, but I don't know how else to put it. What do you think of my story?"

I shrugged.

"No, really. I want to know."

"I always thought slot machines were manufactured to make us all losers," I said. "I never held much stock in fortune telling. It sounds like you asked a one-armed bandit to read you a permanent horoscope."

"I am guilty as charged," he said. "Do you judge that to be a mistake?"

"It's like asking a tractor to confirm your religion."

"Oh, that's a simile or a metaphor. But that's not my question. How do you interpret the message?"

"How do you define lemon? It could be a complement to rum, a car that needs constant repair, a natural curative, a deodorizer..."

He raised his drink as if saluting a monarch. "Go back to constant repair." The drink spilled down his arm.

I suspected that Copeland Cormier had fallen victim to Key West Syndrome. Many first-timers, surrounded by strangers and what appears on the surface to be a free-for-all atmosphere, shed their common sense and inhibitions. They thumb their noses at morals, bouncers, clocks, laws, cleanliness, sunburn, and the fact that other people can detect the booze and drugs. It's when they thumb their noses at hoteliers, cops, bouncers and spouses that fireworks really start to fly. Cormier hadn't mixed it up with the badges—that I knew of—yet. He sounded as if he had pissed off his wife.

"You better have a cocktail before I drink all the hooch in this saloon," said Cormier. "Tell the man here what might be your pleasure."

I looked at the bartender. He gave a quick shake of his head then rolled his eyes toward the glass door behind Copeland, the door that led to La Trattoria's dining room. I slowly moved my head to that direction. The moment Lisa saw me looking, she crooked a finger and vanished back into the restaurant.

"I don't want to sound rude," I said. "I've got a dinner date in a half hour."

Cormier leaned back to better focus on my face. "You came in here for some damned thing. Near as I can see they're only selling drinks. Does my gregarious nature put you on edge?"

Hell yes, I thought. Being around him, the smell of him, wore me out. "I came in to meet someone—to discuss business," I said. "For some reason she's not here. I must have missed her, but I can't wait around."

"I can tell you're a man on the move, sir. More power to you, in this town."

"In this town," I said, "power is a razor-edged boomerang."

That one stumped him. Me too, if I'd thought about it.

I escaped through the door I'd entered, came face to face with the old concrete rectangle that once was Wax, long before that the Bamboo Room and lately Club Zu. I hiked between the buildings, the evening air smelling of nearby rain. Tourists on Duval walked in the late-day haze, searching shop windows for life-affirming products. Mile Zero decals, hookahs, palm tree trivets.

LISA CORMIER STOOD ON the sidewalk in front of the restaurant. Elegant among the unwashed but a haunted look on her face. "I was shopping at the other end of this street today," she said. "I bought one of your fine art photographs." She pointed at the former Strand Theater. "It's that place before it became Walgreen's."

The owner of Oops Gallery, an old friend, had asked me to frame two dozen ten-by-seven prints—all island scenes. He sold them often enough to keep me in his shop. I replenished his walls when he asked.

"Did you take any pictures today?"

I had forgotten the photo of the Dodge Charger. It was still on the printer tray in my office. I shook my head. "Can we walk away from here?"

She started toward Fleming. "Whatever you had to deal with, I apologize."

"You didn't do it."

"I got there early to meet you and he was already there, drunk as a skunk. He told the bartender I was a whore he'd met at the Casa Marina last night."

"What's he call you in a good mood?"

We walked around a dreadlocked busker on a folding chair who played a plywood guitar and sang the worst version of "Come Monday" I had ever heard.

"Whore is his favorite name for me. He knew when we met that I'd already lived with two different men, one for three years and one for six years. Since we got married, I've hardly even told a dirty joke. I sure as hell haven't slept with anyone. Which is not to say," she added, "that I wasn't in the mood yesterday at the Afterdeck. But as you know, nothing happened."

"Not while I was there," I said.

Lisa waved her arm, motioned us up Fleming. "Spoken like a true private eye. Did you have any luck today?"

"The girl I'm looking for—you know about that?"

Lisa nodded.

"She must have been into monkey business. I saw an unmarked car following her father. Aside from that, zilch."

"We therefore assume he was into monkey business as well?"

"Why is your husband acting the opposite of what I saw yesterday?"

"He's upset because his charity operation is coming unglued. Did he tell you that we haven't heard from Sam Wheeler today? He never radioed in."

"No, he didn't say that. He told me about cherries and lemons."

Lisa stopped under an overhang, crossed her arms and stared at a bike rack. "Are you married?"

"No," I said.

"Do you want to walk over there and check into the hotel? You can have me any way you want, do anything to me, with me, whatever. With you I would be a virgin, not a lemon, not a gutter slut."

"I have a dinner date in twenty minutes," I said. "And I've had a long day."

She got a rain-check look in her eye.

"Plus," I added, "I slept with one married woman years ago and regretted it ever since. Someone once said to me, 'Do a married man a favor and...'"

"'...don't fuck his wife for him. I heard that one too. Could you at least tell me that I'm worth considering?"

"You're more than that," I said. "And you're better than that, too. Please don't go gutter-slut just to get even. Especially here on Duval."

"Thank you. Please have faith in my husband's project, despite his behavior. Have a nice dinner. I'm going to lose myself in that book store across the street."

MARNIE DUNWOODY WAS SITTING in her Jeep in front of my cottage. She closed her cell phone and quit poking at her laptop keyboard.

"You live within crawling distance of a major crime," she said. "Fill me in."

"Jerry Hammond of Eaton Street, found cold, I believe, in his dining room. My bonus was a female detective running hot and cold on my porch."

"When was the last time you saw Mr. Hammond?"

"In another life," I said.

"Can you give me a date that's less metaphysical?"

"Never met my neighbor."

"He worked at the post office," she said. "Everybody knew him."

"That's what I hear. How could I possibly know more than Carmen? You're here for today's Sam Report."

"Spill."

"I saw him on Sugarloaf. He was driving a borrowed car. I don't know what kind of jam he's in or how he's thinking, but the wheels are turning. He knows there's a problem and he doesn't want to drag you into it."

"Bullshit in every breath you take."

"Marnie, it's me. We both know that if, two days from now, everything turns out fine—an explanation, an apology, all that— you'll still kick my ass. Literally karate-kick my ass if I'm bullshitting you right now."

"That's right," she said. "Damn it." She pondered it all for about ten seconds. "So what are you doing? Why were you on Sugarloaf, for instance? Where is Sam staying?"

"Every time I've asked you not to put something in the newspaper, two things have happened, right?

"Well, I've waited—until you gave me the green light."

"And you've gotten a big scoop out of the deal."

She pushed the shift lever into reverse, started the Jeep. "Don't even tell me. That way I won't have to kick your ass no matter what. Because you'd know for months that I had done it." She backed out of the lane onto Fleming without looking first.

I went inside to change my shorts—and my shirt for the fourth time that day.

Sam hadn't radioed in?

10

BLUE DUSK COOLED THE Fleming sidewalk. I walked toward Margaret, toward the restaurant under purple thunderheads haloed by orange and yellow vapor. Why, after several years, was I always surprised to see Cobo Pharmacy gone? So many homes in renovation, a dawn-to-dusk percussion of power nailers, saws, portable drills—the island's constant sound track. Rhoda Baker's Electric Kitchen, where Hemingway took his 1930s fishing "Mob" to breakfast, was now a private home. At least the building was intact. I knew its owner, knew she appreciated the history.

Bobbi and I had walked this way to dinner, library events, friends' parties. A few times, on cool evenings, we invented reasons to hike to Fausto's or the book store, or to stroll around, chat and take pictures. This time I felt uneasy, as if I had been naughty, was being summoned to present myself for punishment.

How—on short notice—could our love affair be so close to teetering? Certain things had changed. The fun quotient was down. Support had displaced laughter. She needed a shoulder to cry on more often than an ass to grab, a smile to share. What had begun so well now felt habitual, draining. I wanted to yank her away from routine, put spark in our time together. But there was a new complication, according to Liska. An old friend had reentered her life.

I wasn't ready to quit. I didn't want to be another lover-gone-sour on her life list.

The people I had seen waiting for tables at Michaels in recent months, sipping wine outside at twilight, wore tropical formal. Men in pressed trousers, exotic-print silk shirts, shoes a step above casual. Women in designer sundresses and tasteful, abundant jewelry. I entered in my usual fishing shorts, frayed polo shirt and beat up deck shoes. I love this island. The woman at the podium told me that our table was ready but my date had phoned. Bobbi would be ten minutes late. She seated me under a canvas umbrella, gave me a wine list and hurried off before I could order one of each.

I let my brain drift, ignored other diners on the patio, and began to feel what Sam calls short guilt. My first mission was to make it work, to figure how to salvage my relationship with Bobbi. I also wanted to see what she knew about the roadblock at Bay Point, details of circumstance, victims and on-scene teams. I wanted to help Sam Wheeler, but I couldn't push too hard. Keeping secrets was part of her job. I didn't want to shaft her work ethic.

A server—whom I knew as Suzette—appeared, snapped me out of my dream state. "Mr. Rutledge..." She touched the wine list.

Bobbi enjoyed white wine with dinner while I preferred reds, a problem solved easily at home by opening one of each. I decided to let her order a full bottle if she wanted volume. I pointed at the "by-the-glass" list, picked a cabernet at random.

"The Beaulieu Latour," said Suzette. "A fine choice."

A cynic's translation: my snap selection would hurt my wallet.

I felt myself deflating, releasing wire ropes that had been muscles and tendons that morning. The past ten hours had been an ugly run. Beth Watkins and Julio Alonzo at the door. Catherman in the post office. Cecil blithering in his nasty office. Frank Polan in his Speedos. Sam Wheeler on Sugarloaf, battle-alert in spite of his carefree tone, his turmoil, perhaps even fear, locked up for the sake of clear thought. Copeland Cormier's performance at

Virgilio's. He would pay the devil at dawn, no doubt. I hoped he wouldn't chase me down to explain himself. Exhale new flavors of bad fumes while promoting his mission.

When Suzette returned with my glass of red, she also carried a bottle of white. "We got another call. Your friend will be another fifteen minutes. I was asked to have this Chalk Hill Pinot Gris ready for instant consumption."

"It might be gone by the time my date arrives," I said. "What are we hearing?"

"Sirius Pure Jazz. I think it's Channel 72."

"I wish all restaurants..."

"I'm glad this one does. You okay with the cabernet?"

I was so okay that I may have dozed though I can't recall. I remember hearing "Take Ten," by Paul Desmond, something by Miles Davis, then Bud Shank and "Little Girl Blue" by Chet Baker. And a breeze that rattled the tree tops but no longer threatened rain.

FORTY MINUTES LATER I was okay with my second glass of cabernet when Bobbi arrived. She looked tired and smelled of cologne and conditioner, her hair still damp from showering. She angled her shoulder for a no-wrinkle hug, then sat and mimed a frantic expression. Cast an admiring glance at the Pinot Gris.

I poured.

She took a substantial sip and held out her glass for more. "You don't want to know." She faked a laugh. "It was a bullshit day."

She was right and I knew the second part.

Suzette appeared to offer appetizers. She did not mention that I had already eaten and paid for an order of scallops and brie. Bobbi picked onion soup; I chose shrimp with mango sauce.

Then it became the two of us. I let Bobbi shoot first.

"It started yesterday," she said. "Some rich pest reported his daughter missing. Today he downgraded his problem to a stolen car. He came to me first and I blew him off. Then he suckered a rookie at the Freeman Substation into believing him. It cycled back to my desk, so I made a call. Sure as hell, Storms TowCo had it in their No Name impound lot. I think the car broke down and the complainer wanted us to pay for the tow truck. He'll get a knock on the door tomorrow. He can learn all about false reports of missing persons."

"Why did you say 'liaison' when you answered your phone today?"

"My ever-expanding job description. The glamour of coordination, the thrill of reports, the invigorating meetings. The chain between my ankle and my desk gets shorter by the week."

"You signed up to fight crime," I said, "and you're good at it. All this chicken shit, it sounds like they're buying your soul—whether you want to sell it or not."

"I never looked it at that way, but they are. They're chipping away. I know it probably impacts you once in a while."

"We live with each other's flaws and joys and jobs," I said.

"And celebrations and pain. Meanwhile, you've been gallivanting around the Caribbean. Who hired you?"

"An ad agency in Clearwater. I wasn't in the Caribbean."

"Why didn't you say so in the first place? I pictured you cavorting around with every spinnaker bunny southeast of Cuba. You went to which Bimini, the one in Lake Erie?"

"Bimini is fifty miles east of Lauderdale. The people who don't have satellite watch Miami TV stations with old-fashioned rabbit-ear antennas. It's no farther away than West Palm Beach."

"Okay," she said, unsure. "Why Bimini?"

"I don't know. I didn't argue and I ate great food, drank Kalik, and put about fifteen miles on a rented bicycle. On an island with one road, that's yo-yoing, but the scenery came to me differently each trip up and down the island."

116

"Lovely."

"It wasn't all roses. There's still a sense of gloom over there. The islanders suffered back-to-back tragedies in 2005. A Chalk's seaplane crashed and killed eleven locals, then The Complete Angler Hotel burned down."

"Bad news happens around the globe, Alex."

"Bimini's small, like an extended family. It hit them hard."

"I stand by my first view."

And those six words are a clue, I thought, that she's treating our quiet meal as she would a departmental meeting. Some habits become ingrained.

Our food arrived. We agreed that it looked great, that it tasted just as good. I waited until her spoon had done a few round-trips to the onion soup. She sampled the bread and drank more wine. I should have waited longer.

"Did you connect the names," I said, "the guy wanting the free tow and the girl that may have been harmed at Bay Point?"

Bobbi's face froze. She stared at me and chewed her soup. Her face became harder as five or six seconds ticked by. "You had an agenda for this meal?"

"Not at all, Bobbi, and you invited me. All I had was that question, but fair enough. Here's where it came from. On Monday a Mr. Catherman offered to buy my house for an exorbitant sum. On Tuesday I saw the squib in the *Citizen*—about the roadblock and all. This morning Bob Catherman showed at my door and told me his daughter was missing."

"That makes it your business?" she said.

I reminded myself to tread easy. "Okay, here's another one. Did anyone in the office suggest that the car at Storms TowCo might belong to a crime victim?"

The hint of a pause made me glad I hadn't pointed my finger.

"Alex, if it was an official case I could tell you. I *would* tell you. Maybe this will answer your question about liaison. I was specifically asked not to reveal any aspect of the joint investigation, including agencies' names. Are you through with your questions?"

"Bobbi, do we have a romance or not?"

Her face kept its toughness. "Don't forget, Alex, we're trained in interrogation techniques. I've been sent to schools in Miami. I learned how to be on both sides of the table. And you—you're not a stupid man—wouldn't ask that question if you didn't already know the answer. That makes it fair play for me to ask you the same thing. And none of this 'I asked first' business. What's on your mind, since you just took me by surprise?"

"I want us to work," I said. "Walking from the house I felt alone without you. I'd rather not feel that way going home. Did the feds ask you to shut down your private life, too?"

"This is bullshit I don't need right now."

"Look, Bobbi. If you want to take a break from the relationship, if you want to call a 'time-out,' please say so."

"You're the one taking breaks, rambling around the Caribbean, or the Bahamas, whatever."

"We both work for a living. I may have a few more enjoyable moments in my job, but..."

"Right," she said. "My work doesn't offer built-in vacations."

"Does it make any difference that I thought about you in Bimini, when I saw things that I knew you would enjoy?"

"It's a good line," she said.

"I didn't intend to deliver a 'line.' I meant to suggest that my feelings haven't changed since..."

"I think I'll skip dinner." She stood. "If you'll put this on your card, I'll pay you back this weekend."

"What happened to your rule, one-drink, no-drive?"

"I shouldn't stay over. I would have to leave at 5:45."

"Never bothered me before," I said.

"I might get a phone call during the night."

She walked.

I said, "Work or personal?" but doubted that she heard.

I STAYED LONG ENOUGH to finish my shrimp. A man needs suste-nance. Looking around, I recognized six, maybe eight faces at other tables. I assumed the rest to be newcomers or tourists. I wondered if they looked at me and thought the same—or didn't care. Several times in recent years I had felt that once-familiar streets felt changed in subtle ways that threw my balance, made me the tourist. Passing the old Cobo Pharmacy building on my way to the restaurant, I had stifled a weird impulse to pound on the door, demand that the clock be turned back. Maybe my subcon-scious was trying to whisper to me, tell me to slow down. Or speed up. Or quit worrying about it. I wished I was back on Bimini where my biggest worry was bird crap on the bike seat.

As I left the restaurant a woman seated close to the door tapped my arm. "It's okay, darling," she said. "She was just suffering a short nervous. She'll be fine in the morning."

I thanked the woman for her support.

Short guilt, short nervous, short night. Walking home with the half-full bottle of Pinot Gris, sipping from a roadie cup, I wondered if I had stomped too hard by suggesting that Bobbi might be mar-keting her soul to the boss, though I also could have asked why she didn't just go to jail. Bound to a desk, how was her life right now different from those of criminals she sent away? Or I could have shown more sympathy, been less imperious about telling her where Bimini was located?

Shit, I thought. She could have asked where my life was stuck.

I was bogged down looking for Sally Catherman. I could call her father in the morning, find out her class schedule, professors' names. I could dream up ten ways to keep my search going. I tried to picture Bob Catherman doing identical grunt work but couldn't.

The clock had ticked. Too tired to care, I wanted to hide in my cave, master the horizontal. I had failed to patch up our romance.

WISPS OF POT SMOKE floated in the lane, probably drifting from a rear cottage of the Eden House Hotel. Then I found Mikey Bokamp cross-legged on the recliner. She grinned when I stepped inside the porch screen door. She wore a CAN'T THINK STRAIGHT T-shirt and cut-off jeans and wasn't holding a joint—only a Smirnoff Ice. I saw no evidence of a roach, but the silly grin remained. I would have to inspect the yard in daylight. In my new line of work, with badge thugs tailing me on the highway, I would have no warning if some officer felt compelled to throw a surprise inspection, turn up trace evidence of massive drug use. Not so much to pitch me in jail—but to twist my arm, make me tell secrets, back off from my mission. Or throw me in jail.

Mikey saw my wine and lifted an Ice salute—down to its last ounce. I heard soft music, saw an iPod on the table, wires leading to miniature speakers.

"It's not a school night?" I said.

She pretended to rub her chin, wiped a dribble. "I quit going to class. I couldn't concentrate."

"Doobies are hell on grades," I said. "It was that way twenty-five years ago, too. And one other reality. You don't want to be exhaling pot fumes if the cops ever take interest in your missing friend. They tend not to believe anything you say. They take you to the station to dig for truth."

"If anyone whips a badge on me," said Mikey, "I can flash flesh Kevlar." She lifted her T-shirt to bare one lovely breast, half of another.

"Very sweet, but it doesn't always work."

She covered herself, sneered, put a blasé look on her face. "I can deal with gay cops, too. You keep looking at my iPod, those speakers. Sometimes ear buds make me batty, like when I need more

120

chill than hyper."

"Your mood tonight," I said, "you're more relaxed than in the grocery."

"Oh, I wasn't alone, sir. You walked out his office door looking like every poor fool that met Cecil for the first time. Uptight, out of sight. What are you doing?"

"Recovering from a dinner date."

"You don't bring your dates home?"

"The idea crossed my mind," I said. "We had words."

"Gotcha. So what are you doing in general, looking for Sally? You don't look to me like a friend of her father. Why isn't he out asking questions?"

"He wants to hang close to the phone, wait for news."

"Like he doesn't carry a cell?" she said. "What do you do for a real job? Do you own this place?"

I nodded.

"So how did you get to be his friend? Did Mr. Catherman pound on your door and demand to buy your house? What did he do, buy you too?"

"Not exactly," I said. "I'm a photographer."

"That's it?"

"I take pictures."

"Bullshit. You're some kind of private eye. I think that's cooler than shit. Can I take lessons?"

"How do you know he offered to buy my house?"

"That's what he did to Honey Weiss. She owns a cottage right across Fleming on Nassau Lane. She hasn't been there for five or six years. She rents it out these days for the high dollar and lives on Middle Torch. But she was pissed that you didn't recognize her today. She used to see you all the time on your bike and your motorcycle. Did Mr. Catherman tell you that I used to ride to school with Sally?"

I nodded.

121

"And because I got to know her, all those miles between home and school, you figure that I would know if she was dating someone."

The night wind blew a gentle gust at the screens. I nodded.

"So maybe I do. But she told me that if her father found out—especially that she was doing this particular guy—he'd quit paying for college. She's got two and a half years to go. Why don't those wind chimes make any noise?"

"They were a gift," I said, "but I don't care for wind chimes. I glued plastic straws up inside them. They click, if they make any sound at all."

"What's wrong with wind chimes? You're not into sharing beauty?"

"It's not sharing, it's imposing," I said. "It's audible trespassing. With houses this close together, my neighbors would be forced to hear mine and vice versa."

"I like men who think clearly." She reached under her chair and pulled out another Smirnoff Ice, twisted off its cap. "These, for me, are like peanuts. I can't have just one. Would you like to see my boobs again?"

"I would rather continue your conversation."

"Yes," said Mikey. "I tend to carry momentum. And I'm seeing someone right now, so I shouldn't be offering what I can't deliver."

"Why did you come?"

"I thought you were cute and I'm worried about her. I figured what the hell."

"Obviously you know some things," I said.

"There's this older guy. I mean like thirty. But you can't tell her father."

Make an end run, I thought. "She could be in real danger, Mikey. Why did she come to the Keys?"

"My impression was maybe she had a little breakdown—and I don't mean a babbling idiot kind. It was more like wanting to distance herself from something. Mommy drama. Her mother's disgusting boyfriends, something in that area."

"But her father thinks she's a Goody Two-Shoes?"

"Oh, God, the idea that she'd had a dick in her hand or anywhere else. I don't know what century he came from, but... Now I could get in real trouble."

"Lips sealed."

"That guy she buzzed had, like, 'good fuck' written on the pupils of his eyes. Like you got it, too, but don't get the wrong idea. I started with girls, still in high school. Then I went hasbian long enough to sleep with three guys. Then I fell in love with Honey Weiss. That's who I live with on Middle Torch."

"Does this guy work around here, live in the Keys?"

"They call it the Mansion, the place where he works, her boyfriend. Even that nickname for the house is like the big shit secret of the universe. She freaked and told me she slipped when she said it, and I wasn't supposed to repeat it. Anyway, he keeps a motorboat at a friend's house somewhere on Sugarloaf. They go out and drift and mess around and she works on her all-over tan." Mikey took a long slug from the Ice bottle. "One time driving to the college she said, 'He loves to snorkel.' She made it sound really good and dirty. Well, damn, I thought, who doesn't?"

"How did Sally meet this fellow from the Mansion?"

"The first time I saw him in the grocery, she acted like she already knew him. Maybe they met one day when I wasn't working. Or when I was back in Cecil's office."

"When did she have time to be dirty?" I said.

"I knew you were going to ask that. She didn't work all the hours her father thought she did. Wednesdays she got off at 7:15 instead of 9:15. On Monday she didn't come in until a quarter to five but her dad thought she started at two."

"Surely Colding knew her schedule," I said. "He must not have compared notes with Mr. Catherman."

"He was sort of in on the thing. He got his jollies in the back room."

"That room didn't look too accommodating for jollies."

"He's a titty freak, like me. So... she let him look but no touchies."

"She pulled up her shirt for him?"

"We all mess with him, give him shows every so often. He tries to be such a hardnose. It's a hoot to watch him get flustered. Anyway, if her dad called when she was supposed to be there, Uncle D. made up excuses like he'd sent her on an errand or she was helping a customer. Happened a couple times."

"Uncle who?"

"Uncle Disgusting. Don't tell him that one, okay? She called it a pole dance without the pole—thank God, especially his. One time she came out of his office and she was like, 'Oh my God, he wanted to see my little rug.'"

"Was that his term?"

"I guess. She called it her Mohawk, and it looked like its name, and no, I never did her. I just watched her change into her bikini a couple of times."

"Should I talk to Alyssa?" I said. "Did she know Sally at all?"

"Our checkout wizard. She wanted you to buy lunch at Mangrove Mama's. We loved that. She's a dyke-in-training and deep in the dark. She might sneak up on a few facts but she'll twist them to fit her TV philosophy of life."

"I'd be wasting my time?"

"Never know. We don't hang with her all that much. I don't know where she goes." She checked her Swatch. "I gotta get back sometime."

"How did you get here, drive?"

She nodded. "Honey's car is up at the Sunbeam Market. Actually, being fucked up so slightly as I am... I was hoping I could crash here a few hours, drive home whenever I wake up."

For a scary moment I began to weigh wisdom against sport.

"Gotcha," she said. "Okay if I nap here on the porch?"

"Might be best."

"Look, please don't repeat about Cecil's cheap thrill sessions. It'll come back around to me, and I need my job even though it's a beer and cigs gallery. Uncle Disgusting thinks his sty is a fucking salad salon, a thick-cut beef boutique. We'd all rather work at Murray's Market, but you take what you can get. But I've got to ask this, now that I've blabbed my ass off."

"Ask away."

"I'd like a ride on your motorcycle some day."

"That's a question?"

She laughed. "You're so right. Ask me your answer."

11

Upbeat Cuban music, the great Ibrahim Ferrer, strong decibels and what will the neighbors think? Smells of dark coffee, warm Strawberry Pop-Tarts. No shirt, no shoes, parched throat, damp sheets. Damp sheets? A thick coat of night varnish on the teeth. Sensory overload when I might rather lighten up.

The sun fought its way through slits in the mini-blinds. Bobbi Lewis, dutiful and tough, would be at her sheriff's office desk by now. Lisa Cormier, holding to her husband's subterfuge—if not his heart—would not have come to my home. End of list, and so much for plausible alternatives. I couldn't recall the departure of my late evening guest.

Oh, Mikey Bokamp, what have we done? Please give me details. Honey Weiss will kick my ass.

A closer inspection offered token comfort: I was still wearing the shorts I had worn to dinner. A soft, feminine voice said, "Don't worry, I haven't been watching you sleep."

"What the hell have you been doing?"

"Keeping my distance." Beth Watkins leaned against the bedroom door frame, a sultry pose, especially for that hour of the morning. She wore form-fitting khaki pants, a snug, badge-logo polo shirt and her black belly pack. "Just standing here I should be wearing an oxygen breathing apparatus."

"I stayed up late," I said. "Drank fancy wine."

"You should clean up your lifestyle."

"Every day I try."

She laughed. "You make it a constant process." She wiggled the photo of the Dodge Charger that I had left on my printer tray. "Surveillance?"

"Someone watching me—not the opposite. And, I might add, a huge relief."

"You took the picture, right? It's a Rutledge original taken by you?"

"Call it countersurveillance. I'm going to get up now."

"Of course, I have to ask," she said. "What relief?"

"If you've been rummaging around my home without first presenting a search warrant, I'm no longer a person of interest. I beat the murder rap. Huge relief."

She shook her head. "I'm from California where people are even more transient than Key West. That made it easier to believe that you never met the man."

"Aside from believing that I tell the truth?"

"Allow me the slack. My disbelief makes me a better cop."

"I now intend further relief."

"Your coffee awaits. After your third sip I'll tell you why I'm here. Don't take a shower yet."

"That's an ominous request," I said.

"I'm in sort of a hurry. I like these Pop-Tarts. I've never had this flavor."

I washed my face, brushed my teeth, pulled on a KWPD T-shirt, and presented myself.

"Humorous," she said.

"Ominous."

She poured two and we took them outside. Even with the sun up, the porch still smelled of fresh, damp night flowers. A throaty, high-revving motorcycle over on Fleming field-tested its compact exhaust system. Mikey Bokamp's empty Smirnoff Ice bottle sat on the table, full of sugar ants.

Beth inspected it, turned her head and fixed her eyes on me. "A fine vintage."

"Please state your mission," I said. "Any leads, any suspects?"

"Nada. But I've rethought my decision not to use your immense photo talent. I have an offer for you."

"If it's a vanity portrait of your motorcycle, I can discount my rate card."

"I logged onto the department's secure server," she said. "One of our ghoulish sergeants took bad pictures."

"Surely the body's been moved by now," I said.

"Long gone. We've got dozens of body shots and six or seven of the immediate crime scene. I want a post-forensic review. Every room in the house."

"What are you after?" I said. "A certain class of suspect?"

"I'm thinking druggies looking for stuff to resell. With the jails overcrowded, you can't believe how many dopers and burglars get early release."

"Okay," I said, "but it didn't hit me that way. Addicts and heavy users know what flips fast—iPods, game consoles, hard drives, laptops and cameras. They don't care if someone gets busted going online with a stolen computer. It's gone, out of their hands. But over at Hammond's place it was strange. The laptop was still on its desk. There were plenty of things that dirtbags would have scored, small objects of value. How was he killed?"

"For starters, he was hit on the head with a candlestick."

"Sounds like a childhood board game."

Watkins ignored me. "That was step one—it knocked him down or out cold. He was strangled—garroted—with an electric cord attached to a hair dryer."

"A hair dryer in his dining room?"

"How do you know where it was?" she said.

129

"Colonel Mustard told me."

She wasn't humored.

"Your words, detective," I said, "as Julio Alonzo would be my unwilling witness. You hoped Carmen's ill will didn't extend to the man's dining room. Maybe not your exact words, but close."

"Okay, okay. I don't know why the hair dryer was in his dining room, but you asked the question and none of my people did. That's why I want you in there to look around. You're good for a full-day rate if you can start in half an hour and work for two. Or less if that's all you need."

"You want my photos in your files so the sheriff's office won't claim-jump your case."

"That might help... I'll admit that," she said. "They'll be less likely to steal my thunder. The sheriff or the state. If the pictures give me ideas or, better yet, clues."

"I have to face a motivational issue. If I didn't care about the man prior to his death, what compels me to give a crap now?"

"Forget him," she said. "Care about murder, the crime, the manner of death."

"But you said his lifestyle could have contributed."

"Do it for me. Make his life the pavement on the road to my approval."

"You set the bar so high," I said. "How long did you watch me sleep?"

"Don't worry. No tent poles, no audible rudeness."

"Does your approval win me free coupons and fun tickets, or fewer felony accusations?"

"He was your neighbor..."

"Even though I didn't know him," I said. "I'll do it for his dog."

"That dog's going to need a new..."

"I travel too much. She'd spend her whole life at the kennel."

Watkins went for the door. "Take pictures. Help me find a killer."

"Just like that? B follows A?"

"Remember this about cops, Alex," she said. "Having unsolved cases or being proved wrong makes us feel useless. More important, we don't want bad guys to get away. Who's driving a Dodge Charger and watching you?"

I clammed.

"You asked what I knew about Bay Point," she said.

"That I did. And you paired that with the Charger? Now we both have secrets to discuss."

"Later. After Jerry's mess."

THE KITCHEN WALL PHONE buzzed. I didn't recognize the local number on my Caller ID. Facing down my intense, debilitating fear, I picked up but said nothing.

"At noon, let us pray," the man's voice said. "Yes, no?"

It was Copeland Cormier wanting to meet again at the chapel.

I paused for a mental picture of Sam driving away on Bad George Road. "Yes," I said and hung up, stepped away. The phone rang again.

Sally Catherman's name on the ID. Her father, trying to weasel a status report.

At this point did I owe him that? I'd warned him that I'd be solo for a day or two. My main concern was for Sam. If I answered to comfort Bob or to learn anything he might have for me, how many other people would listen in? I knew for sure that I was wallowing in bad soup. His daughter was probably dead and her car was locked in an impound lot. What the hell else did I need to know?

I let it go to my message service. The listeners probably got to hear it anyway.

Sorting my camera equipment took a few minutes. The bag was still filled with gear I had taken to Bimini. Flash deflectors, a diffuser, a mini-tripod, Ziploc bags. I whittled it down to two cameras, backup batteries and two oatmeal raisin granola bars for emergency use. I added my digital voice recorder, a twelve- and a six-inch plastic ruler, a notepad and a pen. If she wanted me to wear them, Watkins could provide rubber gloves. I changed into dark shorts and a shirt that couldn't be ruined by leftover finger-print dust. The last thing I did was to print out a full-day job invoice, no location fee, no mileage charge, payable in thirty days.

WALKING GRINNELL, I WATCHED traffic crawl each way on Eaton. Gawkers drawn by instinct to yellow crime scene tape. Fortunately there wasn't a crowd when I turned the corner. A uniformed cop whom I knew only as Frinzi stood on Jerry Hammond's stubby walkway, face-to-face with a man of medium build, high blood pressure, short light brown hair, and a tightly trimmed beard. Frinzi looked displeased and bored. The belligerent man claimed to be a "soul-pal, and not what you think" of the deceased. Beyond a quick solution to the heinous murder, he demanded a first search of Jerry's home for "mementos."

I stood away from the men, scoped the house. By Key West stan-dards it was a modest one-and-a-half-story Classic Revival. By the look of its paint it probably was restored in the 1990s. The front door—and corresponding interior hallway—was offset to the right. The window curtains at the peak suggested that Hammond had converted his compact attic to a sleeping loft. Every window in the house was wide open—either a devil's swap of reducing death stench by turning off the air conditioning or—more to my liking—fresh plus cold air and a big utility bill for Hammond's estate. I looked up to see Watkins at the front door. She directed the officer to let me pass.

"No drop cloths, brown paper to walk on?" I said.

"Useless out here from the get-go," said Watkins. "The sidewalk was open to use before he was found. Three different mail carriers, a UPS delivery woman and who knows who else. I was the first detective on scene, so I disqualified it."

"Mail carriers he worked with?"

"You're here to bring me up to speed?"

"If it pissed you off, you can fire me," I said.

"We checked them out."

"The front porch?" I said.

"Documented and processed. Cat piss, lizard skeletons and toxic dust bunnies. That residue circle under the trellis is dried tequila, no salt. The snoop team leader claimed he tested for sneaker tracks and scrape marks."

"How do I treat it?"

Watkins shrugged. "Inside and out, you walk anywhere. They did their thing, they gave the whole place a green light. Could I ask you to look at these?" She motioned me in the door, opened a manila envelope and pulled out a half dozen five-by-seven informal portraits of men, one per picture. Each faced the camera and sat or stood in a local setting—or somewhere that looked just like Key West. "You're a man about town," said Beth. "Do you recognize anyone?"

"I'm a what?"

"You know a lot of people."

"This is an outdoor town, Beth. Everyone knows more people than if they lived somewhere cold or rainy."

"Speech over? Tell me if you know these fellows."

I knew two by name—a charter boat captain and a Duval Street shop owner. Three I didn't recognize. I looked carefully at the last one. "I know his face but not his name."

"Know him from where?"

"He hangs at the Green Parrot. I saw him once at the Half Shell and wondered how he had unglued his regular bar stool from his ass."

"You never spoke with him?" she said.

"Never introduced. I can't recall even nodding hello."

"That's Jerry Hammond."

"So I knew him but I didn't know him," I said. "Who are these others?"

"People we want to talk with."

"Look on the laptop for his Christmas Card list."

Her face tightened, then relaxed. "Okay, assuming you weren't being facetious, that's a good idea. That's why you're here. The charter captain and shop owner, do you know if they're gay?"

"I have no idea. Who was the guy on the sidewalk when I arrived?"

"We interviewed him yesterday, and I just took his picture. He had a rock-solid alibi which, like his name, we don't need to discuss just now. Do you want some mint toothpaste?"

She smeared a streak just under my nose and led me inside.

Hammond's decor confirmed that our tastes varied in more ways than music. I quickly absorbed the scene analysis mess—lengths of disposable plastic measuring tape, a crop of small flags, mini-memorials to mark spots of interest (though I saw no blood), fingerprint lift kit smudge and general disarray. Beyond that, his front rooms had the warmth and coziness of a hotel lobby. But it all looked fresh, new.

"He did this on a postal worker's salary?" I said.

"We're looking into his finances. We've heard there was an inheritance. He was about the right age to have dead or dying parents. You want to start work, Alex?"

I opened my camera pouch. "It doesn't matter that I don't know forensics? The tech people have gone into overdrive since I started this little sideline. I feel a bit intimidated here."

"Techs are good at identifying perps," she said. "That's not enough."

"That's more than you could get ten years ago."

"Screw history. I want more than just locating bad guys. I want evidence I can use to grab juries by the short hairs. I want arrests but I also want to convict the fuckers."

"So you want me to photograph motives?"

"That would be a good start," she said. "Motives in high-resolution, full color. Compulsion snapshots, psychopathic portraits, whatever you think best. I need to make a call. I'll leave you to it."

I wanted to walk the house, do a general survey. But first I quit moving, stood in one spot. It was a trick I had learned from Bobbi Lewis several years ago when she was in a mood to share. She had counseled me to get a feel for a place where someone had died, to attempt a higher level of focus, to know another dimension of a room I had never seen before or observed carefully, and absorb a sense of what belonged or didn't.

Right away the living room bothered me. There were no pictures of people, no family, no friends. Maybe I would find them in other rooms. Hammond had installed high-traffic carpeting, tables with rounded corners, four chairs and twin sofas designed for hard use, and bland knick-knacks positioned to fill space. He had hung a jumble of opulence: primary-tone abstracts, watercolors of Old Island facades and backcountry scenes, and swirling art deco prints. Expensive-looking, no doubt hip in some circles but, to me, visual cacophony.

His CDs and DVDs also bothered me. Unlike the orderly state of the tasteless room, they were strewn in disarray on two broad shelves and, while the stereo and TV looked expensive, new, there weren't many movies or music disks. Why own upscale electronics and not have a media collection? The room had a split personality. It held no clues to direct my thinking. All I knew for certain was that the air conditioning was not in use.

I walked the hall past the dining room where Hammond had been strangled, where Beth now stood in a far corner talking into her phone. I passed a half-bath with a walk-in shower under the loft stairway. A square pantry gave to the master bedroom at left

135

and the kitchen to the right. My powers of observation dwindled as I walked. Chemicals used a day earlier by the city's forensic team were making my eyes water. The mint toothpaste wasn't working. I might have been smarter to push wasabi up my nostrils. Even with cracked windows and the mint, the death stink still registered. Beth had done me a favor by advising me not to shower. I wondered if a complete interior repainting would fix the home's odor, or if the IRS would allow me to write off my clothing. The prospect of inhaling fresh air drew me through the kitchen, out the back door to a small porch.

A narrow deck with a short sloping roof bordered the rear wall of the house. I was surprised to find that Hammond had a remarkably clear view of my yard. I was never able to see though his hedge, but he could easily see the area around my shower and the classy little shed that housed my Triumph motorcycle. It was time to grow my own shrubs, consider a fence if it wouldn't kill the breeze across my screened porch.

I saw no ashtrays, but the back porch smelled like one. I caught a reflection of sunlight through the deck slats and knelt to lean far enough over the deck edge to see what was there. A beer can had rolled under the porch stairs. I jumped to the ground and looked carefully. Cigarette ashes were stuck to the can's lid. Odd that the techs hadn't found it, taken it for a DNA check against the FBI's database system. Maybe an animal had nudged it out from under the house. All I knew was that someone had been banished to smoking outdoors. Looking around, I saw no cigarette butts. None under the porch, none in the tiny yard of bricks and spindly grass.

I opened my phone, dialed Carmen's cell.

"I'm supposed to clock out for personal calls," she said.

"This is business. Did your recently deceased ex-co-worker smoke?"

"He quit about five or six years ago," she said. "For a while there he went from being a complete asshole to a total, all-encompassing asshole. Then he went back to being a regular, smoke-free ass-hole."

"That's all I needed," I said.

"Maria asked me first thing this morning if you would take her to borrow that DVD from Jason Dudak."

"I'm on a shaky schedule. I'll do it if I'm at home or as soon as I get home. Tell her to keep checking on me."

I hung up and again braved the inside of Hammond's home.

ASIDE FROM DIRTY DISHES left over from two or three meals, the kitchen came off as the chow hub of a fitness nut and comfort-food maniac. It reminded me of the old stories about hippies who never ate meat but snorted cocaine every night.

One side of the fridge held five Chek Vanilla Colas, a bucket of leftover Kentucky Fried Chicken, and a half-eaten twelve-pack of Little Debbie Swiss Cake Rolls. On the other side cottage cheese, a half-gallon of soy milk, orange-pineapple juice and a bowl of seed-less grapes. One vegetable bin held bacon, a dozen eggs, hot dogs, and two kinds of sausages. The other bin contained plastic bottles of fish oil, niacin, multi-vitamins, glucosamine, saw palmetto cap-sules, and something called CoQ-10.

I opened the freezer. A sealed sixteen-ounce plastic bowl of Hershey's Kisses. A carton of Haagen-Dazs Mocha Almond Fudge. Six boxes of "No Sauce" Bird's-Eye vegetables. Two boxes of Amy's natural, organic meals. Magnets on the refrigerator door held a diagram of the food pyramid, the six food groups, a short article on the benefits of oat bran and a "healthy salad" recipe clipped from a magazine.

I checked a cabinet. Kellogg's Smart Start cereal, four metallic packets of tuna fish, green tea, whole wheat vermicelli, and Sunmaid raisins. In the next cabinet canned soup, instant ramen noodles, barbecue-flavored potato chips.

Truly a bipolar food collection. Fat, salt and cholesterol versus anti-oxidants, regulators, neutralizers and gruel. There were no compromise foods, no low-fat ice cream or Healthy Choice cookies. It was an all-out war. Longer life versus clogged arteries and booming blood pressure.

Risking a huge backlash I redialed Carmen's cell.

"What now?" she said.

"This is all to get you off the hook," I said. "You're a suspect."

"Kiss my ass and tell that to the city."

"Eating habits?"

"He brought unidentifiable things to microwave for lunch. Veggie this and germ that and meat-free burgers and we could never decide if the food smelled worse than he did after he ate it."

"Nothing in the junk category?" I said.

"If he saw one of us eating M&Ms, the world would end. God help us if we grabbed a Whopper while running an errand. He had opinions."

"Thank you," I said.

Carmen had closed her phone before I said "you."

I WANT TO CLAIM that I did a thorough job in the loft. But the temperature was close to boiling and four pieces of furniture told me nothing. The "double" bed—smaller than a queen, larger than a cot—a small bureau, a nightstand and an old rattan rocker all looked less than fresh but unused. The bed had a mattress cover but no sheets or pillows. The nightstand held a cheap table lamp. The sole article of wall decor was a pen-and-ink drawing of a classic yawl in a driftwood frame. I retreated before I turned into a puddle of my own sweat.

The small bathroom had a sink, an under-sink cabinet, a toilet and a walk-in shower. A rack above the toilet held towels and face cloths. I could see an assortment of soaps, shampoos and condi-

tioners that filled a rack in the shower. Without entering I photographed a vertical view of the shower then a horizontal view of
the flooring and cabinet door. I caught a reflection off the floor
close to my camera, so I elevated my hands and reshot. Still the
odd brightness. I kneeled and looked closely. A sprinkling of dust
or bath powder covered the floor. I tried another angle then
checked the camera's LCD window. Even on the tiny two-inch-
square I could see blank spots in the powder, small foot-shaped
smudges just inside the doorway. I took four more photos to
ensure that the flash was catching what I could see.

A king-size bed with six pillows dominated Hammond's master
bedroom. Set into his front wall was a wide closet with sliding
doors. The rear wall had a slim French doorway to the outside
deck. Sure as hell, the same great view of my yard. Stuck into a corner was a filing cabinet and an oak table where Hammond kept his
Apple laptop computer. Beth had mentioned a missing hard drive.
I could tell by the number of USB, Firewire and power wires to
nowhere that more items were missing.

I sat at Hammond's desk, made another attempt to find the
"zone." I gave it a half-minute but didn't feel a grand moment of
insight. I slid open the top drawer of the two-section oak file cabinet. Behind a pile of his bills and bank statements was a file jacket full of folders in clear plastic sleeves. I leafed through and found
instruction booklets, warranty cards and receipts for every
damned thing he had purchased for years. The man was organized.
He had pamphlets on everything from his Hitachi cordless drill
and Braun coffee maker to his cordless phone, Craftsman electric
hedge trimmer, a convection oven, Bose bookshelf speakers and
two "some-assembly-required, do-it-your-damn-self" bookcases.

Who could possibly need instructions for bookshelf speakers?

Midway through the stack I found pay dirt. Installation guides
for two hard drives—a one-terabyte Western Digital and a twenty-
gig Toshiba. And booklets for a CD burner and a DVD burner—

139

both LaCie brand.

The only things from that group left on his desk were the low-capacity Toshiba and the Epson printer. I pushed the chair aside, sat on the floor and slid under the desk to unscramble a jumble of wires that led to his power strip. After a minute of deciphering manufacturers' labels on the step-down units, I concluded that the wires for both drives and both burners were still in place.

With a new-looking MacBook Pro laptop on the desk, why would a thief swipe only the peripherals plus waste time by not stealing the power and connection hookups? Proper wires can cost as much as basic equipment. The other odd sight under the desk was the telephone cord. Hammond had used a dial-up service for the Internet rather than cable or some other high-speed mode.

"What are you doing down there?"

I explained my discoveries then led her to the small bathroom.

"My camera flash lighted some powder." I pointed to the floor in front of the cabinet. "It looks like one, maybe two sock or moccasin prints."

"Damn," she said. "I asked those guys to bag up the carpet section that was right on top of those prints. It was their last effort before they quit the place. They didn't check the floor under it."

"Why would the carpet be this close to the door? Wouldn't it be closer to the cabinet and mirror or over by the shower? Unless someone in a hurry to grab the hair dryer kicked the rug. But that begs the question, why socks?"

"No sneaker prints to run through our database," said Watkins. "You'd be amazed how many break-ins are solved by identifying high-end shoes."

Beth went to her briefcase, came back with masking tape. She wrote her initials on the tape then stretched two lengths in an X across the doorway. "I'll get a tech to come back and process that footprint."

"Was there anything of note in the medicine cabinet?"

"A ten-year supply of Viagra," she said.

"You had those six pictures in the envelope, but there are no pictures displayed in the whole house."

"Why would that be suspicious behavior rather than choice?"

"You confirmed that he lived here alone?" I said.

"Two close friends volunteered information. Both said that was the case. There was a woman several years ago who owned a condo here in town. She spent half her time here, and he spent half his time at 1800 Atlantic. The romance went south and they went their separate ways. She confirmed it and no one's contradicting."

"Did you ask the neighbors if anyone else was spending noticeable time here?"

"The neighbors on each side are seasonal. One's due back next week, the other after Christmas. Across the street, nobody knew or paid attention."

"What would you think looking into a fridge that held a bag of take-out from Kentucky Fried Chicken and a container of Dannon Plain Yogurt?"

"The man had good intentions and bad cravings. How do you read it?"

"I think someone who was a guest here—short-term, long-term, whatever—knew a time when Hammond wouldn't be home and started to rip him off. He interrupted the thief. The murder wasn't supposed to happen."

"But if this person panicked, killed the guy, then it stands to reason that the perp left in a hurry. Why no evidence?"

"The killer knew he had time and knew how to clean up a crime scene. But he didn't think to cover the fact that he was staying here. Or he ran out of time."

"We got dozens of fingerprints, hair samples, other sources of DNA."

"Did your people find any cigarette butts?"

She shook her head, pondering.

I told her about the beer can out back, asked her to bag it for prints and DNA. "If someone stole computer hardware, they might be back for the wiring. Is there a night guard posted on the place?"

"Only until I finish with the scene. Once we study the bathroom floor, we're done."

"What do want me to do with these pictures?"

"Have you got backup media for your camera?"

"The one in the camera's a four-gigabyte card. I've got a couple two gig cards at the house."

Beth returned to the foyer and took a three-inch by five-inch Photo Safe from her briefcase. "Give me yours and bill us for a replacement. I'll dump your photos onto this portable drive and seal your chip in an evidence bag. That way, back in the office, I can drag the pictures from this thing to my hard drive and back them up on our system. We'll have something to carry into court if the digital prints are challenged."

"When you open them, don't resave them as JPEGs. Save them as TIFFs so you don't degrade the quality."

"What?"

I handed her the memory from my camera. "Call me. Don't launch your photo program until I talk you through it."

"Yes, boss."

The uniformed officer from out front stepped inside the door. "Detective, the county is here."

"Hold them off," said Watkins. "Tell them to come back in an hour."

"Frinzi used to work for Liska," I said. "He'll let the county in."

She blew air out the side of her mouth. "I'll go defend the fort. You didn't call your girlfriend, did you?"

"I had to get permission to work for you."

Her face fell. "You didn't... oh, right," said Beth. "If you want people to really take your bait, you better thin out your bullshit."

"We need to talk about Bay Point," I said. "How about a late

142

lunch?"

"You sound like you're scraping for inside info."

"You make me sound sneaky. I just want an overview on ground rules, seating charts, manpower and contingency plans."

"I hate to say it," she said, "but I don't know. I was fishing too."

I handed her my invoice. "Let's ride our cycles up the Keys when this crap lets up."

"The crap never lets up," she said. "Let's run our lives so that riding always comes first."

A woman after my heart.

12

I HAD FORTY MINUTES to kill before I had to meet Copeland Cormier at St. Paul's Church on Duval. Sam Wheeler's friend Captain Turk had been on my mind from the moment Sam asked me not to bother him unless "odd shit" went down. But I hadn't taken Sam's directive to mean that I couldn't drop by Turk's boat slip, give him a chance to confide in me. Any "odd" detail would be better than a blank slate. I was fresh out of sources, kicking myself for not having taken Catherman's call before I left to take pictures. My search for Sally, from the start, was a search for peripheral info. Cormier, on behalf of Sam, had asked me to take the gig. Sam, for reasons he had kept to himself, had asked me to forge on, to keep looking for a dead girl. Cutting Bob Catherman out of the loop was a mistake. Blame it on my hustle to help Beth Watkins. I needed my brain to catch up with my actions.

And I wanted to ride the motorcycle. A quick run to Turk's slip, a fast chat, should eat up a half hour.

Years ago, in the spirit of job security—to keep my cameras and lenses out of the crackhead barter system—I built a lockbox into the false base of a homemade waist-high cabinet. It sits in my bedroom, looks—as it should—like the result of bad carpentry. It's too ugly and heavy to steal but it's kept my gear mine during two break-ins in the past ten years. I stashed my stuff in its spot,

145

grabbed my helmet and walked out back.

One look at Jerry Hammond's fence reminded me that fragments of my life had been on display. It wasn't a big deal that a stranger might have spied my bare ass en route the outdoor shower. That was their fault for looking. But the privacy of my guests and safety of my home needed fixing. As soon as I could find time.

THE LIGHT TACKLE SLIPS at Garrison Bight are a mile from the lane. There was no way to avoid traffic. I dodged the Palm Avenue bridge by ducking southward on Eisenhower and going left on North Roosevelt and it still took me ten minutes to get there. I didn't see *Flats Broke* as I drove up US 1. There was always the chance that Turk was on the water, earning a day's pay. When I eased into the center lane, to turn left into the charter boat lot, I saw that Captain Runaground's, the floating restaurant next to the road, had blocked my view of the white Ford Crown Victoria snugged up to Turk's dock box. The cruiser was unmarked except for the inverted flat black spotlight next to the driver's-side windshield pillar. But I was stuck. If I tried to rejoin the fast lane, I'd be pancaked. I had no choice but to turn.

I crossed the southbound lane, veered away from the skiff slips and aimed for a slot too narrow for a car in the "paid trailer" section. I wedged the cycle between a Dodge van and a Toyota pickup, set the Triumph on its stand and pretended to check my rear wheel for a problem. Barely hidden, I scoped the dock.

Black taillight trim, yellow county tags on the Crown Vic. I remembered seeing the car in front of Louie's Backyard the day the drunk had interrupted Chicken Neck Liska's liquid lunch. Now Liska's Crimes Against Persons Unit boss, Lt. Dick Wonsetler, and Captain Turk were chatting, passing the time of day. The main reason Sam had given me for not going to Turk was that he could "get a little frantic." He sure as hell didn't look frantic at the moment.

146

Sweat streamed out of my helmet. I needed to remain unseen, get out of the parking area. I wished to hell I had a distant-eaves-drop device—if only to assure myself that Turk wasn't being recruited to shaft Sam. I remained kneeling, shifted my focus for a moment from the dock conversation to the paved area around me. I must have stared at the Dodge van's white license plate for ten seconds before its words sank into my skull. "US Government. For Official Use Only." A white Grand Caravan with tinted windows? What kind of official use requires tint?

"You got a problem?"

The midday sun tripled its warmth. I looked up at a Florida Fish and Wildlife officer. His shadow fell across my upper body. I didn't have to squint, but I had to think fast for an answer.

"The rear end felt wobbly and mushy," I said. "I figured I had a slow leak, but I don't see a screw head or roofing nail in the tread. Must've been my imagination."

"Wouldn't happen here anyway." The officer pretended to have his thumbs hooked in his belt. He was ready for any move I made.

Certain that his words had a double meaning, I expected to be arrested for a bogus charge of stalking deputies on the job. "Why not here?" I said.

He pointed to the Shell station across the intersection. "Too close to where they might patch your tire. Flats only happen in the middle of nowhere, or your driveway." He laughed at his own humor.

"Got that right," I said. "I should probably go over there and borrow a gauge."

"You local?" he said.

I nodded, felt sweat splash onto my shirt. "For years."

He pointed at the dock. "You know that cop's name?"

I pretended to not know whom he meant, then let myself focus on Wonsetler and Turk. "It's Wonsetler. He's one of the sheriff's top boys."

"Son of a bitch," said the officer. "I've known that man's name for ages and I'll be damned if it'll stick in my memory. He looks like a barracuda standing next to Captain Turk there. Past hour or so he's been talking to all the boat captains. Kind of my job, I thought. Thanks for your help."

He walked slowly past the dock security office, climbed into his F-150XL pickup, drove toward the lot exit. I felt light-headed from loss of body fluids. No matter how fast I drove downtown, my shirt wouldn't dry.

I PARKED NEXT TO a bike rack in the shaded alley next to La Trattoria, carried my helmet in the rear door of Virgilio's. My sinuses flexed to block the stale smells of dried booze spills and a pine cleaner that hadn't worked. The bartender who had suffered Cormier the day before was setting up for his afternoon business.

"Your chum coming back to meet you?" he said. "No pun intended."

"I accept no blame. But I will accept a glass of water and a shot of Bacardi 8. What inspired him to get so toasted? Did he say?"

"His wife hates him for being an egghead dork, or words to that effect."

"How long did he stay?" I said.

"Maybe twenty minutes after you left. We showed him the exit after he experienced an unintended and spontaneous urine flow."

"Pissed his pants?"

"And a charming dude he was."

I shot the rum, put a ten on the bar and asked the man to guard my helmet with his life.

"It'll be here. You can keep your tip if you send me back that guy's old lady."

"You're better off this way," I said.

"I'll be the judge." He laughed. "This job, I see all kinds."

I walked down Duval and found myself unable to invent a last-minute strategy for dealing with Cormier. My mind wandered back to Jerry Hammond's computer rig and the router he'd installed for his "wired" network. Why hadn't he upgraded to the more common wireless type, if only for his Internet hookup? With only the one laptop plus a printer and a couple peripherals connected by direct wires, he didn't need a network. If his friends had brought computers into his home to transfer or swap files, he could have done the job just as simply by burning CDs or DVDs. The mish-mash of wires called out for an explanation.

POSING AS A MIND-NUMBED tourist, Copeland Cormier walked out of St. Paul's. He must have been studying stained-glass windows, watching the sidewalk for my arrival, timing his departure. My clothing smelled of my brief time in Virgilio's, tainting the fresh, warm air on the church walkway. I wondered for a moment if I had carried around that morning-after stink of beer slop and cigarette smoke when I had bartended years ago.

Pretending not to notice me, Cormier said, "Pier House Beach."

"Bullshit," I said. "This sneaky crap is getting tiresome."

Copeland stopped, scanned the architecture. "This is for him, not me." He tried to keep his lips from moving as he spoke. "He's my friend and he's yours too."

"You and my friend have your gig," I said. "I have mine. I hope both succeed. If there's an overlap, I don't want to know. I sure as fuck don't want to get caught in the middle."

"You're already there, Rutledge."

"And you can count on my silence. But you can't dick around with my time or my mind or my future."

He gave up trying to hide our conversation. "Is this because of yesterday afternoon?" he said. "I can't deny I was way out of line."

"No, Dr. Cormier. This is a lifetime of stress reduction and jail avoidance."

"You could be hanging your friend out to dry."

"Or I could be just like him," I said, "trusting his wits to keep him where he feels most secure."

"So you've spoken with Captain Wheeler today?"

That stopped me short. I heard it as a dead-end question. If he was Sam's ally no answer mattered. If Cormier, by some convoluted strategy of self-preservation or greed, wanted to pinpoint Sam, wanted him arrested or hurt, either answer could work to his favor—and against my friend.

It wasn't dead-end. It was dangerous.

"Two days ago you were straight out of a Le Carré novel," I said. "Yesterday at Virgilio's you were a Graham Greene character. You drew attention to yourself. You ignored your own insistence on secrecy. Weren't you risking your charity plan, the whole operation? Screwing yourself, your wife and Sam?"

"I suppose..."

"That's what I thought."

"I'll finish my sentence," he said. "You're going too cerebral on this, Rutledge. We don't play brains. We don't employ spycraft. It took research and knowledge to launch our operation, and it takes a shitload of money to stay in gear. Sam doesn't pay for his gas, for instance. If he has to cancel a charter to make a delivery, he is paid back to compensate for his missed date. Then we pay him again so he can give the client he stiffed a free day on the water. We maintain all this with street smarts, grunt work and balls. That's what my team employs and it's what the other side uses."

"So yesterday..."

"I fucking got ripped, but that doesn't mean I spewed top secrets all over the saloon. Maybe I've got issues on the home front and it's my problem, nobody else's."

No comment.

"Meanwhile," he continued, "I believe our friend has allowed his wits to put the worst possible spin on recent events. I'm not saying it's stupid not to trust me. But I assure you, all choices considered, all spin aside, it's a gambit of risk."

"These church meetings, you and me acting like intelligence agents, why not make our risk go away? Why don't we chat on the radio?"

"Radio?" he said, wide-eyed.

"Sure. We can talk in pre-designated non-sequiturs, we can't be tapped, and we pick the frequency and time of day."

"Who told you about all this?"

"I was in the Navy. How do you think we communicated ship-to-ship?"

Cormier locked his eyes on mine for five or six seconds then looked to the sky, shook his head. He walked away, going north on Duval.

I had guessed right. His squad probably checked in clean and simple on an open circuit. Maybe UHF Channel 16. For all the Keys to hear and not a soul to understand, no one able to trace senders or recipients.

BACK IN THE LANE, I coasted the motorcycle past the porch.

"Party time," said a man's loud voice that I didn't recognize right away. With bright reflections off the screening, I couldn't see inside. The porch rear door opened. "You've still got time to catch up," said Marnie.

I stopped the Triumph, pulled off my helmet. Captain Turk stood behind Marnie. Each had a beer in hand.

"Did you hear a loud fluttering noise?" said Turk.

"Fifty air conditioners at the Eden House?" I said.

"Nope."

"What, a helicopter?"

"Not quite like that," said Turk. "It had a much tighter rhythm.

We can't decide if it was the fan hitting the shit or vice versa."

I put the motorcycle in its condo-shed and locked the swinging door. Marnie handed me a beer when I entered the porch.

Captain Turk looks like his nickname should be Turk. I had never heard him called by another name, first or last. He goes about two-forty, all muscle and bulk and his neck size matches my hat size. Over the years anyone who had thought that his appearance connoted a lesser intellect was proved wrong in decisive ways. Or ignored like a dead leaf, because he didn't care about much beyond fishing and friends. Turk wore his usual lightweight fishing shirt, blue jeans, and brown deck shoes. Wrap-around sunglasses hung from his neck on a leather cord. White skin, goggle-like around his eyes, offset his dark tan. It had been a while since I had socialized with Turk, not that this surprise get-together qualified. I saw for the first time light-toned hair that could no longer claim to be sun-bleached.

In her wrinkled polo shirt, khaki pants and ratty sneakers, Marnie Dunwoody looked as if she hadn't slept for days. I had never noticed the spider webs next to her eyes. Never seen her mouth tremble with sadness, or sensed defeat and bitterness in her body language.

The porch air was only a degree or two cooler than outside, but the change felt fine. I sat on a threadbare canvas captain's chair, declined the beer Turk offered me from a paper sack. I already had a shot of pre-noon Bacardi in my system. It had fueled me through my encounter with Copeland Cormier, perhaps with a shade too much confrontation.

"What's up?" I said.

"It's down," said Turk. "The Marine Patrol found a Maverick half-sunk south of the Saddlebunch Keys. It was full of water, sitting just under the surface. The only things visible were the poling platform, a Yahama motor cover and the top of the console. It's got Sam's hull registration number."

152

"Sam just bought a 115 to replace his worn-out 90," I said. "He kept saying, 'Thirty more pounds and three miles an hour.'"

"He claimed he would save on gas," said Marnie, "enough to pay for the motor in ten months. Now that's shot to hell."

"I have a hard time believing it's really Sam's," said Turk. "There's talk that he destroyed evidence," said Turk. "Evidence of what crime, we don't know."

"You got that from Wonsetler?"

"I knew that was you in the parking lot," he said. "I figured you were rolling low-key. I didn't want to scream out your name and draw attention."

"How do they see it?" I said.

"There are people who wonder if Sam's into human trafficking. They think he might have dropped a boatload of Cubans in the Marquesas last Sunday. Nine new citizens of the USA."

"Oh, horsecrap," I said. "We know he's not a coyote. Someone's trying to twist his arm—and not the sheriff's office. They don't give a shit about refugees unless they're swiping shirts off clotheslines in Marathon or hitchhiking up US 1. Plus, what idiot would sink his boat with a new motor and the hull numbers intact? Even the dopes who abandon cars along the highway take their tags along."

"So if Dick Wonsetler is just a messenger," said Turk, "what's the message? He sure as hell knew I wouldn't turn in Sam."

"And sure as hell Sam knew you can't really sink a Maverick," I said.

Turk agreed. "Wonsetler asked me about that. I told him it would take 1,000 feet of anchor chain and a V-8 block jammed in the console. But it probably would roll over and dump all the weight."

"What the fuck is Sam up to?" said Marnie. She leaned forward, focused a cold gaze on me. "I have this horrible feeling that you know what's going on, Alex. You and I have been friends for a long time and that's why it's horrible. You've been told to keep it from me. Please tell me I'm wrong."

"I have *not* been told to…"

"Okay, Alex, *asked* to keep it from me. You can count on one hand the crimes someone might commit in a boat. You get technical, two hands, but you don't run out of fingers. I managed to adjust to the idea that he isn't seeing another woman. You were right the other day when you said he wouldn't do it that way. Now the only thing left to think is that he doesn't trust me. Why is he not coming home at night? Answer: he's doing something after dark. Is he afraid I'll smear his privacy on the front page of the *Citizen?*"

She stopped talking and stared. Challenged me to respond.

What had Sam said when I asked about his boat?

"Hung on a davit in suburbia, where it will stay. Totally out of sight."

Years ago, when I had needed help sneaking ashore on Summerland to snoop the beach property of a car thief and killer, Sam had been there for me. We started with Sam stashing his boat on the bay side of Cudjoe during daylight hours. Later we had gone to the canal adjacent to Johnny and Laurel Baker's home on Blue Gill Lane, picked up the boat and run our deal on beginners' luck.

"There's another way to look at it," I said. "It doesn't impeach trust."

"What?" said Marnie. "He doesn't want to stretch his ethics and pitch me a load of bullshit?"

"That's close," I said. "If you held back on a story because Sam's your partner, how would you feel about yourself for the rest of your career? If you knew your reputation was as bogus as a plastic mango, could you go in the restroom at work and look in the mirror every day?"

She sat back slowly, allowed some of her steam to waft away. "What's with his boat being half-sunk? If evidence is destroyed, evidence of what? If it's really his boat, did he try to sink it or did someone else? If it's not his boat, whose is it?"

"Those sound like a reporter's questions," said Turk, "rapid-fire style."

"No offense," she said.

Turk ignored her sarcasm. "If it's a stolen boat made to look like Sam's, the real owner doesn't matter."

"If someone other than Sam scuttled the boat, no matter whose it is," I said, "it's an attempt to set up Sam for a bust he doesn't deserve."

Marnie crunched her beer can to an hourglass shape. "Great logic, Alex, but your phrasing tells me he deserves to be busted for something."

"Who found it, the Marine Patrol?"

"Good question," said Turk. "Wonsetler didn't say. All I know is they found it south of Saddlebunch, and that's anywhere from Geiger Key out to Pelican Shoal over to American Shoal and back up to Sugarloaf Creek. That's thirty square miles of long-term parking, but more important, it's Hawk Channel. That makes it a hazard to navigation, so they must have towed it to shore."

"How did they find it with just the platform and engine cover sticking up?"

"Better question, unless someone saw it being sunk. Which, after dark, is not a reasonable assumption."

"Unless it had a GPS transmitter aboard," I said. "Maybe Sam found out it was there."

Turk shrugged. I looked at Marnie. Her questions told me she was keeping a tight grasp on her grief, her bewilderment. The most telling detail of her state of mind was that she hadn't asked me about the Jerry Hammond case. She had no way to know that I had spent the morning in his home. But there was always the chance that, as a neighbor, I might have heard a rumor, a hint of motive, a tale of comings and goings. I never had known her to put private life, convenience, or personal safety ahead of her profession.

"What makes you so sure that the boat isn't Sam's?"

155

"He wouldn't let it happen," said Turk. "It's too easy for a boat handler like Sam to make *Fancy Fool* invisible."

"So if he got jumped mid-stream or, say, on Sugarloaf, he might hide his skiff on..."

"Oh, maybe Cudjoe," said Turk.

We understood each other. I had my suspicions and he knew— or had figured out—where Sam had stashed his boat. "Let's take my truck," he said. "It's a nice day for a drive."

Marnie came out of her reverie, picked up on our tone. "Am I being taken for another ride?"

"This time," said Turk, "it's only forty-six miles, round-trip."

"And if we don't find what you think we might find?" she said.

Turk chuckled. "It's a nice day for a boat ride, too."

"Hell," said Marnie. "Are we going to criss-cross thirty square miles?"

"I wasn't the only captain he talked to," said Turk. "Maybe Dick Wonsetler let slip a detail or two to one of the others. We can try to piece it together. Enough to go looking. Maybe find a buoy."

She wasn't pleased. "Sam could tell us where it is with one phone call."

"My phone isn't ringing," I said. "You never know what we might learn. The boat's location could be a clue for us all. It might tell us something about the other team—if one exists. It might help prove that Sam's in the clear."

"In that case, count me in," said Marnie. "And not as a reporter." She pointed toward the lane. "Here comes your fairy godmother."

I hadn't heard Bobbi Lewis's county vehicle stop in front of the house. She held a phone to her ear, and didn't get out of the Explorer.

Turk said, "I hope she isn't following up for Wonsetler."

"Why don't you two go on ahead?" I said. "I'll ride my motor-cycle, catch up with you."

"It won't take three of us to check those davits," said Turk. "It's on Blue Gill, right? I'll call if we decide to take the boat ride."

I asked for his number, punched it in, pressed my call button. A moment later his cell rang. I hung up. "We've got each other memorized," I said.

Turk grinned and stood. "Forget all you know."

"Marnie, when you've got computer problems," I said, "is there anyone in this town you trust for repairs?"

"Your friend," she said. "Duffy Lee Hall."

"My darkroom guy?"

"Ex-darkroom, since he got digitized out of a job. He's been doing Macs and PCs for, I don't know, at least a year. When all his photo processing competitors went out of business, he saw the writing on the wall."

"How could I not have known?" I said.

"You stopped shooting film and nothing went wrong with your computer?"

Turk and Marnie walked past the Explorer on their way out to Fleming Street. I watched Bobbi wiggle her fingers at them, but she made no effort to roll down her window to speak. Marnie looked back at the porch, let her disgusted expression convey her opinion of Lewis's rudeness.

"I OWE YOU FOR a three-course fiasco last night." Lewis opened the screen door. She held out a hundred-dollar bill. "This might not be enough," she said. "I need to use your facilities."

She walked out carrying the photo of the Charger that Beth Watkins had left sitting on the kitchen counter. "Why are you taking pictures of Marv Fixler?"

"I don't know Marv," I said. "I like the car. I'm thinking of buying one."

"You best keep your distance, Alex. Matter of fact, keep your distance from both of us. I never thought of you as a stalker, but I can revise my opinion as fast as a phone call."

"If I could find someone worth stalking, I might give it a try. Is he the reason you've been tied up lately? Or should I say the liaison that's kept you so busy?"

She thought for a moment, slowly hardened her eyes and tensed like a deputy prepping for conflict. She finally blew air outward and said, "Do not push." She twirled the photo toward the porch table. It missed, but she wasn't there to see it land face-down on the floor.

I watched her march back to the white SUV with its roof bar, its departmental green and gold paint scheme. My lover had acted and looked like a stranger.

My ex-lover, apparently.

13

"ALEX."

In the peace of my screened porch, the bark of a drill sergeant. A summoning with indignation, impatience and belittlement. As a teenager-in-training, Maria Rolley had mastered her own intonation, the accusatory one-word command.

"That's not what you used to say when you knocked on my door."

"Can you drive me to get the DVD?"

"Let's take our bikes," I said.

"That's not the point."

"The point, I believe, is that your mother doesn't want you to go alone. It has nothing to do with how we get there. Since they're bike riders, the boys probably will be impressed by yours."

"Cool. What did I say when I knocked on your door?"

"Once upon a time..."

"Give it a break, Alex," she said. "Make it prime-time with no big lead-up."

"Tough audience."

"Every one of my friends is chatty beyond belief, Alex. I go insane."

"I taught you to read," I said.

"I know. You picked me up from day care when mom was at work. My favorite book was *The Case of Og the Missing Frog* which I memorized when you read it out loud. So after a few days, when you turned the pages, I said the words. You thought I knew how to read, but I didn't."

"You wouldn't sit down to read before you had your dish of dry cereal."

"Cinnamon Life, right? I still like it."

"One day your mother let you walk down the lane to visit me. I heard a knock at the door and stepped onto the porch. You looked up at me and said, 'Life.' That was your entire greeting."

"Sounds like a short haiku."

"That's close and very good," I said. "It was a Zen moment."

Maria, emotion-free: "Cool. Can we go?"

I SAW JASON DUDAK'S road-worn Honda parked on Elizabeth Street, the Marion County tags, a Sonic Youth decal on a side window I hadn't noticed before.

"But that's not the house number," said Maria, reading my mind. "It's got to be... There's Russ."

It was a tall, unrestored Conch house on the west side of the street. Russell Hernandez sat low on the outdoor stairway to a second-floor apartment. He was cleaning mud off his shoes. We walked our bikes into the yard and the boy held out his arms to give Maria a friendly hug. She backed away, turned to me. "He's gross all sweaty."

"I've been mowing lawns since 6:45 this morning," he said, "I'm lucky the EPA doesn't track me down as a public menace. I may last another week if I make it through tomorrow. I should be renting out sailboards, selling two-piece bathing suits. Dirt work is not my calling."

"Did Jason find it?" said Maria. "The DVD in his trunk?"

He gave her a one-shoulder shrug. "Visitors coming up," he shouted.

No answer for an awkward ten seconds. Why the warning?

"Umm, umm... okay," said Jason. "Who is it?"

"Princess and her escort."

As I ascended the wood stairs, I felt a twinge of déjà vu. Fifteen years ago, I had dated a woman who lived in this apartment. I knew the two-room layout, the found-object decor, and I feared that nothing had changed. Or maybe I hoped it was all the same. It had been a fine relationship until she left for dentistry school. A dose of nostalgia.

We peered through the screen door. Cigarette smoke wafted outward. Jason Dudak sat with his back to us, playing a game console on the far side of the main room. He was shirtless, skinny as a rail and had a four-inch rocket ship tattoo on his shoulder. Maria strolled in and went straight to his elbow.

"Cool," she said.

I went inside and let the door close behind me.

"He's married to that game," said a young woman in the doorway to the front room. She wore a low-cut tank top that read WHO'S YOUR CADDY? and no bra, which allowed her small breasts free rein when she moved even slightly. She wore black men's swim trunks low on her hips. Her straight dark hair was parted to one side and hung neatly to her shoulder. She held a cigarette in her teeth, Keith Richards-style.

"Give me twenty-two seconds," said Jason. "I'll get it for you."

Music—some kind of Celtic dirge—played from miniature speakers on the kitchen counter. Above the counter a hand-scrawled sign: NO PISSING IN THE SINK.

"Jason's too rude to introduce anyone," said the girl. "I'm Brandi."

"This is Maria," said Jason. "That's Alex, her mom's friend."

"And that," said Brandi, pointing to a mattress on the floor in a corner, "is the famous Cally Piper."

Cally, in a black sports bra and neon green thong underwear, slept atop a pink floral-print sheet, one foot against the other knee, a forearm over her eyes. A few blonde tufts had escaped her thong. Apparently the group's living arrangement dictated that modesty was a non-issue. Next to the mattress were the duffels I had seen Jason loading into his car and two of the packed Hefty Bags.

"Famous for what?" I said.

"Surviving a deadbeat mom," said Jason.

"She's transitioning," said Brandi, "from coming in at sun-up to going back out at eleven."

"Cally likes the island?" I said.

"Oh, God, yes. We've been here six weeks and she hasn't missed a night. This is a peaches-and-cream image of innocence that fools a hundred men a night. The only thing she learned her sophomore year was how to suppress her gag reflex."

"A fine talent," I said.

"And, Jesus, I'm glad I don't have her roster of conquests," said Brandi. "But I wish I had her boobs. She calls them her opportunity knockers. Her name is a contraction of 'cat in the alley.' Or that's what we decided."

As if she'd heard Brandi but had no desire to respond, Cally rolled over. A big lipstick kiss was tattooed on her milk-white right-side bun.

Brandi kept talking. "I love this island, too. I can do the shit my mother never let me do. Not wash my hair for five days. I can eat Vienna sausages. I might get a nose ring."

I sensed that I wasn't free to ask too many questions, but I said, "Where's the Ukrainian?"

"He's at work," said Brandi.

"His second job," said Jason. "He's a bar-back at Rick's. Brandi, why don't you offer Alex a beer or something?"

"I might," she said. "I mean I really might do that. I mean, I have thought about that so very many times."

Maria turned, regarded Brandi with a bored expression.

"Jason's loaning me the Simpsons Tenth Season," she said.

Brandi's eyes narrowed on Jason. "So you're loaning out my fucking DVDs?"

"Hey, whore," said Jason.

"Yes, girlfriend," said Brandi.

"It wouldn't be yours if I hadn't saved it from your old landlord."

Maria looked at me with disgust and consternation in her eyes. She pointed at the counter. "I've never seen an iPod like that," she said. "Is it a Nano?"

"It's some offbrand mp3 player," said Brandi. "My mother wanted to surprise me with it. I think she bought it at a goddamned yard sale."

Jason shoved back his chair, marched into the dark front room, and returned with the DVD in hand.

"Christ," said Brandi. "You'd think I wasn't paying the rent."

Maria was out the door, halfway down the steps, studying the back of the DVD box. I held open the door and turned back to Brandi. "You feel a great compulsion to educate the young ones?"

She looked at me and said for Jason's benefit, "He can't stand dirty words. Fuck him."

"I've been using worse language since before you were born," I said. "But you need to remember—if young Maria gets too smart too soon, she'll be stealing your boyfriends for the rest of your life."

She kept her eyes on me, but her puffiness deflated. "He's got a point."

"Good on ya, Alex," said Jason with a fake Aussie accent.

WE SAW NO SIGN of Russell when we retrieved our bikes.

"Gross," said Maria.

There was a certain element to the whole scene that reminded me that all four of them were almost still kids—midway between Maria's age and graduate school or parenthood. I rode away feel-

163

ing like an old fogie, some buttinsky who had tried to discipline other peoples' children. Like grown-ups did before the media enabled all children to sass back.

Just before we got home, Maria said, "Alex, I knew that all boys my age were disgusting but those two might be just as bad. What do I have to look forward to?"

I gave her my best answer: "The great long search for perfection."

"How do you know when you find that?" she said. "Is it like deciding whether to rent or buy in Monopoly?"

I pretended I didn't hear. She hurried home to check out her entertainment.

I POPPED A BEER and called the number I had for Beth Watkins. She picked up on the second ring. "I was beginning to think you'd never call."

"Sounds like you're in a saloon," I said.

"A late lunch and an early white wine at the Turtle Kraals," she said.

"Have you got that envelope full of pictures with you?"

"If I do?"

"I borrow."

"Bullshit," she said. "Unless I accompany. What's on your mind?"

"Let me call you back."

I called Duffy Lee to make sure he was home. We caught up our hellos, and he told me to come by.

I redialed Beth. "Have you got forty minutes?" I said. "Pick me up when you finish eating."

Eight minutes later Beth Watkins's city Impala appeared in the lane. I stuffed my compact camera in a pocket of my shorts and locked up. She pushed open the passenger-side door for me.

"You left the restaurant in a hurry," I said. "Did you grab a toothpick on the way out? Cops chew toothpicks."

"It's a trait I've escaped so far." She backed around and eased toward Fleming. "I don't belch in meetings and I don't scratch my nuts. I'm not one of the guys."

"Pardon my attempt at humor. Go up to White, down to Olivia and take a left. I got an inspiration about ten minutes ago. Sitting there on my porch."

"Mine usually come in the office or the bedroom," she said.

Did I dare let my imagination dance with hers? I wanted to envision acrobatics, nude yoga on a wide mattress, solo of course—but my mind could picture only a pissed-off Bobbi Lewis striding toward her Ford Explorer.

"You're not laughing," said Beth. "Did I cross a line?"

"It's a matter of timing," I said.

"Trouble in paradise?"

I held back for a few seconds then said, "Also known as palm-tree purgatory."

"A friend of mine was in Michaels last night," she said.

"I wondered if there had been witnesses." I began to sweat. I blamed the sun's reflection off the dashboard, the heat baking downward from the car roof.

Beth kept her eyes on White Street's oncoming traffic. "She showed up late and left early, the word I got. Given her job description and your laid-back approach to life in general, an intelligent person could almost guess the script."

"Why would an intelligent person want to do that?" I said.

"Living next door, I never got the warm and fuzzies. Not that people are real neighborly on Big Coppitt. I saw her one time in her yard going back and forth. It looked like she was practicing her cop walk. I've wondered—hell, ever since I met you—what you saw in each other. To almost answer your question, I don't steal men from other women, married or not."

165

"How does a cop walk?" I said.

She hung a left on Olivia, ran a slalom-gauntlet of curbside trash cans up the narrow street. "Like they just had a hemorrhoid operation and their leg muscles stiffened up in the hospital."

I ran the mental movie again, Bobbi strutting back to the Explorer, and found the description accurate. "Bobbi said you moved into town."

"The rent on Aquamarine kept creeping up. I bought a cottage smaller than yours, at the end of that dirt path off Passover Lane. One bedroom and a yard the size of a card table. My ex-roommate in Petaluma bought me out of the condo we owned. That California money put me into my new house like a charm."

I pointed at a parking space. She nailed it, nudging only two trash bins.

DUFFY LEE HALL AND his wife own a large two-story house on Olivia. We found him on a cushioned Adirondack chair on his broad front porch. His Volvo station wagon, long in need of a paint job, sat in his short driveway.

"This guy did all my film processing and photo prints for years," I said. "Once in a while he worked with Liska and a few other detectives. Now he fixes PCs and Macs."

Duffy Lee stood as we approached. I've always assumed he was about five years younger than me and a lot smarter with a patient manner, a fine intellect. He was four inches shorter than me but probably matched my weight. A good man to have alongside in a tough moment.

I made the introductions.

"I haven't seen Alex lately," he said to Beth, "but there's an upside. I haven't had to look at dead people pictures. I'm afraid you're here to change that."

Watkins showed him the manila envelope. "All these fellows but one are alive, as far as we know. Nothing gruesome."

Duffy Lee took us inside and arranged the photos on his kitchen counter. "I know these guys," he said. "They've all come to me for help and repairs. Why don't you tell me what you're after?"

Beth explained Jerry Hammond's murder and the fact that the photos were in the victim's possession.

Hall shuffled some of them to one side. "These four had a virus last spring. The same virus, almost like they'd given each other the clap. Once I'd fixed one, the others were a breeze."

"Did you ever wonder what they might be passing around?" said Beth.

"Maybe they had a genealogy club," said Duffy Lee. "Key lime pie recipes. In this town I don't want to know a thing. I don't look at content. In this new profession, like my old one, privacy is king. It's far too easy for customers to accuse me of peeking into their business and financial matters, their confidential emails, their Internet searches. I go to extremes to assure my respect for content. I mean, the last thing I want to receive is a summons to an IRS hearing, you follow?"

"So far," said Beth.

"I install larger hard drives. I purge viruses, do software rehab and save data from crashes. I try to save data from jump drives that went through the laundry. I download updates when people are too busy to do it themselves. I'm learning to write programs. Not many of my clients need that level of work. I stay clear of prospecting and peeping. Truth is, I don't have time."

"Gotcha," said Beth, her tone impatient.

"But there's one thing," said Duffy Lee. "I've been working my way around to this and I'll probably be sorry I mentioned it."

"Will it help solve a murder?" said Beth.

"You knew Billy Blanco, didn't you, Alex? He worked at Key West State Bank before it became First State—before he retired."

"He wrote me loans for camera gear."

"His next-door neighbor owns Reef Pawn in Habana Plaza," said Duffy Lee. "The old guy's in ill health and his wife's in worse shape, so Billy's been in the shop almost full-time the past couple years. I don't think he even collects a pay check. I do favors for Billy, except not really favors because he pays me. He sends me electronics and computer gear to check out and clean before it goes up for sale. The stereo stuff, he waits until the owner blows deadline. The computer gear, he wants to make sure it doesn't have virus infections or bad crap installed. Most of the time the operating system is skunked." Duffy Lee pointed at Jerry Hammond's picture. "This dead guy, I went to his house—over on Eaton—twice, to get his laptop to synch with his printer." He pointed to a shelf and tapped his finger on a hefty-looking, black-cased hard drive. "I could swear this Western Digital drive was his. He had the first one in town. The only one I ever dealt with."

Beth nodded.

"It showed up in the pawnshop yesterday. Billy sent it over, and I checked it out. It has the oddest damned thing—a hidden partition. If you didn't know it was there, you'd never see it on your desktop. You'd have to access it like something on a network. The only way I noticed it was the drive's capacity was lower than it should have been. I mean, all the companies lie. They sell a terabyte drive like this that holds 960 instead of 1,000 gigs. But this drive was way less than true capacity. I was afraid it was carrying spyware or a trojan horse archive, so I ran a diagnostic program. It found a large section almost totally hidden. But no dangerous-looking file types."

"What kind did you find?" said Beth.

"Quicktime movies and photo files, TIFFs and JPEGs."

"Can you show us?"

"Not without the owner's permission, the sick old man. Even permission from Billy isn't enough."

"You didn't erase it?" said Beth.

Duffy Lee shook his head. "I kept the data intact because I wanted to figure out how he ghosted that partition."

"I might have to get a search warrant," said Beth. "Keep it legal for all of us, in case we find crime evidence. We don't want to taint a future court case."

"Fine with me," said Duffy Lee. "It's not going anywhere and we three are the only ones who know where it is. I've got a feeling I'm not going to make a buck on this job."

"I have to consider it crime evidence," said Beth. "I have to get a collection bag out of my car, so please don't touch it."

"My hands have been all over it," said Hall. "Are you going to drag me downtown to ink my fingers, or is that digitized too?"

Beth cracked a huge grin. "I haven't revved up my Perry Mason today," she said. "Don't we have you on file as an evidence tech?"

"It'd be news to me," he said.

"We may have to scrape your tongue for a DNA sample, to establish a positive negative."

"Oh, that's perverted," said Duffy Lee.

Beth smiled. "How about consulting work in the future?"

"That'll work, if you shitcan the scrape routine."

Beth went to her car, left me with Duffy Lee. "One other small favor?" I said.

"You've gone quota."

"But you're more resourceful than I am. Can you do a web search on Copeland Cormier?" I spelled the two names. "His wife's name is Lisa. Also the names Marv Fixler and Cliff Brock. And let me call you for the info instead of you calling me."

"What the hell are you into?"

"Quicksand with an ocean view."

"Treat it like the swamp it is, Alex," said Duffy Lee.

"How's that?"

"Swim your ass out."

14

SPEEDING FROM DUFFY LEE'S place to Dredgers Lane during the after-work rush hour, Beth Watkins proved again that cops fear no tickets. She drew a bouquet of hitchhike thumbs from a pack of shirtless military men jogging toward us on Palm Avenue. At drunk man's curve—where Palm bends into Eaton—three bike riders saw her coming and steered for the sidewalk.

"I won't have time to drop paper on a judge today," she said. "I can write the warrant request before I go home, have it ready for the crack of dawn."

"You might make the pawnshop before it closes," I said. "See if Billy Blanco remembers..."

"He'll be there tomorrow. He'll give me a description and the fake name some doofus used. Bang, bang, brick wall. First things first."

"If anyone can spot a phony photo ID, Billy..."

"You should see the stuff coming out of Thailand," she said. "They bring the blanks ashore from cruise ships like decks of cards. A couple backroom operations do the rest of the work. A ten-year-old could buy beer in church. How about lunch tomorrow?"

"I have to go to Cudjoe in the morning."

"On your Triumph?" she said. "I'll take a long noon hour on my road rocket."

How could I take her to Polan's for my cash replenishment? Or to Colding's to make an appointment with Alyssa?

"We have secrets to discuss," I said.

"Bay Point and a Dodge Charger?"

"Those are my secrets. What are yours?"

She stopped to let me out on Fleming near the lane, kept her gaze on the street ahead. "Is that a proposition, Alex?"

No, but your question is.

"Am I out of line asking how you rate time off?" I said. "Your two-day-old murder is turning into a cold case."

"It's a two-day-old investigation, Alex, but a five-day-old murder. Taking me to Duffy Lee—and your ideas inside Hammond's house... You've given me my best clues to solving it, so I want to hang close. I'll be here at ten ready to ride, unless I have to call and cancel. Is that early enough?"

"Ten's fine," I said, not meaning it. "As is hang close," I added.

That part I meant.

I WALKED TO THE house under the cyan heat lamp. Parched crotons were grateful for the late afternoon shade. I flipped open my cell and punched in Turk's number.

"We found it," he said. "High and dry and wrapped in a mildewed Sea Ray boat cover."

"Marnie feel better?"

"I dropped her off fifteen minutes ago. She thought she could finally take a nap."

"So what did they find in the water?" I said.

"A piece of crap," said Turk. "Maybe Sam's old ninety-horse motor on a junker flats skiff. I just pulled into the Bight lot. Maybe these captains who talked with Wonsetler will have some ideas."

"If you come up with anything, want to form a search party, count me in."

172

IN MY HUSTLING AROUND, I had forgotten to check the garage that I rent behind Carmen's home. I had no doubt that Sam could leave me a weapon, hide it inside without being noticed. Skills he had learned long ago served him well today.

I walked toward the lane's end and pondered my dilemma.

Aside from absolutes—the deaths of Jerry Hammond and maybe two others on Bay Point—I felt stuck in an awkward charade. I had endured three days of vague threats, hollow fears, hints of violence, and tales of do-gooder crime. I had been offered sex, a huge fee for not taking pictures and a generous price for my home. I had a friend in hiding, an exact copy of his boat sunk in Hawk Channel, his partner baffled and brokenhearted. I sure as hell hadn't made progress in my dead or alive search for Sally Catherman—even if only to find out how she died. I felt as if I had walked waist-deep against a current for sixty hours, lost ground, and didn't know why I was there. I had a feeling it would happen but not how soon I'd be over my head.

On my third day as an illegal private eye, I knew little beyond my ten fingers and toes. Surrounded by unknowns, I felt that Sam's pistol might offer reassurance.

I always leave the combination lock's dial on 43. No one knows this, not even Sam. If I find it pointing to another number, someone's been curious. Someone not smart enough to return the pointer to its resting place, though Sam likely would take the precaution.

This time I didn't like seeing the dial where it was supposed to be. I unlocked the doors, swung them open far enough to let light inside. My antique wooden crate looked untouched. I groped the wad of towels, didn't find a pistol.

On a whim I opened the Shelby's driver-side door and felt under the seat. No gun—just the long, heavy flashlight and the sheathed hunting knife I keep for day or night emergencies. I closed up the garage, reset the lock.

"Am I moving or not?"

Carmen stood on her back porch. She held a half-empty glass of red wine.

"You're standing still," I said. "Are you about to fall down?"

"I called the number on the guy's card. When he answered he sounded like he was down in a well, or at the other end of a long tunnel. He said, 'It may happen. I gotta go,' and he hung up on me. I called back twice more. He wouldn't pick up. Hell, it's not like I'm calling him to ask for a date."

I didn't have a fast answer, but Carmen deserved a warning.

"My mother's already packing the house, deciding what stays here and what goes to Ocala. Carol Anne faxed me a real estate form. You can buy a place in Ocala for what people on Shark Key pay for a car. That house near her, I can make my offer contingent on selling this property under our feet."

"Do it," I said. "What's to lose? If your mother's already boxing the dishes, she wants a change. Even if Catherman flakes on his offer, Hector and Cecilia might gain a whole new social life. They'll see less of Maria, but she'll be off to college in five years, right?"

"And if my house doesn't sell?"

"No big. You can figure a way to afford two houses. For starters, put off buying that Ferrari. If they hate Ocala, your folks can always come back to the island. The whole exercise will give them something to do."

She drained the wine from her glass. "You want a glass if I refill this?"

I shook my head. It might have adjusted my think pattern—for good or ill—but more than wine I needed porch time. A tall glass of Arizona Green Tea, a pad and paper, a mental recap.

"What if one of them gets sick, or both of them?" she said.

"Bring them back down. Good reason to keep both houses right here."

"You piss me off, Alex. I haven't slept for two nights. You make it all sound like I'm buying a second tube of toothpaste. Is this Catherman asshole going to flake, as you call it?"

"I wish I knew."

"Will you sell out?"

"No," I said. "It's like when I quit taking flying lessons fifteen years ago. I did dozens of touch-and-goes, my solo flights, my cross-country up to Pompano Beach and over to Naples. I logged in 40 hours. I was supposed to go to Miami and stay in a hotel for a week and eat restaurant meals while I took an expensive cram course and the pilot's exam. At that point I didn't have much money. I had no place to go, no relatives to visit and I couldn't afford a plane. All my friends who didn't live in the Keys showed up like clockwork every year. I'd have to sit around and invent trips I couldn't afford to justify a week in Miami I couldn't afford."

"I don't mean to sound like my cynical, sarcastic, lovely daughter, but what's your point?"

"I already live in paradise," I said. "Where would I go if I sold?"

"Thank you, Alex."

BY THE TIME I reached my porch, I knew that I needed much more than tea and quiet. Over the years, therapeutic hours behind a lens have paid me fine rewards. My safaris rarely last more than an hour. They begin with the goals of capturing light and color. I follow my nose to places on the island I haven't visited in a long time and wind up with the flavors of Key West. Once in a while I'm inspired to projects I couldn't have imagined back on the porch.

I enjoyed the camera I still had in my pocket. It fit in my hand, weighed less than a beer, had plenty of battery power, megapixels and memory. Its image quality was fine for my personal shots. This time I had a place in mind—a narrow street between and parallel to Duval and Simonton.

No one can ignore changes in Key West. In the past twenty years the island has suffered growth, wealth, demolishing, remodeling and idiots. The worst change I've noticed is the number of rules. I made it through the first thirty years of my life with very few of them. If you think about it—and I do—the rule about "Do unto others" might be all we need. So I couldn't help noticing the blizzard of "No Parking" signs on quaint, short Bahama Street. I wasn't sure what I would do with the photos, but I wanted a picture of every sign.

If I had left the house closer to sunset or walked instead of riding my bike, I wouldn't have had time to photograph them all. I locked the Cannondale in front of the bank on Southard and began walking, documenting. To call it a wealth of material would be corny and ironic, but damn... Two towing companies had given away colorful "Tow Away Zone" signs, one pale aqua on white, the other medium blue on white. Pure coincidence—each promised an $85 minimum tow though a sign down the block touted a $300 release fee. When I first arrived in Key West, a $300 release fee would have effectively totaled my car. One sign read, "You WILL be TOWED without a displayed permit. Another read, "Permit Parking Only. Cars without parking permit will definitely be towed away at owner's expense." Only in the Keys could we have a threat of indefinite tow.

I needed only three or four more to hang a gallery show of nothing but signs. But my project stopped abruptly when someone tried to kill or injure me, or warn me off. Technically, I was jaywalking, crossing Fleming in front of the antique shop. I also was showing a nick too much faith in my fellow man.

We trust vehicles around us. We co-exist on sidewalks, in parking lots, on the shoulders of highways. No damn choice, right? But it's always a shock to hear that some jerk in a distant city has jumped the curb, struck down people at a bus stop or in a street market. So call it habit when I failed to think that the funky Taurus might hit me, especially with so many witnesses, so much room for both of us on the street. Only at the last moment, when the vehicle faced me, accelerated like an oncoming bull, did I perceive it as a threat.

There wasn't much to question. It drove toward me, picked up speed. For some reason I noted that its hood paint was sun-faded and its grill resembled the mouth of a bluefish. I could see the driver's eyes enough to sense his focus. If you asked me two minutes later to describe him, I could have come up with a face anywhere between Gary Busey and Adam Sandler.

It was his focus that got me.

Everything in my mind slipped into slow motion. Not just slow but drawn-out, filled with elaborate reasoning and moves that, in a less-dangerous instance, might take me ten minutes of logic and choreography. As if a clock ticked in my subconscious, I recall taking each moment in order, anticipating events and my reactions.

The first three things I wanted to protect were my camera and my knees. It might take me the rest of my life to figure out why a point-and-shoot camera took precedence over my arms or my head. Perhaps I had developed an instinct after decades of holding my gear clear of solid objects, wrapping cameras and lenses in plastic when rain or ocean spray was a threat.

My knees—no-brainer. They bend in one direction, break in the other. Broken knees on the island would be worse than a revoked driver's license in Los Angeles. My only sensible move was to turn away and raise my arm to keep the camera from colliding with the hood and grille. Call it a pirouette, the twist that offered the backs of my calves to the crunch. Mix in the luck of timing, the jump I made, off-balance and more an ankle lift and a push of the toes. In my drawn-out logic the jump made sense because it dropped my chances of being knocked down, wedged under the car, scraped on the pavement as tire treads turned my limbs into waffles.

I probably had cleared the ground by fewer than four inches

when the Taurus hit. Its bumper's impact launched me upward, and I remember bystanders' tardy yells of warning. I rolled and tried to imagine a Hollywood stunt master playing it for drama, somersaulting backward. None of it was acrobatic or much in my control. I remember thinking that if the car had an antenna on its right front fender, I could be impaled. Then my left shoulder bumped, slid off the windshield, my left ear whacked the right-side mirror. I can't recall my legs going over the top or the moment I landed cat-like next to the curb. I was crouched like a wrestler ready to rumble, my camera at eye height and pointed at the escaping, swerving Ford Taurus. A spray of sand and gravel hit my hand and shirt. I hoped that my lens would be spared. On impulse I pressed the shutter button, lifted, gave the auto-focus a fighting chance and pressed again. A Good Samaritan on a yellow motor scooter took off up Fleming in chase of the Taurus and blocked my last few photographs.

I was still catching my breath when a city squad car appeared. Only one officer. He hooked his microphone to the dash, got out slowly and motioned for several cars to proceed up Fleming.

"Gimme a sec," I said. "I'll give you a license number."

He ambled toward me. "Man called the city, said it was a green Ford Taurus."

"Taurus, yes," I said. "Color... Hold on." I clicked my camera's review button, clicked back four or five pictures and pressed the zoom. "Yes, green. The tag number starts with L-six-eight."

"Forget it then," said the cop. "It was stolen at Searstown twenty minutes ago. It's been dumped already. You can bet he turned onto a side street up there and jammed it into the first open spot."

Shit, the motor scooter was the Taurus driver's escape vehicle.

"Does that mean you've downgraded my near death?" I said.

"Lost you there, pal."

"An assault with a deadly weapon is really just an unsolvable hot car beef?"

"A bit worse than that," said the cop. "It's a hit-and-run with no apparent injuries. But you're asking me to assume that it was intentional. How will you prove that in court? Or how will I?"

I looked around. Astonished onlookers stared from the sidewalks and Fausto's parking lot. I locked my eyes on the La Concha where a day earlier I could have performed back flips in a top-floor suite with Lisa Cormier. Something compelled me to raise the camera, zoom on the hotel, snap a photo. I kept going on zoom, photographing gawkers across the street, in front of the book store, the grocery, back down Bahama Street.

"Could I see some ID?" said the cop.

I threw him a look of disbelief.

"Sorry, it's the rules."

"Today's my day to hate rules," I said. "Are you going to arrest me for getting hit by a car?"

"I have to fill out a report."

"And you have no name for the other guy. So bag the rule and call me a hit-and-run victim. I'm going home for a beer."

He puffed up, stepped closer. "I can arrest you for disobeying a legal order."

I held out my arms, wrists together in front of my belt buckle. "Please cuff me. I can't wait to see how your audience reacts. *Key West Citizen* sales will skyrocket. Everyone will know your name."

The officer thought for a moment. "Tell me yours."

"Rutledge."

"You stood up for one of our detectives a couple years back?"

"There was a deputy there, too," I said. "I gave her a little help."

"You saved his life. You need a ride somewhere?"

"No thanks," I said. "But you might call in a BOLO for two guys on a yellow motor scooter."

"I'll do that."

"Now shake my hand and slap me on the shoulder," I said, "like the handcuffs thing was a big joke."

179

I wished I had asked him to slap my right shoulder instead of the one that hit the windshield.

My CELL PHONE CHIRPED while I walked toward Southard to retrieve my bike. A local number I didn't know. Rolling with the concept that a non-communicator can't learn shit, I took the call.

A voice I recognized after three words said, "The second-choice location, thirty minutes, no bullshit." The line went quiet.

Copeland Cormier wanted to meet me at the Pier House Beach.

I called Duffy Lee Hall from a pay phone—a rare item these days.

"Your man Dr. Cormier is quite the humanitarian," he said. "He's done stints in three countries and still oversees the surgery section of a hospital in Georgia."

"Which countries?" I said.

"In the past few years he did three months in Nicaragua, three months in the Dominican Republic, and two Mexico visits for two months each. He traveled under the auspices of a group called Doctors with Deep Wallets."

"Any visits to the Middle East?" I said.

"He spent five months in Iraq, back in 2004. It looks like he took humanitarian leave from the hospital. But he was employed by KRSW Global, an Alabama-based security contractor. Our best presumption might be that he provided in-country medical services to his fellow employees."

"What kind of security did they provide?"

"I can't tell, and the company went out of business last year."

"How about his wife and those other two names?"

"Haven't had time, bubba," said Duffy Lee. "Call me tomorrow afternoon."

I hung up and wondered if Cormier had scuttled a replica of Sam's skiff.

15

RIDING MY BIKE TO the Pier House, I didn't hug the curb. I fought the idea that my attacker might return for a sneak-from-behind rematch, a faster-paced whack. Assuming that the cop was right—the Taurus had been quickly dumped—it made no sense to turn my head. I couldn't guess which vehicle might nail me, and the whole process could drive me batshit. I refused to look backward. On an island known for lunatic action, I chose the comfort of thinking that my up-and-over had been a random, one-time event.

Along with that shot of denial I welcomed the floral air of dusk, my favorite time of day. Cumulus clouds to the north still held the vivid purples and orange wisps of sunset. Minimal action and noise from the Rum Barrel and Two Friends Bar; a slow night in the tourism trade. That would change with Fantasy Fest only six days away, but for now it was a lovely evening—to be targeted in the tropics.

I usually have no interest in motor scooters, but coasting into the hotel lot I noticed at least a dozen. They all sported rental company placards, blocked bike racks and took up car-sized spaces. In the dim light I saw none that were yellow.

Again I begged myself to let it go.

Then, more attentive, I saw a Porsche Cayenne with Florida tags, the same dark metallic gray as Bob Catherman's. I hate coincidence and wished that I had thought to memorize Catherman's license number. To find him in the company of Copeland Cormier would put an odd dimension to my three days of intrigue, although Sam's comments on Sugarloaf appeared to link Sally Catherman to his Cuba trips. Five cars farther down the line, I saw an identical dark gray Cayenne with a Florida tag. Maybe they were all produced in the same color. I hadn't seen more than four or five Porsche SUVs in recent years, so I didn't know. They fit the upscale Pier House demographic, however, so seeing the second Cayenne allowed me to quit worrying about Catherman.

I locked my bike, entered the parking lot hallway, and bemoaned the remodeling that had eliminated the atrium. A group of people ambled around me, all dressed for dinner, wallowing in a force field of cologne and after-shave. I walked past the Chart Room Bar—the ghosts of 15,000 cocktail hours and twice that many love affairs. The room was busy, as it probably would be until the Pier House came tumbling down to make room for a more posh destination.

Outside again, I followed a curving bricked path through a manicured jungle, a mist of chlorine. I went left, looped the pool and hung back from its mood lighting. A security guard approached, eyed me without smiling. I offered a quick, confident nod to assure him that my presence on the property was more important than his gig. He kept on walking.

Cormier sat facing away from me in the open-air Beach Club. Another man at the table took no notice as I stopped and turned back to circle the pool in the other direction. I wanted to see if anyone was watching Cormier—or if he had other team members around the hotel. For all the Garden Building's ground-level patios, the beach area's square footage, there weren't many hiding places for observers.

I entered the Beach Building and followed an inside hallway to a double door that gave onto the sand five yards from the tideline.

From that vantage point I studied the bistro. Two men and two women I recognized as locals sat at the bar. The bartender spoke into a portable phone and a tourist couple three tables from Cormier looked as comfortable in their Bermuda shorts, flowery shirts and sandals as they might in medieval armor. An unskilled acoustic guitar player with a snare drum in his iPod sang an insipid version of the Piña Colada song.

Not five yards away from me a thin boy sat cross-legged on a coral rock toking a joint. Closer to the restaurant, a lesbian couple, arm-in-arm on a raised walkway, stared down at playing tarpon teased to shore by underwater lamps.

Not just a slow night on the island, but a dead night. No one appeared to be shadowing Cormier. Our meeting would be private—except for the other man at the table.

Cormier stood as I approached the Beach Club's raised decking. He wore his fashionable fishing outfit minus the long-billed cap and smug confidence of our first meeting. "Alex," he said, "thank you for taking my call, for coming to see us. You're just in time to meet Ricky Stinson."

Stinson wore a black, long-sleeved crew-neck T-shirt, camo hiking shorts and what looked like a matte black stainless steel wristwatch. He half-stood, supported his weight on the table and made a token effort to extend his arm. I circled the table to shake his hand and saw he also wore black high-top sneakers. We sized up each other without speaking.

"Ricky's part of our support team," said Cormier.

"Why just in time?" I said. "Is he leaving?"

Stinson sneered. "I told Cope I was out of here if you didn't show in the next ninety seconds. You hit the mark a half minute too early."

"That's what my old girlfriend used to say."

No laughs, no smiles. My sharp dart of levity hit a shield of contempt.

Cormier shoved a chair with his foot. "Please join us."

An attractive server in her twenties appeared next to the table. Her accent was eastern European, her manner graceful. Cormier asked for a refill of his vodka and tonic. I ordered a Bacardi 8 on the rocks. Stinson didn't look up, didn't speak, but pushed his empty Heineken bottle toward her. She took it away, showed no offense and hurried to fetch our drinks.

Aside from his failed sense of humor, Stinson was hard to peg. My guess would be forty, give or take four years, with a fitness center build. His full head of brown hair started high on his forehead. It looked uniformly dark as if to mask premature gray. His eyes were sunken, unreadable. Except for an inch-long scar below his left ear, his cheeks and jaw were strong and smooth, with smile lines out of the question. A master of the frozen expression.

"What are we here to talk about?" I said. "Sam's not making his voyages."

Stinson looked to Cormier for the answer. Or silently told him to answer me.

"As I assured you two days ago," said Cormier, "you're helping an admirable cause and helping your friend as well. We put our campaign on pause. We're not in the business of instant results, so we took a breather to let some heat dissipate."

I thought about Sam's description of the ugly boat with four motors.

"I guess you'd call a high-seas boat chase an example of heat."

Cormier nodded.

"You and Sam," said Ricky Stinson, "you've been friends how long?"

"It doesn't matter," I said.

He stared at the table. "The boss here says you stepped up to help the man. No hesitation. What did he do, once or twice save your life?"

I said nothing. Tried to figure out his up-north accent.

184

"You two old pals from jump school? Swamp training? Same tank in Kuwait?"

The server returned and smiled at Cormier and me as she placed our drinks on the table. She dropped the smile and handed Stinson his fresh beer. Something about her got my attention. Only after she walked away did I get it. She had Beth Watkins's eyes. She also had Bobbi Lewis's rear view, but those eyes...

"Back to business," said Cormier. "I spoke with Sam. I have been castigated for underestimating you. He asked that I apologize on his behalf for making the same mistake. I asked you to help us with the long-term payoff of self-satisfaction. But I failed to emphasize risk. By withholding information, by trying to protect you, Sam and I could have put you into greater danger. If you want to hear more about what we're doing, I am prepared to tell you everything I know. I will answer all of your questions."

Stinson shifted his downward gaze to the tabletop in front of Cormier. "You're talking to this shitbird like he's one of us."

Cormier gazed off at the dark harbor, said nothing.

"I know we're not counting days," I said to Stinson. "How many hours have you been in the Florida Keys?"

"Long enough," he said, sliding his eyes to the drink in front of me. "I hear you're a groupie for the she-cops."

"Where did you study medicine, Ricky?"

He joined Cormier in staring into the distance.

Cormier said, "That's not his field, Alex."

Like a savvy lawyer, I knew that before I asked. I almost said something about Sloppy Joe's calling their bouncers "emotional control technicians," but I held my tongue. Stinson was one of those boys born with a "use-by" date.

The alleged entertainer began to moan the Buffett song, "Tin Cup Chalice." Far too slow, off-key and ill-timed. I wished I could give him a sample of what I now knew to be Stinson's expertise.

"Copeland," I said, "I appreciate your willingness to answer my questions. You didn't have to expend all this effort. But now it worries me that you did. I don't want to know more than I already know. I wish to hell I didn't know any of it."

Cormier kept his eyes on the water.

Stinson's phone buzzed. He extracted it from a side pocket of his shorts and didn't check the window before he flipped it open. He grunted, listened for maybe ten seconds, snapped it closed, returned it to his pocket. I knew from shaking his hand that he had laborer's calluses. I could tell by the way that he handled the phone that he also had the grace of an aristocrat.

Or a martial arts expert.

"So, one more time," I said, "why are we here? I got turned off by your drunken performance yesterday, so now you want to play me with intimidation?"

Still no response from either man. I dug deeper.

"Okay, play me. When I'm through shivering in my boots, will I be compelled to try harder? Get scared away? Maybe leave town? Did you ask me to this dream resort so we could all go backward?"

"Whoa," said Ricky Stinson. "With the doctor, here, you might get away with that kind of yammering. But don't think you can jack me around."

"I don't recall talking or referring to you," I said. "Are you over-compensating for a poor self-image, or just trying to justify your salary?"

"Boys, boys," said Cormier. "You keep pissing at each other like that, your splashing might soil my drink."

Stinson let a huge belch. Not too damned aristocratic.

FROM SOMEWHERE IN THE restaurant, three college-age girls stumbled onto the beach singing along with the last few lines of "Tin Cup Chalice." They looked to be children of wealth, dressed for dinner and fortified by drink. As the lyric ended they began their own song—a sorority ditty, part foul-mouthed, part cute—about searching for their dream date in Nantucket. Performing for themselves and anyone else who cared to watch, they struck jutting-ass and tits-up poses, tried to look alluring, or helpless when they sang their naughtiest lines. At the end of each verse the women removed an article of clothing. None of them wore bras. If their goal was nudity, it would be a short song.

A crowd of maybe ten or twelve began to assemble, to offer applause and hoots of encouragement. When the ladies were down to their panties—or thongs for two of them—one reached into her stack of duds and pulled out a small camera. She ran around the others, snapped a half dozen topless photos. She put the camera in her shoe as they started the verse that promised full nakedness. On the final line, they paused as if the big moment had arrived. Then they burst into laughter and knelt to pick up their garments. One counted to three, at which point they stood up, faced away, mooned the Beach Club and ran toward the Beach Building annex.

Our eastern European server went onto the sand to collect the plastic cups tossed there by the girls. She lifted a thong by her pinkie finger, gave it a look of disgust then dropped it.

"Assholes," said Stinson. He reached over and flicked his fingernail against my drink glass. "Did you think we didn't see you cruise the pool when you got here?"

The phone call. An observer had watched me arrive.

"I trusted you out of the gate," said Cormier. "I told you everything."

"And I assured you that I'd keep my mouth shut. I'd do nothing that might put Sam in jeopardy. Now you're going a step beyond my loyalty to Sam. You're trying to force me into keeping my mouth shut."

"Crossed my mind," said Cormier. "And Ricky's, too. You don't think Sam still needs your help?"

Shit, I thought. Good guy, bad guy has gone to bad guy, bad guy.

"It's not what I think," I said. "It's what I don't know. I thought we were in agreement—neither of us would endanger Sam. Now your mind is envisioning a possible betrayal, and I have to think the same of you, Dr. Cormier. From now on it's what he tells me, not you."

Cormier said, "Don't think for a minute that Sam is our only resource. You don't think that five or six other honest boat owners live in the Keys? We knew from the start that we'd have to be flexible."

"Starting now," I said, "I'm out of your loop, deep in the dark and five steps removed. I don't want intrigue, insider knowledge, fail-safes, plans or tough guys. Thanks for the drink."

Cormier glanced at my empty glass. "By the way, Rutledge, my wife, for all her upbeat alertness, her good looks and positive take on things, has been an alcoholic since college. I still love her dearly and I would hope that anything you might witness, anything in questionable taste, you might keep to yourself. Grant her the sadness she has never outgrown."

I nodded.

"Should she take a liking to you, please know you are not the first nor last. I ask only that you do us a favor. Treat the situation with dignity."

"My shoes will grow wings," I said.

The remark puzzled Cormier for a moment, then he appeared to accept it as I had meant it. He stood and his expression changed, became hard. "You want out," he said, "but there is no out." He began to walk and Stinson stood to follow him.

Stinson leaned toward me so Cormier couldn't hear him. "You're easier to read than a stop sign. If I ever see you again and you still got that mouth, you're going to wish you grew wings."

"And here I was, about to throw you an attaboy," I said. "You keep your boss on such a tight leash."

As if addressing an audience of hundreds, the singer thanked us for listening. He invited us back for tomorrow's happy hour, told us not to fear the tip jar.

WHEN I WAS SURE that Stinson and Cormier had left, I wandered back into the Beach Building annex. With the crazy laughter and an upbeat Supremes song echoing from the second floor, I had no problem finding the three drunk girls. I climbed a stairway, found them running between two rooms, one still in her panties, one buck naked, the other wearing a pair of boxer shorts.

The naked one saw me in the hall, put her hands up to cover her face and said, "Oh, I feel so violated."

From inside a room one of the others shouted, "I'm next."

I wanted no part of their party.

I checked their room numbers and split. My banged-up leg muscles forewarned that I would not enjoy getting out of bed in the morning.

16

IN THE PIER HOUSE parking lot, the Cayenne farthest from the door was gone. I wished I had read both license tags and not blown off my initial suspicions. I also wished I could quit thinking like a private eye and go have a quiet beer.

My cell phone rang as I started up Front Street. I pulled it from my pocket to inspect the little window, but I was too close to a loud saloon to hold a conversation. One block up Simonton I returned Beth Watkins's call.

"The telegraph has you smacked by a car," she said.

"I'm fine, no problem."

"See, Alex, a cop thinks differently. It's more like the victim is lucky but there's still a problem because hit-and-run is a crime in Key West. It could have been a mistake and the driver panicked. Or it might have been intentional, assault with a deadly weapon, and the schmuck could try again. It sounds like you're not at home right now, for instance."

"Okay, you got me. I just turned around to look."

"Can we meet somewhere for a drink? I need to pick your brain."

"I feel like hiding in my cave," I said.

"That's understandable, given that I just goosed your fear factor."

"I'll meet you at my house in ten minutes."

"Nine?" she said.

"Eleven."

I detoured to the package store behind the Bull & Whistle, bought a cabernet sauvignon. I was a block from the store when I turned back to buy a second bottle. Call it contingency planning. Wishful thinking.

The island's highest elevation—Solares Hill—is seventeen feet above sea level. My ride home—going away from the high point— felt uphill every inch of the way. Fleming Street's bike lane was an obstacle course of drunken moped riders and drunker idiots trying to parallel park. Carrying wine added to my clumsiness, though tropical evening fragrances lightened my load—not including fabric softeners in the block between William and Margaret.

I tried to pre-plan my encounter with Beth Watkins—lovely cop that she was—and to figure out how to answer her first question, one that I should ask myself.

How in the hell did I flip over that car's hood?

And her probable second question. What the hell's going on?

I now knew that Copeland Cormier wanted me off the hunt. He had wanted to assure himself—and Ricky Stinson—of my silence and to ensure it with a hammer-slam threat. The silence was a given. I would never cross Sam Wheeler. But Cormier's heavy crap had backfired, had ignited the idea that everything he had told me for the past two days was bullshit. Including the short speech about his alcoholic wife. The rare bulb popped on. Her proposition had been planned to rope me in—in some way, for some reason.

With you I would be a virgin.

I had confused them by declining her passionate come-on. Was she more to be pitied than scorned? Had Cormier's speech about her sadness been a ruse to whitewash their treachery with a tale of affliction? Was she even his wife? Was he more a pimp than humanitarian?

Had he spoken with Sam, or thrown that in as part of his ruse?

I saw Beth Watkins hurrying up Fleming in the glow of the Eden

192

House lobby lights, lightly tapping her hand against each of the six vertical columns out front. I stopped alongside of her, climbed off my bike. She said, "Handy man," and patted the wine bag, then checked me for damage, squeezed my arm when she saw that I was okay. As we started down Dredgers Lane she bitched about having to park a block away on Grinnell.

"You smell that?" I said. "We're downwind from a rain squall."

"They're talking a tropical storm near Haiti, and I saw a bunch of lightning off Higgs Beach. I hate it when people I know get run down on purpose."

"Ahh, you get used to it."

"Don't even joke," she said. "We found the Taurus in front of Carmen's house."

"Jesus."

She began to speak but stopped. We both saw the prowler skulking in my yard, peering in a window.

Beth motioned with her hand, palm upward, to ask if I recognized the man. I shook my head, and she placed both hands against my chest, silently told me to stay put. In the next several seconds I learned about the arsenal in her black belly pack. She slowly, quietly peeled open its top Velcro closure. Its face flopped down; even in dim light I saw "POLICE" in reflective letters facing outward. She reached down with both hands, came out with a mean pistol in one hand, a Mini Maglite in the other.

She took four steps into the yard, switched on the light. The flash illuminated the man's upper body. "Police," she said clearly. "Don't move."

Bob Catherman turned his head toward us, looking sheepish, a bit defiant.

"You know the man, Mr. Rutledge?" said Watkins.

"Yes," I said. "He shouldn't be a problem, but make sure he's unarmed."

"Look, lady, you want me to strip naked, I will," said Catherman.

"But I don't have a weapon on me. I don't even have fingernail clippers. Or a ballpoint pen."

She barked: "Tell me your name, where you live and what's going on here."

"Bob Catherman, Cudjoe Key. I wanted to talk with Alex."

"Through the window?" said Beth. "Were you going to open it?"

"Look," he said, "I didn't want to wake him if he was already in bed. I saw a light on, but I didn't hear a TV or a stereo. At this hour, I didn't want to be rude and bang on his door."

"People knock on doors all the time, Mr. Catherman. It's only 8:15."

"Lady, in my business people leave their homes with me for months at a time, fully furnished, personal items all over the place. I don't have to be a B&E boy."

"Defensive are we?" she said.

"Sorry. I'm trying to sell you the idea that I'm trustworthy."

"I get it. You're not breaking in, you're just looking in."

Now looking haunted—as he had when he first tried to hire me—Catherman leaned to look around her, to appeal to me. "Alex, tell her I don't like guys."

"I don't know that, Bob. You were married but people change."

He turned to face Beth again. "Okay, point B, with the beaches we have in the Lower Keys, there's no percentage in being a window peeper. Wouldn't you say?"

"I don't know," said Beth. "I'll have to research the pathology."

Shit. I was all for giving him a rough time and finding out why the hell he was lurking in the yard. But she was about to arrest the bastard. I didn't want to interfere with her professional duties. I also didn't want either of us to spend the evening at the cop shop. I sure didn't want the wine to go unused.

"Mr. Catherman," I said, "did you have some information for me?"

"More questions than anything else," he said.

I felt fat raindrops and picked up my Cannondale. "Let's move inside."

Beth opened the screen door, Catherman went in, and I carried my bike onto the porch. We'd been under my roof fewer than fifteen seconds when the sky let loose. After ten more seconds the downpour settled into a steady drizzle.

I didn't invite them into the house. My porch furniture sat far enough away from the screening to keep us dry. I wanted Catherman to feel unwelcome, and the rain's white noise plus the lack of visibility through the porch screens gave us an illusion of isolation. Or, in Catherman's case, claustrophobia. He and I sat while Watkins remained standing, repacked her cop gear into her belly bag, but didn't close it up.

"Rutledge, I know you wanted to work alone," said Catherman, "but I was going stir-crazy in my house. My mind's been whirling around like a ball at the end of a rope. I felt worse than useless. Maybe I made it worse. I had a cocktail or two around sunset."

"Did I see your Cayenne parked at the Pier House an hour ago?" I said.

He looked genuinely puzzled. "No. I just drove into town."

Beth said, "Have you been driving intoxicated, Mr. Catherman?" She leaned toward him. "Endangering our citizens on the streets of Key West?"

He didn't flinch. "If you mean blowing a bad breathalyzer, I doubt it. I ate some chips and dip before I got in the car."

She stared at him then let it go. He didn't appear drunk, and I suspected that his mention of "work" had piqued her curiosity.

Catherman stared at Watkins, then gave a what-the-hell shrug and turned to me. "I guess I'm looking for a progress report. What have we learned about Sally? Any news at all, official or otherwise?"

Hot damn, I thought. If Beth hadn't been curious, she was now. "Nothing of substance," I said. "A couple of interviews set up for tomorrow. What's been going on with you since we last spoke?"

"You know they found her car, right?"

I nodded.

"They came and took my fingerprints so they could eliminate mine from prints they found in her car. It wasn't that nasty detective, but her name came up. The technician said they had to get the images to Lewis as quickly as possible. I was worried that someone considered me a criminal suspect, but the techs told me that was a foolish notion."

"Mr. Catherman," said Beth. "Would you mind if we compared your prints to the ones found in that Taurus?"

"Taurus, like a Ford?"

She stared him down.

"It was a Mazda Miata," he said. "Where does a Taurus come in?"

It was a smart move on her part, a good try. But he was honestly baffled, and I couldn't see logic in his wanting to hurt or kill me. It was also a bad move because it stopped my momentum. Not that I was in a hurry. I was enjoying the constant patter on the porch roof, the thick humidity and gust-driven crescendos, the fresh smell of wet leaves in the darkness. And the fact that Beth was there. Aside from my total concentration, the only thing missing was an open wine bottle and one less person.

Sensing the power balance on the porch, Catherman shifted his attention to Beth Watkins. "My daughter's gone missing. It's been almost three days, officer..."

"Detective."

"Sorry, detective. What are the stats? Maybe you know the numbers, you know, the odds of finding her."

"Where did she live, Mr. Catherman?"

"In the guest room under my house on Cudjoe. A legal enclosure, I might add."

"You reported her disappearance to the sheriff?"

He sneered. "Like getting a busy signal fifty times in a row."

"He had a tough time generating concern," I said. "They finally

196

took a report. Then they found her Miata abandoned at Mangrove Mama's."

"How have you been following up?" she said.

Catherman looked away. "Same damn woman at the Sheriff's Office."

Beth raised one eyebrow, gave me a glance. I nodded once.

"I know that stats exist on some categories of missing persons," she said. "I never memorized them."

"I can't tell you how much I miss her," he said. "I don't know where I'll get the courage to tell her mother about this."

Beth said, "Maybe her mother knows where she is."

"Sally wouldn't go this long without calling me."

I tried to imagine the ex-wife, their existence in Clearwater where he had been fired from a printing plant. The divorce had been recent—or so he'd said—so that ruled out child support for Sally. I wondered if he still paid alimony, and whether the tough real estate business was providing him a decent living.

"What was that SUV you were driving?" I said. "A Porsche?"

"I owe a lot of money on that ride. I have to mind my pennies."

"You saved a bundle by opting out of the kangaroo guard," I said. "Still, you got those oval-shaped dual exhausts. Those are sexy."

"A seminar instructor in Orlando told everyone in the class to buy expensive cars. He told us to go out on limb because home buyers like to impress wealthy people with their money. You stand a better chance of getting a listing and making a sale if you look successful. Hell, I might have to give that back. I could be sporting around in a Honda Civic by Thanksgiving."

"Your offer to buy my house," I said, "are you on salary?"

Catherman nodded. "Except I can't keep my mind on work." He stared at the rain-drenched screens, then at the table, the plastic bag that held two wine bottles. He looked like he could use a shot of rum, but he didn't dare ask in front of Beth Watkins for fear of setting himself up for a DUI citation. "If we're through talking," he said, "I better get out of your hair, head back to Cudjoe. Could I use that plastic bag? You know, my wallet and watch and phone."

I gave him the bag then flipped the lid of a two-by-four-foot teakwood box that I keep on my porch. I'd placed a half-dozen cheap umbrellas in there a year ago for situations like this. Grasping it like treasure, Catherman said, "Have you had any expenses we didn't anticipate? You need a booster for that package I gave you?"

As if I could bribe my way to non-existent info, I thought. Or squander five grand in thirty-six hours. I shook my head. "We're okay, Bob. I still owe you a day and a half."

He turned to Beth Watkins. "Lots of female detectives around here. I've been dealing with one from the county three times too often. Very unpleasant. So I can personally thank you for being friendly, less on edge."

"No problem," she said. "We try to comfort our suspects every chance we get."

Her remark blew past him. He stepped outside, popped the umbrella with his back to the wind and almost got dragged down to Fleming Street.

"THAT WAS ODD," I said.

"No shit," said Beth. "I never sensed that he was feeling grief. With all that business jargon, I expected him to ask for a loss-prevention status report. Why would a man with a missing daughter worry about being cited for a ground-level apartment?"

"I've known the man for two and a half days. If I had to sum him up, I'd say his priorities are in the wind."

"Did he drive his daughter away?" she said. "Is that why he acted so guilty?"

"The way he phrased his questions, it sounded like he was looking for what the authorities knew instead of what I'd learned.

Maybe he keeps all of his emotions in a filing system and calls up what he thinks people expect. His personality demands that you follow the bouncing ball."

"It took me a minute or two to figure why you kept us all on the porch," said Beth. "You wanted to knock down his comfort factor. That was good."

"Thanks."

"But now he's gone and it's fucking hot out here. Could we take off our clothes or else go inside to the air conditioning?"

I hoisted the wine bottles. "I'm going to need a corkscrew."

"On second thought," she said, "let's not get ahead of ourselves. Or does that sound horny, too?"

I UNLOCKED AND SHE went first. I had left a lamp burning in the main room, saw no reason to turn on another, but I closed the front and side window blinds. Don't want to give window peepers a reason to hang out. Beth took off her belly pack and went to use the bathroom while I uncorked one of the bottles.

When Beth returned to the living room, she stuffed her bra into the belly pack. "My least favorite part of the uniform," she said.

I handed her a glass and tilted mine to toast. The glasses came together with a light chime.

"A-sharp," she said. "The Restaurant Store, twenty-one, ninety-five each. Fine glasses make fine wine taste so much better."

I asked how she had spent her evening after our visit to Duffy Lee Hall.

"We'll get to that, Alex. Let's stay with Catherman another minute or two."

I knew full well where she was heading. "Can we talk about it tomorrow?"

"What was that all about, Sally Catherman and Bobbi Lewis and him paying you money?"

"Does your badge come off when the bra does?"

"Is that like, when I go off duty, what time do I get off?"

It was funny but I shook my head, refused to laugh.

"I'm sorry," she said. "Yes, this can be unofficial. I assume he wants you to find Sally. Why in the world did you take the job?"

"To help a friend. He might have a tangential involvement."

"That can only be Sam Wheeler."

"Have you ever heard of the Mansion?"

Beth said nothing.

"What's that look on your face?"

"I went out with a guy three times back around March or April," she said. "He works there. On our third date he got what he wanted. I did, too, I suppose, but I was sure as hell expecting more. I never heard from him again."

"Can I ask his name?"

"This will sound like I'm dodging, but he asked me not to say his name and his workplace in the same conversation. In spite of his poor behavior, I still believe the part about national security."

"Okay," I said, "I'll say a name and watch your reaction."

"I don't think..."

"Cliff Brock."

Beth sipped her wine. "Horndog bastard. I heard he had a thing for young ones, going out lately with girls half his age."

"I'm afraid it was Sally Catherman."

"Oh, shit." She studied my eyes. "Past tense. Did he do something to her?"

"I don't believe that's the issue."

Her facial expression went from worry to full shock. "Oh, my God. Is Sally the reason you asked about Bay Point? Did someone kill Sally and Cliff?"

"Only the feds know that answer," I said.

Beth got a pensive look on her face, pursed her lips and pressed them to the side of the wine glass. She finally shook her head. "I don't know anything. I was faking, working off rumor and what I read in the *Citizen*."

She stood, walked a circle in the living room carrying her empty glass, then went to the kitchen, tapped her finger on the wine bottle. "May I?"

"Have at it. Weren't we going to discuss Hammond? Did you show anyone those pictures in the brown envelope?"

"Quick and artful change of subject, Alex, but okay. It brings us right back to young ones."

I clammed up, allowed her to think her way into her answer.

She returned to the living room, kicked off her shoes, sat across from me. "I spent the early evening showing those pictures in bars," she said. "Hangouts for locals—the Parrot, Schooner Wharf, that place at Truman and Grinnell. I even went to the yacht club for a few minutes. You knew two of the men, and I got names for two others. The more I learned the less I saw any of them as suspects."

"The tie-in to young ones?"

"They all had a taste for younger women. Not jailbait, but fresh out of high school, maybe in college. Women beyond twenty-two were over the hill. Based on the bar chatter I heard, they weren't the irresistible studs they thought they were. They'd pick them up on Duval, then parade them around until the girls got fed up. Once in a while they got lucky, but a couple people suggested they were swapping porn instead of swapping dates. Three of the four are married."

"Maybe Jerry Hammond strayed from their fold," I said, "got into kiddie stuff. They all felt threatened."

Beth shook her head. "With legal-age girls—or legal porn, if that's what they were into—they weren't breaking laws that we enforce. I don't see a threat there."

"Okay," I said, "if the others are married, how about blackmail? Or maybe they were making porn."

"We didn't find video equipment or duplicator machines in Hammond's house. His gear, he was more of a low-level consumer, not a distributor."

"Unless his killer cleaned the place out, took the exotic stuff and left enough components to deflect our focus. Why do you think Hammond had their pictures filed away?"

She thought, then shook her head. "Those pictures could point to a murderer, or mean nothing, or anything in between. We can talk about that tomorrow."

"Shall we make our own little movie?"

"Soon, perhaps, with the lens cap in place." She sat back in her chair, put her feet on my knees. "I feel like we're on an island of calm with wreckage all around us. Thank you for being here right now."

"Easy for me," I said. "I'm here because it's home. You're welcome to stay."

A sly grin. "I sure don't want to drive and I'm not too damned excited about walking."

"Would you like me to refill your glass?"

"Oh, I don't know," she said. "Once you pass the age of thirty, getting drunk first is overrated. Maybe your friend can write a revisionist song. 'Why Don't We Get Drunk and Snuggle, Then Rip Off a Wild One at Dawn?'"

"Tough rhyme."

"And too long to wait," said Beth. "Is your girlfriend going to show up?"

"Ex-girlfriend, by her words and actions."

"Burst in here with her gun blazing?"

"Her mouth, maybe, but not her gun."

"Can I borrow a sleep T-shirt in case I get cold before you wake up? That way I can wear this top when I do the walk."

I laughed. She knew the lingo. Key West residents call the early morning drag back home after an unplanned all-nighter the "Walk of Shame."

We stood, embraced, and with a certain nervousness kissed lightly. The kiss went long and our anxiety vanished. Our hands touched new territory and a mutual comfort lifted the room temperature.

She finally backed away slightly. "Kissing is sometimes underrated, yes?"

"And it happens too seldom," I said. "Like learning to play the oboe, you can't practice too much."

"Why did I think you were a bassoon man? You don't, by any chance have..."

I knew her next word. "I might even have two."

"I hate them," she said. "They feel like sausage wrappers and smell like inner tubes. Actually, I was going to ask if you had a bottle of water to put next to the bed. I hate to wake up thirsty at four AM."

She disrobed as if I wasn't there or had seen it all a million times. I sat on the end of the bed and watched. Stunned by her lovely figure, I tried to comment but couldn't cough up a word.

"Force of habit," she said. "For the moment, think of it as a nude beach. Inspect every square inch, but don't assume knowledge or possession."

"You've been saving that speech for a while."

"Far too long. Do I pull down your pants or do you?"

"I've always believed in teamwork."

"Perfect. Please kiss my nipples while I do your belt."

"How about I do both?"

I tasted the perspiration under her breasts and touched the wonderful muscles on the insides of her thighs. Kissed her abdomen and moved my hand to find soft shallow curls, fragile skin and dampness.

"Keep doing that."

"This?"

"Yes, for like the next thirty-six hours. But I should warn you. I might start to sound like women's pro tennis."

A minute later she lay beside me, a moment after that pulled me in. Our first loving wasn't frantic but our pacing gave way to need, to pushing and squeezes and quiet words and floating and catching our breath. I stayed inside her, not wanting to leave, and began again to move.

"Let me turn over."

I pushed upward with both arms.

"Damn," she said. "My leg is caught in the sheet."

"No hurry."

"Maybe not for you."

And the second time, more rhythmic, more sensuous, took us to exhaustion, a tangle of sweat and caresses, and more touching to make sure we were real, not imaginary, not illusions. We lay awake for a long time.

"Give me a hot snuggle before you pass out," said Beth. "Are we still riding our motorcycles tomorrow?"

"Sure."

"Remind me in the morning that people who worry about little things—like zoning citations—are often afraid of background checks, large black marks in their past."

"Like illegal immigrants who refuse to jaywalk?"

"Like convicted felons who never let their license tags expire."

A minute later she shifted her head on the pillow. "He said he didn't know where he'd get the courage to tell her mother. Does he already know she's dead?"

I had been asking myself the same question and didn't have an answer. I was too tired to speculate so I kept silent.

"How did you manage a backflip over that car's hood and fender?"

That was her last question.

I feigned sleep for the next five hours.

———

AT 5:15 THE HOUSE phone rang. I had a feeling it was Sam Wheeler, which meant one kind of news at that hour. I reached to check the incoming number and felt Beth sit up and roll out. She walked toward the bathroom, her bottom in dim light worth the million I had kissed goodbye in refusing to sell my house.

I didn't recognize the Caller ID but answered anyway.

Captain Turk said, "Dress yourself for yachting, mate. The bus for dawn recon leaves in two minutes. Bring photo ID."

"Dark clothing?" I said.

"Don't bother. White boat."

"Where are you?"

"On your porch, watching the scenery."

If that was the case, he had a clear view of my bedroom door and a wonderful view of Beth Watkins wearing only a T-shirt.

"Don't let her know you're there, please." I hung up.

I looked up.

Beth stood at the bedroom door. "Was that who I think it was?"

"Please get in bed so I can explain."

"I'll stay right here, thanks."

"I was trying to protect your modesty. There's a man on the porch staring at your lovely bare buns."

"I'm not falling for it," said Beth. "If he's really there, he won't see any more in the next ten seconds than he saw in the last ten. I want a straight answer. Was that Bobbi Lewis?"

"The call came from the porch," I said.

"Okay, I'll look. Only because I want to go back to sleep."

She turned her head, saw Turk averting his eyes.

"Shit." She walked into the room and lay down next to me. I felt her body heat, smooth legs against my skin. She put her lips against my ear. "Does this mean you have to go away and not be here?"

I rubbed my hand along her hip. "I'm not sure what time I'll be

205

back. Do you know, by chance, where the Mansion is located?"

"Cliff never told me, so I didn't ask."

"I'll lock the door behind me," I said.

"Since we won't need that second condom…" She hesitated. I felt her swallow.

"What?" I said.

"Do you have a vibrator?"

17

Turk sat on the porch, twirling his keys, broadcasting impatience. The last three things I grabbed were Polarized shades, a pocket-sized digital camera, and a Ziploc pre-packed for boat trips. The bag held bug repellent, a flat plastic whistle on a woven lanyard, sun block, a chromed bosun's knife, a keeper string for my sunglasses, and two empty Ziplocs. The whistle's distress signal was more effective than shouting, especially in darkness. It was loud at a pitch more easily heard over wave noise. It didn't suck up your energy when survival was the point. The spare bags would hold my phone, camera and wallet if we got into a squall.

My usual yacht rides tended more to pleasure. The morning call declaring a picnic in the Marquesas, the late-day invitation to a sunset cruise. I had learned in the Navy that preparation pays off. If you don't think ahead, the ocean will bite.

"Foul-weather jackets?" I said. "Bottled water?"

"You're covered," said Turk, "and you can piss in the ocean like a fish. Let's go."

"You want to surprise me with the reason for all this?"

"I can ninety-percent guarantee you surprise," he said.

"What time did you talk to Sam?"

He rattled his keys on the table top. "We can talk in the truck."

Hurrying off the porch, I looked down toward Carmen's cottage.

Had the driver of the Taurus turned into the lane not realizing it was a dead end, then ditched it? That could have happened with someone new in town, but it smelled too much like coincidence. The message was adamant. The stolen car had been left as a further threat to me—or my friends. My activities of the past three days had angered someone with a mean streak. A type known to be persistent.

A follow-up thought: If the driver had been hired to run me down, should I be curious about the value of my death? I hoped it was worth more than the ratty car that flipped me, but I hadn't been there to jack up the bidding.

Turk's pickup was angled into the Eden House "Loading Only" zone, where I had stopped my bike to walk with Beth Watkins seven hours earlier. The hotel's night clerk stood in the central doorway, eyeballing the truck, about to push the buttons of a portable phone. Turk approached him and extended two fingers that held a ten-dollar bill. The man pulled the bill to freedom, smiled broadly, dropped the phone into his shirt pocket.

I would wish that the next seven hours might go so quickly, so smoothly.

The night felt muggy, the temperature in the mid-seventies. Like every night for the past six months except cooler. The squall of earlier had blown away leaving clear air behind it. We said nothing until Turk had crossed Garrison Bight Bridge to the empty, neon-lighted boulevard out of town. Too early for the first delivery vans in from Miami. Not even a stray pink taxi or a city cruiser on patrol.

"We knew from Wonsetler that the boat was awash south of the Saddlebunch Keys," said Turk. "I talked to a few other captains on the docks and got a couple of good clues. One said that Wonsetler mentioned Old Papy Road. Another said that he mentioned eight feet of water."

"Why do we care?" I said. "The swamped boat was a hazard, you said yourself. It's been towed to the beach. For all we know, it's in Miami being refurbished by the brother-in-law of some Marine Patrol officer. It'll be retitled and sold by year's end." I thought for a moment. "What's open water going to teach us?"

"We're going out there to be bait. We want to draw sharks."

"What did Sam say?"

"I didn't talk to Sam. This was Marnie's idea, so I'll let her explain. But, to put this in perspective, Sam warned me last week. If it all slams into high gear, whatever it is, it'll be bigger than we can imagine."

"Our dreams come true," I said. "I hope Marnie's on target, and our bait act doesn't turn us into chum."

"You brought photo I.D., right?"

TAMARAC PARK IS TWO miles east of Boca Chica Naval Air Station's control tower and a quarter-mile west of the Geiger Key Pub and Grill. The subdivision borders Hawk Channel and most of its stilt homes back up to canals, with modest yachts alongside seawalls or boats on trailers in yards. A few mobile homes have yet to be replaced by houses. Manatees occasionally visit. Loud Navy jets often fly overhead in practice patterns. The last time I was there, ten years ago, was to photograph a vacant lot for a real estate brochure. I charged my half-day rate for thirty-six pictures of canalside dirt, marl and scrub grass. The broker was so pleased with my work that she added a ten-percent bonus to the invoice.

After we passed the Tamarac sign, Turk asked me to look for Mars Lane on the right. I cued him and he went left, then right, then into a driveway. Too confusing for me at that hour. The house was dark, but Marnie Dunwoody's Jeep Wrangler was parked under the carport overhang. A flickering street lamp and low-intensity lamps from neighboring yards gave dim illumination.

"I brought the skiff out here before dark," said Turk. "Place belongs to an old friend who hasn't come back from his summer in Montana. I ran charters out of here five or six years ago when I was fighting the city for dock space at the Bight."

Marnie sat upright when Turk knocked on her driver's side door. Bleary-eyed, coughing herself awake, she said, "New Moon Tours at your service. We have black coffee and fat-filled pastries on the floorboard."

Turk opened the passenger-side door and grabbed a Styrofoam cup. "Eat fast," he said. "No food on the boat."

She climbed out of her Jeep. "You're welcome, fuckhead."

Turk jangled his keys then started toward the canal, his feet crunching gravel. Over his shoulder: "That's Captain Fuckhead to you, mate."

Marnie laughed and turned to me. "That's how I felt in the Circle K. Four city cops in there were staring, trying to figure why a news reporter was up at five A.M., looking my worst, and what did I know that they didn't?"

She wore a photographer's vest covered with flap-and-zipper pockets, and caught me staring at it. "A nautical reporter's kit," she said. She walked her hands from her hips to her shoulders, alternating right and left, to explain the pockets' contents. "Portable GPS, digital tape recorder, pepper spray, granola bars, boob, boob, cell phone, digital camera."

"Well-equipped."

"Electronics, indeed," she said. "Other than that, let's get on the boat."

"Can I ask the point of this excursion?"

"I know Sam better than anyone," she said. "I know how he juggles facts and twists logic and still hits the truth. We don't know who left that boat out there, but for a small skiff essentially underwater, it was found too soon. It was meant to be found—with Sam's hull numbers on it—and meant to be a message. It's so off-the-wall, it sounds like something Sam would do. I think its location was part of the message."

"So by going out there, we get a better grasp of the whole mess?"

"Or some idea how to help him," said Marnie. "I'm paying for Turk's gas and it's risk-free. We troll around and maybe draw flies. Maybe I can be less like those cops in the Circle K, wondering what I know that they don't. Because I don't know screw-all, and there's nothing else to do at this hour, and it's all we've got."

Nothing except for an alternate activity I would have enjoyed. But I was there to help Sam, and—with her determined face in the faint light—Marnie was right. Draw sharks... or flies.

Draw conclusions.

THE CONCRETE SEAWALL STOOD five feet above the water. Turk's Maverick, *Flats Broke,* hung on davit hooks, its propeller a foot above the placid canal water. He flipped a breaker then twisted levers on each davit. The winches turned slowly to lower the skiff, their steel cables popping as they untwisted and released tension.

Turk handed us the loose ends of dock lines cleated to the bow and stern. We stood in silence as the boat settled into the water. He shut off the davits, hunkered on the seawall and stepped down to the gunwale. It took him a minute to unhook the lift slings, clear the bilges and start the motor. Marnie and I pulled the davit arms back to the seawall, then she went aboard and I followed, bringing the dock lines with me. Turk flipped on his depth finder, a small compass, and a GPS unit and slipped it into gear. With his running lights dark he idled confidently out of Tamarac Park. I was glad he could do it. I couldn't see shit.

The wind freshened and easy waves rolled as we left the protected canal. Turk aimed a hand-held spot ahead of us and lighted a green "1" marker. He panned a red "2" triangle to our left, doused the beam, built up speed between the posts, brought the skiff to a plane and continued southeast. For the first half-minute he adjusted his tilt and engine speed to balance the hull to our weight, our positions around the console. Once we reached a rhythm with the waves, the ride was a joy.

The breeze on our nose carried open-ocean smells but no pre-dawn chill. The ocean carries a different flavor when it hasn't been sunbaked. I've always found it easier at that hour to differentiate among fish, seaweed, plankton and salt spray. And a new moon it was—with no moon at all—in that period before dawn when the sky is darkest, the stars brightest, more numerous, more mystical.

After a minute or so Turk angled left to take us east at about thirty-five knots. Engine noise and rushing wind made conversation pointless. Lost in our thoughts, we had no need to chat. The only light south of us was Pelican Shoal's red flasher. Ashore, to the north, I saw headlights on US 1 once or twice, but little else in that direction either. Then, southeast of us, American Shoal's automated flashing light popped into sight; and, dead ahead, the flashing white light of Ninefoot Shoal. After about twelve minutes, maybe a half-mile from Ninefoot Shoal, Turk slowed, dimmed the depth finder, scrolled his GPS to highlight our surroundings, and circled slowly back to the west.

"This is good," he said, keeping his eyes on the water ahead. "It'll stay dark for at least another fifty minutes. That's what we want."

Marnie sat in front of the console, hugging herself as if fighting the chill in her mind, the cold fear of what she might learn on the open ocean. Or what she might never know.

For twenty minutes Turk ran a slow yo-yo, a broad east-west grid. He was quiet except once when he muttered, "This isn't working," and reversed course.

During a west leg with the wind to our backs, I said, "Why GPS?"

"Keep us generally north of West Washerwoman. That's the ballpark, according to the scuttled boat report. I'm looking for at least eight feet of depth but no less than that. Once you get a quarter-mile off the beach, it shallows up."

"How waterproof is that unit?"

"If you can trust a salesman," said Turk, "it's supposed to survive splashes. If I drop it in a fishbox, it's probably okay. But if it sinks four feet, it's history."

"So someone could have trashed the boat, then come back and found it later?"

Turk shook his head. "I've been thinking since we first talked yesterday at your house." He tapped his GPS. "This runs off the boat's battery. The battery goes under, along with all the wiring, things go to hell fast. There wouldn't be any GPS."

"So how do we know if someone sees us on radar?"

"Maybe they'll come out to see our real live faces." Marnie had a shiver in her voice. "Can we give it a few more minutes?"

I had learned about underwater listening devices in the Navy, though I'd never heard of any in the Florida Straits. "How about one other thing?" I said. "Set your tilt to make the prop noisy, wake up the barracuda. Maybe cavitate on your turns."

"What the hell," said Turk. He pressed his engine tilt switch, brought the lower unit up a few notches but kept his prop below the surface. He turned to starboard, began a slow circle. The propeller didn't cavitate at that speed but churned loud enough to disturb plenty of fish. Turk straightened his course and motored toward the east.

For the next fifteen minutes, each time Turk turned, the prop burbled loudly—at least to us.

I HEARD IT EAST of us, the flutter carried by wind, muffled by distance. My first thought made it a helicopter. More careful listening killed that guess. Multiple motors and the metallic slap of its hull against the low wavetops had it coming our way. Not directly at us but within fifteen degrees, honking along quickly. I raised my hand and pointed toward the rumble.

Turk pulled back his throttle and checked the ominous throb. "If he kept his course, he'd pass south of us, right?"

Ten seconds later Marnie and I agreed.

"So right now he's fishing."

"Where did he come from?" I said. "Little Torch or Big Pine?"

"If it's the playtoy I think it is," said Turk, "it was docked last night in that marina at the bottom of Drost Road on Cudjoe. You're hearing three 225s on twenty-eight feet. All black paint, no hull numbers, no engine cover logos. I didn't have my tape measure. Might have been thirty-two feet, but born to be mean."

Turk spun his wheel, nudged the throttle lever, cavitating louder than before. He went a couple hundred yards, did it again, then pulled us back to idle speed.

Thirty seconds later we heard the boat shift course, aim directly toward us. It was still dark, and I glanced at Turk and Marnie, looked at my own clothing. There wasn't enough light to make us visible at that range. "Did it have radar?" I said.

"Not the boat I saw," said Turk.

"Are they using night-vision goggles?" said Marnie.

"We'd be a speck on the water at this range," I said. "I think they were guided by a shore facility, and I doubt they'd put Fat Albert's radar on something small like us."

"Alex called it," said Turk. "The beach crew heard us out here and steered him our way. Somebody's listening to hydrophones."

Marnie stared ashore. I saw it, too—the single lighted house on Lower Sugarloaf, west on Old Papy Road.

I spoke so only Turk could hear me: "You think that's what Sam wanted us to confirm?"

"Yep," he said. "And, by doing it, our trip here was a success. Now we have to pay the tab."

A separate, louder flutter approached from the west.

"Shit," I said. "That's a helicopter. Did we bite off more than we can stomach?"

214

"It's most likely another boat, but it's pay dirt," said Turk. He pressed the tilt control. The engine rolled back, the propeller went downward. He brought *Flats Broke* around slowly to point south and flipped on his running lights.

"We can't outrun those clowns," I said.

"We have to act afraid," said Turk. "They're coming right at us and they haven't identified themselves. They'll make it pretty fucking clear in about thirty seconds."

I said, "This has something to do with Photo ID, right?"

"Everybody hold on." He double-checked Marnie's grasp on the console and pushed the throttle full forward.

We traveled less than a quarter-mile, barely got up to speed before the boat approaching from the west blipped its blue light.

The other boat, now behind us, cued a directional loudspeaker. With painful intensity, like a foghorn with words, a voice said, "Police. Stop your boat, captain. Police. Stop your boat." Two focused spots lighted us like midday.

Turk eased his throttle. He made it clear that he was stopping but he didn't risk swamping the skiff by screeching to a halt.

"Turn your boat into the wind, captain. Take it out of gear and rev your prop."

Turk did so.

The boat behind us approached. The one to the west hung back.

"Captain, identify yourself. Did you lose someone overboard?"

Turk remained still. We were all blinded by the brightness.

The voice shifted to a battery-powered hailer. "Shut her down captain. You and your crew on your knees. Hang your arms over the side so we can see them. Hands in the water. We want to see thirty wet fingers, right now."

"My hands are in sight," shouted Turk. "I'm a licensed boat operator. You can read my hull number plain as day. Cut down those lights and come over here and tell me what you want."

"There goes my wild idea of trying to eat lunch today," I said.

The stern voice, as if two feet away: "We want you on your knees, hands in the water."

Turk shook his head. "Ain't gonna happen, Boats."

Long pause. The men on the dark boat tried to figure out how Turk knew the man's nickname—the traditional Navy moniker for a boatswain's mate.

On the hailer: "What are you doing out here, captain?"

"Trying to see who would come out and ask me that question."

"If we have to do an equipment demonstration, captain, the first shot airs out your bow at the waterline."

"Which law does that enforce?"

"Failure to identify yourself to Homeland Security, sir."

They had been well trained—to be courteous to everyone and friendly to no one.

"That's the Border Patrol with a new name?" said Turk. "Do I look like a Somalian pirate, or what?"

"That's the loss of your federally-issued captain's license on first offense."

"Oh," Turk said to us softly. "I guess we can take that as adequate jurisdiction. But don't put your hands under the surface." He switched off the engine.

We knelt and hung our arms over the side.

"I just made it to page one," said Marnie. "Tomorrow, above the fold, for good or ill. I'll either have the byline or be the topic."

We were less than 2,000 yards at sea, in Florida waters. I was close enough to the beach to hear cars on US 1—or at least imagine that I could. I felt very close to knowing an illegal alien's desire and desperation, except I had every right in the world to be where I was. At least the Navy allowed me to believe they held a vested interest in my right to life. The men with automatic weapons and black boats with their blacked-out numbers and motor logos had been trained to make me believe the opposite. Their presence assured me that I had no rights at all.

They flipped off one of their million-candle-power zappers and aimed the other one into the water astern of us. There was still enough light to play a softball game. I could make out at least five silhouettes aboard the large craft. Two held weapons pointed directly at us.

"Now, what are you doing out here, captain?"

"We came out to drift around," said Turk. "Enjoy nature."

"We worship the sunrise," said Marnie. "We come out here often. Do you want to interfere with our religious freedom?"

"We'll get to you in a minute, ma'am. During the past half hour, captain, you were running a pattern, like a search pattern. We think maybe you were waiting to rendezvous with another vessel. We've got some great equipment here. Is there anything we can help you find?"

Leading question, I thought. They know about the half-sunken boat.

Turk shook his head.

They drifted to within fifteen feet of us. Another man said, "Where do you live, captain?"

"Rockland Key."

"And your first mate, there?"

"Key West, Florida, USA," I said.

The man exhaled, disgusted. "A wiscass. And the lady?"

"Key West," said Marnie.

"Where do you work, ma'am?"

"I'm a news reporter. The *Key West Citizen*."

"Would your publisher be happy to know that you're out here?"

"My boss loves good stories," she said. "If he learned how I'm being treated by government employees, he would be overjoyed."

"Captain, we have you coming out of Varadero, departing the Cuban coastline a half-hour after midnight. Can you prove that you haven't spent the past five hours crossing over from Cuba?"

Alibi-free, Turk was silent. I pondered and rejected the idea of

217

tossing Beth Watkins's name into the mess. She didn't deserve to be dragged down by our folly.

Marnie came through. "I can absolutely prove it," she said. "I didn't have any cash with me."

"Okay, honey, what's that supposed to mean?"

"I was in Circle K—the one on the corner of Kennedy and North Roosevelt—at about 4:45 this morning. Four Key West police officers saw me and they all know me. I didn't have any cash, so I paid for three coffees and bad Danish with Visa. I keep all my receipts."

No one said a thing.

After a minute or so, the primary speaker said, "As you were."

"What does that mean?" said Turk.

"Belay my previous commands."

"And what does that mean?"

"Stand up and stand easy, captain. Identify your point of debarkation."

"Jesus."

"Sir?"

We all stood and Turk looked around his boat. "I don't think I have one."

I wanted to laugh at Turk's expense but let the men on the black boat do it for me. They turned down their spotlight and maneuvered to come alongside.

"You want to protect your hull, put out fenders, captain."

Turk lifted his seat cushion and I removed two oblong vinyl-coated tubes. Each had a length of fender line looped through an eyelet. I secured them to mini-cleats under the starboard gunwale and adjusted them so the big boat wouldn't crunch Turk's side rail. Two of the other boat's crewmen used boat hooks to grab *Flats Broke,* to snug us toward them and keep the boats from banging together. When I stood I could see a younger crewman making entries to a laptop. It had a screen dimming overlay so only the person facing the monitor could see what was on it.

The honcho barked his standard speech. "Driver's licenses, passports if you have them. Boat papers, captain. Copy of your most recent Coast Guard inspection."

"I just had that inspection last week," said Turk.

"Didn't see your running lights."

Turk looked baffled. "Maybe we were down in a trough between waves. I know my battery's running low. You saw them when you got closer, right?"

"You were transiting southward when we blue-lighted you, captain. Where did you think you were going?"

"We thought you were pirates coming to hijack our boat to use for highly illegal activities."

Marnie and I gave our licenses to Turk. He reached out to hand the paperwork to the main man. That man, in turn, passed our I.D.s to the kid with the laptop.

I spoke up: "What makes you so certain that we came out of Varadero and so clueless to our departure an hour ago from Geiger Key?"

The man hesitated, then said, "When was the last time you had an all-American knee in the balls?"

"Two years ago," I said. "Wouldn't you know, it was a law enforcement officer. Poor guy lost his job. When he tried to hire on with JIATF, they turned him down."

The Joint Interagency Task Force, based in Key West, coordinates at least fifteen federal agencies and military branches to fight illicit trafficking. They're our big fist against incoming drugs and illegal aliens. I had no doubt that the ugly black boat worked with the task force.

"What do you know about JIATF?"

"Their phone number," I said, "for starters."

He turned back to Turk. "Any weapons on board, captain?"

"The gaff, if you use it right," said Turk.

"I've got a knife," I said.

"We'll have to take that."

"Bullshit. I've owned it for twenty years and never harmed a human."

"Sir, we'll have to..."

"I keep it for personal safety, like every boat captain and fishing enthusiast in the Keys. You want to go on record as depriving me of safety equipment?"

"Religious freedom, safety on the high seas," said Marnie. "Anything else you gentlemen wish to revoke this morning? It all makes for a better headline."

The kid with the laptop spoke up. "Skipper, slight glitch here. You want to look at this?"

The pair with the boat hooks kept their eyes on us while the other three black-clad men huddled around the computer. Only then did I notice the matte-black weapon held by the shortest huddler. I was no expert but it looked in the dark to be an automatic rifle—nasty and lethal.

The agent in charge quit studying the monitor and approached Turk. "We've got a case of mistaken identity, captain. We're going to have to ask for your understanding in this matter."

"It'll cost you."

"Pardon me, captain?"

"My friend here wants an explanation of another topic."

"We're not in the explanation business." He turned and smiled at me like I was a long-lost friend. It was all self-pride. I was a mouse on downers and he was a six-pack of cats.

I asked anyway: "That underwater music festival at Looe Key every year... Do you have to put plugs in your underwater ears?"

He handed Turk the sheaf of boat documents and our licenses then faced me. "Don't ask that, bubba. I mean, you have every right to ask but, if I gave you the answer, we'd have a long day ahead of us. You folks enjoy the holy sunrise."

18

THAT HALF HOUR BEFORE sun-up, a pale cyan haze of vacant sky and light-chop water, no visible horizon. Nasty and full of thunder but hauling less emotional punch, the black boat roared eastward. Its wake a pale, turbulent strip in the monotone ocean. The agents had their job to do and we weren't it.

Turk restarted his motor, slipped it into gear, idled slowly toward Geiger Key.

"Not to be unladylike," said Marnie, "but what the fuck was that? Those faux-ninjas called me 'lady.' Ladies are dumpy old broads in grainy movies who wear bowl-shaped hats with veils. The other bastard called me 'honey,' like he's buttering up some waitress in a diner. Or talking to one of his daughter's playmates."

"They protect our nation's coastline," I said. "Did you copy their chatter?"

Marnie yanked a zipper, pulled out the digital voice recorder then an earpiece from another pocket. She fitted them together and tested. "I got every word. They sound like they're on the boat with us, but I'm not too sure I got a story. Your all-American knee in the balls, however, might go to the Sports page."

"Do we have time for a short cruise up Sugarloaf Creek?" I said.

Turk eased his steering wheel to starboard. He'd led me to think he knew more about Sam's caper than I did. He certainly understood my curiosity.

"Can we head back?" said Marnie. "My piece on Jerry Hammond's murder hits this morning. I need to be in the office for feedback calls."

"This man, Mister Alex, has a fine idea," said Turk. "The first part of this tour was sponsored by Ms. Dunwoody. The second and final segment will be hosted by the world-famous photographer."

"What birds will we see on this daybreak excursion?" I said.

"Maybe a fish hawk—an osprey," said Turk. "Perhaps the odd cormorant. If we venture close to Sugarloaf Shores, we might see a fluffy-titted skinny-dipper."

"Quit screwing with me," said Marnie.

"Why do you think they let us go so quickly?" I said.

"I'm a reporter."

"That helped," I said, "but they were looking for lumps. We were a wrinkle."

"Can we go with facts instead of imagery?" she said.

"Some file on their computer gave us a free pass. One of our names or Turk's hull number... something waved a green flag. With their clout, they may have confirmed on the spot that you used a credit card at the Circle K. Once they decided we hadn't crossed the straits, they lost interest."

"Or they got redirected," said Turk. "They left here fast on a single heading. That team on the beach found the real boat that departed Cuba. This won't add an hour to getting back to Tamarac Park."

"Does this detour relate to our reason for coming out here?"

"The ninjas pretended not to know about the sunken boat," I said. "We came out here to draw attention. The swamped boat was meant to do the same. We weren't the right flies."

"And this creek we're exploring leads to Bay Point?" she said. "Is the sunken boat connected to that fiasco on Sunday?"

"It crossed my mind—and I think Turk's, too."

"Does any of this intrigue lead us to Sam—or help him out?"

"I have no idea," I said. "But we're here. There's not much else to do at this hour, and it's all we've got."

Marnie recognized her own words, bit her lip and nodded. "All right," she said. She made a grand "Onward" gesture and moved sideways for a better grasp on the console.

Turk asked me to kneel on the bow to watch for coral heads, then brought *Flats Broke* to planing speed. With a freshening wind on our starboard quarter, it took five minutes to cover not quite three miles to Lower Sugarloaf. With shallows in sight, Turk dropped speed, raised his prop and let momentum carry us inshore.

At the inlet, with little headway in eighteen inches of water, I slid off the boat, held us in place, and looked around for prop scars in the grassy shallows. I saw old scrape marks but no torn grass, nothing recent. If Sam had taken this channel to duck a chase, he had done a clean job of it.

"How far north is open bay water?" I said.

Turk shrugged. "Couple hundred yards, if that."

"Is there more than one way to cut through here?"

"Yes and no, depending on silt build-up," he said. "Storms blow it open but quiet weather shuts it down. The locals know the way through." He pointed to our right then swung his arm to the left. "They also know the shortcut to Bay Point, off that way, and know when to use it. A kayak would love it, but not this boat with the sun low and the creek in shadows. We'll go the deep route."

I pointed at a white one-by-four slat that stuck maybe fifteen inches above the water's surface. "What the hell? Is that supposed to mark the funky channel?"

Turk said, "I don't remember a post in here."

I let the boat drift and wandered up the shallow cut. "Seems like a confusion factor, and a dangerous one," I said. "Some innocent newbie could mistake it for the safe way to go. Maybe I should yank it out and toss it into the mangroves."

"Leave it," said Turk. "Somebody put it there for a reason. You might cause more trouble than you think you're saving."

I wiggled the one-by-four. It was jammed tightly into the sandy bottom. I left it alone, waded back to *Flats Broke* and rolled onto the bow.

THE NEXT TWENTY MINUTES offered us nothing. Turk knew the perimeter channel, zig-zagged expertly around the open bay south of US 1. We motored to Sugarloaf Shores, made a long, slow S-turn then ran westward parallel to the road. He pulled power to go southward, seventy-five feet off the east shore of Bay Point. We passed a vacant, storm-shuttered home that stood out oddly among the show places along the waterfront. It looked especially weird because of signs of recent activity on the seawall—scrape marks, a small, fresh oval fender left hanging on new-looking yellow nylon line.

Turk and I exchanged glances, shared the thought that Sam's friend Cliff Brock and Sally Catherman had died there—or were killed elsewhere, perhaps not far away—and were found in that yard. Then I recognized the place as a crime scene I had observed sixteen months earlier. A man had been hung on his boat lift davit, murdered because he knew too much about other murders.

The dropping tide and tough visibility into the sun forced Turk to take a circuitous route back to the creek. We approached its northern mouth this time from the west. At that angle, from my side of the boat, the bay bottom gouges were easy to spot. In recent days a single-engine speedboat—such as Sam's Maverick—had barged through the creek, gone toward Sugarloaf Shores, then angled west. Turk saw me checking the scrape marks and slowed to look but kept quiet.

"Have you two accomplished what you wanted?" said Marnie. "I think that coffee went to yesterday instead of today. I have to piss bad and I'm getting a caffeine withdrawal headache and my hurry didn't disappear."

Running south, pushed by the outbound tide, Turk fought to maintain steerage. "We're almost there," he said.

We swatted aside low branches as the skiff snaked down the creek. I wouldn't admit it to either of them, but I felt more hungry than enlightened. I had learned only that Sam, if in fact he'd come this way at speed, had all-American balls, size large.

"I feel like the cheese in a mangrove sandwich," I said.

"You're on my boat," said Turk. "What's to worry?"

"Just about everything," said Marnie, looking away from both of us. "Can we tie up to a tree and talk a minute?"

Turk looked at the back of her head, his expression stating plainly that women fall back too easily on emotion. He pulled his shifter out of gear, reached outward, caught a branch and let the boat drift against the mangrove roots. No one spoke at first. We sat listening a few moments to wave slosh and bird calls.

"Starting now," said Marnie, "I want to stop feeling like a three-year-old being dragged around a county fair." She gave me a hard stare, turned to do the same to Turk. "You two have been holding out on me. I don't deserve this."

I felt her stare return to me. I fixed my eyes on the boat bottom. She had every reason to be pissed off. We'd held out on her—on Sam's request.

"You think I can't handle the truth?" she said. "Where the fuck is Sam? What's going on in Monroe County that has law enforcement agencies locked in their own handcuffs? Why did a boatload of tooled-up feds become our long-lost pals? Why do we know lots of shit, but we don't know the reason for all of this?"

Neither of us responded. I peered over the side and watched a barracuda drift with the current.

"Okay, I admit," she said, "it was my idea to come out here—at least to Hawk Channel. And if that swamped boat was really

225

found—which I now question—I still believe that Sam left it there."

"You through?" said Turk.

Give her credit, I thought. No one else had suggested that the sunken boat was raw fiction. All pressures aside, I had to admit something, too. The possibility that she would go to press with anything to injure Sam was miniscule.

"Why this creek?" said Marnie.

I said nothing.

"There must be some reason why your idea was pure genius. Did you get a tip through the grapevine, or what?"

I raised my shoulder. I shouldn't have moved a muscle. Having been a reporter for years, she was expert at reading body language. My slight movement had rung a warning bell.

"Okay, Marvin Gaye, you heard what through the grapevine?" she said. "Don't shut up on my account."

I looked over her shoulder. Turk shook his head, warned me off. But he was too late. "Someone we know got chased by a boat," I said.

"Go ahead, say the name 'Sam.'"

"It was similar to the black one we just saw thirty minutes ago. His local knowledge saved his ass. I'm not sure exactly where..."

"Chased, Alex? Are the pieces coming together now? Did the elusive 'they' have him coming out of Varadero by chance? Is that what he's been up to? Is my man a smuggler?"

There must have been a hundred ways to dig myself in deeper. I couldn't think of a single word to save my ass.

"You bastard," she said. "You talked to him, didn't you? That's why you were so sure he didn't have a girlfriend, that everything would be all right."

I had no answer. Even my silence was a lie.

"You make me wish that man had kneed you in the balls. I'd try it right now if I didn't think I'd fall overboard."

Turk kept quiet. His tactic worked, though his guilt matched mine.

She ignored him and stayed focused on me. No words. Just daggers. From a woman who, for a time, had kept up her black belt status in karate.

"The only thing you don't know," I said, "is that he was taking things into Cuba, not away from there. He was working with some do-good doctors, delivering drugs to legitimate doctors down there."

"Bullshit," she said. "He makes damn good money chartering. He lives to fish. They couldn't pay him enough to risk it all."

"My impression is they paid for his gas. That's it."

"So it's community service in Castroland?"

"Sums it up," I said. "Except something got screwy Sunday night. I got the impression that he didn't expect to be intercepted. He got away by running through a creek. It could have been this one, it could have been any other cut between the mangroves from Key West to Bahia Honda."

"Well, fuck," she said. "Are the do-gooders local?"

I shook my head. "One of them is here in town, somewhere. He's a surgeon from Georgia and he's worried just like us. Everybody's waiting for another shoe to drop. I'm just afraid it'll be five shoes at once."

Marnie ran out of questions. She turned to look at Turk. He faced her eye-to-eye, stonefaced, a bit sheepish and—I could tell—not convinced that I'd done the right thing in telling her all. Or almost all.

"Let's go home," she said. "I hear my office phone ringing."

THE DAY HAD BEGUN for the rest of the Lower Keys. Nearer Geiger we could see highway traffic, the inbound rush hour from Cudjoe and Summerland and Ramrod suburbia, the day's first tourists who had made it only to Key Largo from their late evening landings in Miami. Now we were navigating under the plane traffic, take-offs from Boca Chica, arrivals to Key West International's landing pattern.

I tried to think again about what we had learned—if anything—and what I had done. It added to zip—except for jamming a white marker stake next a shallow channel. Perhaps it might make a small difference, misguide a non-local, provide an advantage for Sam the next time he had to evade pursuers, if there was ever a next time.

We returned to Tamarac Park each in our own world. One more quiet period in our collection of silences. After we entered the canal, I readied the fenders to protect Turk's gunwales when Marnie and I climbed from the boat.

Alongside the seawall, Turk said, "Marnie, please take Alex home and meet me at the Bight. I'll need to come back here to get my truck. We can stop at your office if you need to pick up messages."

"Thank you for making the trip, Turk."

I was sure she meant it, though her voice sounded stiff.

The dropping tide put us a foot lower than when we'd left. Marnie went first. I gave her bottom a chaste flat-hand boost up the wall then handed the fender lines to Turk.

Under his breath he said, "The weapon that dude was holding? A Heckler & Koch 416 assault rifle with the ten-inch barrel. Very high end. The fucker weighs less than seven pounds. Even cops can't get them. It's Delta Force-level stuff."

I must have looked puzzled by his sudden expertise.

He shrugged. "I read magazines. Keeps me out of the bars at night."

I grabbed a cleat on top of the wall and hauled myself up. Turk drifted several yards while he re-stashed the fenders, then chunked *Flats Broke* into gear and headed back out the canal.

"You're stuck with me," I said.

"Good," she said. "I can disable the passenger-side air bag. Shit,

I don't have one, but don't worry. I'll aim for a soft tree. Wait in my car while I urinate behind those bushes. It should only take me about six minutes."

Another silence. No further discussion for eight or nine miles.

Driving down Palm Avenue, a quarter-mile from my house, Marnie said, "I'm sorry for screaming and whining. Whatever Sam's doing isn't your fault. It's his decision, his ass and my heart, and you're the bystander who was ordered to keep me sheltered. I don't know what I'd be doing without you. You wanted to be straight with Sam and straight with me and you were caught in..."

"Quicksand?" I said.

"I was thinking something more septic, but okay. After I shuttle Turk back to Tamarac, I'm going to blow off my job and go home to sleep for eighteen hours."

"I want you to be careful. Be aware of your surroundings."

"That's my job description, Alex. Are you saying I might be in danger?"

"Just pay extra attention. Consider the chance that your knowledge or your sources could make you a liability. Don't assume you're always safe."

"Thank you for thinking of me. I will now transfer your debt."

"What's that?"

"I'll kick Sam in the nuts. If you see him, tell him not to wake me if he comes in late."

"Right."

"Wrong," she said. "I'm starting to get hysterical."

A NOTE WAS WEDGED into my screen door. My first thought was that Bobbi Lewis had come by to make nice. In the past year she had left me humorous, often risqué notes in that same place. But that wasn't it. On an unused *Harper's* subscription card: "Call or come by." No signature, but I knew the scrawl. Duffy Lee Hall would not

229

have visited if he hadn't dug up some background info.

I got his answering service. I said, "Call my cell, please," and hung up.

Someone—either Beth or Carmen—had left the front section of the *Citizen* on my porch table. I dropped my shades, small camera and boating essentials next to the paper, went inside and started a strong pot of Cuban. Too tired to change out of my salt-stiff clothing, I returned to the porch to read Marnie's front-page Hammond story. A quick scan found, to my relief, no mention of Carmen and only one quote from Beth. I had every intention of finishing the article, drinking all of the coffee, trying again to reach Duffy Lee. Maybe checking off ten other things on my list.

I WOKE FROM A dream in which a man was knocking at the screen door. I figured it was Bob Catherman with a get-rich-quick offer, but it was Bobbi Lewis's lover, Marv, whom I didn't know.

Like the ringing phone in a dream that's the real phone next to the couch, there really was a man at the door. I didn't know him either. He didn't look like a vinyl siding salesman, religion peddler or real estate broker. Then I broke out of my dream fog and saw the Dodge Charger parked in the lane.

"Hello, Marv."

"Yep, Bobbi said she blew my cover. Got a minute?"

"Last name?" I said.

"Fixler. You won't remember and you won't have to."

Marv Fixler looked like a military man in civilian clothing. A plaid short-sleeve shirt with only the top button undone, once-washed, creased Levi's, a close-cropped crewcut, bulky forearms. You would call him "medium-build" and admit that you'd hate to tangle. He appeared capable of defending himself—perhaps in surprising, unorthodox ways.

"Look," I said. "If this about my relationship with Detective

Lewis, you need to know..."

"It's not about that," he said. "I don't want to punch you in the nose or compare dick length. I came here for the open exchange of words and ideas."

"That's wonderful, Marv. Come on in. I may not be at the top of my intellectual game this morning. I didn't get a healthy night's rest."

He pointed at the Ziploc full of nautical gear, the bosun's knife and whistle in plain sight. "Been out night-fishing?"

"Helping a friend look for her dog," I said. "Contingency planning always pays off. What's up?"

Now inside the porch, looking part paratrooper, part thug, Marv stood with his boots just far enough apart to be ready for anything. Real cowboy boots—rare as snowshoes in the Florida Keys. He had the eyes of a Boy Scout, the sneer of a street punk. Old damage to his nose suggested real rumbles—not just sparring. His left ear was much larger than the right one.

"Mr. Rutledge, you've come recommended by the Monroe County Sheriff."

"Why do I need a reference? Which law enforcement mob do you work for?"

"I'm not at liberty to say right yet."

"It's a free country, Mr. Fixler. You can say anything, and I can say nothing. If you don't tell me who you work for, I don't want to talk to you."

"Yep, you look distracted," he said. "What's on your mind this very moment?"

"How do hydrophones work, triangulation?"

Fixler shook his head. "Ancient technology. You know how to dig a foxhole?"

"You want to show me a badge?" I said. "Something official... a note from the teacher?"

He blew off my humor. "Just a few questions about yourself," he said. "A little background. It's in your own best interest to cooperate."

I wasn't sure how long I had slept before Marv's arrival, but I came wide awake. "What the fuck do you know about my best interests?"

"On the scale of national security priorities," he said, "they rank for shit. I think you discovered that at dawn this morning. Did you enjoy meeting those defenders of our coastline?"

"They had a nice yacht," I said.

He crossed his arms, widened his stance by an inch or two. "That yacht is the nautical equivalent of a Stealth bomber. It's so loaded with tech gear that we know the location of every one of those in the world. They have satellite tracking tied into their ignition and steering controls."

"You're spreading them around?"

He shook his head. "We're selling them to friendly nations for coastal duty, for right-now response and agile security. But we've got one off the reservation. It was stolen from a dock in Belize."

"Why do I need to know this?" I said.

"The Keys have seen a series of odd events in recent days, all related to boat thieves. We aren't sure who they are and we damn sure don't know what they want with that boat. But they knew enough about electronics to leave the GPS transmitter on the dock and still be able to start and steer the craft. We hate the thought of having our front-line weapons used against us."

I had no response for that, so I waited for him to continue.

"You've been going around asking questions," said Fixler. "Just the asking could jeopardize our recovery mission. How did you happen to photograph my car while I was running surveillance?"

"Happenstance," I said. "It was just another car."

"You made a five-by-seven of it. Why?"

"If Bobbi told you every last detail about me," I said, "you know the answer already."

"How often do you meet Robert Catherman in the Summerland Post Office? Or were you following him, too?"

I pointed at the screen door. "My invitation to leave. I insist."

"There's a saying among upper echelon snoops, Alex. They say, 'Born to Black.' It means some people—one out of ten million—are cut out for sneaky shit and the others are general fuckups. You've made it far too obvious that you're tracking the evidence of... Call it an unknown crime. Am I getting through, here?"

"You talk tough but I hear generalities. Have the facts eluded you, too?"

"You have a nice face."

"Odd adjective."

"A little faggy-sounding, I admit," said Marv, "but pertinent. I expect you'd like to keep it that way."

"This isn't going well, Marv. You walked in saying you didn't want to punch me in the nose."

"Fuck me, I lied."

"What do we do now, whip out our weenies and a ruler?"

"Wouldn't be fair," he said. "You've been stepping on yours for three days. I hate to start with a disadvantage."

"You're coming from a position of horsepower, near as I can tell. Traction and torque and all those manly metaphors."

"Glad you understand that," he said.

"Why talk to me in the first place? Why can't you take me out with a trumped-up arrest or a spinal cord injury, a simple hit-and-run?"

He smirked and went for the door. "I'll get back to you on that. Might have to fix you up with a blind date."

"Is this the way you treat your girlfriend?"

"Rutledge, your friend Sam Wheeler is a killer who's in it for the money. It's general fucking knowledge that he's been out of sight for four days. Why do you think he's hiding? Take a guess."

"I don't guess," I said. "I don't ask why."

"Ask your buddy why he doesn't want to get rich, why he's kissing off an early retirement. He knows the program. No strings, no risk. Hell, once and for all he could pay off that place in Alabama."

Marv was either ten steps ahead of me or tonsil-deep in horseshit. I couldn't believe his indictment of Sam Wheeler, but he had confirmed the cover-up of at least two murders.

"You should let the cops do their job, Rutledge. What do you do for fun, ride your motorcycle? Take the rest of the day for a ride."

"Maybe I will."

"If you don't back off, we don't do forgiveness."

I was going to say, "Give my best to Bobbi," but I didn't want to spoil my opportunity to see him leave.

His engine started as he approached the car. I guessed it was a remote switch on his key ring until he opened the passenger-side door, got in and slammed it. The car was already pointed out of the lane. It was gone in ten seconds.

19

MARV FIXLER LEFT BEHIND a fog of gym-locker cologne and a new assortment of puzzles in my mind. It wasn't so much a straightforward list, but layers with edits, corrections, and arrows in the margins. A smoke screen with sharp edges. Fill in the blanks—or else.

Buzzed numb by fatigue, I gazed from my porch, studied the short shadows of mid-day sunlight and cobwebs in the crotons, and tried again to sift facts from bullshit. Ugly assumptions came to me moments before I heard the motorcycle downshift on Fleming.

Beth Watkins's tomato red Ducati sounded like a dozen lions growling through a ballpark sound system. She gave it a quick, precise throttle burp and shut it down on my walkway. She wore a sly grin and gunmetal-tone leathers, her silhouette an exact match to the immodest one I had seen—and Turk had enjoyed—six hours earlier.

"Killing the noon hour boredom?" I said.

"We talked yesterday about riding up the Keys," she said. "I'm taking an all-afternoon lunch."

I wanted to retrieve my cash from Frank Polan. Awkward with a witness. I also needed to connect with Alyssa at Colding's Grocery, but having Beth along could make it complicated, if not kill the whole interview.

"I thought you had a murder case to investigate," I said.

"I've got two people on it, and they're waiting to budge a judge. I want to scope out that non-crime scene on Bay Point, if we can figure out where it was."

"Your bike looks different. You grew an extra headlight."

"I love a man who notices small details," she said. "My SS-800 was an '03 with forty thousand miles. This 848 is a benefit of the constant paycheck."

"And you kept the color to match your hat?"

She glanced down at her helmet. "Paint code rosso seven-four-nine-five. There were two choices and white didn't light my fire."

"New leathers, too. You're worried about road rash?"

"Oh, I have scars," she said. "Remind me to show you my ass when the lights are on."

A vision filled my mind—for the second time in a minute.

I could think of no graceful way to dodge a two-bike excursion. Checking out Bay Point made sense. "It'll take me a minute to liberate my ride," I said. "Let me make a phone call first."

"Thank you," she said.

"For what?"

"For not saying that I showed my ass the other day, with Julio in tow, when I first asked you about Hammond. I was Ms. Mega-Cop for a few minutes. I don't need reminding of that, at least from outside my conscience."

Another moment custom-built for silence.

I went inside to brush my teeth, change my shirt, put a fresh battery in my pocket-sized camera and smear goo to mask my own gymnasium effect. I grabbed the house phone to call Duffy Lee Hall and found a message from Carmen: "Have you heard from that real estate dude who's making us all wealthy?"

I dialed Duffy Lee and reached his voice mail. I said my first name and hung up.

Beth was around back sizing up my motorcycle's mini-garage. I felt disloyal suspecting a possible ulterior motive. Was she also checking out my view of Hammond's yard and home? If so, she covered herself well.

"My new yard on Poorhouse Lane has a perfect spot," she said. "The paint on my old Ducati was iffy before I got to the Keys. Then the tropical sun played hell. I like the tin roof. Who built it?"

"Man named Tim Dunne. He lives on Stock Island. His nickname used to be 'Un' Dunne and he lived up to it, but lately it's 'Gitter' Dunne and I trust it's just coffee. He looks like an axe murderer but he's a puppy dog and reasonable and an absolute artist."

Beth looked around, walked toward the outdoor shower, opened the door and stuck her head inside. "Heaven on Earth. A bench, twin massage-style shower heads. The more I learn about you..."

"I just installed new all-weather stereo speakers," I said. "Maybe they'll last longer than the last pair."

She pushed me up against the shower door and kissed me, held it, pressed her fingers into my shoulders, her hips against mine. "That's just music, those speakers," she said. "Let's make sure your new girlfriend lasts longer than your old one."

"Fine by me."

MY 1970 TRIUMPH AND Beth's sparkling Ducati were like a '65 MG-B and a new Ferrari running the streets out to Stock Island. She suggested that we take Flagler up the center of the island instead of North Roosevelt. "I'm a spine rider," she said. "Two wheels are two too few on the boulevard."

Crossing Big Coppitt Key, trailing the Ducati's snarling tailpipe, I wanted to hear Tom Rush's song "On the Road Again" or "Blues' Theme" the fuzz-guitar instrumental from *The Wild Angels,* the Fonda biker movie that pre-dated *Easy Rider*.

Once we hit the 55-MPH zone past Shark Key it became more a matter of daring than equipment. Beth had a GET OUT OF JAIL FREE card in her pocket. She would get a courtesy warning while I might receive an expensive high-speed driving certificate. She remained ahead but didn't leave me eating her dust. On U.S. 1 you travel at the speed of the slowest common denominator. Most of the time slow-moving cars and double-yellows kept us in check.

A briny tang hung in the air through the Saddlebunch Keys. The view to the northeast was misty, almost gray—ominous for a sunny day—with pale aqua in the shallows. To the south was the sprawling green-gold mangrove forest—vegetation held by roots instead of land, plants capable of forming their own islands and always more fascinating up close. This uninhabited section, minus the roadway, is what the Keys had looked like for centuries before Flagler's railroad jerked the island string into the early 20th. The islands farther north—Sugarloaf, Cudjoe, Summerland, Ramrod and Little Torch—were irregular splotches of land split by the main highway with a few short roads reaching like tentacles to the north and south. They were scattered with businesses and homesites—from trailers on blocks to elegant estates, though most were canalside two- or three-bedroom houses on stilts.

I thought back to Jason and Russell loading their car in Carmen's driveway, extolling their first impressions on arriving in the Keys on Sunday. Russ had called the briny smell a combo of fish damp, salt and seaweed. Jason Dudak had enjoyed the magnificent view from a bridge peak. The olfactory certainly came into play during my first drive down the Overseas Highway, yet—as with Jason—the visual captured my soul. Two palm trees with nothing behind them but endless green and blue water. That was the clincher. Up to that moment I'd been an Ohio boy. After that I had sand in my shoes, a camera in my hand.

My sunsets-and-coconuts vision of paradise, stained so often in recent years, had taken a hit that morning as I faced government gun barrels aimed at my head and body. It also stood to suffer when I arrived in Bay Point where a probable double-murder was discovered and hushed. What was happening to my Keys, the Keys of Carmen, Hector and Cecilia? For that matter, the adamant, born-on-island Julio Alonzo's Keys? I've never envisioned myself leaving and I dislike clichés, but too often I've caught myself wondering whether bad island days really are better than great days elsewhere. I hoped to hell it held true.

I WAS SO LOST in thought I almost jammed into Beth's Ducati. She had signaled and slowed—she knew where to turn. West Circle took us to Bay Drive, a stretch of high-ticket homes with well-maintained yards so lush and perfect they could be murals in the La Concha Hotel lobby.

A quarter-mile down, Beth stopped to speak to a man cutting his lawn. The guy wore a "banana hammock" bathing suit and Doc Martens boots. Even from a distance I saw sweat flowing from his forehead and bare chest. His house—if it was his—was elegant, but I couldn't remember the last time I had seen a push-it-your-damned-self mower. I sure didn't expect to see one in that neighborhood. Nor did I expect a man with his flabby buns hanging out.

I couldn't hear what they were saying, but the man pointed across the road. I looked where he pointed and recognized, as I had that morning on the boat, the former residence of the late Lucky and recently widowed Tinkerbell Haskins. The large, elevated home—seemingly vacant—sat on raised ground on a double lot. It had become the local slum. I rolled past the conversation, parked in its driveway, removed my helmet.

The yard had gone to seed, untrimmed and weedy, especially compared to the homes on either side. I recalled its white five-foot fence, healthy palms and new shrubs—all gone. The mailbox with hand-painted tropical fish had become a mildew farm. One smiling, toothless grouper with faded lavender lips oversaw the single remaining stick-on house number. A realtor had stuck a sign on a post in dirt near the road.

Beth ended her chat and rode over to join me. She had already pulled off her helmet. Damp ringlets of blonde hair hung over her forehead and ears. The sweet smell of feminine perspiration added to her beauty. She unzipped the top of her riding suit, wore a sweat-damp KWPD T-shirt underneath.

"How romantic," she said. "This is where we first met."

More of it came back to me. I was on my motorcycle that time, too. A Carolina Skiff had rested on a trailer under the house. Bobbi Lewis was the officer in charge of the crime scene, and she had allowed Beth, then a rookie Key West detective, to observe the county's crime scene procedures. Beth had complimented my Triumph and asked—already knowing—if it was a 1970 T-120R model.

Beth said, "Bobbi Lewis introduced us."

I winced. "Can we celebrate our first date instead of this crime scene?"

"You're good," she said. "If you had come up with anything but those words, you were in the deep."

"Want to leave?" I said.

"Yes," she said. "After I look around."

Closer to the water, the place didn't look like most of the unoccupied homes in the Keys. The feds—or whoever they were—had cleaned up. The patch of grass had been raked, the patio swept. One section of concrete near the seawall was bleached to pure white. The place was as neat as a rich man's desk.

"What do you think happened?" she said.

I reminded myself that Beth had dated Cliff Brock. "Processed, documented and vacuumed," I said. "No one would do this for a robbery or a stolen boat."

"Empty house," she said. "Nothing to steal."

I couldn't look at her face. "That's all we're going to learn."

"I agree," she said, "but I can't believe they clamped down a murder scene. It's way too much like a spy novel."

"Where did you go boating with Cliff Brock?"

"Actually, we only went once, on a weekend. We went to some remote island called Marvin."

"What kind of boat did he own?"

"Brand name?" she said. "I don't know motorboats. It was like the smaller guide boats in the Bight. Flat on top, big motor."

"Where did he keep it?"

"On a trailer he towed with a black Ford pickup. He launched it off a ramp by the Sugarloaf Lodge."

Shit, I thought. The sunken skiff really had existed. It had been Cliff Brock's boat with Sam Wheeler's registration numerals stuck to its hull. It was no stretch to guess that Cliff and Sally been killed on the skiff, then their bodies moved to Bay Point.

"Want to leave?" I said.

She zipped up her leather top. "Oh, yes, now I do."

Why had it been so important for the two bodies to be found? Had someone wanted to learn how law enforcement might react, put the security machine into action? Lay the groundwork for the next step, whatever that might be? Why did it have to begin with Cliff and Sally?

What if they succeeded? What if they now knew what they were out to learn? And how, from false hull numbers to forced hiding, did the whole mess come snaking back around to Sam?

THE MAN ACROSS THE road was still cutting his lawn. I placed my helmet on the Triumph and walked over to speak with him. It took me a second to recognize the drunk who had pestered Sheriff Liska at Louie's about the roadblock and cops with pizzas and Pepsis on the hoods of their squad cars.

"Hard labor," I said.

"A few people here in ritzy Monroe still work in their own yard."

He used his forearm to wipe sweat from his brow. He left behind a smear of tan dirt and grass confetti. "Also, I'm sweating out a three-day bender." He pointed back to where Beth stood with her Ducati. "Same house where some poor rich bastard hung himself two years ago."

"Were there any helicopters?" I said.

"What do you mean, this week?" He shook his head. "I got it all second-hand, but there was no talk of that."

"An ambulance?"

"Not that either."

"Can I ask who told you about it?" I said.

He jacked his thumb toward the house just north of us. "Dude next door. Boy hid behind his mini-blinds and watched the damnedest parade. He left yesterday for Wyoming to go hunting for a week, and don't ask your next question. He don't have one. If I answer my cell phone while I'm talking to him, he gets offended like I cut the cheese and he walks away."

"WHERE TO NEXT?" said Beth.

I told her about Sally's job at Colding's, along with Mikey Bokamp, Honey Weiss and Alyssa. I explained why we had to be careful about socializing with the women if the boss was around.

"Who is this Colding?"

"A sleazeball," I said. "He cons the girls into his back office so he can ogle their bare titties. They put up with it for fear of their jobs."

She clenched her fist. "My kind of guy. After we fry the bigger fish, I'll hook his ass."

"They'll all lose their jobs," I said.

"They'll own the grocery."

THE TWO ROADS THAT connect Bay Point to the Overseas Highway straddle the land triangle occupied by Baby's Coffee. Just north of that triangle, at the end of a gated, unnamed stretch of gravel, is a broad field of antennae and triple-story white buildings. Years ago I heard it was a Navy Communication Station. I have never met anyone who works there, don't know anyone who has been down that one-lane road. Based on acreage, it's a huge government presence, and it's been there for decades. It became a piece of scenery that I quit noticing. Hell, I had passed it two days ago without a second thought.

If that was the Mansion, its presence and size could be the reason for all the hush-hush, and the source of all the mysterious, unmarked vehicles.

It was on a damn long gravel road.

I KNEW THAT CECIL Colding bullied staff he thought to be socializing, so I played customer, went straight for the grocery's candy bar rack. Beth Watkins studied the bananas on an end cap display. The place smelled of garlic and the Clorox used to disinfect floor mats and cooked coffee. I saw only Mikey Bokamp and Honey Weiss on the job and no other shoppers. Honey, behind the deli counter, wore a dark red T-shirt with the Sugar Daddy logo. I got the joke. Again unzipping, Beth wandered farther away, pretended to peruse the granola bars.

Mikey sidled over from the pastries section. "I expect you're here to talk with Alyssa, but she's back there reviewing her time sheet— or whatever—with Uncle D." She pointed at Beth. "Is that the one you had trouble with two nights ago?"

"No, she's the one I had fun with last night," I said.

"I thought you looked ready." She looked at Honey then turned serious. "We would have heard if you found Sally, right? The boss hired a new girl who starts tomorrow. She's some mama's baby but she's got the devil in her tush. And nipple rings, I think. Cecil took forty-five minutes to interview her."

Alyssa exited the narrow door of Colding's office, her face beet red. Flustered and ashamed, she looked downward and hurried to the register.

I tapped my fist on Mikey's forearm. "Hang with me on this."

"What a deal," she said. "I can't have your front, I got your back."

"What's her last name?"

"Navarro. Alyssa Navarro."

I took my purchase to the register, making sure Mikey stayed close. We got an odd, disapproving look from Honey. Distracted, hugging herself, Alyssa didn't recognize me at first.

"You still want a free lunch?" I said.

Alyssa shook her head. "Look, I just got warned. If he walks out and sees me having a 'gab fest,' I'll get docked."

"Right," I said, "you've got all these customers to take care of."

Alyssa checked the office door. "The clientele is last in our job priorities."

"How about lunch at Boondocks?" I said.

A flicker of disappointment. "I have to work until three."

Mikey said, "I get off work in twenty minutes, but I'll cover you 'til three."

"Cool," said Alyssa. "I'll ride my Vespa. See you in a half hour."

OUTSIDE, BETH SAID, "How does she eat cereal with that barbell in her tongue?"

"I expect her meals are yogurt-specific. Might be a problem at Boondocks."

"I say she gets tuna salad. I hope that thing doesn't short out her electric toothbrush."

Cecil Colding flung open the grocery's front door. He barged toward us like a confused farm animal. "I told you not to come around pestering my help."

"That you did, Cecil, baby," I said. "I heard you loud and clear, so I came into your slopchute today only to buy this Payday bar. Here's the receipt, Cecil, so get out of my face."

"You fucking weasel," he said. "You talk to me like that, I'll shove that candy bar down your goddamn throat." He lunged for the Payday.

I stepped back. "Whoa, big guy, that could hurt. This is worse than having an automatic weapon pointed at my gut in the middle of the night. I could even die."

"I'll leave that up to you," he said. "Just don't do it in my parking lot. It's sure to fuck up business."

"Don't ever lose sight of that bottom line, Cecil." I turned to Beth. "Which law did he just break?"

"Florida section seven-eight-four-point-oh-one-one," she said. "Second degree misdemeanor assault with the intentional threat to do violence coupled with an apparent ability to do so, and doing some act which creates a fear that violence is imminent. But he can get only sixty days max."

Colding eyeballed the silver leathers. "You travel with your attorney?" he said.

"She's not a lawyer, but she's a highly-credible witness."

Beth jerked the stub of her banana up and down suggestively and waved her receipt.

He kept staring, approaching drool stage. "And you're too pussy to slug it out?"

"Not at all," I said. "It's just that smacking you around would be a pain in the ass. It's hot out here and I could break my hand. Why should I worry about the challenge of a schmuck?"

"Oh, poor boy, break your hand," said Colding.

"And I've got stuff to do because I'm still curious about Sally Catherman. You didn't ask how that was going."

"She's an ex-employee, that's all I know." Colding turned and charged toward the store entrance in a half-controlled stagger. He pounded the heel of his fist on the door's aluminum frame then yanked open the door. I assumed that his act was mostly for show and didn't think he'd be stupid enough to get physical with the three women inside, but I decided to hang close for a couple of minutes.

Beth grinned widely.

"You had a moment of triumph there?" I said.

"Not what you think," she said. "That deli woman admired my riding leathers."

"So did the bellowing butthole," I said. "I expect it's universal reaction."

"You are the man with the golden tongue. Where to now?"

I wanted to retrieve my Catherman money from Frank Polan, but I didn't want to implicate Beth. I envisioned a prosecuting attorney asking her, a year from now, *"When he counted out $4,000 in hundred dollar bills, Ms. Watkins, did you wonder about the source of all that cash?"*

"Look," I said, "I've got a couple errands to run that might bore the piss out of you. Maybe you could go to Boondocks, get a good table and hold it for us."

"Alex, tune up your bullshit dispenser. This ride today is pure 'out-of-the-way.'"

"One errand might get weird," I said.

"Weird is that you don't want me there. Just tell me her name ahead of time, okay? I'll be cool. I just don't want to be introduced and not know she was the cause of my broken heart."

"I have to see a man about money," I said.

"Have we got a conflict?" said Beth. "Say, between this money and a certain highly-credible witness?"

"Call it potential. With downside to said witness."

She covered her ears with her hands. "Can the witness pledge blindness and a shaky memory?"

246

20

I CALLED AHEAD TO make sure Frank Polan was home.

"You coming by with a couple of lovelies?" he said.

I watched Beth climb aboard her Ducati. "Only one, but she's very good looking."

"Did I hear a truck?" he said. "You're by the highway?"

"Ten minutes away," I said.

"I'll clean up the big boat."

"We won't have time, Frank. We're moving fast today."

"Just as well," he said. "Waste of time if you only have the one, so I know why you're coming by. I still have most of your cash."

Colding had told me to stay out of his grocery store. To avoid a possible trespassing beef, I asked Beth to look inside, to ensure that Cecil wasn't browbeating or physically beating his employees. She checked, backed away from the door and shrugged.

All was quiet.

I HAD ONE STOP to make before going to Polan's. I had stashed Catherman's envelope in my helmet and forgotten to remove it. It held Sally's car registration, a copy of the picture page of her passport, her drivers license renewal notice, and three copies of a head shot photo. I hoped that its contents hadn't turned into a sweat-saturated mass of fiber and bled-out, unreadable inks.

I peeled back the lining pad and found what I needed—as legible as my thumbnail: Catherman's address printed on the upper left corner of the envelope. Scabbard Road, and why hadn't I been able to recall that? I'd dug out the address when I had seen the tow truck haul Sally's Miata away from Mangrove Mama's.

"Bob Catherman lives five minutes from here," I said to Beth. "Before we go to Frank Polan's, I'd like to see how he lives."

"Is this the life of a private eye?"

"I think so," I said. "But I left the instruction book in my other briefcase."

I'VE NEVER UNDERSTOOD WHY people with loads of money are compelled to buy cute mailboxes and live on streets with cute names. The folks assigned to name streets on Cudjoe must have been enthralled with swashbucklers, despots and their related gear. We ran south on Cutthroat and west on Jolly Roger. The short streets that ran northward to dead ends off Jolly Roger alternated with stubby canals that gave each home in the area salt water access. We passed Arrgh Lane and Eyepatch Street before finding the right area.

To assure myself that we were observer-free, I scouted the streets just east and west of Scabbard. There were no Dodge Chargers parked on Gangplank Lane, no Chevy Impalas on Grog Road. No other faux-stealth sedans on either street, but rolling slowly on Grog we found a spot where we could look through a spacious yard for a cross-canal view of the Porsche Cayenne parked under what had to be Catherman's home. The elevated house was no palace compared to its neighbors, but the boats tied alongside his seawall spoke of wealth and adventure.

I pulled out my Canon PowerShot, zoomed to optical max, and took several photos of the Catherman Yacht Club. A center-console

38-foot Fountain with three Mercury 275 Verados on its transom; and what looked to be a 28-foot Skater—probably the smallest model made, but it carried two Mercury 300 OptiMax outboards.

"Living the life," said Beth.

I agreed. "That Fountain is a seventy-mile-an-hour monster, but it can be used for deep sea fishing. That little Skater is even faster—but strictly a hot rod. Impractical and expensive."

Beth showed a sly grin. "Bet it's great for trolling."

I reminded myself that she worked in a male-dominated profession. She had heard it all.

"For the money that bought those boats," I said, "we could lay back in the most luxurious hotel in Paris, eat the best food and drink the finest wine for about two years."

She held her right hand to her heart. "Any chance of making it one boat and one year in Paris?"

WE RODE AROUND TO the house on Scabbard, pulled in alongside the Cayenne. Aside from the hot boats floating out back, nothing under the house or in the yard gave clues to the pastimes or personalities of the home's occupants. No kayaks or flower plantings or decorations. The only indication of Sally's "legal" ground-floor apartment were mini-blinds in a two-foot-square window facing the street.

Bob Catherman descended an outside stairway and walked toward my motorcycle, nodding in admiration.

"You're a man of fine taste," he said. "I didn't have time to check out this baby at the post office the other day."

"You had other matters on your mind," I said.

"Still do." He paused and regarded Beth, pretended to be admiring her Ducati. She kept her eyes down, feigned attention to her gauge cluster.

In his navy Bermuda shorts, yellow button-down shirt and tassel loafers, no socks, Catherman looked like an oil executive on vacation. "Look, Rutledge," he said, "I owe you a mess of apologies. One is for that first day I knocked on your door. I treated you like a hayseed. I shouldn't have been so high and mighty."

"We're even. I reacted as if you were a sleazy solicitor full of promises and horseshit."

He shrugged it off. "Another apology, obviously, is for last night. I can't even begin…"

"Then don't. It was awkward for all of us, but I don't believe for a minute that you're a window peeper."

"Your meter runs down about this time tomorrow, right?" he said. "I assume you've been talking to Sally's fellow employees."

"The young women in Colding's are torn up by all this," I said. "It's been a task to gain their confidence, and I think there's more to learn. I would hate to see my efforts tank before I get to dig deeper."

He kept his eyes on Beth. "What are you saying?"

"Let's not upset them more than we have to," I said. "I'd appreciate your shopping at Murray's Market for a few days."

Catherman faked a chuckle. "What am I, a loose cannon?"

"Just the sight of you will stir them up. No disrespect intended, you're also a man with emotions. We boys think we can stifle them, but we can't fool all of the women all the time."

"Gotcha," he said, "and well-put."

"Couple of fine boats out back."

"And I wish they were mine." Catherman pointed to a work site two homes to the north. "My neighbor is having new davits installed. I'm temporary parking, but it sure classes up the real estate."

"Bob, about that subject," I said, "you made several offers on Dredgers Lane three days ago. I've known my neighbors for years, and several of them are making plans that amount to life-changing moves. Are those offers good to go, or is there something we all need to know?"

"All on the level," he said, "though we can't close all the deals on one day. There will be appraisals and due diligence and such. I'm sure you're more up to speed than some of those... your neighbors."

"Could be true," I said.

He shifted his eyes back to Beth on her Ducati. "Can I ask one favor?"

I tilted my head, non-committal.

"Maybe I don't have to say this, what with our working arrangement." He paused to form his phrasing. "If something—anything— pops up that's, say, south of the law, my daughter in a jam, but not only that, I'd like to get a call before you notify the cops."

I couldn't imagine the mess of guilt and helplessness and denial in his mind. Yet something about his phrasing caught me wrong enough to instantly ease my mind about accepting his nickel—to work, in truth, for Sam.

"You bet, Bob," I said. "I read somewhere that good private eyes always report first to their clients." I was fairly sure I'd seen it in a detective novel written eighty years ago.

Missing the sarcasm, he checked his watch. "I've got a lunch meeting in five, just up the road at Square Grouper. I'm going to have to let you go."

"Do you mind if I ask—is Sally your only child?"

"Yes, she is, Alex. I'll wait for your call."

So patient, so social and businesslike, I thought—as he runs task delegation to a new low.

FRANK POLAN'S HOME WAS a half-mile from us—across Cudjoe Bay— but a two-mile ride on the island's streets. I planned to make it quick. I didn't want to be late for lunch at Boondocks.

Even people who own homes in the Keys dream of a place like

Polan's. His double lot is low on the ocean side yet faces north-west—away from the neighbors—for plenty of sunset cocktail hours. There's a boat ramp—installed before rules about such things changed—a T-shaped dock with two elegant boats along-side, a dozen mature palm trees, a scattering of shaped shrubs and—always a sign of sophistication—an outdoor shower. As a small matter of fastidious obsession, he keeps his home in great shape. I imagined that five or six weeds a year might sprout in Polan's pea rock and be annihilated within fifteen minutes of their discovery.

We parked our motorcycles under the house behind Frank's spotless SUV and a mid-sized, freshly washed, two-door Mercedes. Climbing the stairway to his open deck, Beth paused to unzip her riding suit and admire the placid bay view. The earlier clouds had scattered. Two kayakers paddled westward along the far shore near the waterfront homes we'd just passed on Jolly Roger. An elderly heron atop a dock piling watched a lone cormorant skim the flat water.

"I could stand it," she said.

"Wait until you meet Frank. He'll flat steal your heart."

"You own the damn thing," she said. "I hope you'll defend it."

I almost tripped up the steps.

"Or at least get a good price on the flip," she added.

Frank had heard our arrival. "The slider's unlocked," he called out. "Come on in."

The house smelled of chicken that Frank had grilled on his porch, on a small propane-fueled hibachi, and of broccoli he was steaming in the kitchen. The cold air in his living room fogged my sunglasses but I couldn't miss, dead center on the Persian rug, a workout rowing machine.

"It's a light lunch I have three times a week," he said. "Six ounces of chicken and eight ounces of broccoli. Which, of course, I pee out everything except the good protein and antioxidants."

"Chicken's a known oxidant," I said.

Polan's voice a drawn-out, distressed whine: "No."

"You could know this but you refuse to recognize the existence of the Internet," I said. "You've never heard of H-two-cluck side effects?"

He rolled his eyes, whispered, "Fuck you," slipped me my wad of hundreds, and turned his attention to Beth. "So what magazines have you been in?"

"None, I hope," she said.

"You're not a fashion model?"

"You were right, Alex," she said. "I like this guy."

Frank patted my shoulder. "See, Alex? I'm not so bad. They all like me—like that one last night. She and I got very drunk so we quit after the first try. She got dressed and went home at two then called me at ten to apologize. Talk about your perfect date. I might call her again. Plus I'll put her in my book."

"Doing some writing, Frank?" I said.

"I'm a thinker, I know that about myself," said Polan. "I've been thinking about starting my autobiography. I've lived an interesting existence, and I think it's time. I'll call it *Snowball to Hell*."

"How does Hell relate to your life?" she said.

"I'm not sure yet. But you have to agree, it's a catchy title. When I'm drinking, I'm prolific and I make a lot of sense. I figure the meaning will come to me while I'm writing the book."

"May I use your bathroom, Frank?" I said.

He screwed an odd expression onto his face. "Can I tell you something first?"

"About the bathroom?"

"No, I've heard you're an expert. But let me say, I always knew you took pictures, but I never knew you were so good."

"How did you find out, Frank? I hope you didn't take someone's word for it."

"I was walking around Key West a week ago, you know, killing time and I like to walk. Sometimes I walk three or four hours in a row, so I went into this little art gallery on the south end of Duval. That's not a weird or faggy thing for me to do, is it? Go into an art gallery?"

"I don't think it is, Frank. In recent years I've seen numerous heterosexuals in art galleries."

"So I'm in this gallery and really liking the pictures on the wall. I asked the fellow working there if he knew the artist. He tells me they're photos by Alex Rutledge, so I told him you were a great friend of mine and I bought one of them. Right there and then I paid him cash. Maybe you'll make a few bucks, put some gas in your motorcycle. Then I found the perfect place to hang it."

"You're making me feel good, Frank."

"But don't take this wrong, because I really like the photo. And it's black and white so it matches the tile in the master bath."

"Wonderful, Frank. My art found a place in your home."

"So you're not upset, it's in the bathroom?"

"Well, I should tell you, the bathroom is a very humid place, Frank. The damp air could damage the mat and the photograph."

"Well, I can live with that. If it gets fucked up, I'll just buy another one because I can afford a few more. I'll take the chance that the price doesn't go up, and either way you'll make more money. Am I talking to the soul of the artist here?"

"Loud and clear, Frank. As only you can."

I returned to the living room to find Polan washing dishes and Beth studying the framed reproductions of classic paintings on his walls. "Frank, what kind of fish do you catch off your dock?" she said.

"I don't fish," he said. "Not off the dock, not off the boats. It's far too messy. When I want fish I go to the store. Better yet, I go to a restaurant. I can afford to eat out, so why catch fish?"

She watched him finish the dishes. "You're a man who thinks things through to their completion, I can tell. If you don't mind my asking, why two boats?"

"Luxury and sport. The one with the forward cabin is for overnights or supper parties, if the girl wants to cook. The other one will do fifty-five knots and it draws only eight inches, perfect for the backcountry."

"Frank, we've got to go," I said. "I'm glad to see that you're eating healthy food, treating your body well. You'll live longer."

Polan shrugged. "I don't know about that. It's not like they splice ninety days into your fiftieth year. I want to see proof that the time I add to my life doesn't come smack at the end. I don't want four extra hours of twilight on my dying day. I'll be too feeble to think back between drools and appreciate this broccoli."

21

NORTHBOUND TRAFFIC HAD PICKED up after the noon hour. We tagged along like freight cars hitched to a long train until we turned into the Boondocks Grille parking lot on Ramrod, taking care to keep our tires vertical through gravel patches. Beth found us a car-width spot next to a pickup that bore the bumper sticker: WOMEN WANT ME, FISH FEAR ME.

It must take a hell of a man to sense fear in a fish.

The restaurant is a huge tiki hut with a bricked patio at ground level and an elevated open-air bar and restaurant. To the mellow tones of "Summer Breeze" by Seals and Crofts, we climbed to the dining area—to six flat-screen TVs and that many women in red tank tops with "STAFF" printed on their backs. We approached one of the tall round tables surrounded by bar stools.

"This won't work," said Beth. "She won't feel comfortable perched high on one of these."

"Don't tell me you've had a witness interrogation course, too."

She looked puzzled then figured out that I was referring to Bobbi. "A couple of years ago, in California. But this is your gig. I was just thinking ahead. You're doing all the talking today."

The music segued into "The Weight" by The Band. We walked back down to ground level and chose a square green Formica table with four green plastic yard chairs. Next to us stood a rusted-out four-foot pedestal fan that breathed a dull whoop sound as it twirled. It still did its job. We sat back and ordered iced teas from an on-the-spot, red-shirted server, a woman in her mid-thirties.

We'd arrived four minutes late for our meeting with Alyssa. Not really enough time to piss her off to the point of splitting. Now, apparently, we were early arrivals by ten full minutes. I worried that the young woman might be a no-show.

"Shit," said Beth "I just remembered that I'm scheduled to go next week to a county class for handling semi-automatics." She paused. "Which brings me to that remark you made to Colding about a gun at your gut. That wasn't conjecture?"

"You're a newcomer, so you probably won't be apprehended and prosecuted," I said. "It's illegal to use words like 'conjecture' in the Florida Keys."

Her eyes bore a message into mine. Wrong time for humor.

I explained, condensed, about taking Turk's boat to the middle of nowhere and drawing attention from heavies with motors, guns and computers.

"And that was it?" she said. "They held you at gunpoint and ran your names and numbers and went away? They didn't come aboard the boat, give it a phony safety inspection?"

"I guess we were lucky," I said.

"You couldn't even get arrested?" She exhaled, shook her head, worried. "This is something way beyond your friend Sam's midnight runs to Cuba."

"You're serious."

"Worse. I'm worried."

What had Sam told Turk? "If it all slams into high gear, it'll be bigger than we can imagine."

OUR SERVER BROUGHT LARGE plastic cups of iced tea and departed. Beth tore two paper towels from the roll at the table's center and wrapped our cups the way Cubans wrap their beer bottles—like wrapping a towel around your waist and tucking in the final corner to hold it. A simple theory, too seldom used: the wrap absorbs condensate that evaporates and cools the liquid inside.

I said, "Have you hit on any theories yet—on what happened at Jerry Hammond's house?"

"I forgot to tell you something, but thank you in advance."

"My expert photography solved the crime?"

"More your judgment," she said, "but those sock prints in the dust on the bathroom floor? The floor was covered in talcum and plain household dust, but the socks left behind a chalky substance that our scene team also found near Hammond's body."

"Laundry detergent?"

"No," she said. "Pizza cheese and flour."

"We've got scientists in the Keys who can tell the difference?"

"Pizza cheese is a processed cheese that mimics mozzarella. High-end pizzas use real mozzarella with maybe a blending of parmesan and romano. These days most shops use the processed variety that we found. We lucked into a quick confirmation from the Florida Department of Law Enforcement. We're working up a list of every employee in every Lower Keys pizza shop or Italian restaurant."

"That'll be a long list."

"It's a start," said Beth. "We got a customer list from a food distributor out of Miami. Anyway, the sum of evidence—or lack of it— suggests that Hammond knew his killer. If we factor in strangulation by a cord from a hair dryer, an object usually stored in the bathroom, his murder may have been spontaneous, unplanned, and the dryer was a weapon of opportunity. If he and his killer knew each other, something changed quickly in the relationship and brought on the violence."

"Sounds reasonable, except for lack of other evidence."

"And that could make it the exact opposite, you're right," she said. "It could have been well-planned, including the use of the hair dryer cord, and either way the killer had time to remove evidence traces—as well as steal the computer items you noticed."

My mind went into high gear for crime analysis. "Or a third choice," I said. "Maybe he arrived home and surprised someone in the house."

"Roll with that," said Beth.

"Okay, maybe someone wanted to steal the whole computer but had to kill him and get out of there fast. Took what they could. Or someone knew that he had porn photos on his hard drive..."

"...and the gay element isn't completely out of the question..."

SOMEONE NEARBY—OUR SERVER—said, "Hey, babe."

Alyssa patted her forearm and said, "Lookin' good."

The women gave each other the foxy eye and approached the table. Alyssa went straight to Beth Watkins. "Thanks for checking on us before you left, to make sure we were okay. The sick puppy was majorly steamed. As Honey, our supervisor, says, he went to stew in his cauldron."

Beth turned her hands palm-up and shrugged. Nothing to it.

Alyssa's coral-toned top read ONE DAY I WILL MAKE IT ALL UP TO YOU. Her pastel green shorts hung low, almost to Panama. She had to have spilled something from every aisle in the market on her white sneaks. She sat next to me, touched my arm. "I'm not hungry at all." She held her touch and said, "That's just my first lie."

"Then let's order our food and start talking," I said. "I want the whole fib symphony."

Alyssa looked up at the server. "I'll do Mountain Dew and twenty mild teriyaki wings, please." She pointed at Beth. "You should get the Tuna Tempura. Just order the appetizer with two cups of honey soy sauce."

Beth did a repeat of her palm-upward shrug. I ordered a fresh fish sandwich with potato salad. The server gave us an I-like-locals smile, took back the menus and departed.

I finally picked up on the most significant change in Alyssa—the removal of her tongue ornament. Was the stud only a part of her work uniform or had she removed it to speak with us? No matter. Her words came through clear as hell.

From that point on we mined unexpected gold. People-watching as a matter of habit, sipping our drinks, the three of us in the shade occasionally wiping sweat from our brows with paper towels. The constant rushing sound of highway traffic to one side, easy oldies off a satellite from inside the restaurant, the unplugged version of "Layla," obscure songs by John David Souther and Marshall Chapman, a country-tinged Mac McAnally song—all of it okay except for a syrupy John Denver tune. Beth rolled her eyes at that one, too, a gesture that boded well for our relationship.

NERVOUS, ALYSSA FIDDLED WITH the catsup and condiment jars in a table-center plastic bin. "I feel like a ropey donkey today," she said. "That stupid job can be a ball-buster and this morning was a shit storm."

Beth and I kept our mouths shut.

"So you don't want to hear about that," she said. "You need to know about Sally, and this discussion stays at this table—or at least anonymous, right?"

"Sure," I said. "Were the two of you friends?"

"She was a twit. I wasn't down with her bubbly act. You don't know how bad I wanted to pour Tabasco down her ass crack, light that little twat on fire."

"Down her coin slot?" I said.

Alyssa looked startled—surprised that I knew the slang. "She was such a tight-ass sometimes," she said, "I don't think a coin could slip through."

"So you two didn't get along?"

She raised her gaze upward as if beseeching the heavens to relieve her of a sour memory. "We monkeyed around."

"The two of you?" I said. This was not at all what Mikey had described.

"No fucking way, just the two of us. She invited me on a boat ride, like a double date, two boats, and I had to promise not to blab. It turned out to be a few Jello-shots, skinny dipping, getting it on, watching each other do it. Sunburn, for sure."

"How long ago?" I said.

"I don't know, a month?"

"Was she with her boyfriend?"

Alyssa nodded. "That guy she dated from the Mansion, Clifford. My guy was named Constant Johnson. He really couldn't decide which name he wanted to tell me, but whatever. He paid for the beer and he didn't try to be a bone-star."

"Did he work at the Mansion, too?" I said.

"Yep. He was actually a fun jump except he sneaked way too many peeks at Sally on top of Clifford. Like I was having sex, but he was watching TV."

"Where did all this happen?" I said.

"Some place called Picnic Island except it's not an island. It's a shallow spot, I guess by the end of Summerland. I'm not sure."

"Do you remember what kind of boat it was?" I said. "Did it have a name?"

"I don't know boat brands or how many feet, but he had the name 'Maverick' on the side. I told him that was a cool name for a boat. Not like one of those cutesy names like *Swizzle Stick* or *Wet Spot*."

"Did they mention the Mansion's location?" I said. "Is it on the bay side, that fenced-in land opposite Baby's Coffee?"

"No, it's on the front side, on that stretch of Sugarloaf that goes to nowhere. You go down the road from the lodge and go right at the dead end, then go a long damn way. But oh, Jesus, they treated it like the biggest secret in the free world. Of course, I already knew where it was. Everybody at that end of Sugarloaf knows, but they all call it the Porcupine because of all those spooky antennas sticking out of it."

"The Porcupine."

"Right, it's a manufactured house on stilts way down by the creek bridge. We all knew it had to be something. I mean, it's on the ocean and they trimmed all the mangroves down by the water. That's so illegal. You didn't read about that in the paper. Nobody got popped, nobody caught a fine."

"The people who work inside call it the Mansion and their neighbors call it the Porcupine?"

She stuck out her chin and gave a single nod.

Our food arrived. We were all so hungry, no one spoke until two-thirds of it was gone.

"TELL ME ABOUT YOUR boss," said Beth. "How sick is he?"

"You really want to know? Today he had his usual look at 'the girls.'" Alyssa cupped her smallish boobs to cue us to her meaning. "Then he wanted to finger me. How gross is that?"

"How did you react?" I said.

"I told him I was the only one allowed to do that. Plus, I got me a nasty daddy and I'm an ace at becoming the wallpaper."

I suddenly had more respect for Alyssa's wisdom and smarts, two different things, both substantial.

"The girls call him Uncle Disgusting," I said.

Alyssa leaned toward Beth and lowered her voice. "He gives a twenty-dollar bonus each week for a ten-second look at the 'angel beard.' He once gave Mikey fifty dollars to grow hers back. It took so long they both gave up on the deal."

Beth stared ahead, unfocused. Her neutral expression, I could tell, masked a fundamental disgust. We were all finished eating. I gave the server a check-please wave.

"I need to get back to work," said Alyssa. "Mikey covered for me, so I promised her a one-hour break. Was I any help? I can't believe I told you about Sally boinking her hot fellow. She does have a cute ass, tight as it is."

Good for her, I thought. She had used the present tense—"tight as it is"—instead of the past.

BACK OUT IN THE parking lot Alyssa drove northward while Beth and I started the motorcycles and fed our helmet straps through their loops. A red Mini Cooper pulled up facing me, a lovely woman with silver hair at the wheel, the lawn-mowing guy from Bay Point hanging out the passenger side window.

"Lucky thing I saw you two standing out here," he said. "Out of the blue my neighbor who saw it all calls from Wyoming. He thought he left his trickle hose running in his sago palms. He said a helicopter landed in the water that day and a dude got off and into a fast boat of some kind. The chopper took off, the boat brought the man to shore and the boat went away. That's all I know. See you."

The Mini Cooper scratched gravel on its departure.

Everyone in a tropical hurry.

"WHERE TO?" I SAID to Beth. "It's your turn to guide us onward."

"You're plum out of gumshoe errands?"

"I get three thirty-minute breaks every twenty-four hours."

She wiggled the twist-grip throttle, barely revved the engine to three grand. She went full-bliss at the sound of it. "Well... there is one thing."

22

Eight minutes south of the restaurant, on Cudjoe Key, Beth Watkins signaled a right turn onto Blimp Road. It's a traffic-free straightaway just short of two miles in length, and it ends abruptly at Florida Bay—hard pavement into choppy salt water. She led me a hundred yards northward and pulled her cycle to the shoulder.

"I've been thinking about this for three weeks," she said.

I knew what she had in mind. Twenty-four hours earlier she had said, *"The crap never lets up. Let's run our lives so that riding always comes first."*

I pointed at the ground. "I'll wait right here."

"I'm not trying to make my dick bigger than yours, Alex." She smiled and snugged her helmet strap. "I just happen to love this machine. I won't kill myself."

I said, "Okay, please survive." I wanted to tell her that I'd once seen a car go off the boat launch ramp at road's end. But she went belly-down to the tank, lifted the revs to hot-launch the Ducati, controlled her rear wheel spin like a champ and became a receding speck in four seconds. Under the twin exhaust tips' intense blast I heard chirps of rubber. She hit her shift points and stayed gracefully shy of spinning her rear tire in each gear. I suspected she'd had lessons from a pro.

Even with the diminishing noise I barely heard my phone rang.

Duffy Lee Hall's number showed in the window: "I've had a few successes online," he said. "Those topics you asked me to research. You probably want the details face-to-face."

"You're the renaissance man, Hall," I said. "Transforming your obsolete occupation into numerous others."

"Well, I miss my darkroom," said Duffy Lee. "I curse the words 'digital camera,' even though I own three of the fuckers. You want to come on by?"

"I'm up on Cudjoe," I said. "I'll call when I get back into town, precisely at beer-thirty."

"I'll take that as your offer to buy." He clicked off.

Duffy Lee had mentioned something that caused a distant bell to ring. Or a bell in a distant part of my brain. What the hell had it been? He'd been online; he'd had success; he cursed digital cameras; he'd wanted not to discuss anything over the phone... Bang.

I'd forgotten to chase an important detail. I needed to go home, clean up and follow up.

TWO-THIRDS OF THE way back from the water's edge, Beth cut her throttle and coasted the Ducati, then braked to a quick, firm halt. She lifted her helmet, shook out her damp hair. "I want a road with corners," she said. "I really need a performance driving school. Meanwhile, I treat the machine with respect."

"And so easy on the tires," I said. Heat radiated off the Ducati. "Did you work off your hate for Uncle Disgusting?"

"He'll get his due." She unzipped, pulled up her T-shirt to mop sweat from her face and from between her unadorned breasts— also damp, a dazzling cream color in direct sun, and obviously delighted by the fast ride.

Her phone rang. The T-shirt fell to spoil the view. She checked the Caller ID, frowned and took the call. I stepped away to give her privacy. She clicked shut her phone twenty seconds later.

"I've got to go," she said. "They found my murderer. The pawn-shop paid off, thanks to you. Some shitbird from up north named Hernando DeBary. He's denying everything, but the pawnshop has him on video."

"Nice fake name. He tried to hock the hard drive?"

She nodded. "He brought in items from five different B-and-Es over the past six weeks. He claims he bought all the swag from some black guy on Whitehead Street, but they suspect him for a half-dozen other burglaries. God these criminals are dumb."

"It can't wait until..."

"He's asked for an attorney. I need to convince a judge that he's a murder suspect before he posts bond. I'd like to interview him right away, too, while he's still scared. Get him to ignore his lawyer and spill his guts. And I've got to run through the rain locker before I meet with anyone."

"Any clue to his connection to Hammond?"

"No mention," she said. "How do you know it's a fake name?"

"It's a county north of Tampa and a city near Daytona. Where did you pick up Navy lingo for taking a shower?"

"I never told you? I'm a military brat. My father was an admiral, retired now."

She zipped up, looped her helmet strap, cranked it up and left. I could hear the Ducati accelerate clear down to the Bow Channel Bridge, echoing off the puffy cumulus cloud that hung above the William Freeman Sheriff's Substation at Drost Road.

I STOOD ON THE roadside surrounded by sago scrub and marsh flats, alone but for the blimp in the odd quiet. The breeze carried no scent though I might not detect smells that a newcomer would notice. I had piled up lot of information to digest. The location of the Mansion—a/k/a the Porcupine; Sally's misbehavior, her defi-nite link to Cliff Brock; the idea of a murderous home invasion within forty yards of my own living room; Bob Catherman's odd detachment from his daughter's disappearance.

My phone rang again. Marnie said, "I think someone was in the house."

"If you report it to the cops, do it in person."

"Me go to the cop shop instead of them come here?"

"You don't want them in your house, anyway," I said. "They always find more than they were searching for. You want to be at the police station anyway."

"I thought I picked up something on the scanner," she said. "Where are you?"

I explained myself and told her that I'd check back in an hour.

I TRIED TO ASSESS the fool quotient in cruising Old Papy Road to search for the Porcupine Mansion. I wouldn't learn anything beyond confirming its site, and the motorcycle provided the opposite of anonymity. Still—as if seeing it could provide a miracle insight, take me a single step closer to answering fifty questions—I wanted to view the source of all this official confusion and deception.

I pocketed my phone, began with the helmet, then saw the Monroe County green-and-white coming toward me, moving slowly down Blimp Road. Fifty feet away, the deputy lit up the car like a Tokyo disco. The roof rack, the grill flashers, the wig-wag headlights. I was surprised he didn't have blinking blue neon under his rocker panels.

He angled the car so that its nose crossed the center line, perhaps to block an escape attempt though he must have known it was ineffective. When he exited the vehicle, I recognized Chris Ericson, a former city cop.

"Little over the top this time, eh, Mr. Rutledge?"

He could have been talking about any of ten infractions in the past three days. "How so, deputy?" I said.

"We had a report a couple minutes ago. A motorcycle doing a hundred and... at least a hundred and twenty, maybe one-thirty out here."

"I didn't know Fat Albert was that good," I said.

"Let's just call it documented," said Ericson.

"This Triumph is older than you are, Deputy. Does it look like it's capable of running over a hundred?"

He stared at the motor and pondered the concept.

"Does it smell like a motorcycle that just did a high-speed pass?" I said. "You'd think it would heat up after quadrupling the speed limit. The motor, the brakes... I mean, I've been riding it today. But if I abused a leaky old beast like this, you'd see an oil puddle for starters."

Ericson gazed up at Fat Albert, the tethered surveillance balloon. "I see your point." He didn't look down at the single drop of oil under the crankcase.

"Have you got an eyewitness to back up this report?" I said.

"I know you're a friend of Sheriff Liska," said Ericson. "And a closer friend of the lady detective. I know the game."

I shook my head. "No game, Deputy. But I think the sheriff trusts me. It goes back to when both of you worked for the city."

Ericson studied the flat land east of us, clusters of pisonia and pigeon-berry bushes, a line of sweet-bay hardwoods and a single unmolested manzanillo tree.

"So, hypothetically," I said, "if Fat Albert had a video of an alleged speed event on this roadway, would someone in the blimp control building send it to the Mansion for relay to the county?"

The deputy kept his gaze on a distant point but tightened his jaw. "It's logical. I suppose it's possible."

Pushing my luck, still guessing, I said, "Straight to one of the comm guys, the men who run the radios and monitor the fax?"

"I've only been inside once, at 3:00 AM for a cup of coffee."

"Shame about that guy."

269

"It's a bitch, but we don't know about that. We don't know shit."

"With you on that."

"You didn't notice another motorcycle in the vicinity, did you?"

"It might have been one of your tin-bearing brethren," I said.

"Shit, that detective downtown?" Ericson pounded a fist into a flat hand. "Man, I'd like to nail her. I'd like to give her a speeding citation, too, but I have to respect the badge."

I RODE SOUTH TO the end of Sugarloaf Boulevard then turned right—as Alyssa had directed, although you can't turn left. It's designated Florida 939A, but its name on the maps is Old State Road 4A. Locals don't do route numbers. They call the dead-end stretch Old Papy Road, after a powerful state representative who brought loads of postwar improvements to the Keys. I supposed the naming confusion suited the Mansion. With its antenna array largely hidden by vine-woven vegetation, no passer-by could claim to have seen anything unusual—except for the green-and-white county vehicle guarding a sturdy electric gate at the top of a two-rut driveway.

Not recognizing the deputy inside the car, I drove past and took several sweeping curves to the dead end a mile away. Stopped there, absorbing the quiet, I took a moment to palm my small camera. I wasn't sure what I might document, but I wanted to sneak a few photos of property near the Mansion.

It didn't happen. From a quarter-mile off, scanning the crest of the Sugarloaf Creek bridge, I saw the deputy leaning against his cruiser, arms crossed, eyes locked on me. It's a free country and I can take pictures anywhere on a public road. Except... I slipped the Canon back into my pocket before I crossed the short bridge.

Was it Butch or Sundance who said, "Who are those guys?"

The other then said, "They're very good."

23

I HAD HOPED TO sift facts and sort thoughts on my ride back into Key West, but the dead-ahead sun was a blinding bastard and traffic was haywire. My concentration went to simple survival—staying awake, remaining vertical, winning the inbound demo derby.

Except for the morning nap that Marv Fixler interrupted, I had been in Hawk Channel or on the motorcycle for most of twelve hours—after four hours' rest. I had reached the point where my crusty logic required assistance—a legal pad, a felt-tip pen, a rocking chair and a cold beer. I still had to follow up with Duffy Lee Hall, but I wanted to park the machine and chill a few minutes before barging onward, trying to connect dots, make sense of too much info and too few confirmed facts.

I ROLLED THE TRIUMPH behind the house, my legs still vibrating, face caked with dried sweat. Someone should create a mesh crash helmet for ventilation. A patchwork of Kevlar and inch-square solar panels to power eight miniature fans inside the shell. Hell, if I turned myself into a back yard inventor, I could quit leaping into misfit occupations.

What was I thinking? Every meth lab dope rat in the hemisphere was a back yard inventor, of sorts...

271

I sensed change in the yard, something askew. A detail was off, something as trivial as a dead frond canted oddly or grass mashed flat, trampled where it might stand tall to remind me to mow. I hung the helmet on the handlebar and checked for a puddle to ensure that a water line hadn't split under the shower, searched the mango tree for cracked branches, partial loss of crop. A siren cried several blocks away, but its wail faded. Beyond the details I sensed a vibe of regret in the still late-day air.

Then I saw a glitch more odd than panic-inducing. My storage box lock was gone.

Except for overnight trips, I've never relocked the shed while out riding. I've never kept anything in there worth stealing. A Windex spray and a half-roll of paper towels to clean dust and dampness off the motorcycle's seat. An antique electric weed trimmer with maybe two feet of monofilament left on its spool. A plastic watering can; a trowel for digging weeds; one of those squirter nozzles you screw onto the end of a garden hose. My habit has been to spin the tiny dials to conceal my combination then hang the lock on its hasp. Not once had I put it inside the box. I always found it where I'd left it.

I glanced around, didn't see it in the grass. I hoisted the Triumph onto its stand and reached to swing open the shed door. I hadn't cracked the door more than an inch when a latrine stink wafted upward. Dread grabbed me—as if a huge person had enclosed my arms and chest in a bear hug. My eyes adjusted to reduced light, and I saw a woman's bare knee and slim nude midsection. Fearing that I'd smudge prints, I lifted my fingers from the pull handle. In that moment—against logic, against the obvious—I wanted to know if the crime victim inside was still alive.

I looked around for something other than my fingers to open the shed door. For all I knew, even a twig could be crucial evidence. I pulled out my keys, used one to snag and move the door another couple of inches. My first reaction was relief. It wasn't Beth—nor

Marnie, Bobbi, Carmen or Maria. My second was the horror of strangulation and the awful knowledge that my four-day paranoia was justified.

I felt powerless and numb—as alone as I had ever felt this close to my home. I needed comfort, a reassurance that the island had not tilted, poured compassion into the sea. I would welcome the company of Jerry Hammond's brown and white springer spaniel poking its nose, its eager, lonesome eyes through the fence. That was a small impossibility. The larger one would be to bring Lisa Cormier back to life.

I didn't want to be the one.

Someone else could tell the man that his wife was dead.

WHAT HAD MARV FIXLER said about fixing me up with a blind date?

I pulled out my cell, punched in Beth's number. It rang five times and went to voice mail. "This is urgent," I said. "Call immediately or come to my house. Call me back before you come into the yard. This is no-shit police biz, right now."

I pocketed the phone then stayed put, stuck in a forensic nightmare. I stared at the shower, the back of my house. I was afraid to walk around, foul up footprint evidence, compromise the scene. I felt like a man who had painted himself into the center of a target— put himself smack in the bull's-eye. Or what was certain to become the center of a stadium.

My mind raced, confusion tried to take charge. When had Lisa Cormier propositioned me? I had photographed Hammond's place yesterday, then taken Maria to get that DVD. So the "chance meeting" in front of the La Concha was two days ago. Had Lisa come to the house today to apologize or to see if I would reconsider my rejection? Had Copeland followed, become angered, killed her in the yard or on my porch? It wouldn't make sense that he had killed her elsewhere and made a difficult special delivery. Too easy to be seen by neighbors, plus how could he have known that I had a shed for my motorcycle? It isn't visible from the lane, so how could anyone but a friend know about it? Or someone who had been on my porch and had a clear view of the back yard. Hell, if I made a list, just from the past week...

I remained still, breathed deeply, listened to typical neighborhood noises—car horns on Eaton, a moped accelerating on Fleming, the nervous Sheltie barking on Nassau Lane, the hum of air conditioners. Someone a block or two away had caught a steady rhythm popping a nail gun. With little breeze, murmurs from the poolside cocktail hour at the Eden House drifted over along with dinner-prep smells from Azur on Grinnell—the sauce for the restaurant's osso buco.

Jesus, I thought. My stomach was growling while I analyzed gourmet scents. Meanwhile a woman with whom I'd shared drinks twice in four days lay dead at my feet. I hadn't caused her death but felt guilty performing the tasks of the living, studying the world that Lisa never would hear or smell again.

I CALLED MARNIE DUNWOODY'S cell.

"What now?" she said. "Sam's waiting at the bargaining table?"

"No, that's not it. Anytime from the next few minutes to—I don't know, the next hour—I will call again and hang up. When that happens come straight to my house and be ready to work."

"Reporter work?" she said. "What did you do, find a body in your bathtub?"

"You're getting warm. But do not come here until I call, agreed?"

"Have you spoken to him today?" she said.

"No, I was..."

"Thanks for thinking of me."

My phone beeped—a disconnect.

———

KNOWING THAT LATE-DAY darkness might temper the view, I used one of my keys to snag and reopen the shed door. It wasn't scary in there like movies with discordant cellos and tympani, sound tracks of terror and unreality, noir lighting. It was sad and final. No matter how she had lived her life, it sucked.

I nudged the door shut. I had learned nothing in gawking. I'd merely ratified my intolerance of senseless shit.

My phone finally buzzed. I answered Beth's call.

"What's up?" she said.

"A dead person in my motorcycle shed."

"Did you call 911?"

"From a cell phone? How do I know they won't answer in Arizona?"

"Technology has its ways," she said. "I'll get there as soon as I can. Our scene techs might arrive first."

"I hope they're not the same ones who missed the pizza cheese at Hammond's house."

"You bet," she warned. "It's good to have top-notch personnel."

"WHY ARE YOU STANDING there, sir?"

A man crouching near the porch aimed a pistol at my neck. At his left hipbone a badge hung from his belt. My brain had been spinning for maybe ten minutes, speculating on hows and whys, and I hadn't heard his approach. He looked ill at ease, unaccustomed to crouching and aiming—which made him especially dangerous. The last time a man had pointed a gun at me in my yard, I had come within a quarter-second of visiting my personal eternity. Thanks to a quick-thinking friend, the gunman had gone to visit his own.

"There's a dead woman in this storage box," I said. "I don't know who put her in there, but I didn't want to shuffle around and fuck

275

up potential evidence. I called the city and spoke with Detective Watkins."

He scanned the yard, left to right. "You think we're going to check each blade of grass for DNA? Maybe pull forensic fibers off the backs of lizards?"

Why not, I thought. It might snare a murderer. But the rational Rutledge said, "I would never presume to know your job."

He held the gun with only one hand. "Do you know the dead woman?"

"I know her name," I said. "I wouldn't call her a close friend. I also know her husband."

"Where is he? How can we reach him?"

"That I can't tell you."

"Why not?" he demanded.

"Because I don't fucking know."

"Where did you buy the attitude, numbnuts, New York City?"

"No way," I said. "I got it on loan from Lieutenant Julio Alonzo."

The pistol quivered in his hand. "He's my father-in-law."

Oh, fuck, I thought. That's how this guy got his job. He should already have run procedures second nature to any cop—ordered me face down with my fingers laced behind my neck, made sure I wasn't armed. Instead he asked how I knew Alonzo. I figured the fellow would panic if I told him that Julio had come to my home two days earlier to question me about another murder. He might shoot me for drill, go for his hero merit badge and guarantee his job for twenty-two more years.

So I guessed and lied: "I think I met Julio playing softball about ten years ago. He was one hell of a competitor."

"Too bad his knees gave out," said the tech. "He flat loved the game."

Good guess. The pistol barrel dropped an inch. It was pointed at my groin. I wanted it back up to my neck. Where the hell was Beth?

Her voice came from out front: "Alex?"

"Back here," I shouted. "Back here talking sports."

BETH ASSURED THE SCENE tech that he could put away his weapon. She asked his permission to approach the shed, then used her laminated I.D. card to pry open the door.

She lowered her voice: "Do you know her?"

"Lisa Cormier from Atlanta, the wife of Dr. Copeland Cormier, one of Sam's fishing clients."

"Sam knew her?"

"I believe so," I said. "I'm not positive."

"Go on."

"That's all I know."

We looked over at the scene technician. Next to him stood Julio Alonzo in his lieutenant's uniform, his eyes on me like grease on a T-shirt. We hadn't heard Julio arrive.

Julio said, "How long has the body been in there, Detective?"

Beth held her answer long enough to show that she wasn't buying the sexist demands of an underling. "My guess is less than four hours, *Lieutenant.*"

Julio backed down a notch but not completely. "Has Rutledge shared with us how he spent his day?"

I glanced at Beth. Her wary expression translated to a request. Please leave her out of it, if possible.

"I loafed around the house all morning, Lieutenant. About 11:30 I took my motorcycle out of this shed and rode up the Keys. I visited two friends—Mr. Bob Catherman then Mr. Frank Polan, both on Cudjoe. I had a late lunch at Boondocks and paid the bill about ninety minutes ago. I've got a credit card receipt in my wallet. It probably shows the date and time. Forty-five minutes ago I had a conversation with Deputy Chris Ericson—one of your old department colleagues—on Blimp Road on Cudjoe. After that I rode down Old Papy Road and the only person I saw was another

TOM CORCORAN

deputy parked, I assumed, on a detail. If he can't recall my motorcycle, he certainly can verify his presence at that remote spot. Then I drove straight back here and found the body."

Alonzo looked at Beth Watkins. He shrugged, disappointed, and said, "We'll have to check all that. Come out to my car, Rutledge. I've got a few more questions."

"I need him right here for the time being, Julio," said Beth. "Plus, alibis don't come much tighter than that."

Alonzo angled his face and talked to the ground. "I hear titanium alibis eight hours a day, Detective, all due respect."

Beth Watkins stared at Julio until he walked away. She kept her gaze on the scene tech. He stepped back about ten feet.

"Who knew we were gone?" she said.

I'd already formed the answer—while waiting alone with the body. "Colding, Polan, Catherman and the three women in the grocery. Unless someone saw us ride out of the lane or you gave your name to the man mowing his lawn on Bay Point... but he doesn't know my name. Other than that, no one."

"You went inside to get a shirt before you rolled the Triumph out of this shed. Did you call anyone?"

I thought back six hours. "I called Duffy Lee Hall. I didn't mention our ride up the Keys."

Beth peered around my shoulder, asked the scene tech to give her two more minutes, then said, "Before more cops show up, tell me again what you did after I rode away from Blimp Road."

I told her about Deputy Ericson's accusation of my flaunting the speed limit, our exchange of words, and my trip to Old Papy Road, wanting to take a picture of the Mansion but being bluffed off by the deputy I didn't know.

"Perfect," she said. "And simple. Polan, that lunch receipt, and Ericson will make your alibi. Unless one of them mentions my name, we don't have to connect the two of us—officially."

"Give the case away," I said. "Why risk blowing it? I can take the

278

heat."

"It's not like you're a suspect, Alex. Let's see how it unfolds. But promise me you understand that keeping our ride confidential is a workplace tactic—that's all. I don't like my personal life juked around the office."

"I don't blame you," I said. "And I promise not to blame you for having a murder dropped in my lap. My privacy's sure to suffer for a while."

Her eyes thanked me. "Now comes the difficult part. It's hard enough to move dead people at night. How did anyone get her into your yard in broad daylight?"

"I've mentally worked every possibility." I pointed to the hedge and fence.

Beth shook her head. "Hammond's place is on Eaton Street, Alex. There's no driveway—only the front door and the gate alongside the house. Unless they carried her body down the sidewalk, she would have to 'arrive alive,' as your Florida license tags used to say."

"Okay, let's back up a bit," I said. "Why was she put here except to screw with me?"

"Maybe she came alone and her killer found her here. Would she have any reason to come to your home?"

I said it too quickly: "Persistence."

"We're making progress," said Beth, mock optimism in her voice. "She hit on you."

"She asked once, two days ago."

Beth set her jaw, dropped her eyelids as if focusing. A professional pose for a personal question. "Did you..."

"I got the impression she wasn't used to being turned down."

"I'm being stupid and out of line," she said. "I apologize." She pulled the Maglite from her belly pack and opened the shed door for another look. The light showed the weed trimmer's power cord around Lisa's neck.

"It looks—or was made to look—like she was killed right here," said Beth. "Choked with an electrical wire." She looked over at the fence. "A fresh version of Jerry Hammond's murder, except the public doesn't know how he was choked."

"I think it's phony," I said. "Two bits says that the power cord is too rotten to hold tension enough to strangle her. It would break apart before it did the job."

"Okay," said Beth. "Let's hold that thought, because what I'm seeing as a first impression, it almost looks like she undressed herself. I don't see any bruises or scratches. In a violent sexual attack, buttons and clasps are the first things to go. But the front-hitch bra is undone instead of ripped. Her pants are off both legs instead of just one, and they're here in the shed. Her panties are pulled down instead of torn off or pushed aside. Her pubic hair looks clean—it actually looks freshly combed. This is totally unlike any other rape-murders I've studied or seen."

"You think the scene is staged?" I said.

"It's as if she was undressed to make it look like a sex crime. I think we'll find out she wasn't raped. Also the power cord is not the only similarity in the two. With Hammond there was a sex angle we haven't divulged."

"Evidenced by?"

"Exposure," she said. "His unit was out of his fly. He died with his dick out."

"Those are legal terms, detective?"

"What do you want, Alex, penicular appendage? At this stage of our investigation I'm aiming for clarity."

"Maybe he was aiming for the toilet, taking a pee."

"He wasn't found near the bathroom," she said.

"So... he was surprised while pissing and chased to another room by a pizza cook. The hair dryer now becomes a weapon of opportunity. Did anyone check the commode water for content?"

"A favor just for me, Alex. Stop theorizing right now."

"Okay," I said, "but I still need to ask a couple of questions. Is Hammond's house vacant now?"

"Far as I know."

"I probably should have asked you this one yesterday. Did Jerry Hammond have a girlfriend or a part-time roommate?"

"None that we discovered. Why?"

"Someone else was spending time there. There was food for two. One was a health nut. The other was purely opposite—a comfort food junkie. If there's a link between the two murders, it may be that second person."

"You forgot to tell me about food for two?" she said.

"I'm sorry. I was too wrapped up in the computer, the missing hard drive. But I noticed the other day that this shed can be seen from his rear deck. Whoever killed Jerry could have staked out my yard for the next murder to happen."

Beth pinched her lips together in a tight line. "I'll think about it. This afternoon one of his pals offered a $25,000 reward for information leading to his murderer. It'll be in the *Citizen* tomorrow."

"Maybe you'll get a worthwhile tip," I said.

"Never happens. I'll get two dozen bogus leads which will waste my time. Rewards always carry the blatant message that the cops aren't capable of doing their job."

I pointed at Lisa Cormier's body. "Where's her husband right now and who will notify?"

She thought a moment. "I hope to hell that's not my job."

I WALKED AROUND MY house to meet Julio, feeling as if I was being sent a scolding stool in a classroom corner. But there was no sign of him, and unmarked cars, squad cars and vans had invaded the lane.

I excused myself from penance, and finally remembered to call Marnie. I let her phone ring once, hung up, and walked over to the home of Carmen's parents, Hector and Cecilia Ayusa.

Cecilia opened her front door as I climbed the stairs. "Don't tell me why the police, Alex. I don't want to know."

"How about Hector?" I said. "Is he interested?"

"He's takin' a nap," said Cecilia. She gave me what looked like a thumbs-up but angled her hand and raised her elbow so she could mimic someone drinking from a bottle—his precious Spanish brandy. She kissed the tip of her thumb and said, "You come back at suppertime, one hour, Alex, see my grumpy husband."

"Did you see any new people in the lane today?"

"No, Alex. I been packing my sheets and my dishes, not looking out windows. You know we going to Ocala, don't you?"

"I would miss you if you moved. I'd think about you up in that cold weather, all your porch plants freezing at night."

"No, they won't do that, Alex. It's still Florida."

"They had frost warnings in November last year."

Cecilia looked baffled. "Frost?"

BETH WATKINS STOOD IN the lane staring at me as I left the Ayusas' porch. My eyes were distracted by two cops stringing plastic yellow CRIME SCENE tape around my screened porch.

"The forensic boys kick you out?" I said.

"For an hour or so," said Beth. "Speaking of which, I have rough news for you. Your home is part of our investigation. You won't be staying there tonight."

"Well, shit."

"You'll just have to bunk with the investigating officer."

"I can't even go inside for my toothbrush and a change of under-wear? I really need to get a portable flash drive off my desk."

"I own one of the largest toothbrush storage facilities in the Keys. Dr. Goldner gives me one every time I get my teeth cleaned, but I use a battery-powered model. I take home all the freebies in hope of a situation like this."

"Why do you still have so many on hand?"

"I'm as fussy about my sex as I am about my teeth. And you won't need underwear unless you've browned-out the pair you're wearing. I don't allow clothing in my bed." She checked her watch. "I've got at least forty minutes. Let me show you your mandatory accommodations for the evening."

"Do you have that device with you?" I said. "The one that downloads a camera memory card?"

"It's in my car. I've also got a portable flash drive."

"Can I borrow both?" I said. "I need to run a quick errand."

"Just as well. I need to sit in my car and think this through."

"Think about the proximity factor," I said, "a possible connection between Lisa Cormier and Jerry Hammond."

"The timeline doesn't work," said Beth. "We arrested the guy who did Jerry Hammond three hours ago, thanks to the pawnshop video and his fingerprints on the hard drive. He's a young punk full of wise-mouth and denials. I've got to get up early tomorrow to interview and intimidate him."

"Hernando DeBary?"

"You were right about the fake name. It's Russell Hernandez."

"That's who pawned the hard drive?"

"Got him on video. He's admitted buying the drive from what he called a street person. And he's claiming innocence on anything else. I'll rip his story like a wet Kleenex."

"He does yard maintenance, not pizzas, Beth. Did you compare his shoe size to the footprints?"

"How do you know this?"

"He and his buddy Jason were Carmen's houseguests for the first couple nights they were in town. They've been on the island less than a week. I think they got here Sunday."

"Fuck," said Beth. "You're sure?"

"Easy enough to check out. Jason Dudak's mother is Carmen's

best friend. There must be some way to track their travels."

"Well, double-fuck." She inhaled deeply then exhaled slowly. "That screws up the murder and the string of burglaries."

"It might save you from a dead-end Q-and-A session," I said.

She inhaled deeply then exhaled slowly. "Maybe you got it right when I asked who knew we were gone. It's some kind of horseshit set-up. Someone saw us ride out of the lane."

24

THE POLICE ALLOWED ME into the yard to retrieve my Triumph and helmet. They looked like kids but I could tell by their approach, rigging lights—stadium lights, I thought—dividing my yard into sections, that they meant business. One tech wore a blue nylon jacket with CSI: CAYO HUESO on the back. Probably custom-made on Southard Street—at Ramona's Shirt Put-On. It spoke to the man's affection for his job and the sense of humor the techs must need for continued mental health.

It helped my humor that I didn't see the one who had pointed a gun at me.

Beth was waiting by her parked car on Fleming. She smiled on one side of her mouth and handed me a small thumb drive and her image storage device. "Be home in time for dinner, honey. No fair buying pajamas."

"I'd better find some curbside Viagra," I said.

She licked her index finger, touched it low on her right hip and made a sizzling hiss through her teeth. "I will make sure you don't need it."

I grinned, and she grabbed my arm.

"I'm under so much damn pressure right now," she said. "Tell me you like me. Tell me I'm not making an idiot of myself."

"I like you very much. Thank you for asking. I'd kiss you right here but we don't know who's watching."

"Where *will* you kiss me?" she said.

"On your cute boca chica."

I RODE DOWN EATON trailing crab-slow traffic, along Simonton past evening cruisers, people walking from sunset at Mallory Square. Four weeks into autumn, the temperatures hadn't changed much but the evening air smelled colder. Not like chimney smoke cold, but crisp and welcome in the year's last days of Daylight Savings.

The Pier House entry gate dude gave me a hairy eyeball. I told him I was a Chart Room regular, and he waved me through. No fools, several other cycle owners had claimed the best spots in the lot. Defensive parking is wise in a town catering to drinkers. I settled for a remote corner shielded by an oversized croton bush and chose not to leave my helmet behind.

With Happy Hour in full swing on Duval, I wasn't sure I would find any of the party-hearty college girls in the Beach Building annex. I rode an elevator to the second floor where a bedraggled young woman answered my knock. She wore a long, flimsy robe and looked like the aftermath of a long and voluminous intake of shots and drafts. Air escaping the room carried odors of a morning saloon. I was reminded of a Navy ship's forward berthing compartment at six A.M. in a foreign liberty port.

She looked at my empty hands. "You're not the food. Bitches said they'd send up food."

"No, but..."

"What," she said, as a statement of fact. She apparently didn't have the energy to make it a question.

"My name is Alex Rutledge," I said. "I live here in town and I'm here to ask a non-sexual favor for which I'd be willing to shell out some cash."

"First things first," she mumbled. "Why not sexual?"

"You're not a hooker and I don't buy fucks."

"Good answer. My name is Barb. Do I smell bad?"

Bad is the smell of death, I thought. "No, Barb, you don't."

"So what are you buying?" she said. "You mind if I sit down?" Without waiting for my answer she slid down the door jamb and plopped her butt on the floor, stuck her legs straight out. The whoosh of wind gave lie to my last statement.

I said, "You and your friends were taking pictures on the beach last night..."

"Whoa, that sounds sexy to me. Or pervy. We were flashing our twins and buns."

"I was sitting with two men at a table in the outside bar. I'd like to see if one of your snapshots showed their faces."

Barb burped. "Very mysterious."

I feared that her next burp might come up in Technicolor.

"A little mysterious," I said. "One wants to sell me his boat, but I think he's a boat thief."

"His price is too good to be true? My dad used to sell boats in Milwaukee. Your name again?"

"Alex."

She sized me up, calculating her next move. "I smell, don't I?"

"If you really must know..."

"They're all at the Hog's Breath or Captain Tony's, and Patsy's got her camera with her," said Barb. "But she might have moved her pictures onto her Viao. Please help me up. I still have shame left in my conscience. You're going to have to wait two minutes while I shower."

The room looked as if a small waterspout had come ashore and had its way with a dozen duffels and bags. Again, no big deal, the nudity. She dropped the robe, grabbed a hairbrush from the top of the television and plodded to the bathroom. Below her chin, a pleasant figure, the start of a beer belly, not a hair on her body.

I appreciated her graciousness in washing up. She came out in less than a minute wrapped in a towel, soap-scented, her walk an uncertain hula, her ample bottom two-thirds exposed. She went straight to the laptop on the small desk, pulled a chair close, turned on the computer.

"You just want to see it, right?" she said. "I don't have a blank CD to burn."

"I've got a jump drive in my pocket."

Barb quickly found a photo file dated only six hours earlier. "We might be in luck," she said. She launched a Picture Manager utility that sequenced the photos forward in time, starting with several in another room and the adjacent hallway—a faux strip show from one of them, two others mooning the camera. "That's what my ass looked like when it was drunk two days ago," she said.

"Better than some girls' faces," I said.

"You're so kind." She scrolled onward, skin and smiles, go cups and attitudes. If photographs still cost what I used to pay for film and developing, the women probably couldn't have paid their hotel bill. She finally found a series that went from outside Sloppy Joe's, then inside the Pier House restaurant, then their beachside song and dance routine. "There's you," she said. "Sitting in the shadows, gawking at Patsy's little bitty titties. That's not good of the other men, but... There." She stopped the photo sequence. "You've got those two other men and four ta-tas, including my chubby babies."

Sure enough, the faces of Copeland Cormier and Ricky Stinson had been caught straight on by the camera flash.

"It's Alex, right?" said Barb. "You said you'd be willing to... what did you say, shell out cash?"

I pulled the tiny flash drive out of my pocket. "Yes, I said that."

"I will make you a deal. I will copy this picture to your thumb device if you buy me a food delivery and a six-pack of Cokes from the best deli in town."

I handed her the small drive, picked up the phone, dialed 9, then the number I had memorized for Damn Good Food To Go. The

288

place was great and only three hundred yards away. I ordered a turkey melt with American cheese on sourdough, macaroni salad, a fresh fruit cup, chicken noodle soup, a large café con leche and the Cokes. I hung up, took forty bucks from my wallet, put it next to the phone.

Barb had copied the photo for me. She also had zoomed on the picture, blown up Ricky Stinson's face to fill the monitor.

"It's photo number DSC-3031," she said. "Is this guy your boat thief?"

"That's him."

"I never would've remembered it happening."

"It?" I said.

"He came to the door this morning—I don't know how early. We were still passed out, except I'd gotten up to barf for the third or fourth time. I cracked the door and he offered to buy our cameras for five hundred bucks. I figured he was nut case, so I closed the door in his face, hooked the chain and went back to bed."

Stinson—with something to hide. My gig as a private eye might be a washout, but my instincts still were tight.

Barb looked at my expression. "Why the look?"

"Please believe me," I said. "Except for your friends or a Russian kid waving bags of food, don't open that door again, okay?"

Barb leaned forward to study Stinson's face. "He's worse than a boat thief, eh?"

I TOLD MYSELF IT was rational caution, not blatant fear, that had me pacing the Pier House lot in search of Porsche Cayennes. Either way, it was pissing up a tree. If I found one—even if I was sure it was Catherman's—I wouldn't learn a damned thing.

The lot, given its proximity to Lower Duval's standard battle of the bands, was oddly quiet. The walk offered me a pause to think ahead so I might, for the next few hours, act instead of react.

My first stop would be Carmen's cottage. Her yard was the safest place that I could park my Triumph overnight, and she needed to know about or be comforted regarding the second neighborhood murder and Russell Hernandez's arrest.

The city had posted a uniformed officer at the lane's entrance. I was asked to show photo I.D. and to remove my helmet for visual verification to ride past my own home. Carmen did not come out to her back porch to greet me. I assumed correctly that comfort was required. Carmen was in a massive funk. Beth Watkins had visited first, to verify the information I'd given her about Jason and Russell's arrival in Key West, so she knew about the newest killing, too. More crushing was the big picture now planted in her head: her parents would not be moving to Ocala.

"Scam, scam, scam," she said.

Maria sat at the kitchen table, trying not to stare at her mother, doodling on her homework, unsure how to respond.

"You had a good plan in motion," I said. "Don't let one rotten deal keep you from following through."

"You say, but somehow my mother got the idea that she'll be cold in her bones that far north. She's having second thoughts. Other than that, I'm having doubts about my job. And other than that, Carol Anne—Jason Dudak's mother—is pissed at me because Russell's in a jam."

"You've got a job for life, Carmen... Are you catching shit because of Jerry?"

Maria sat up and pointed at the cuss kitty, an empty rum bottle now half-full of dimes. I added my ten cents and turned back to her mother.

"Surely you can't be held accountable," I said.

Carmen dug around in her purse, pulled out a dime, walked to the cuss bottle. "A few people at work actually liked the asshole." The dime made a dull click as it joined the others. "The cops don't have a suspect, so to them I'm the next best fall guy. And now

Carol Anne blames me because Russell bought a stolen hard drive. That's just plain stupid. Thank goodness she paid for a tank of gas when they left Ocala so they'd have cash to rent a place when they got here. She still has the receipt from Sunday morning, so she's going to email me a copy to show Detective Watkins. At least my daughter didn't borrow a cartoon DVD from a murderer."

"Was there any sign of Marnie during all the confusion?" I said.

Carmen shook her head. "There was a guy from the paper who stuck around maybe five minutes. I think they ran him off."

I asked Carmen to plug my thumb drive into her computer and locate photo DSC-3031. She found it and told Maria to stay in the kitchen.

"I'll explain when it's no longer highly classified," I said.

"I've already reduced its status," she said. "No class at all."

We cropped the photo once to show both men and saved it as a new file. Then we cropped to show only Ricky Stinson's head and shoulders and saved that. There wasn't much usable resolution in either close-up. Carmen printed two copies of each on postcard-sized photo paper, closed the file and extracted the thumb drive.

"Don't debase yourself," she said, "wasting money with these young tourist chicks. Any time you get the urge to see bare breasts, bring me a free bottle of Estancia Meritage."

I WALKED FOUR BLOCKS to Beth's and arrived as another man—a young, athletic-looking fellow—was leaving, looking smug, counting his money. It was the Russian delivery man from Damn Good Food. I don't hold stock in telepathy, but I mentally predicted that my supper would be a turkey melt on sourdough with macaroni salad and a fruit cup.

Beth gave me a hug and led me to her kitchen. She had ordered more adventuresome food: it was a Reuben by the Sea—blackened grouper, melted Swiss and coleslaw on rye. I would get four bites then wait twelve hours to finish it.

I'd put my cell phone on vibrate instead of ringtone. It buzzed in my front pocket. Once again acting counter to common sense, I dragged it out, saw the number and whispered, "Damn."

"I know that 'damn' tone of voice," said Beth. "If it's Bobbi Lewis, she probably heard about the body in the box. You may as well talk to her."

I shook my head and took the call.

"Where are you?" said Sheriff Chicken Neck Liska. "On the island?"

"Yes, camping at a friend's home because my place is a crime scene."

"So I heard," he said. "I need you at my house right now. I trust the words 'need' and 'now' carry a little weight."

"Any clues as to topics, et cetera?"

"You know me," said Liska. "Master of the party surprise. Use the gate through the fence around back."

"Will the county cover my cab fare?"

"I arranged for a ride. Call Lewis on her personal cell."

"Oh, wait a minute," I said.

"Put aside your issues for the greater good." He hung up.

I faced turf packed with land mines. I explained my dilemma to Beth. It prompted a sympathetic expression.

"I'm okay with it." She opened a cabinet, took a spare house key off a rack, handed it over. "You're a man at the plate with a fastball headed for your elbow. You're going to take one for team."

Beth's phone rang. She picked it up from the counter and walked from the room. "I'll get this while you make your call."

I brought up Bobbi's number and pressed the green button.

"I'm outside your house," she said, "looking at yellow crime scene tape. Are you okay?"

"I'm fine, but yes. The city wanted to secure it for a day."

"I'm your taxi. Where are you?"

I could tell by the echo that she was in her SUV.

"Does it matter?" I said. "I'll meet you in front of Mangia Mangia."

"Give me more credit than that, Alex. I lived next door to the woman for a year, and I sure as hell know where she bought her new house."

I knew Bobbi was a good detective. This was too good.

She knew I was stymied. "I had a chat with Deputy Ericson at the substation an hour ago. You two were out riding?"

"Yep," I said. "I'll meet you in front of Mangia Mangia." I shut off the phone, stared at my sandwich.

INTENT AS I WAS on keeping things businesslike and impersonal, I was stumped for words. I opened the passenger-side door of the SUV, nodded hello, climbed in and hooked the seat belt.

Bobbi turned right onto Margaret. Slowing for the stop sign at Fleming, she said, "Are we history?"

So much for my high-road intentions.

"I suppose so," I said.

"What about my Montana trip? You always said you would drive me out to Livingston. You were going to introduce me to all your artsy lit-type friends out there."

"You made your choice," I said. "You tossed a fit and walked out of the restaurant. Did you assume I'd be overjoyed to reconnect?"

"You had nothing to talk about except your questions about that missing Catherman girl."

"I asked if we had a romance. I said that I wanted us to work. I told you that while I walked from the house to dinner I felt alone without you there. Your exact words were, 'This is bullshit I don't need right now.'"

Bobbi let the dust settle for a minute or two before saying, "I'm not allowed to be tired, worn to a fucking frazzle?"

"When you walked out of the restaurant you made it clear that you didn't want much to do with me. Right behind that came an alternative, an acquaintance that turned into a closer friendship. That's when I made my choice."

"Nice word for the girl, 'alternative.' Although, I will admit, she is a good cop."

I felt a moment of déjà-vu, which wasn't too difficult on a small island. We were on Flagler, the road Beth and I had taken out of town that morning.

"By the way," said Bobbi, "I got only two sets of fingerprints in the Miata. We matched Sally's to a hairbrush in her bedroom, and the other set belonged to her father. It looked like the steering wheel and door handles had been wiped clean."

"Tell me about Marv Fixler," I said.

Bobbi hesitated, perhaps wondering how I knew his last name. She said, "A brave man, sharp as a tack."

"Law enforcement career man?"

"Oh, yes. Went to college for it."

"Where did Marv go when he left the sheriff's office?"

"That's confidential information," she said.

"A government job, then."

"Indirectly."

I made an authoritative-sounding guess. "Was he contracted to the government for security work?"

"That's quite simply not your business."

A second impulse: "Has he spent time in third-world countries?"

"Again, classified."

"I guessed as much. He came by the house today."

"He what?" she said. "I don't think so."

I pointed at Liska's house. "I think we're here."

"Hang with me on this, Alex."

"Hang for what, more shit you don't need?"

"The whole time we dated I lived on Big Coppitt," she said. "I felt so removed from the city and from you. I wondered about you on the nights I didn't see you."

"We talked every night, unless one of us was working. Did you want me in your sights constantly?"

No answer.

"So you worried that I was running around?" I said. "Should I have worn a monitoring device? An ankle bracelet?"

"Did anyone talk to you?"

"What about?"

"Maybe someone I work with told you I might have had issues in the past… With a man who wasn't as true as he claimed."

Liska had, indeed, counseled me to go easy and extinguish her fears of abandonment if I wanted the relationship to continue.

"What prompted this?" I said.

"I don't know. I talked with a couple people today about that Jerry Hammond murder. You asked me, you begged me never to call you again for a death-related photo job. Then a city detective gets a case and suddenly you're Johnny-on-the-Spot."

"I went there a day after Hammond was found. I had her assurance that the body was gone. I didn't want to see a dead person this week, or ever. I shot the surroundings, not the corpse."

"Why didn't you take real crime scene shots?"

"Because of my proximity to the dead man."

"Were you a witness or a suspect?"

I shrugged. "I guess her SWAT Team boys did the dirty work."

"I know the SWAT guy who takes the photos. He's very good. Why did she need pictures without her victim around?"

"She didn't think it was random. She wanted to tie motive to lifestyle or vice-versa."

"She was opening the door," said Bobbi. "To hit on you."

"So you think that's my pattern, I wait for offers? I have no taste, no say in the matter?"

I saw the look on her face and knew I had gone too far—or struck

295

too close to home. Because Bobbi had taken the first steps in our relationship.

She stopped in front of Liska's house. "Do you want your say? Do you want to share your feelings?"

"I feel like a scuffed pair of shoes you've put in the back of your closet. You might wear me once or twice next year if you get in the mood."

"Marv is a flu bug I've got to get out of my system."

"That doesn't sound like a spectator sport, Bobbi. Thanks for the ride."

"Thank my boss," she said. "I was just doing my job."

25

I HAD BEEN TO Chicken Neck Liska's home on Eagle twice before. Each time, in late evening, I arrived to find him alone in his living room, drinking in near-darkness. This time I would blaze a new trail, as would he. His front yard was dark as a cave. The narrow driveway was bordered by crotons to one side, an eight-foot wood slat fence on the other. He hadn't spent a cent on shrub trimming or security lights.

I fumbled my way around his personal sedan, nudged the tall door set into the fencing, almost caught a mess of pine splinters in my palm. The gate's electronic lock made a soft click but gave and let me enter.

If Monroe County's residents knew that Sheriff Fred Liska had tucked a mini-paradise into his secluded yard, his image would be shot to hell. The money he had saved out front had been well spent on accent lighting, a narrow lap pool, a guest cottage and a cabana. The yard smelled of freshly watered plants, damp earth and a night bloom I couldn't identify. I heard vintage West Coast jazz turned low—a Henry Mancini melody off "Music from Peter Gunn."

The luxury was not enough to worry me about ill-gotten cash. I knew Liska to be a rule-bender but never had questioned his basic honesty. Still, none of it matched the former Key West detective who, before his election to sheriff, was famous for eccentricities, including his habit of wearing vintage—and garish—disco attire.

I found him in a teak armchair on a softly lighted patio studying pages spread atop a square glass-top table. He looked up at me, unsurprised.

"Your dutiful servant," I said. "You needed me now?"

"Among others. I also called this guy." Liska jacked his thumb toward a sliding glass door. Sam Wheeler stepped outside with a beer in his hand. I hadn't noticed his borrowed Mustang parked in the street, but I'd been distracted by Bobbi's awkward plea for reconciliation or forgiveness—I wasn't sure which.

"You knew his number, Sheriff. That was more than I had."

"It was my phone," said Liska. "A personal line I've kept active but haven't used since the county gave me a freebie. We've been in touch for three days."

"I followed your example, Alex," said Sam. "If you're going to have a friend on the good side of the fence, why not the top guy?"

"Does he know?" I said.

"All four trips."

"I figured two at the most."

Sam reached to slap Liska's forearm. "I fooled Rutledge. I told you I was good." He handed me the beer and went to get another for himself.

"Sam brought along two assistants," said Liska. He stood, led me inside to a small room off the kitchen. We found Duffy Lee Hall working with a Macintosh laptop and Marnie Dunwoody in front of a corkboard thumbtacking lists and grainy photographs printed from web pages. She gave me a wry, harried smile that bordered on grimace.

"You were on to something, Alex," said Duffy Lee. "Most of what they asked me to do were the same things you asked about, so a lot of it was already done. I filled them in on Cormier's travels to the various countries. I printed out everything I found, but I was touching on web sites that locked everyone out if they detected a snoop. If the authorities want to, I suppose, they can track me down."

"From here on out, " Liska said, "let me worry about that. You're all special deputies working on my orders." He tapped my arm and pointed to a second corkboard on an adjacent wall. It held a small nautical chart surrounded by three-by-five cards, each with names and arrows in red or blue Sharpie ink. Like a loose storyboard for a three-act play.

I sipped my beer, looked back at Duffy Lee, turned my head to watch Marnie, then gazed into the kitchen where Sam stood, his butt against a counter, tapping the neck of his beer bottle against his chin, deep in thought. I didn't say a word. I drank another slug of beer and considered their homemade Command Center, their assigned tasks with bulletin boards, printouts, the computer. The room remained quiet until Marnie looked at me and lost it. When she laughed the other three joined her.

I didn't get it.

"Okay," said Liska. "That's our last chuckle of the evening." He faced me. "Marnie predicted you'd be pissed that we started this— and got this far—without you."

I shrugged—a silent agreement.

"We've been at it less than two hours," he said. "When I heard you'd found Lisa Cormier in your motorbike box, I made the calls. After an extended prep time, the other side is moving fast."

"Like hounds are on their trail," said Sam.

"The ones that caught Lisa," said Marnie.

Sam caught my eye to confirm the fact: "And Cliff Brock and Sally Catherman five days ago."

"I assume they were found at that house at Bay Point," I said. "Were they killed somewhere else?"

Liska nodded. "Each shot twice by someone they probably knew, probably on open water fairly close to shore. They were naked with sun oil all over them. Sally still had her iPod earbud wires strung around her neck. The feds never found their clothing, and the killer tried—but failed—to sink Cliff's boat."

"With Sam's hull numbers on it?"

"We can't figure out why they did that," said Sam, "except for the sake of confusion, which worked."

"I spoke with Alyssa Navarro this afternoon," I said. "She works at Colding's Grocery, where Sally worked, and she went on several of Cliff and Sally's skinny-dip excursions, on double-dates with a friend of Cliff."

"Dates as in group mambo?" said Marnie.

I nodded. "More like voyeur stuff than clusters. The guy gave her a fake name which didn't bother her. She knew that Cliff and her party partner worked at the Mansion."

"My deputies have been getting rich on overtime guarding that driveway dusk-to-dawn for months," said Liska. "And lately during the day... but you know that, Rutledge. You drove by this afternoon and did a piss poor job of concealing your camera."

Our side is good, too, I thought. "Can you take a half-minute to explain the Mansion's mission?"

"It's pure, broad-reach surveillance," said Liska. "It's run from the top of the intelligence mountain but manned by a civilian out-fit that employs contract workers. That gives them two degrees of deniability, perhaps more in a legal sense. Cuba—for sure—is the main target. They've never confirmed it, but I think they track GPS transmitters on vehicles down there. They track every boat in the Florida Straits. They monitor underwater listening devices and match surface data—radar—with satellite info. I have no idea how much they pull off Fat Albert. They may even watch people in the Keys, but I would be the last person they'd admit that to."

"What about all those rafts that come ashore with half-starved refugees?"

"My take is, they target security threats and felons, not families."

"If Alyssa can identify her party man and she's still alive," said

Sam, "he may not be the shooter."

"But that gets to the core of our problem," said Liska. "We don't know shit. We don't know whether they planned all this to happen right now or they're panicking. We're looking at histories, stolen boats and smuggling. We're looking at outbound pharmaceuticals as pure distraction. If we figure out their hurry, create a plausible scenario, we might get an idea of what they're really doing."

"Isn't all this Homeland's job?" I said.

"First off," said the sheriff, "they're agents from Customs, the DEA, Immigration and Transportation. Mostly Customs, but they just don't have the teamwork that any of those groups had before they got thrown in the blender. They're ninety-nine percent straight, but they depend too much on contract workers. There's too much room for lone rangers and renegades... and assholes. Second, they specialize in the one-way street. I'm supposed to hand over every shred of background and evidence, and they won't give my office the time of day. I don't like working with them."

"How can I help?"

"Start looking at all of this," said Liska, "reading it and piecing it together. Keep an open mind. And don't be misled by appearances right here at this moment, the beer and all. We're in a state of total panic. I don't want more people to die in my county."

"What am I looking for?"

"Connections," he said. "That page right there is a timeline. Our target names are Cliff and Sally and the Cormiers, and the father, Bob Catherman."

"Let me ask first," I said to Sam. "Was Cliff your inside man at the Mansion?"

Sam nodded. "We timed our runs so he'd be on watch when I ran south. He'd pocket outbound notifications sent by the Cubans, and give me all-clear signals for my return runs. Your next question is how Cormier recruited him."

"Yes, but go ahead."

"They met a few years ago in Nicaragua. Copeland found out that Brock was going to be transferred up to the Keys, and he knew that Cliff's employer had won the contract to monitor north-south surface traffic on the Straits. He told Cliff about his desire to move legit drugs into Cuba. He recruited him to help with the altruistic end."

"I found two photos of Copeland Cormier on the web," said Duffy Lee. "In Baghdad and in Nicaragua, both times posing with regional hospital honchos. While he was offshore, Lisa Cormier was misbehaving. She got three DUIs in the Atlanta area, plus resisting arrest without violence and providing a false name to law enforcement. I got good hits on Bob Catherman, too. He was in the printing business in Harrisburg, Pennsylvania, then Kingsport, Tennessee, and for a while up in Clearwater. Then he showed in a court case in Fort Myers. It looks like he was a nautical repo man with a company called Aquatic Liquidators."

I pulled my camera out of my pocket. "I have a couple of photos that might tie into that, except I don't have my wire to run from the camera to the computer."

"You're an ace photographer, I know," said Liska, "but maybe you can tell us in words."

"I saw two boats today parked in the canal behind Catherman's place on Cudjoe. I saw him an hour later. He claimed they belong to a neighbor, which could be true..."

Duffy Lee pointed at the laptop's monitor. "Was one of them this ride, stolen last month out of Naples?"

It was the Fountain that Beth and I had scoped from the other side of the canal.

Liska read my reaction. "Progress with teamwork," he said. "Let's go sit outside and talk this through."

"One more thing for the bulletin board," I said. I went back into my pocket, removed the picture that Carmen had printed. "It's a photo of Ricky Stinson that might come in handy."

302

No one reacted. Sam finally said, "Who?"

"I met him with Copeland Cormier last night at the Pier House. He made sure to let me know he was your good friend and part of the deal. He knew all about your Army training and the boat you outran last weekend."

Sam shook his head. "Never heard of him."

"They wanted to know if I'd heard from you."

Duffy Lee held out his hand. "I'll stay here and search for Mr. Stinson. And whatever else..."

I gave him the photo.

WE MOVED TO THE patio and used cook's tools from Liska's gas grill to keep papers from blowing off the glass-top table. Sam Wheeler remained standing but stuck close, a determined, pensive look on his face.

My first question was for him. "At what point did you know that your last trip was screwed?"

"I got my radio 'all-clear,'" he said, "but it wasn't like the three I received from Cliff before that. Someone had the right code but the wrong format. I wasn't a hundred yards off the Cuban beach when I started running a random zigzag toward Marathon. Two-thirds of the way home, I cut northwest toward Big Pine. I'd checked the Lower Keys tides so I knew from that point I could haul ass down Hawk Channel and beat a chase through one of the creeks."

"The cargo was strictly one-way?" I said. "You never brought anything back?"

Sam looked at Chicken Neck and Marnie, cracked a smile. "The boy's a thinker," he said.

"He'll love this," said Liska.

"Two things came back on every trip," said Sam. "Letters for me to stamp and mail from here. They had Keys return addresses, and were going to people who had made it out of Cuba. I also brought back the snap-shut boxes used to transport their heat-sensitive drugs. They have some kind of space age insulation and a rubber seal around their edges—like that waterproof suitcase you used to carry for your cameras. They cost like crazy, and the Cubans had no use for them, so I'd deliver one or two full ones and bring back one or two empties, whatever they handed me."

"Who would you give them to?" I said.

"I'd put them in a funky Styrofoam cooler in my Bronco, park in the Half Shell lot right after I returned, and go have breakfast at Harpoon Harry's. I'd come back after eating and drive home. They told me if the container was still there, I should have breakfast the next day, but it was gone all three times."

"You didn't connect the fourth time?"

"I waited for someone to arrive, to find out what they knew about my being chased. They never showed up, so I kept it." He leaned over to a shelf of potted plants and lifted an oblong, hard plastic box. It was maybe sixteen inches long, four inches wide, not even two inches deep.

"It's empty?"

"Unless you tear it apart—which the sheriff, here, made me do back there." Sam pointed to a far side of the yard. "He was afraid it might explode, so he wouldn't stand near me."

"Okay, drama champ, you survived," I said. "Was it empty?"

"Once I peeled back the lining, sure as hell."

"Empty."

"No," said Sam. "Sixty thousand dollars."

I took a moment to digest the news. "You think every box you brought back..."

"My best guess is that I unknowingly smuggled in three hundred grand, minimum."

"Could those airtight boxes have held more than charity drugs on the trips south?" I said.

Sam shrugged. "I made them show me the pills and vials, just like I made them introduce me to Cliff Brock. I wanted to see my lifeline face-to-face. I have no idea whether they put anything in the linings on my southbound trips."

"Surely the government wouldn't kill someone for letting a boat slide through. That's a bit severe, even for the old administration. Any idea who gave you the phony 'all-clear?'"

"The last thing Cliff said to me was, 'Something's funky in the Mansion. Be careful.' Turned out we both needed to be careful. I had the double-whammy on me. If I survived the chase, I was the perfect murder suspect. If the cops didn't catch me, the bad boys would shut me up ugly. Triple-whammy."

No one spoke for a minute or so. The light jazz had ended. We listened to burbles from the pool.

"Had to be a rat in there," said Marnie.

"I think Cliff suspected one or two of them were doing a similar dodge," said Sam," but not for the good of mankind."

"Speaking of not for good," I said to Liska, "your ex-employee, Marv Fixler, paid me a visit this morning."

"Was this in regard to another of my employees whose name, Lewis, shall not be mentioned? Can this wait?"

"He claimed not. He talked about a government go-fast boat that was stolen in Belize. He said it was an ocean-going equivalent of a Stealth bomber."

"I've received a stack of urgent situation reports on that one," said Liska.

"Fixler said that my snooping and meddling could jeopardize the government's recovery efforts."

Liska shook his head. "Hell, you should be proud. That's what they say to entire civilian law enforcement agencies."

"He also suggested that Sam might be involved in the boat theft. Or he offered the possibility to see if I'd agree."

"Okay, let's work with this," said the sheriff. "He left the Sheriff's Office before I won the election. I barely knew him, never learned much about him, except social rumors. After he left we received background and reference requests. I heard maybe a year later that he became a security professional. At some point he went to Panama, then to the Middle East. Now he's back, supposedly working for the government, but there's no way to verify that. He could be Homeland or Defense Intelligence or a contractor. I happen to know that one day last week he wore a T-shirt that read: DAD MADE ME CRAZY. Sam tells me that these days, among warriors, 'Dad' means 'Baghdad.'"

We hadn't seen Duffy Lee Hall poke his head out the sliding glass door. "Speaking of which, Sheriff," he said, "I've put Ricky Stinson in Baghdad at the same time as Copeland Cormier."

"Tell us more," said Liska.

"Richard M. Stinson ran a construction company called Rampant Eagle, LLC, licensed out of Fall River, Massachusetts. Near as I can tell, he had a state department contract to build latrines and chapels."

"Poetic," said Sam. "That's the military I learned to love."

"Duffy Lee, run another search for me," said Liska. "See if Belize has a Coast Guard or the equivalent. Look for mention of a high-tech boat missing or stolen from that country."

"WE'VE SIFTED THE SHIT down to basics," I said. "Boats, bucks and Iraq. Whatever they're doing, they've invested a lot of time and money, a lot of forethought."

"And they've killed people to cover it up," said Sam.

Liska nodded. "Killed them on my turf. Keep going with this, Rutledge."

"Okay," I said. "Where's the easiest money these days? You run cocaine, you have to work with the Mexican Mafia, whichever family hasn't been decapitated this month. You run heroin, you have to be cousin to someone in the Middle East or the Far East. Why screw around with something you have to resell? Why not bring in dirty money and spend it clean?"

Marnie leaned forward. "I thought crime gangs were desperate to get cash offshore."

"The risks are different these days," I said. "When Noriega tumbled, the dope profits in his banks went up in smoke, so to say. The ultra-secret banks in Europe and the usual offshore havens have succumbed to pressure from Interpol and the banking system. They're giving up names to stay afloat."

"Let's go back inside," said Liska. "Let's shuffle three-by-fives and draw more arrows."

"Could I ask one question before we move?" I said. "What are we going to do with all this speculation? What if we come up with a credible scenario? We're not a bunch of swashbucklers or snoops with next-generation tech toys. And you said yourself, Sheriff, you don't like working with the feds. We're going to be like the dog that caught the car it was chasing. How will we act on it?"

"We'll know the truth," said Sam Wheeler. "After that, we'll follow our noses."

"Well put," said Sheriff Liska. "Alex, thank you for asking."

"MORE ON RAMPANT EAGLE," said Duffy Lee. "I found a link to a *Vanity Fair* magazine article about billions of impounded Iraqi dollars that disappeared when we sent the money back there for reconstruction. Cash was being tossed around like beach balls, and the period in question matches the time-in-country of both Cormier and Stinson. And get this. It also matches the time when troops from Nicaragua were sent home. Then, right about the time the money dried up, the Dominican Republic withdrew its troops, flew them out."

"And you placed Cormier in both those countries doing his so-called volunteer work?"

"Where he could reconnect with one or two bad colonels."

"If Fixler was in Iraq back then," said Liska, "we've got a trifecta. Anything on that go-fast boat stolen in Belize?"

"Nothing official, but I found an unclassified blog on it," said Duffy Lee. "The boat was a Keeltec Yachts triple-inboard equipped with a constant-transmit GPS and a disconnect alarm. Someone was able to duplicate the signal, install a substitute ignition and engine management system and make off with the boat. They left behind the old system hooked to a solar-charged twelve-volt battery. Anyone monitoring its GPS transmitter would think the craft was at the dock—right where it was supposed to be. The blogger also said that a non-military boat with a compatible ignition was stolen in Naples, Florida, four months ago. That boat's electronics came from the same company. It was a customized Fountain."

"Who was the blogger?" said Marnie.

"No way to tell," said Duffy Lee. "Anonymous and truly weird. He signed in as 'slut-virgin.'"

Lisa must have sensed an ill wind blowing. She wanted an ally, not a lover. If I had taken the bait, I could have wound up dead in my shed.

"That report you found of the Fountain stolen in Naples," I said. "Was there any mention of a performance hot-rod, a Skater?"

Duffy Lee nodded. "All told, Alex, three gone at once. A Skater and two Fountains. It doesn't paint a good picture of Catherman, the former nautical repo man. He probably had the dockside skill to pull and replace a complex electrical system."

"So there are four players," said Marnie. "Four that we know of, and one of them killed Sally Catherman. One of them—maybe the same bastard but not necessarily—killed Lisa Cormier."

"The feds are searching for a stolen boat," I said, "and it means more to them than solving two murders. This is far bigger than the boat."

Sam tapped on the corkboard. "But not bigger than this chart."

"Keep at it, Duffy Lee," said Liska. He motioned the rest of us into the kitchen.

"I THINK WE JUST proved the value of teamwork," said Liska. "We've got Sam's Cuba trips; Alex's investigations; one, maybe two moles in the Mansion; cash in the lining of that sealed box; Duffy Lee's electronic sleuthing; and Marnie's summary. For right now, I'll buy Alex's suggestion that dope smugglers don't spend much time on strategy. Human smugglers, coyotes, barely plan past reaching the beach. But I think these dudes are smart. So here's our major presumption. They got their mitts on a shitload of money in the war zone, moved it to Third-World countries, and intend to bring it ashore in Monroe County."

"Where we have plenty of money to go around," said Sam.

We laughed for a moment, and half-proud, looked around the room, catching glee in each other's eyes.

Sam added, "Plus everyone in the Keys stole theirs legally."

DUFFY LEE WALKED INTO the kitchen, handed a computer printout to the sheriff. "So much for scenario," he said. "We're less than spectators. Whatever was going to happen already did."

We all looked at him, stupefied.

"This just popped up on a Miami TV station web page," he said. "A boat chase in Hawk Channel ended an hour ago. It reads like a three-ring circus."

Liska studied the printed page, pulled out his cell and, punching in a number, walked out to the yard.

"I just want to think that those pharmaceuticals helped one or two sick people down there," said Sam.

Marnie rapped her knuckles softly on the back of his hand. He grabbed her hand for a moment then let go.

Liska returned. "The feds tracked their Keeltec Coastal Pursuit out of Varadero, Cuba. It went slowly for the first two hours. They thought it was a fishing punt with a small outboard headed for the Marquesas. Then it kicked up speed, veered northeast and met a local boat twelve miles south of Big Pine Shoal. They spent fifteen minutes together—plenty of time for a transfer. By the time the Marine and Border Patrols launched their boats, the go-fast was screaming east toward Cay Sal Bank and the other craft went west toward Boca Chica. They caught the Keeltec with two Nicaraguans and two million bucks aboard."

"That explains some of the bad boys' urgency," said Marnie.

"It sure as hell deflates ours," added Sam.

"The other boat was chased into the mangroves," said Liska. "It failed to navigate properly. They're choppering some guy to the hospital in Marathon."

26

"How did this happen again?" I said. "How the hell did I get neck-deep in your occupation?"

"Someone should have warned you."

"You did," I said. "I didn't listen."

"No need to apologize," said Liska. "We need citizen volunteers to run interference for us. It notches down our peril and you break rules that we can't break."

"I didn't apologize. I just whined."

Duffy Lee and Marnie had gone home to bed. Liska, Sam and I sat at the glass-top table, passing around the news print-out and alternating shots of Haitian rum and sips of Beck's Light—the only brand the sheriff had left in the fridge, but fine with me.

"For all the times you shamed me," he said, "picked up sticks I had dropped, I finally got to this moment where I'm sitting on my ass, drinking beer, doing my job about as well as I've ever done it."

I wasn't convinced. "How could any of us—me, Sam, or you with your badge—have been of assistance to the Homeland people? We don't have training, knowledge, background or weapons. We were going to get in their way. They proved tonight that they'd trample us to reach their target."

"My main thought," said Liska, "was they aren't from the Keys. We know how things work down here. We know how things appear to be strange and aren't; or how they look normal when they're bent all to hell."

"Let's hear it for equipment," said Sam. "We solved fifty riddles in less than four hours, and those bastards got the arrest."

"Why did you have Detective Lewis bring me here?" I said.

"Purely a matter of convenience, Rutledge. I knew she was running an errand on the island. I asked her to do us the favor."

"Part two of the story?" I said.

"She figured out that you and Watkins were riding your motorbikes on Cudjoe this afternoon. She wanted to take the Cormier murder case away from Watkins because Beth is your alibi."

"Talk about conflict of interest," I said. "Marv Fixler might have been..."

"Don't even voice the word," said Liska. "I decided for now to leave the case in the city."

"For now?"

"I may change my mind if it's connected to the Hammond murder. Two bodies six days and six car lengths apart. That's major."

"You've got more to say, I can tell."

"You want to know?" he said. "You want Sam to hear this?"

"Sam can hear it, too."

"One of my green-and-whites had to go by Bobbi's house on Aquamarine, to drop off some paperwork. There was old Marv, out in her yard hosing off his flippers and spear gun and snorkeling gear. Like he was on vacation at his own personal resort. Marv acknowledged the deputy but didn't recognize him. I guessed he assumed the deputy didn't know him, either. Two days later the deputy came back for the paperwork and there was Marv, sitting back by the canal bulkhead, wearing his Baghdad T-shirt, drinking a beer."

"Living there."

"I offer facts but no opinions," said Liska.

In the parlance of diplomacy, she had run a multi-level liaison.

We sat for several minutes, listened to the pool filter gurgle. It was the most peaceful moment I'd had in a week. After my ride across town in Bobbi's SUV, while finding my way up Liska's dark driveway, I had felt a question park itself in the back of my mind. I had wondered about my decisions—to stop seeing Bobbi and to begin a romance so quickly with Beth.

Liska's well-intended gossip had eased my dilemma.

SAM WHEELER STARED ABOVE the treetops into the distant night sky. He tracked the downwind leg of a private jet in the airport landing pattern, but he wasn't pondering air travel. I knew the gears were still grinding.

"Pretty quiet over there," I said.

"All the years of forethought," said Sam, "recruiting each other, gathering their equipment... That gang got caught like a bunch of high-schoolers."

"Maybe they lost their cool at crunch time," I said.

"I think it's a cowboy movie," he said. "They went that-a-way."

Liska wasn't convinced. "You think someone fell for a diversion tactic?"

"They stole an unsellable boat," said Sam, "a military craft with minimal radar presence. Paint it white, put red cushions aboard, it's still a weapon. They needed its utility. They wanted to move fast and undetected, which we have to assume they've done. When the boat was no longer of use, they gave it back, more or less."

"Along with..."

"Two Nicaraguan mules, a busted-up stolen boat, and chump change."

"Two million... chump?" I said.

Sam shifted in his chair, sat up straighter. "Four of them, right?

313

Copeland, Catherman, Fixler, Stinson. But we can't count out Lisa because she was a co-conspirator before she took dead."

"Okay."

"Divide two million by five and run it against the years they've been plotting this caper. Not much of a paycheck, eh?" He waited and got no answer. "Also, there's at least one other stolen boat still out there. We may be the only ones who know that."

LISKA PULLED OUT HIS phone, keyed a number in the cell's memory. He identified himself and asked to speak to the duty officer. After a short wait he said, "Sheriff Liska, here, Commander. Trying to avoid a conflict. I scheduled a dawn-light marine training exercise for my boat teams in the Lower Keys, but I understand you fellows had a confrontation a few hours ago. Have your personnel cleared the area?"

Sam glanced at me, flashed an expression of admiration.

Liska listened a minute then said, "We won't be launching until five A.M.—I'll check back again before we roll."

He clicked off and we stared at him.

He raised his hands, an I-dunno salute. "The boat that crashed in Sugarloaf Creek came up on the radar several times as two blips. A bit later they noticed a smaller boat heading north out of Kemp Channel. When it didn't try to run north into Florida Bay, they decided it was local. They think it looped east to the north side of Big Pine. Whatever, it fell off the radar."

"Two targets and two hits," I said. "The feds have gone home to celebrate their victory."

"Smaller boat, like a reduced radar image?" said Sam. "Anyone feel like a boat ride?"

"I feel like shit," I said.

"Rutledge," said Liska. "Did you really get hit by a car?"

27

"I saw an odd channel marker in Sugarloaf Creek this morning."

"You didn't move it, did you?" said Sam.

"I left it alone," I said. "Turk said he'd been through that creek a few times, and he had never seen a stake."

"It's a mystery to me," said Sam. He sounded insincere.

"As a senior member of local law enforcement, I didn't hear this conversation," said Liska. "Let's not mention it again."

We motored slowly in the canal behind Johnny Baker's home on Cudjoe Key, the waterway illuminated by the outside lights of homes to either side. Open water would be less friendly until the sun came up. The new moon had worked to our benefit on Turk's boat that morning. This time, in shallower waters, darkness gave points to the other team. They also had a head start.

This was not vigilante action. Liska had called out three of his two-man boat teams, each equipped with semi-automatic weapons and infrared viewing scopes. The skiff launching from the Drost Road ramp, on Cudjoe, had made it to Niles Channel before we were out of Key West. Two units out of Big Pine were instructed to search Pine Channel, Coupon Bight and the Content Keys. They were looking for performance boats that appeared out of place or abandoned, and told not to use spotlights.

We had driven past Catherman's place on Scabbard Road to

assure ourselves that the Fountain and the Skater I'd seen earlier now were gone. From there to *Fancy Fool,* on the hooks at Johnny Baker's place, was less than three minutes. Our time from Liska's home to being underway was forty minutes flat. Not that we were hurried. The real chance that our opponents could have full-automatic weapons and night scopes prompted us to caution. We had one pair of daytime binoculars and two pistols among us.

Liska sat on the bow, talking to his crews on a hand-held VHF radio. To thwart eavesdropping, they used a digitally scrambled, police-only channel.

"What's your guess, Alex?" said Sam.

"Take it one step at a time," I said. "Idle over to the top end of Knockemdown, let our eyes adjust to the dark. Take a look at that man-made channel through Tarpon Belly, then go up the east side of Sawyer Key. They could be north of Sawyer, waiting until dawn to pretend they're out fishing."

"I like staying east," he said. "Too many lobster trap floats to the west. If I snag a pull rope and foul my prop, we'll be useless."

Liska half-overheard us. "Let's work our way out toward Sawyer Key," he said.

"Aye," said Sam. "Splendid concept."

"If you think about it," I said, "Catherman lives five miles from here. If he ever went boating, he would have visited Tarpon Belly. He would have seen that odd canal cut through its center."

"The alleged shrimp farm of 1973," said Sam.

"The worst-kept secret in pot smuggling," said Liska. "You think Catherman believes, like everyone who finds that canal, that he's the first one ever to see it?"

"Great way to vanish off the radar," I said. "Do we know he's not the one they took to the hospital?"

"I just got the word," said Liska. "Cormier died before they got him there. Head injuries. Skull versus vegetation."

Knockemdown Key failed its name. Sam shut down his motor

well south of the oblong island and let the northbound current take us inshore. We couldn't see a thing. No lurking bad guys, no pale boat hulls in the mangrove overhang. We didn't hear birds or fish. Worse, we couldn't tell if someone was watching us.

Liska twisted around, took bearings on headlights on US 1 to the south and a radio tower's flashing red light to the west. "We could practically drift to Tarpon Belly, the way the current's pushing."

"I like that," said Sam. "If anyone is on that island, the forty minutes it takes would be worth the surprise factor. It's just, if we're a hundred yards off our mark, we'll have to crank the engine to get close. Adios surprise."

"I'm all for doing a fly-by at dawn," said Liska. "One pass would cover all of these islands."

"Tarpon Belly's inside the no-fly zone around Fat Albert," I said. "You're talking a couple days' paperwork—beforehand."

Liska grunted. "Your thought patterns remind me of a kid playing with a light switch."

"If we really want to find them," I said, "we could call and ask. I've got Bob's cell number in my phone."

"What'll you ask him to do?" said the sheriff. "Shoot up a flare?"

"Maybe just strike up a chat, bend the conversation," I said. "If he doesn't hang up on me."

"Nothing to lose but your dime," said Sam. "I love technology when it's somebody else's"

I called but got no answer. It went to voice mail. I said, "Top o' the morn, Bob," and closed my phone.

We drifted, whispered among ourselves for twenty minutes.

"Wish I'd brought my jacket," said the sheriff. "The coldest it gets is just before dawn."

"It's October in the Keys, Sheriff," said Sam. "We're not freezing our butts in Minneapolis. Or sitting in a Seattle rainstorm."

"Point taken."

My cell phone buzzed.

"Oh, Jesus," said Liska. He keyed his radio, spoke quietly to his teams.

Catherman said, "Is that you just north of the blimp?"

I looked at Tarpon Belly, six hundred yards distant. "That's us, Bob. My friend Sam Wheeler and I are night fishing. What have you got, infrared binoculars?"

"Wheeler's a son of a bitch," said Catherman. "He knows who killed my daughter."

"Is that why you hired me to find her?"

"That was two-thirds of it. I guess I won't make you rich, after all. I was going to own every house on Dredgers Lane."

"I don't get it," I said. "You're helping to make Fixler rich. How can you partner with him?"

"He's got my back."

"He saw your daughter naked," I said. "Every square inch."

"Where do you get that shit?"

"Working on your nickel. Sally had a secret boyfriend named Cliff Brock. Cormier's inside guy at the Mansion."

"Horseshit," said Catherman.

"She got her co-workers to cover shifts a couple times a week while she went boating with Brock. You never questioned her suntan after all those long hours inside Colding's Grocery?"

Silence.

"Fixler was there one time. He went out on the water with Sally and Cliff and the one from Colding's that he was screwing. They all took off their suits and got it on."

"Crock."

"That's how he was able to approach Cliff and your daughter on the water on another day. He knew he could shoot them with no witnesses. He told his girl his name was Constant Johnson."

Catherman said, "No fucking way." I heard him cough and sob. Then he said, "Constant Johnson was always your joke, Marvin."

Fixler's voice came back, distant, argumentative, adamant.

I heard the gunshot through the phone. I also heard it through my other ear. Sam and the sheriff turned to look at Tarpon Belly.

"Strife," said Sam.

"Catherman shot Fixler," I said. "That's my guess."

"Drops the prosecution budget," said Liska.

We sat for a moment, pondering what happened. Then a quick burst of gunfire—from one weapon—echoed across the flat water. Had Catherman shot Stinson, too? Ten seconds later the gunfire came more focused, with no echo—straight at us.

"We're out of range," said Sam, cool to the point of boredom.

Liska spoke into his hand-held in a measured, forceful voice. He asked his teams to hold back and wait for daylight. "They've got a Fountain, but they're not moving," he said. "We don't need to occupy Tarpon Belly. Post two teams at Kemp Channel bridge and send one north of Sawyer. Watch yourselves. We're outgunned."

Through my cell I heard crunching sounds, footsteps on gravel, then thuds like closing doors or objects dropping onto a fiberglass boat deck. Someone—perhaps the last man alive—was carrying Catherman's phone, trying to hear what we were saying. I tugged Liska's sleeve, showed him the glow of my still-open phone.

Liska turned off his radio, thought for a moment, leaned closer to my cell. "You're right, Major," he said. "We'll circle the bastards and bring in SWATs and SEALs on the Navy's helicopters at day-break. They can lay on the firepower. No sense putting our people at risk." He paused, then said, "This isn't a case of needing them alive to explain their scam. That Cormier schmuck is talking like a speed freak in the emergency room."

He tapped my hand and whispered, "Done."

I clicked off. One way or another, we'd find out if it worked.

"Thank you, Alex," he said. "Inducing panic is a wonderful tactic when you're this far away from it."

Two minutes later we heard the Fountain's three 275-horsepower Mercury engines start, one by one. They weren't particularly loud, but their bass notes rumbled with muscle.

"That second motor put us in a dead heat," said Sam. "The third gives him twenty-miles-per-hour more than my skiff."

"Chase him anyway," said the sheriff. "Maybe you can inspire a navigational error."

The Fountain came out of the Tarpon Belly canal at idle speed but kicked up to full power immediately, headed directly south.

Sam started his engine, knocked it into gear, flipped on his running lights and brought us quickly to planing speed.

"Turn off your lights," shouted Liska.

"Open ocean, Sheriff," Sam shouted back, "and your boat teams are out there somewhere. It's easier for them to collide with me than for that maniac to connect with a bullet. This way, he knows we're coming."

"Good thinking, Captain," said Liska. "Very good."

Even in the dogleg channel south of the highway, the Fountain pulled away from us. We were joined, then passed, by boats from the Sheriff's Office and Border Patrol. As we transited from Hawk Channel into the Florida Straits, Sam pulled back his throttle.

"You're giving up?" said Liska.

"We won," said Sam. "We inspired that navigational mistake, so he's doing the tough work for us. Running wide open, he'll burn at least eighty gallons per hour, and he's already been out front for that rendezvous. He'll be out of gas before he gets to the Cuban coast. They don't like boats that stop offshore. They want them to come to the beach so they know what they're up to. The Cubans will deal with him, and he won't like it. Their ancient Soviet PT boats have modern Chinese guns."

28

Sam hit the steering wheel, "What's that word, fear of spiders?"

"Arachnophobia," I said. "Don't ask me to spell it."

"Is there a word like that for people afraid of the speed limit?"

We were rolling behind a long line of slowpokes.

"I believe it's fleetaphobia. I may be wrong."

"The Florida Keys thrill me," he said. "You can be stuck behind a slow-moving, fume-belching old pickup truck on US 1, and get tailgated by a Bentley convertible. I love living with diversity."

Sheriff Liska stayed on the phone the whole way into Key West. He was mopping up details, delegating follow-up. The unit he had sent to Sawyer Key had gone ashore on Tarpon Belly and found the bodies of Marv Fixler and Bob Catherman.

"Stinson ran out of gas halfway to his safe haven," said Liska. "They found a ton of money in the Fountain."

"Two thousand pounds?" I said. "How much is that?"

"Actually four-fifths of a ton. One of my men calculated seventy million in hundreds, but it might be seventy-one."

Sam laughed. "Surely, that's not..."

"Yes, it is," said Liska. "The lunkheads weren't just smuggling a little money into Florida. They were moving a damn fortune. They would've been mega-rich when everyone else was poor."

I could barely get my voice to work. "Can we go back to Tarpon

Belly and see if any green debris blew over the transom?"

"It doesn't work that way," said Liska. "I can get you citizen-hero commendations for your input, but you'll have to wear coats and ties to the ceremony. And regular shoes."

"We handed the feds a money bust on a silver platter," said Sam. "Let's make them come to our ceremony. Flip-flops required."

"By the way," said the sheriff. "He shot at us with an HK-416 rifle. That's Delta Force gear. Those boys had strong resources."

"I guess we weren't out of range," said Sam.

"Lucky me," I said. "I got hit by a Taurus instead of a Hummer."

I DRAGGED MY ASS up the dirt path to Beth's house, brain-fried and half-starved, too tired to be jubilant. She didn't answer my knock. More than gunfire, poverty or arrest, I feared dropping the key. I wasn't sure, if I bent over to retrieve it, that I had the strength to stand up straight again.

A note next to the kitchen sink said, HEAT UP YOUR LEFTOVERS. TRY ONE MINUTE AT HALF POWER.

The microwave was too complicated for my state of mind. I went flat out on her bed quilt, realized I hadn't closed the blinds, and fell asleep before I could muster the energy to get up and darken the room.

I woke to find Beth Watkins staring down at me with fondness in her expression, as if regarding a precious child in a day bed. I didn't understand. Even in deep drowsiness I knew that I smelled like a goat. She appeared bedraggled as well, with ringlets of hair stuck to her forehead, her eyes reddened and bleary.

"What are you dreaming?" she said. "You've got a rise in your shorts."

"Oh, Jesus." I reached into my pocket, pulled out my camera. It looked ready to shoot. I pressed a button and the telescoping lens retracted. "I must have rolled over and hit the 'on' switch."

"Well, that's no fun. I understand you had a busy night."

"Some of us have to work," I said.

"I put in a good morning, believe me," said Beth. "You forgot to tell me about food for two at Hammond's house."

"We've been through that."

"Well, I forgot to tell you something," she said. "We reviewed the stolen hard drive. It held a half dozen porn clips, amateur but close to slick. They all had two females doing each other, and they were shot on several occasions in Hammond's home."

A barrage of possibilities zipped through my mind: Mikey and Sally; Honey Weiss and Alyssa; Mikey and Honey. "There's your strong motive for stealing that drive," I said. "Jerry's murder may have been unplanned."

"If someone regretted their acting career, exactly," said Beth. "And one other factor came into it. That was Carmen Sosa on the phone, the call I got as you left to meet Bobbi at Mangia Mangia. Your young friend, Maria Rolley, is quite the sleuth. She was upset that Russ Hernandez was a murder suspect. She liked him because he called her 'Princess,' and liked Jason because he loaned her a comedy DVD. She told her mother that, if anyone was a killer, it was probably a girl named Brandi."

"Jesus, yes," I said. "Two girls were living with the boys on Elizabeth Street, or else the boys moved into their place. The other was named Cally. Were they budding actresses?"

"Part-time. Cally worked in a pizza kitchen, but quit four days ago. Now both girls are guests of the county. Hernandez is still in trouble, but not for murder. He'll get off with probation. And Maria is much richer now. I spoke with the man who offered the $25,000 reward. He's going to open a college pre-pay account in her name. Do you want me to warm your sandwich?"

"A sexy response comes to mind," I said, "but I doubt I could fulfill my offer. Yes, I would love a sandwich."

I took my time getting up and was still in the bedroom when the doorbell rang. Beth told the visitor to come in. I plodded my way to the front room to find Beth and Bobbi Lewis staring at me.

"I survived machine gun fire and a hit-and run," I said. "Now I'm going to die by visual daggers."

That got a laugh, and I detected mischief in their eyes.

"We're about to take inter-agency cooperation to new levels," said Bobbi.

"I didn't wake up?"

"It's not a dream," said Beth. "When I reviewed Hammond's sex videos this morning, I found a dozen files on the hard drive with odd names. They weren't numbered like the others. The first one I checked showed Alyssa looking unhappy but stripping down to her panties. It appears Cecil Colding has been secretly photographing his employees, selling videos to Jerry's gang of horny old men here in town. So... the city has the evidence and the grocery's in the county. Detective Lewis had to secure the search warrant. We're going to pay Cecil a social call."

"Um, look..." I said to Bobbi.

"Don't even start," she said. "Marv Fixler will be an easy one to get over, and I brought this on myself. Also, I heard from a head-hunter today. I'm in line to become a detective in Pinellas County, up in St. Pete. I'll find out next Tuesday, but it looks good. You and I would have had to deal with that fact, but... we don't. I'm glad you two are happy."

Bobbi turned and walked outside.

Beth gave me a bewildered look and blew me a kiss.

"If it gets weird," I said, "please don't go solo. Don't try to be a hero."

"At work, I'm a team player." She touched one index finger to her hip and made the sizzling sound with her mouth. "I'm a hero only with you, dear."